THE RESTLESS EARTH

Although a work of fiction, *The Restless Earth* is based on actual events. The author has endeavored to be respectful to all persons, places, and events presented in this novel, and attempted to be as accurate as possible. Still, this is a novel, and all references to persons, places, and events are fictitious or used fictitiously.

THE RESTLESS EARTH

a novel

ALAN COCKRELL

WordCrafts Press

In honor of a bygone species—the wildcatters.

They managed to survive wars, wild market swings, regulation, imports, depletion, and shrinking hunting grounds. Their extinction began when somebody figured out how to bust shale.

And for Bob Schneeflock, wildcatter extraordinaire and my inspiration for this story.

The Rocks

In a small corner of a pre-historic continent, hulking dinosaurs, stuffing their jaws with plant life and with each other's flesh, were oblivious to the unhurried but relentless upheaval happening under their feet. A colossal column of salt, a mile or more in diameter, had begun a slow rise through the Earth's crust. It took the overlaying rock layers with it causing them to bulge upward. Enormous temperatures and incomprehensible pressure built in the rocks resulting in a hot-blooded affair.

Carbon atoms in the organic-rich rock married hydrogen atoms and gave birth to a dark, slimy irascible liquid laced with petulant, restless gases. These new tenants of the rock's pores expanded and wanted out—wanted out now, and their host rock barely contained them.

Long after the great lizards died out, the submerged mound that sat atop the salt dome—a few miles across and few dozen feet high—became home to millions of fish that schooled around the reefs that grew on it.

And with the small fish came sharks, tens of thousands of them, growing fat on the fish, tearing at their prey, tearing at each other, dying and sinking, their soft bodies decaying, leaving only the razor teeth in the sand.

The sea withdrew again, and forests grew. The rains poured, and when the swollen streams cut down through the sandy soil—a hundred thousand years after their owners died—the sharks' teeth sprang free. But the seething fluid trapped far below bided its time.

The passing of the ages held no sway with the evolving planet until humans came. Only then did time seem to count for something. In their ephemeral thoughts, the humans could fathom neither the eons that went before them nor those to come, although their allotment of a few decades of occupancy on the planet seemed to them an eon. But they were too busy surviving to ponder it much.

A group of them settled on the small mound above the salt bulge because waters that flowed from the ground there were believed to be so pure they had a healing power—so they built a village. Then men with guns came, drove out those with arrows, and built a town and a resort hotel. Others of their kind came from afar to soak in the restorative waters.

But interest in the healing springs waned when men swinging big hammers laid a railroad through the town. With so many new opportunities to travel to more fascinating places, the town became just another hot Southern settlement that made its living sharecropping and milling timber. Children grew up vowing to leave as soon as they could, but most ended up as farmers and lumbermen, or their wives—just as their parents did.

Many of the town's children who played along the nearby creeks were fascinated with the shark's teeth and other fossils they dug from the sandy banks, but one girl became more than fascinated. The fossils obsessed her. Her collection grew bigger than others'. She talked about them to anyone who would listen—the postman, the milkman, the neighbor lady, and her friends.

When the others lost interest, Laura Hamilton stared at her collection and handled it for hours on end. She read all she could about her specimens in the town library, which wasn't much. When she asked her daddy how the sharks got in the sand, fifty miles inland from the Gulf of Mexico, he told her they were left there by the great flood of Noah.

She daydreamed a lot too. She sat in church and imagined the seas being there, right there in the town, as they had once been, the big predators swimming casually down her street, into her church, up the isle toward the altar.

Men were warring when Laura turned eighteen—the second of their big wars—but that didn't stop her from going down to Spring Hill College. She wanted to be a science teacher. Sim Hamilton wanted in a mighty way for his daughter to be the first person in the family's history to go to college, and he spent every cent he could scrape up for the tuition, but it wasn't enough so she worked in the shipyards.

After college she taught in a couple of schools around Mobile, but when her daddy took sick she found a job teaching at the middle school back in Fossil Rim so she could look after him. She moved back into her old room and found the collection. After Sim died, orphaning her, she sat evenings swinging on the front porch sifting through the old box, remembering the happy, carefree trips to the creek to search for the fossils, wondering if her own teeth and bones would be all she had to show for her life at its end.

When men started slaughtering each other again in a far-off Asian peninsula something happened that excited her. An oil company put up a drilling tower near the south end of the town. Her curiosity drove her to ask the men on the tower questions, but they just laughed and cajoled her. She nearly panicked when she realized they thought she had come to sell herself to them. Then the boss told her to leave—told her that a woman had no business on a work site like theirs, and besides, what they were doing was a company secret. She went back out there after they left—having found no oil—and stared at the place where the hole had been, wondering how far down they had dug and what fascinating fossils their bits had pulverized.

When Laura came back to Fossil Rim, she found her old boyfriend, Benny, had been rejected by the army for some reason she didn't know and went quickly through several jobs, finally becoming a decently successful fertilizer salesman. But agriculture wasn't his forte, and he wasn't the least bit interested in taking over his father's farm. Selling it, when he got it, was his plan for the farm. He told her with a wink the farm would fetch a tidy sum.

Benny had been married and divorced already, and that troubled her too, but more than anything else, she thought it was his lack of ambition that made him ill-suited as a potential mate. But then, no empires had fallen to her sword lately either.

Laura spent countless evenings sitting on her porch swing reading, sewing, or handling her collection. Sometimes Benny would come by and ask her to go for a ride. He never wanted to simply sit and talk. He would yell from his car window. She would see him raise a paper bag to his lips. She would smile, shake her head, and go inside. When he left she would go back out and sit, ponder her future, and make plans to leave and follow her dreams.

But the plans always needed more study. More time. More money.

Money matters were never much of a concern for her. She would make do no matter what she decided. But time was a genuine concern. She was approaching middle age and had seen little of the world yet.

For the rocks she lived above, time was endless. Yet in a way that only fate or providence would bid—and if asked, she would claim the later—their time had come as well. The work of the salt, three miles below the town, was finished. And someone had noticed. Yet another bull's-eye was being drawn, and Laura and her friends lived in its crosshairs.

2

The Map

The geologist sat on the edge of the chair, elbows resting on khaki-clad bony knees, staring at a turquoise and white checkerboard floor. His toes and heels, with a mind of their own, rocked back and forth in opposite directions—a habit that annoyed people.

He looked up at the calendar on the wall and studied the picture over the month labeled DECEMBER 1955. Hard-hatted oilmen, faces stained with grime, stood grinning in the sun in front of their gigantic drilling rig. He envied them. Theirs was the job of running the equipment—making hole, as they liked to say. When they made hole fast and without problems, they were happy men. Whatever might lie at the bottom of their hole—or whatever didn't—was somebody else's concern.

He cupped his hands over his nose and mouth, swallowed hard and thought about that last dry hole—the last of a string of them since he left Phillips Petroleum and struck out on his own. And that was one of his best prospects yet. A "slam dunk," Noble had said. But when it, too, turned up dry, Noble had turned somber, which was uncharacteristic of him. He might not open his checkbook again for the next deal.

He sighed and glanced at his watch. The notion haunted him again. Everybody got dry holes. But twelve straight dusters? He blew out a deep breath and ran his hand across his brow. He knew the stakes. In this business the last thing you wanted was the odor of incessant failure wafting about you.

And now here he was again, he mulled, knocking at the door of another big oil company, hat in hand, asking for a morsel of that vital life blood an independent needed—information.

He recounted his phone call to Gulf's exploration manager. The man had cheerfully agreed let him see the data. "Sure!" he had said. "We're not too interested in that area any more. We'll work a deal with you if you like it." He imagined he heard a subtle chuckle.

The door opened and a man came in carrying a long cardboard tube with a bold red label on it that read *Gulf Oil Company: Confidential.*

"Mr. Purvis is in a meeting," he said as he led the geologist to a small work room. "He said he won't be able to see you, but you can examine the lines."

The guy complained that it took some time to find them, sending the geologist the subtle message that his presence here was a burden the man would rather not have to put up with. He shook the tightly rolled, long pieces of paper out of the tube, opened them, and laid them on a large drafting table. He reached into a drawer and got out weights, placing them on the corners of the paper so it wouldn't roll back up when he let it go. "I believe these are the ones you asked to see, Mr. Bonner. And here's a shot-point map you can take notes on and keep."

Ethan nodded and thanked him.

Then the guy added, "But, of course, you can't keep the lines themselves."

Ethan flashed a derisive glance at him, snubbed that the guy said that, as if he were a greenhorn at this business.

"Yell if you need anything else," the man added.

How well Ethan Bonner knew this was the way of the oil business. A deep-pocketed major company goes in on a hunch, shoots seismic lines, and gets excited about what the data shows. They usually picked the low-hanging fruit, the obvious prospects that pop out of the data screaming, "Drill here!" The company sends out landmen, leases the minerals under their prospect, and sinks a hole.

When they hit oil or natural gas, they started a feeding frenzy that drew in other companies, big and small. When they missed—which was most of the time—they packed up and left, sometimes after trying one or two more holes. Gulf called it quits after only one hole. *There must have been a good reason for that,* Ethan thought. He knew the big boys always performed a postmortem after a failure to figure why it was dry. The bosses demanded explanations of their technical staffs and sometimes a pound or two of flesh.

That's when the little wildcatters like him closed in. Like skulking coyotes sniffing around a plundered kill, they came looking to see if a morsel was overlooked. Outsiders, like Ethan, kept an opportunistic eye on the big companies' drilling operations. They did their own independent autopsies on the dry holes, which they hoped would reveal some potential still hiding in the depths, perhaps a few hundred feet in some other direction. Or deeper. The big companies—most of them—allowed the scavengers their pickings. A deal could always be made. Something salvaged from it.

Ethan slowly nodded to the clerk, his eyes cast aside and riveted on the big paper sheets. The man went out of the room and sat down at his desk with a clear view through the door he left open. Ethan glanced at him and saw that he was being casually watched.

He always marveled over the chaos the seismic records seemed to portray. The uninitiated eye could make no sense of the marks on the big sheet. They looked like a ridiculous jumble of squiggly lines in tightly packed vertical rows. But the geologist knew he was looking at a sonic record of a selected slice of the earth's crust.

The paper print-outs he studied were the result of a man-made mini-earthquake. Explosive charges had been set off that were spaced at intervals along two lines on the ground, each several miles long and intersecting at roughly their mid-points. Instruments had recorded the travel time in milliseconds of the energy imparted into the earth as it went down and reflected off of the various sedimentary rock layers. The paper print-outs in front of him were the recorded raw returns. Their interpretation was entirely up to him.

An alcoholic-like buzz crawled up the back of his neck, as it did in most of his breed every time they saw a new piece of seismic information. But the stuff was often hard to figure out. He might see a promising feature that others have pored over and missed, or dismissed. New possibilities sometimes lurked. His eyes, eager for discovery, darted from one feature of the seismic records to another, like a kid tearing through Christmas gifts, casting aside one by one, hoping for that special one. Then he saw it.

He moved to the side of the table and lowered his head, turning it slightly sideways to better see the minor variations in the geometry of the lines. He smiled. His hunch was correct.

He knew Gulf would never drill foolishly. There had to be something here to draw their attention—thus what he saw was no surprise. But what did surprise him was its size. He had never seen a sub-surface feature this big.

About half way down from the horizontal line that represented the surface he saw a bright reflection that formed a long but subtle arch. Faint whispers fell from his lips, as if remarking to an unseen partner leaning over the records alongside him.

"The Lower Tusc."

The Lower Tuscaloosa was a thick sandstone that Ethan and many of his peers thought was deposited in Cretaceous time, about 100 million years ago, by raging rivers, overflowing deltas, and vast ancient beaches. Like most rock formations it was named after a city near which it outcropped on the surface. But here, much farther south than its namesake, the Lower Tuscaloosa plunged far below the coastal plain sediments, to a depth of about 7,000 feet, he guessed. Productive of oil far back to the west, it was Gulf's target. But when they drilled, instead of oil they had only found the remnants of an ancient ocean in the grainy pores of the Lower Tusc—saltwater.

Yet Ethan knew all that. Everyone in the business knew that. He wanted to know what was deeper. Shifting his scrutiny lower he saw some weak evidence of the arch in the reflections below the Lower Tusc—depths unexplored and unpondered.

He unrolled the other seismic line and laid it on top of the first one. Again he lowered his head at the edge and looked along the traces. He saw another crest. He knew it was the same one, only seen now from a different angle.

But Ethan knew he couldn't raise any money telling investors to trust that he saw the promise in the data. He needed hard evidence. As the clerk had said, Gulf wouldn't give him copies of the seismic, but they would allow him to make his own map from whatever interpretation he could conjure from them. And to help him raise the necessary cash for another hole, they would even allow third parties to come in for a verification look. They still had some unexpired leases in the vicinity that Ethan's efforts might help them evaluate.

That's why they had given him the shot-point map to pore his visions upon with his own pencil. He could show it to potential patrons. That required tedious work, but it was work he reveled in. He unrolled the shot-point map the clerk had given him and got out his pen.

Near the place where the two lines intersected, he saw a small circle with a short vertical line and a similar horizontal line through it—the standard map symbol for a dry hole. The label next to it read **Gulf Oil No. 1 Buchanan, TD 7012**. He noted the total depth Gulf had drilled to: 7,012 feet. He whispered to the map, "Only a couple thousand feet deeper, boys, and you'd have found it."

He selected the sharp reflection he thought was the Lower Tuscaloosa, which Gulf had proved to be dry. The deeper rock layers appeared weak and disjointed on the seismic records—so much so that he couldn't reliably identify them. But he figured they should logically conform to the Lower Tuscaloosa's geometry. If they did, then maybe they contained oil. Thus he would map the Lower Tusc and assume the unexplored layers beneath it conformed.

At each shot point he picked the reflection that he thought was the top of the Lower Tusc and projected horizontally to the scale at the edge of the sheet to get the reflection times. He jotted that number down beside the respective shot point on his map. He did that for each shot point—dozens of them.

When at last the tedious job was complete, he put the two seismic records aside and sharpened his pencil. His stomach growled. Lunchtime had gone by, but he didn't care. He sensed the payoff was coming. He began doing what he loved best—contouring. His pencil inched across the white paper map connecting points of equal travel time.

Time and again, he mumbled a mild curse and erased a few inches of line, then resumed the slow snaking movement of the pencil. His trace curved and jogged, but it slowly circled the map, finally meeting where it started. He grinned. His contour formed a crude, oblong bull's-eye. He selected a longer travel time and added another contour. Then another. His bull's-eye grew bigger with each new contour.

He warmed in the sweet satisfaction of watching his dreams dance through the contours looking for a place to reside. Hope followed the curvy lines, flowing along them, billowing in domes of exhilaration or languishing in troughs of despair. But most thrilling of all, he knew fortunes were won and lost in the contours. He was also keenly aware that he had yet to win a single, humble triumph in this viciously competitive game.

When the Gulf clerk came in and said it was quitting time, Ethan thanked him. The map was complete. He took a last look at the seismic records and nodded, signaling to the clerk that he was finished with them. While the clerk put the lines away, he gathered up his notes and rolled up his new structure map.

He went straight to his hotel room, passing restaurants and cafes along Houston's busy streets, his stomach pleading for a table. The smile lingered, unusual for him.

He knew the bull's-eye on his map signified an enormous swell in the earth's crust, a swell that did not express itself much on the surface. Erosion saw to that. He didn't know what caused the swell—that was a question for the researchers, and he knew some day they would figure it out. But he knew one thing for certain—a dome like the one he had mapped was a preferred lair for oil.

He burst into the room and unrolled his map on the bed. He looked again at the bull's-eye and noted the center point of it—section, township, and range. He pulled out a Mobile county road map and cross-referenced the location. He put his finger on his selected spot and saw that it touched the south edge of a town. Not good. No oilman relished undertaking a leasing effort in a town where prying eyes watched and where mineral ownership was split into hundreds of small tracts. Maybe that was the reason, he suddenly realized, that no one else had followed up on Gulf's failure. He put on his drugstore cheaters and read the name of the town. *Fossil Rim, population 3,532.*

He took out a blue pencil and outlined four sections in the middle of the bull's-eye, a square two miles on a side covering 2,560 surface acres. His grin widened. His head nodded as if acknowledging a completed quest. Now he needed his main investor again, Noble Abrams. But he wondered if Noble would open his checkbook for yet another in a long series of good ideas gone bad. The grin faded.

The drive to Shreveport gave Ethan time to think. Abrams had been good to him. He had provided seed money for all his prospects. He always put up the first quarter interest in Ethan's deals, and after that other investors fell in line. The oil business respected Abrams and usually followed his lead. But how much longer could he count on Noble to bankroll him before he finally found something? More haunting still, was the question of whether Noble would have been as generous if Ethan's father had not given up his own life to save Noble's on that fiery blowout years ago.

Ethan found a parking spot, grabbed his maps, and went in. As he often did, Noble had lunch catered in from a café across the street. Over bowls of spicy gumbo the two caught up, the older man reminiscing at length about the old days when he and James Bonner cut their teeth in the oil patches of Oklahoma.

After the accident, he had picked himself up by his own boot-straps, as he said, and built a sizable oil estate with no college education. Noble said he got his degree from the University of Hard Knocks. When he talked about the blowout he usually choked up. "Your daddy—" He would pause, sniff, and wipe his eyes. "He was something."

When the gumbo and the small talk were finished, Noble pushed away from the table and offered a cigar, which Ethan waved off. He fired the log up and invited Ethan to present his deal.

Noble puffed, listened, and looked over the maps and cross-sections as Ethan unrolled them and passed his hands across them pointing to this and that feature of the geology. When he finished he looked up and saw Noble looking at him, not the maps. Long seconds passed. He felt the jinx crawl up his spine.

A long, uneasy time passed before Noble spoke after Ethan finished his spiel. "Ethan, this one is pretty far out. It's the riskiest one you've done yet."

Ethan nodded.

"The other ones were not nearly as risky as this—on paper, anyway—and you know what happened."

Ethan nodded again and thought it best to let Noble say his piece without interruption.

"I admit, I thought that last one you did down near Brookhaven was a gut cinch. But you know, son, twelve dry holes in a row is a tough pill to swallow."

Ethan did not offer a comment. He knew Noble was averse to excuse-making.

Noble turned in his chair and stared out the window, then examined the tip of his cigar. He wet his lips with his tongue. "Have you thought about going back to work for a company? I'll give you a good reference."

Ethan slowly rolled up the maps. He doubted references would count for much, now. "Well, I guess I have been thinking about that lately. But I don't want that."

Noble turned back to the table and took a deep breath. "Let's do it different this time. You get the leases first, and then I'll sign on for quarter interest. But if it's dry—this is the last."

Ethan's eyebrows went up. He thought about his bank account. He had about $800. That wasn't a drop in the bucket for what he would need to lease the prospect. But he knew the discussion was over.

Noble saw him to the door. "Ethan, I need to see how much you believe in this deal. And in yourself."

Ethan forced a smile, nodded and thanked him.

"Wait," Noble called out. He went to his desk and jotted something on a piece of paper. "I don't know who does your land work, but here is a man who can work miracles. And that's about what you need now."

Ethan read it and shook his head. "I don't know him."

"If he's still alive and you can find him sober, tell him Abrams says Hi."

Noble smiled, slapped him on the back, and gave him his usual send off. "Go find some oil!"

3

WHITLEY

Shivering, Ethan double-checked the western Jackson address and knocked on the dirty, scuffed apartment door. He was a warm weather person and hated seeing his breath fog.

No answer.

He knocked again and after another minute started to return to his car when he heard a rattling and saw the door crack open. A face appeared, a man rubbing his eyes and then squinting at the daylight.

"Whitley?" Ethan asked. "J.D. Whitley?"

The man stared at him as if he were expecting someone else, eyes dull and unfocused. The response came in a voice pitched so low it surprised him. It didn't fit the feeble face scrutinizing him. "Who the hell are you?"

"I couldn't find a phone number. I'm Ethan Bonner, a geologist. I need a landman."

He heard a cynical gurgle from the man's throat, then a wet cough that repeated three or four times. "I'm out of the awl business," he managed to say in a raspy voice after the coughing spasm.

Ethan had seen and heard enough. He was about to tip his hat and turn away when the man opened the door wider.

"Hell, come on in."

Ethan sat on a dirty, tattered sofa. He heard Whitley saying something from some other place in the gloom. He looked around the dark, sparsely appointed apartment and saw a trash container heaped with empty Schlitz cans. Some had fallen off the pile onto the floor. The room smelled of cigarettes, sweat, and beer. Empty food cans and dirty dishes sat in heaps on the dining table and kitchen cabinet.

Whitley came out of the murk from the vicinity of the kitchen and set two cups of coffee down. Ethan thanked him and took a sip. It was lukewarm and bitter.

"Mr. Whitley, I need a landman. I heard you might be available."

Whitley chuckled. "And what jokester sent you to me?" He raised the cup and drank the putrid stuff as if thoroughly enjoying it.

"No jokester. Noble Abrams."

"Ha ha! Is he still kickin'?"

Ethan nodded. "He's had some heart problems, but he's doing okay now, I hope. Look, I know you've had some problems of your own, but Noble said you were a good landman."

Another cynical laugh.

Ethan couldn't get over Whitley's low voice. He would have made a great bass singer on a barbershop quartet. His words came from the bottom of his throat, laced with a deep back-woods accent, yet uncommonly clear, precise, and even articulate. "What problems?"

"Drinkin'."

They looked one another over. Whitley's beaky nose, raked with tiny maroon veins, jutted from a long, pockmarked, and patchy face. The top of the scalp was under attack by creeping baldness. The wide eyes, clearer now than when he opened the door, darted across Ethan's own features as if looking for a weapon.

"Cut through the crap. You wouldn't be here if you weren't desperate. What do you need?"

"I'm starting a leasing program in Alabama."

The laugh started low and deep, then rolled off Whitley's

tongue through a half-opened mouth. His head dipped and shook. He put a hand to it as if the head shake produced pain. He drank another slug of coffee and tried to talk before the liquid had gone completely down. He coughed several times, and started to talk again before the spasm stopped. "Man, I thought you said you were in the awl business."

Ethan, not surprised at the insult, ignored it. "I think the Lower Cretaceous rocks extend that direction—"

"Of course they do," Whitley interrupted, "but does the awl? It's a long way from the awl fields in Mississippi to—where did you say you want to lease?"

"A place called Fossil Rim, in north Mobile County."

Whitley fished in his shirt pocket for a pair of glasses and pulled out a drawer from the lamp table beside him. He withdrew a handful of paper documents and nervously shifted through them until he found a road map of Mississippi. "Let's see," he mumbled. "I think I got me an Alabama map in here." He found it and laid it beside the Mississippi map. Whitley then leaned over the table and aligned the two maps, breathing heavily. Ethan smelled his beer breath. He glanced at his watch. It was still before noon.

"Right here is the Soso Field, which is the eastern-most Lower Cretaceous oil anybody's found yet, if I'm not mistaken, and I could seriously be."

"You're not," Ethan said.

"Not what?"

"Not mistaken, I mean. Right. You're right!"

Whitley wrinkled his brow looked back at the map.

He put his finger on the hamlet of Soso and looked up at Ethan as if to see that his guest was paying attention. He switched fingers, putting his thumb on Soso, and stretched his shaking hand onto the Alabama map. "Where did you say?" He asked without looking up.

"Fossil Rim, in north Mobile County." Ethan knew Whitley was demonstrating a point he already knew, but he let him go on.

"Okay, I see it here." He put his middle finger on the town. Holding the two fingers outstretched, he lifted his hand and, being reasonably careful about keeping the distance between the two fingers, moved it to the scale at the bottom of the map. A heaving chuckle began to climb up his throat. He coughed and looked over his spectacles at the geologist. "That's eighty miles, boy!"

Ethan liked the way Whitley said, *boy*. It sounded chummy, not condescending.

Whitley's brow wrinkled again. "For little operators like you, steppin' out five miles from known production is considered risky. Eighty miles! Hell, that's for a major oil company!"

Ethan got on his knees to better reach the maps and put his hands out. "Look. There's shallow oil production all across south Mississippi now," he said. "But there's only two deep discoveries in Mississippi, so far."

Whitley nodded and said, "Soso and Bolton. But they're back over in oil country. You're eighty miles out!"

"I know," Ethan snapped. He didn't need to be reminded. "Bolton is back here west of Jackson. They found Lower Cretaceous production there. Use your fingers again. Stretch them between Bolton and Soso."

Whitley stretched his thumb and middle finger between the two oil fields.

"Now hold that distance," Ethan instructed, "and slide your hand southeastward until your thumb is on Soso." Whitley did it.

"Look where your middle finger is."

Whitley studied the relationship. He mumbled, "Eighty miles between Bolton and Soso…eighty miles from Soso to—" He looked up at Ethan. "Fossil Rim."

Ethan marveled at how the man articulated words with his deep drawl.

"I don't remember much about the place, even though I know I've been through there to Mobile a bunch of times."

"Got relatives in Mobile?"

"Naw. I used to work with some Mobile people who played oil leases in south Mississippi."

Ethan made a mental note of what Whitley just said. Connections in Mobile might be an asset, but he didn't want to discuss that now.

"And notice how all three spots are in a straight line," he explained, looking at Whitley.

Whitley's eyebrows narrowed into a menacing "vee" shape. "So, you're not really doin' real geology," he said, with a generous ration of sarcasm. "You're just doing trendology. That works sometimes when you're close in, but boy, you're out there in goat pasture—unknown territory. You gotta have more than a couple of fingers on a road map to get done what you want to do!"

Ethan shrugged off the lecture. "I know, and I do." He was surprised at how technically savvy the landman was. "I've seen the structure that Gulf drilled on at Fossil Rim in '51. Been to their office. Looked at their seismic. Mapped it myself."

Ethan didn't intend to get into such geological detail as this. Normally you never discussed such things with a contract landman; you just told him where to lease. But Whitley's unexpected knowledge and questions had led him in to it. Now he began to become concerned that if Whitley turned the work down, he may tip off a blockbuster who might rush in ahead and take the choicest leases. But if sharing the information would help persuade this guy to help him, it was worth the risk.

Whitley nodded. "I remember. Everybody around here was excited about those wells Gulf drilled to the Lower Tuscaloosa across south Alabama. Down to eight or nine thousand, I think. Two of 'em on platforms in Mobile Bay. All dusters."

"That's right. And the one they drilled at Fossil Rim was on a gigantic structure—one that's right on trend with the two Lower Cretaceous discoveries in Mississippi."

Whitley looked squarely at the geologist and cracked a smile. "The silly bastards didn't drill deep enough."

Ethan grinned and nodded.

Whitley put his glasses back in his pocket, got up, and started for the kitchen. Over his shoulder he yelled, "Good luck."

Ethan's grin melted. "But I want you to work with me."

Whitley stood with his back to Ethan pouring coffee. "What's it pay?"

Ethan dreaded this part. He swallowed. "Expenses plus override."

Whitley's shoulders began jumping. Ethan could hear muffled chuckles. He saw the back of Whitley's head slowly shaking.

Whitley turned and leaned against the kitchen counter. His voice echoed off of the barren walls. "Are you serious?"

"Yep. Money is low."

"I can understand why," Whitley sang, then turned up the cup. He swallowed and coughed. He reached for a pack of cigarettes and lit up. "You raised any money?" he asked, emphasizing *any*.

"Kind of."

"Kinda? What kind of money is that?"

Again, the conversation was getting too intrusive, but he reckoned he was in too deep with this guy now to bail out.

"Abrams will buy a quarter of the deal, but I've got to put it together first."

Whitley nodded, the cigarette tipping in his lips. "So, let me guess. You want me to go down there and lease land with no money—try to get free leases and not even get paid for it?"

"That's right. I want you to get me some free leases. You'll get expenses. I can cover those till Abrams comes in."

"Expenses," Whitley repeated, chuckling, "and an overriding royalty interest in a prospect that has about as much a chance of hittin' oil as the Pope holdin' Mass at a Baptist Church."

Ethan forced a laugh. "Bring him on! He can yell Hallelujah with the best of 'em." He paused and got serious again. "I can start paying you when I get some cash."

"Gawd awe mighty," Whitley uttered to the floor. "No wonder you couldn't get anybody else. I'm the bottom of the fuckin' barrel."

Whitley mashed out the butt and leaned back against the counter. He looked at the maps on the table in front of Ethan. He looked at the piles of beer cans. He looked around at his dim, trashy abode and sighed heavily. Ethan sensed the man was evaluating his circumstances: staying here, rotting away. Or taking on one last challenge.

"You gotta understand something. I'm not reliable. I'll let you down—you can count on it."

Ethan nodded. "I'll take the best of you—and make do with the worst."

Whitley lit up another Lucky and tossed the match out the Plymouth's side window. He raised his voice to make himself heard over the wind noise. "How long have you been independent, Ethan?" It was Whitley's first use of Ethan's first name.

Ethan thought for a second or two before answering. It was that word again that stirred him: *independent*. At first he had liked the sound of it, but lately he preferred not to hear it. It had different meanings in the oil business. An independent could be any oil company other than the well-known big ones. Or it could be any oilman who simply forewent corporate security and struck out on his own. The latter was himself all right. But the reality was, he was far from independent. He depended on other oil people to share information with him, to put up lease money, overhead expenses, and ultimately drilling dollars. He was as dependent as a baby to the nipple. Sometimes he just figured "independent" was a way to dress up "unemployed."

"Couple a years," Ethan answered.

Whitley looked over at him. "Found anything?"

Ethan shook his head and kept his eyes on the road.

Whitley sighed and looked out the side window. "Oh, boy!" He took another drag at his Lucky. "Tell me this—you say you are a geologist. Do you have a degree?"

"Yes. University of Oklahoma."

"Geology degree? Not business or English or basket weaving, or whatever the hell?"

"Yes. Geology degree."

Whitley looked relieved. "Did you work for a company?"

"I worked for Phillips for eight years in Texas and Louisiana. Some Arkansas. Later they put me in Mississippi."

"How come you left?"

Ethan glanced at him, grinning. "Chasing the dream, J.D. Chasing the big one."

J.D. shot back a stern look. "You're not holdin' anything back from me, are you?"

"Like what?"

"Like maybe you got fired from Phillips because you weren't worth a shit?"

Ethan looked at him and managed another grin. "You been fired before?"

"Hell yeah!"

"If I was too, would that make a difference?"

J.D. looked aside out the window and mumbled so low Ethan could hardly understand him. "No."

"Let's stop here."

Ethan braked the Plymouth and stopped in front of a weathered clapboard country store festooned with gaudy signs. Inside, J.D. made his way past the beer cooler, and Ethan saw him take a quick, lusty glance at it. Ethan paid, and they resumed their trek southeastward down U.S. 49 with their elbows hanging out the windows.

"How come you insisted I ride with you instead of taking my own car?"

Ethan thought about the answer and decided he might as well be bluntly honest. "Because, I need to watch you work for a couple of days." He looked aside at the landman. "Need to make sure you're on my side."

J.D. nodded. "Understood, loud and clear." He took a swig

from his soda and studied Ethan's buy outline map. "I guess you've noticed this is on the edge of the town."

Ethan nodded.

J.D. sniffed and rubbed his nose. "Now—one more time—let me get this straight. You want me to find the biggest tract in this area that you outlined here, and go and try to lease it for free?"

"That's right."

"Why don't you do it?"

"I'm not good at that. Abrams says you are. Besides, I got a bunch of other stuff to do."

"Am I to assume we will dangle some sort of carrot in front of the owner, since we don't have any money? Like a bigger than normal royalty and a commitment to drill within," J.D. shrugged, "—six months?"

"Six months is exactly what I'm thinking," Ethan said. "We can offer him three-sixteenths royalty. That's a lot better than the usual one-eighth."

"And don't forget to add my one percent on top of that."

"I haven't forgotten."

"You said Abrams seeds all your deals. How come he didn't advance you lease money on this one?"

Ethan drove on, not answering.

"Well?"

"Because I've drilled twelve straight dry holes. And he thinks this one is the riskiest of them all. He wants to see how badly I want this one. When I get a core of leases, he comes in."

"Twelve?" Whitely sighed and shook his head. "Boy, I can throw twelve darts at a map on the wall and find at least one oil field!"

Ethan nodded. "I used to think that, too."

"Damnation alley, who have I thrown in with now?" he asked the wind, shaking his head. He looked back at Ethan. "And on top of your bad luck, you want me to work for free? I can't believe I'm doin' this. In Mississippi you'd get laughed out of the county for even asking for a free lease."

"Let's don't talk about luck. And this isn't Mississippi. The people down where we're going haven't had a taste of oil yet—"

"Neither have you," Whitley interrupted, laughing.

"They've already had the Gulf dry hole drilled under their nose," Ethan continued. "They should know it's risky, and maybe they'll be willing to cooperate to get a deeper test drilled."

"It makes sense to you and to me," Whitley said, "but I don't know if it will to them. If you get me some cash to buy leases, like real oilmen do, I might be able to do some good for you."

"I know, J.D. I'm workin' on that. Oh, by the way. You mentioned last week in your apartment that you worked with some people in Mobile. Do you still have any connections down there?"

"I'm not sure I ever had any connections there. I was just a hired hand—hired to do some leasing in south Mississippi for a bunch of doctors and lawyers. They didn't know what the hell they were doing. Nothing I leased for them ever produced—that I know of." He took a final drag on a Lucky and flicked it out the window.

"So don't you know anybody in Mobile who might be interested in buying in on my deal at Fossil Rim?"

Whitley laughed. "You ain't got a deal yet. You need leases first. But the only person I know in Mobile who has any real money and is interested in the oil business is Matt Chambers, a well-to-do businessman, and some say a big crook. I tend to think the latter. So stay away from him. I don't trust him."

Ethan glanced expectantly at him, waiting for elaboration.

"I was eating with my clients, and he came over to the table. They knew him and introduced him to me. Boy, he was a dresser! Nice clothes, haircut. Thin little trimmed black mustache. I thought, man, here's a fellow knows class and style. Got money too, no doubt."

Ethan marveled at the way J.D. pronounced "money." It came out with a deep-toned rush of hot breath, sounding like, "*mhunnie.*"

"He pulled me aside and asked me to bust a lease block Shell was puttin' together in south Mississippi. I told him I was a professional. Not that kind of a man."

"Good for you," Ethan blurted. Now he definitely felt better about Whitley. He would not likely get double-crossed.

"He got mad," J.D. continued, "but he knew the people at the table were watching us. He held a smile on his face while he called me a slimy no-count son-of-a-bitch. And he told me to not show my face in his town again. Imagine that! Mobile— *his* town!" J.D.'s head performed its now familiar slow shake of disgust.

"Did you leave town?"

"Not right away. The next morning I found all four of my tires cut to ribbons. I went back a few times to finish up my business but—" He paused, reached in the back seat and pulled a Colt 1911 out of his duffel bag. "Because of that, I kept this close by."

Ethan's eyebrows lifted. "Is that loaded?"

"Hell yes, boy! What good's it unloaded?" He put it back and turned his soda can bottoms up. "Anyway, back to blockbusting; I'll starve before I do that. The lowest form of life in this business is sneaking in on somebody else's hard work and risk-taking."

The story about Chambers unsettled Ethan, but J.D.'s disdain for unscrupulous leasing practices reminded him of his own experiences with that loathsome part of the oil business.

"When I was with Phillips," he said, "we mapped a gorgeous feature near El Dorado. Started leasing on it. Word leaked out early, and we got busted right smack in the middle of the block. The guy was a chiropractor, for Pete's sake."

"Gawd-aw-mighty!" J.D. uttered, rolling his eyes.

"Yeah, he was. Busted blocks on the side. He came to us and offered the forty-acre tract he had leased. He wanted a thousand dollars an acre and a quarter override. He didn't know anything about geology. But we knew a fault ran through his forty and we thought we could drill on the up-thrown block, so we wanted it, but we didn't want it that bad.

"We refused him and drilled the forty beside him. We made a

nice little discovery and drilled two more flanking him. We had him surrounded on three sides with wells, and we knew the fault went down-thrown on the forth side, so we weren't interested in that. He kept badgering us and his price kept going up every time we made a new well beside him. We kept saying no. He finally hired a rig and drilled. He was so confident he drilled straight up—paid for all of it himself!"

J.D. looked at him, waiting.

"It was dry—he got faulted out!"

Both men burst into heavy cackles. J.D. slapped his hands together.

"Of course after that he was more than ready to sell out. We bought his lease for ten bucks an acre and gave him a small royalty. We moved 400 feet back off his dry hole, got up-thrown and made a 200 barrel-a-day well."

When J.D. got his breath back he warned Ethan. "Seriously, don't get involved with Chambers. Play your cards close. Maybe word won't get down to the Mobile mafia what you're doing."

Ethan glanced aside at Whitely, eyebrows arched. "Do you really think Chambers heads up a mafia?"

Whitley shrugged. "I don't know. That's just a word that came to mind."

Ethan nodded and watched the road, seeing a green sign flash by.

Welcome to Alabama
The Heart of Dixie
Governor James "Big Jim" Folsom

4

Hull

J.D. protested, but one room at the Do-Drop Inn was all Ethan could afford. At least he got a room with two beds.

"I feel like I'm back in college again," J.D. grumbled, shaking his head as he unpacked. "Got me a damn roomie!"

Ethan turned from his bag, surprised. He never thought to ask J.D. about his background. "You went to college?" Instantly, he regretted putting emphasis on *you*.

J.D. sneered. "Contrary to popular belief, I *am* schooled." He resumed unpacking, grumbling under his breath.

"Where?" Ethan pressed, trying to sound casual.

The response echoed out of the bathroom where J.D. had gone. "Mississippi State."

"Degree?" Ethan yelled, making himself heard over the splash of urination into the toilet.

"Petroleum engineerin'."

Ethan froze. His head slowly turned toward the bathroom. He walked over to the door and stared in.

J.D. zipped up and looked aside. "You like to watch me tinkle, huh?"

"You're kiddin' me?"

"No. I am not," J.D. said, brushing past Ethan to get to his cigarettes. "I'll smoke outside, if you want me to."

Ethan followed him out into the motel parking lot. "I should

"

have known, from all the questions you asked. But why didn't you tell me that?"

J.D. shook his head, chin high, sending roiling smoke clouds to either side. "It don't matter. I don't do that anymore."

Ethan stood dumbfounded. "Why?"

J.D. blew another cloud and coughed. "You ready to get to work?" He didn't wait for Ethan to respond. "Let's go."

Ethan carefully tendered more questions about Whitley's revelation as they drove to the courthouse, but J.D.'s refusal, with a head shake, made it clear the subject was closed.

He dropped J.D. at the courthouse steps and began a slow tour of Fossil Rim, wondering as he drove why Whitley would give up an engineering career for leasing work which didn't require a degree, was irregular, and generally paid less. He couldn't get the questions off his mind.

The town was pretty typical, Ethan noted, of small Southern towns. It had railroad tracks running smack down the middle of Main Street, separating the north and southbound lanes. A few people were out walking along the sidewalks. The Kress department store was doing the best business, but Buchanan's Mercantile seemed to him to be a more inviting store. Its double doors were propped open. Various housewares and garden implements sat outside with bright price tags dangling from them. As he drove by he saw men sitting on stools and chairs just inside the door.

Across the street he saw a barber pole spinning, that door also propped open. A block farther he passed the Farmer's Bank. At four stories, it was the town's biggest building. From there he could see several church steeples in various directions, all jutting above the tall longleaf pines.

Ethan cruised north out of town for a mile and pulled over. He sat and looked ahead at the scenery. The highway fell away to the north, not abruptly, but gently. Still, he could see for several miles. He reached into his satchel and pulled out a topographic map he had brought from Jackson. Yes, the town indeed sat on a high area in the terrain. It wasn't a mountain by any means but a simple rise. This was further confirmation that a large bulge in the earth's crust sat underneath the town and its local area, just as his structure map suggested.

But Ethan knew that such subsurface features rarely expressed themselves on the surface. In fact, this was the first one he had seen in his career. The effects of erosion usually wiped away the evidence but not here. Whatever was pushing up this town was still growing. That might not bode well for oil. Oil needed time to pool up in a trap. The thought troubled him.

Ethan started the car and resumed his tour, seeing more evidence of the high area in other directions from town.

Finally he found Gulf's old drill site. It was a scuffed up acre of land near the south end of town. He knew the hole had been plugged with cement and the casing cut off below the surface. Dirt had been back-filled to smooth the ground. Sage grass and young pines now covered the site.

He felt a rumble and heard a train horn blow, two long blasts, a short and another long—the standard warning engineers used at road crossings. He turned to see red lights blinking. A bell began ringing as a long string of sooty diesel-electric locomotives rolled past him bearing the green and white Southern Railways paint livery. He took note of that. Most railroads owned the minerals under their rights-of-way.

His eyes followed the slow progress of the train heading into town. A gas station sat about 300 yards north of him, and the other buildings sat beyond that. He could almost see the courthouse.

He checked his watch and headed back to the motel. He still had much work to do on his prospect package to get it ready for showing to potential investors. He would do that until J.D. finished up for the day.

He heard heavy snorts coming from inside his room as he inserted his key. J.D. lay outstretched, shoes cast onto the floor, shirt unbuttoned to the navel, the hairy chest heaving. Gurgling snorts spouted one after another from a mouth gaping wide enough to set production tubing into.

Ethan moved to his bed and sat watching, shaking his head, irritation building. His anger at J.D.'s early return from his duty station in the courthouse records room grew worse as he wondered how he would ever be able to sleep. J.D.'s struggle to breathe in his sleep reminded Ethan of a big truck roaring and backfiring as it jake-braked.

His gaze shifted to a table with paperwork on it. Ethan picked up a legal pad and looked over J.D.'s notes. He smiled. The man worked fast. He saw that J.D. had found a large 480-acre tract of land in the target area, owned by Victor Hull. J.D. had marked the acreage "open" on the rough lease map he had drawn. Lands belonging to the Buchanan family were also marked open. Ethan wondered if that acreage belonged to the owners of the mercantile he had passed downtown. Much of the target area was yet unmarked. J.D. had obviously done a quick search, looking only for the big tracts.

Ethan snapped his fingers. Open—not under lease. Here was the core lease he had hoped for. And quick and early, too! He looked back at the sleeping, heaving heap. Now if only J.D. could sign Mr. or Mrs. Hull without giving him cash. He stared at J.D. wondering if he should trust him to try. He sure didn't want to do it himself. He needed Whitley.

That night they fed on pot roast and mashed potatoes at the Wagon Wheel Restaurant, which was a block up the street from the motel. The restaurant was nearly empty, and the few diners inside seemed not to take much notice of them. Ethan told J.D. how pleased he was that he found the information so quickly. "So, when are you going to see Mr. Hull," Ethan asked.

"Already have," J.D. said after washing down a biscuit with a slug of coffee.

"What?" Ethan blurted, startled. "When did you go?"

"This afternoon, while you were out gallivantin' around." J.D. looked at his food and continued to munch as if the subject wasn't important enough to pursue.

"How'd you get there?"

"I borrowed a car from a clerk at the records office." He smiled. "Nice lady—a widow woman." His eyebrows arched. "Right smart looking, too. Her name's Clarice. I'll be needing your car Friday night. She's having me over for dinner."

Ethan put his fork down and forcefully threw his napkin on his plate. "You've got to keep me in the loop, J.D. You're working for me. I need to know what's going on!"

J.D. looked aside at the other diners and back at Ethan. He put a cupped hand to his mouth and jerked his head their direction.

Ethan leaned closer and lowered his voice. "What did he say?"

"Nothing much. I'm gonna see him again tomorrow."

Ethan relaxed. "Oh. Well, what's he like?"

J.D. swallowed the last of his meal and wiped his mouth. He reached into his shirt pocket. Ethan leaned back and held his breath, knowing what was coming. He hated that first cloud smokers made. It contained the nostril-burning, acrid, phosphorus stench of the match.

The blaze flared in front of J.D.'s face. A stinking blue cloud appeared and slowly dissipated. J.D. puffed, sniffed, and coughed. "He's old. I'd say close to ninety. He's an old farmer. Wife long dead. He's got one son—and that could pose a problem."

"How so?"

"Adult children are always looking out for the older parents' best interest when it comes to leasing. Of course they expect to inherit whatever deal transpires. And when you get a really old man like this one, sometimes the kids think he's senile and ought not to be wheeling and dealing on his own."

"You think he's senile?"

"No. I think he's competent. He looked me straight in the eye and talked like he knew what was goin' on. I didn't ask him for a free lease or anything. I told him I wanted to introduce myself, and I told him I was interested in talking to him about his land. He thought I wanted to buy it and told me to get out. I saw a sword hanging on the wall and struck up a conversation with him about it. It was his daddy's. His daddy rode with General Forrest. So did my granddaddy. So we hit it off pretty good. He talked some more about the Civil War and cows and tractors, and he invited me back to breakfast tomorrow."

"Good," Ethan said, slumping, smiling. "It amazes me how you did that."

"Did what?"

"Walked up to a total stranger, got to know him, and got an invite to breakfast without even telling him why you were there."

"I got lucky. The poor ole man is lonesome as hell. He just wanted somebody to talk to. I just mostly listened."

The next morning the phone rang just as Ethan got back from breakfast. It was J.D. "I'm coming back to the motel to pick you up. "I want you here as a witness when I sign him."

"Did you ask him?"

"Yes. He agreed to the terms you offered."

Ethan felt a grin crawl across his face. He couldn't believe the fantastic luck he was having—and so soon.

J.D., driving Ethan's car, picked him up a few minutes later, and they went back to the Hull house. On the way Ethan asked why he was needed to witness the lease signing. He knew it wasn't standard procedure.

"Because it will give us a little insurance if somebody challenges his competency. If something comes up, you can vouch that I did not misrepresent anything, and that he seemed fully aware of his actions. Let's hope it doesn't end up in court, but if it comes to that, it'll be a little tougher for them if we do it this way."

"That's smart," Ethan said. Then, playfully, he added, "Maybe you should have been a lawyer."

"I am," J.D. uttered.

Ethan's mouth fell agape.

J.D. put his hand up. "We don't need to talk about that now. We've got work to do."

Ethan was still wondering what other revelations he might discover about J.D. when he saw Mr. Hull at the door. The sight stunned him. The man was decrepit. His eyes had sank far back into his head, bloodshot and dull. He was tall and broad-shouldered. His skin clung to his frame. His brown-stained teeth—those that remained—protruded unevenly and at unnatural angles.

The man ushered them to his sofa and began chattering in a high-pitched voice. Ethan could only make out about every other word. It sounded as if Hull were forming words from the back of his tongue, the tip of it being numb. J.D. nodded and grunted as if he had no trouble understanding.

The old man launched into the story of how he got his John Deere tractor. "As fine a machine as anything a man ever built," he declared. A salesman had invited him to join a group of farmers to visit the John Deere plant in Waterloo, Iowa, which, Mr. Hull pronounced as "*Iowee*." He was young, then, and a single man. It was his first trip out of the state. And there were girls for them there, too. The salesman saw that they had pleasant company for the evening. The old timer grinned and slowly shook his head.

He wanted to take them to the shed to see the tractor, but J.D. suggested they first sign the papers. Mr. Hull put on glasses, but Ethan wondered what good that could do for such wretched eyes.

Ethan watched as the other two first fixed their signatures to the standard oil-and-gas lease form that J.D. had filled out with the appropriate information. The lease gave Ethan six months from that day to commence a well on any part of the land, or in a forty-acre drilling unit, of which the land was included, in part. If the well was not commenced in that period, the Hull lease would become null and void. Hull reserved for himself a handsome royalty of three-sixteenths. One-eighth was the industry standard royalty for mineral owners. Ethan signed the witnessing clause at the bottom. He noted the date, February 15, 1956. He needed to spud the well before midnight August 15.

They shook hands and went out to the barn where Ethan listened politely to the old man's prattle. But his thoughts were now on the task ahead. He now had a prospect. There was money to be raised and more leases to get. He needed bids from drilling contractors. Six months to go. Already he imagined a ticking sound in his ears.

5

Brubeck

Grover Shine jettisoned a slug of brown spit precisely into the stained coffee can beside the door, then settled into Harry Little's chair.

The barber popped the apron in the air, sending chopped hairs flying and let the apron float onto the farmer's lap. "Well, did you hear the news, Grover?" Harry asked, picking up his clippers.

"Naw. What news?"

"The awl business is coming to town. Again."

"To hell you say!"

"No s'r. I'm not ly'n'. There was an oilman up to Old Man Hull's yesterday morning wantin' to lease his land."

"I knew it! I knew it!" Grover shouted, turning and pointing a bony finger in the barber's face. "I knew they didn't dig deep enough when they come through here a few years back. And I told you so. Remember?"

"If I remembered everything people told me in here my head would be bigger 'n Clew Sheppard's punkins."

Harry began clipping but had to halt and urge Grover to be still. "Why are you so jumpy this mornin'?"

"I ain't jumpy! I'm just studin' on them oilmen. I told you they'd be back. I did."

"Just what makes you so fit to say there's oil down there, deeper? My gracious, they went down more'n a mile! Any further and the devil'll be climbin' outta that hole with a pitchfork a comin' after yo ass!"

"Well, he can have me if he brings sacks of money with 'im."

"He don't need no money to get you."

Grover gazed out the window and turned pensive again. "I can feel it, Harry. I know it's there. Every time I go out on my land I keep thinkin' of that well they drilled—just a mile away. They didn't go deep enough. I got eighty acres. Maybe I'll get a well on every acre. Whew! I'd never have to hitch another plow again."

"They don't drill them things that close together. Do they?"

"Maybe. Maybe not. But I'm tired of being poor. I hope Ole Hull makes 'em pay big for his leases. They'll be more willin' to pay up when they get to me."

"Well, you better be ready to get disappointed, big boy, because Ole Hull leased for nothin'. That's what I heard."

Grover got up and turned. Harry hated it when his customers did that. He backed off and grimaced.

"Harry, you're joshin' me. Harry!"

"I'm not joshin' you. I heard he leased for free. That's all I know. Benny Hull came in here yesterday and told us. He was mad as hell."

Grover threw off the apron and walked to the window.

"I'm not through with you yet," Harry growled.

Grover ran his hand through his hair, what little he had left on top, looking toward the courthouse. "They ain't gettin' my lease for nuthin'. No s'r, they're not."

"I don't blame you. Make 'em pay. Ole Hull don't know what he's doin.' Now get back over here."

"I need that money. I got bills. We get another drought like last summer, and I'll go broke. I need them oilmen. I need 'em now."

Harry strolled to the window and stood beside the overall clad farmer.

"Well, there sure ain't no draught here now. Look there. My barber pole stopped turnin' again. This rain's playin' hell on the motor."

"You don't need no motor," muttered Grover, his frog-like eyes fixed far off.

"I like things to be right," snapped Harry. He stepped back toward the empty barber chair and sank into it. He reached down and picked up the *Mobile Press Register* and scanned the front page. "Birmin'ham's had twelve inches this month, and there's still a week to go. We've probably had more than that here. This is the wettest winter I can ever recollect."

"The Hulls never paid no mind to me," Grover mumbled. "I'm just a hardscrabble dirt farmer to them. They always had the best land, and the most."

Harry rattled the paper some more, cocking his head higher to peruse the upper columns through his bifocals. "What do you think about this McCarthy feller? Says he's go'n get rid of all the com'nists."

"Never heard of'im." Grover's gaze swung inside to the barber. He spat again. "Harry, how long have you known him?"

"Who? McCarthy?" Harry answered, smirking.

"Dammit, you know who I'm talkin' about—Victor Hull," Grover scolded.

Harry removed his glasses. His bottom lip rolled up across the top one, as if attached with a wire to his upward scrolling eyes. "I don't know—twenty five, thirty years."

Grover paced and shook his head. "Finally, the oilmen come back! I feared we'd never see 'em again. Now they're back, and look what Hull does! Stabs the rest of us in the back!"

"Settle down, Grover. You'll get along all right."

They both sat thoughtfully for a while, listening to an approaching train. The horn sounded, and a rumble pervaded the planks under the floor tile. They listened a while longer, as the engine blew again, and the rumble steadily built. A bell on the engine began ringing. The rumble grew heavier, until the storefronts across the street vanished behind an enormous wet hulk dripping with morning rain. With squealing brakes the lone engine glided to a smooth stop in a siding.

Immediately a door opened on the cab. The engineer, brakeman, and half a dozen men from the switching yard south of town clambered down the steps and made their way along the catwalk laughing and bantering, descended the ladder, stepped across the mainline, and headed straight for the cafe.

Harry chuckled. "You always know the blue plate special is on at the Wagon Wheel when the Southern Railroad comes to a screechin' halt, and they scramble off of there like rats off a sinkin' ship."

"Oh, hell!" Grover grunted. "Here comes a pile o' work."

A woman holding her long skirt up stepped across the tracks in front of the idling engine and came toward the shop. "Hey there, Corrine," Harry announced when she came in.

"How do, ma'm?" Grover added.

"Did ya'll hear anything about oilmen in town?" asked the woman.

"We just been talkin' about that," Harry said. "Grover's been telling me how rich he's gonna get."

"I hope we all do," she said. "Have they been in here?"

"No 'm."

"Have they leased your land yet, Grover?"

"No. Just Victor Hull's, far as I know."

"Old Man Hull? How much did he get?"

The two men eyed each other. "Nuthin'." Grover said. "Not a single red cent. He leased for free."

"My God!" Corrine said, shaking her head. "Why did he do that?"

"Who knows what he does. Does he even know?"

"Well, they won't get ours for nothing! I can tell you that! Do you think they might find oil this time?"

Harry shrugged.

"I've got to tell Ben." She paused before darting out the door and turned. "He better not get a notion to sell our lease for free!"

Harry and Grover stepped out front and watched her scurry back across the tracks. "I don't think that conversation is gonna be very tender."

Grover chuckled and fumbled in his pocket for his truck keys.

"Good luck, Grover," Harry said. "I hope you get dirty, filthy rich and put me in your will."

Ethan was working on his prospect package when heard a rattle at the door, someone inserting a key. He glanced at his watch and wondered why J.D. would be coming back from the courthouse so early in the afternoon. Light spilled into the room, and a large lawman peered in.

"Who are *you*?" the officer demanded.

Ethan got up. "Ethan Bonner. What's wrong?"

"Do you know that man?" He pointed out into the parking lot. A deputy was helping J.D. out of the back seat of the police cruiser. His legs were wobbly, and his head listed aside at an awkward angle. J.D.'s lips moved, but Ethan couldn't hear him.

Ethan grimaced. It had happened much sooner than he expected. "Yes. He's my business associate. J.D. Whitley."

"Well, he's drunk. We found him and Mr. Victor Hull sittin' in a truck drinkin' rot gut out of a jar. He told us he was staying here. We fished this key out of his pocket. He didn't say anything about you."

"Thank you for bringing him back," Ethan said after they helped J.D. to his bed.

"I'd a thrown him in jail if I thought he was botherin' Mr. Hull, but they were both havin' a hootin' good time."

They went out into the motel parking lot. "Who are you people?" the sheriff asked.

Ethan told him why they were in town. The sheriff listened sternly, as if he didn't trust the story. When Ethan finished, the officer still looked skeptical. "When we found your friend he told us he was going to make Mr. Hull rich."

Ethan stared at the pavement and shook his head.

"Mr. Bonner," the sheriff said, "oil people came through here about five years ago and got everybody excited. Then they let us down. Said they had a dry hole. They packed up and left. Now here you come promising to make us rich with oil."

"He shouldn't have said that," Ethan interjected. "Every hole drilled for oil is risky."

"I know. But this is my town, and these are my people, and you two fellows—who apparently don't work for a real oil company—are stirring things up."

"What do you mean by that?" Ethan asked.

"Benny Hull, Victor's son, came into my office this morning mad as a wet hen. He told me you people tricked his daddy into signing a lease for free. That's why we were going out to Hull's house when we found them drinking. Now, what you did was not against the law, as far as I know. But I don't like what you're doing."

Ethan felt a rush of anger and embarrassment. He looked at the sheriff and slowly shook his head. He saw the sheriff's name tag, Hub Tant. "Sheriff Tant, if we can sit down and talk about this I think you might understand better what we're trying to accomplish here. We're not here to scam anybody. We're trying to get another well drilled—deeper this time. But money is short because of that dry hole you mentioned."

Sheriff Tant's tongue seemed, to Ethan, to be probing the snuff pooled inside lower lip while he thought. "Okay. We'll talk. But we'll talk in a meeting with the town leaders. We'll let them hear what you have to say. Come on."

"Wait," Ethan said, caught off guard. He tried to quickly think about what documents he should carry with him and what to say. He couldn't believe things were going so wrong, so quickly. Any hope of confidentiality about his work had now evaporated. "Do we have to do this right now?"

"Yes sir, you do. We'll see if the mayor is in." He called the station on the cruiser's radio and asked his dispatcher to contact the mayor. They waited. "Why Mr. Hull?" The sheriff pressed his interrogation as Ethan gathered his thoughts. "You seemed to have picked about the oldest man in town. That's what shysters generally do."

"Sheriff, Mr. Hull has 480 acres right where I want to drill."

The sheriff looked at him and spat. The radio crackled. The mayor was over at another office—that of a city council member. "That'll do," the sheriff said. "Call and tell them, if they wouldn't mind, I'll drop by with a visitor for a few minutes."

Ethan rode with the sheriff to the Farmers Bank. They went up to the top floor and through a door with a sign that read, *Brubeck & Associates, Land & Timber*. A secretary ushered them into a large office. Ethan followed his escort in. A man sitting in a stuffed chair in the corner got up and nodded to the sheriff.

"Mayor," the sheriff said, nodding.

The mayor stepped forward and offered his hand to Ethan. "Mayor Danny Hooper."

The other one, apparently Mr. Brubeck, sat behind his desk, not offering a hand. "Sheriff, is this the man who's been dogging Victor Hull?" he asked.

Ethan felt his blood pressure go up. Just when he thought all was going so well, this happens.

"You know already?" the sheriff said.

"Don't much happen around here that I don't know about," the man said, not taking his eyes off Ethan. "As a matter of fact, we've been sitting here talking about it."

The sheriff turned to Ethan. "Mr. Bonner, this is Emmett Brubeck."

Ethan nodded. Brubeck didn't get up. Instead he gestured to a chair.

"Sit down."

Ethan and the sheriff sat. The mayor made small talk, asking Ethan where he was from, but Brubeck wasted no time getting to his point and cutting the mayor off. "Mr. Bonner, what are you here for?"

"I'm here to lease land and get a test well drilled for oil."

"Really, now." Brubeck spouted. "You're here to get money, aren't you?"

Ethan glanced aside out the office window as if seeking

counsel from an invisible lurking adviser. "No. I'm not here to raise money. I don't think there's much of that in this town to raise. I'm here to lease mineral rights."

Brubeck chuckled under his breath and reached for his coffee. "Mr. Bonner," he said, "you're not the first oilman, if that's what you really are, to come around here promising wealth and riches to us if we'd only give you some money and land."

"Mr. Bonner," the mayor butted, "did you know that way back in the early part of this century this town had an oil lease auction?" Ethan shook his head.

"Right after the big oil discovery at Spindletop in Texas, oil fever swept all across the Gulf Coast. People around here were dirt poor—much more so than today.

Brubeck and the sheriff sank into their chairs anticipating another of the mayor's narratives.

"In the years after the Civil War the northern economy was booming. People up there got rich in the manufacturing business while down here we were still reeling from reconstruction. The Yankees got more leisure time on their hands and looked for somewhere to spend it. After a while they got up the nerve to vacation in the South. They went to Hot Springs, Arkansas, and bathed in the mineral waters up there.

"Well, we got some mineral springs here, too. In two or three places nice clear water rises up. Good water for your health. One day a Yankee got off a train that stopped here. This fella walked around town while the train took on water, and he saw the springs. He bottled some of it up and took it back north with him.

"Next thing you know agents are buying land around the springs and the trains are bringing in construction crews. A hotel went up. Had a spa in it—a big pool where people could soak in that mineral water. Then another hotel went up. People were coming from Cincinnati and Chicago. They thought soaking in that water would cure all their ills." The mayor looked about, eyebrows arched, head nodding. "Maybe it does!"

Brubeck grinned, leaned back, and clasped his hands behind his head. "What a racket! I wish I had been in on that action."

The mayor's history lesson fell as prattle against Ethan's ears, as he tried to concentrate on what next to say, when Brubeck's cross-hairs swung back his way.

"People were making money here hand over fist," the mayor continued. "True, most of it went up north to the investors, but folks around here benefited, too. Some did construction and worked for the railroad. And then—"

"And then it went to hell in a hand basket! Right?" Brubeck guessed.

"Yes. It did. The prosperity left this area almost as fast as it came." He shook a finger at the others. "You see, the Yankees started discovering that we've got the prettiest beaches in the world on the Gulf Coast—bar none."

Ethan almost felt like chuckling, wondering if the mayor intended the pun.

"When the first hotel went up in Gulf Shores, it was all over for Fossil Rim." He leaned back. "The trains started coming through and not even stopping. People fell into poverty. Some sold out and left. Others tried to farm. The lumber industry couldn't support many. This town died.

"But, back to the oil lease auction." All the men perked up. "As I was saying, right after the big discovery at Spindletop, everybody who owned land started dreaming. What if it happened here? And, why not? What's so special about Texas? I suppose people didn't know much about geology back then?"

Ethan shrugged.

"Everybody just thought you picked a spot on a hunch and started digging. Hell, I don't know, maybe they were using a dowser stick for oil out there in Texas. But at least it was a reason to hope. So they all banded together—my daddy, yours probably." He gestured toward Brubeck. "They got together and organized a big land auction one Saturday. They advertised it in the papers in Houston and Dallas. Even in New York. They put on a big festival. Raised every cent they had and put up banners across the streets and on the railroad depot welcoming the oil industry. Booths went up selling drinks and—hell, I don't know if they had hotdogs back then. But it was a festival. They even had a band out playing. At 10 a.m. they opened up the bidding on the courthouse steps."

He paused.

"Nobody showed up—nobody! Not a single damn pitiful solitary soul! From the oil business, that is."

"I never knew that," Brubeck uttered.

"Yes," the mayor said, nodding. "It happened."

"And then, after the War, they came here to drill, and everybody got excited again, but we didn't have no auction. And they come up with a dry hole."

"I know that part," Ethan said. "I've done my homework."

"Now," Brubeck interjected, leaning forward and leering at Ethan. "Mr. Oilman, how do you propose to build on that record of failure?" He pronounced "oilman" mockingly. Ethan wanted to punch him.

Ethan got up and went to the window. "A good start would be some understanding on your part." Brubeck rolled his eyes. "I need leases," Ethan said. "I don't have any money to buy them. I need for people to give me free leases, just like Mr. Hull did."

"Aw—" Brubeck moaned, turning his head in disgust.

"Are you crazy?" the mayor protested. "Why should we trust you? Your own oil buddies don't even trust you. If they did, you would go raise your money before you leased."

"That's not always the way the business operates," Ethan answered. "Look," he said. "What's so crazy about free leases? I've studied the geology. I've made maps. If I can go back to Jackson or Houston with a stack of leases in my hand and with a map that shows a giant oil field under them, there's a good chance I can find some investors that are willing to take the chance. But without the leases, all I've got is an idea. And ideas alone don't sell."

The sheriff finally spoke up. "I've got some land about three miles north of Mr. Hull. If I gave you a free oil lease what would I get in return?"

Ethan perked up. "Nothing—up front. An initial payment for a lease is called a bonus. Over in Mississippi they're getting twenty-five-to-fifty-dollars-an acre. I don't have that kind of money. You give me your lease; I'll have the exclusive right to drill on it within six months. That's all I ask. If I can't raise the money and drill in six months you get it back. If it's a dry hole you lose nothing. If it's an oil well you get a generous royalty. You can't lose!"

"Oh, but we can lose!" Brubeck objected. Ethan waited for an explanation.

"If I leased my—I'm not telling you how much I've got, but let's just say one hundred acres. If I lease my one hundred acres to you for nothing and you get a dry hole, I have wasted my chance to profit off of my lease. Whereas, if I lease my land to another oilman who will pay fifty dollars an acre for that lease, I make five thousand dollars regardless if it hits oil or not. So you see, we do have something to lose."

"But what other oilman is at your door for your lease?" Ethan asked, jumping in on the argument as quickly as Brubeck did. "I'm the only game in town!"

"That's true," Brubeck countered. "But if there's oil under us it's not going anywhere. We can wait until the oil business comes our way. I think it will eventually. You are way out in front of it. If we let you condemn our leases with a dry hole—and we get nothing in return—then, when the oil business finally gets here, it will bypass us and we will have nothing to show for it." Brubeck looked at the mayor, who was nodding vigorously.

"I can't wait, sir," Ethan said. "I have to get in front of it. Following is not an option."

Brubeck got up. The other men got the signal and rose also. "Mr. Bonner, best of luck to you. Now if ya'll will excuse me." He didn't offer his hand.

The mayor left, and the sheriff walked with Ethan down Main Street and introduced him to some other people around town, mostly merchants. They went into the barber shop and talked to Harry Little and his customers waiting for their turn in the chair. They also visited Buchanan Mercantile and met owners Ben and Corrine.

Ethan stayed mostly quiet. He had spent his emotional energy and much of his will at Brubeck's office. The sheriff offered him a lift back to the motel, and Ethan politely refused. The walk would help him think.

"Mr. Bonner," the sheriff said. How long will you and your partner be here?"

"J.D.'s not my partner. He's working for me. But he's a good man—a fair man. You can trust him." The sheriff nodded. "I'm planning on leaving tomorrow to go to Jackson first, then Texas."

The sheriff seemed unsettled. "And your hired help?"

"I'll take him back to Jackson to pick up his car. Then he'll come back."

The sheriff shook his head. "It won't work. I know drunks when I see them. The only way I'm going to be okay with this is if you stay until I get to know him. How do I know you won't ever show up back here again and he stays?"

Ethan tried not to show frustration. He wondered if the sheriff had introduced him to all those people just to be friendly, or to make them aware of him. Might he not later go back and warn them not to do business with him? He could not leave his plan in J.D.'s hands until he established trust in town.

"Okay. I'll stay a few days."

The sheriff nodded then looked stern again. "You'd better be on the up and up, mister!"

Ethan forced a smile. "I am."

Hub sat down to supper that night with his wife, Edna, and his niece, Laura. He told them he'd met an interesting fellow. Edna's eyebrow's raised. But Hub wasn't into matchmaking. When he saw the women's expressions, he paused and said, "All I'm sayin' is I met this fella from Louisiana. He's a geologist—so he says."

Laura's eyes snapped to him.

Edna said, "A what?"

Hub explained that the geologist was looking for oil and thought there might be some nearby.

"Would he be interested in talking to my kids about geology?" Laura asked.

Hub shrugged.

"Would you ask him?"

Hub rubbed his chin and thought for a while, then smiled. "Okay. I'll ask him."

J.D. was laughing at the television when Ethan opened the door to the room. Ethan sat on his bed, leaned back, and joined J.D. watching *I Love Lucy*. At the commercial break J.D. said, "Ethan, I'm about ready to ask Mr. Buchanan for a free lease. Keep your fingers crossed."

Ethan looked up and nodded. "We'll need it." He sat on his bed, then slowly laid back. "I've been with the mayor," he said softly. "And some others."

"Yup," J.D. uttered. "I heard."

Ethan's eyes opened and cut toward Whitley. "How did you hear?"

J.D. shrugged. "I'm already part of the grapevine in this town. It's my job. But why you did it, I'll never know. I thought we were supposed to be discrete about what we're doin' here."

"Discrete!" Ethan roared, springing upright. "What's discrete about getting hauled in for public drunkenness?"

J.D. reached for a pack of cigarettes. "I told you, didn't I?"

Ethan stared at the floor between his legs. "Your—binge is what got the sheriff's attention." His voice trailed off. "He took me in to see the mayor and—and this guy named..."

"Brubeck," J.D. said, nodding. "I know all about him."

The phone interrupted. Ethan answered. He listened, then cut his eyes toward J.D. "When?" he asked, into the phone. "Yeah, I guess so," he mumbled. "I don't know. How about, say, Thursday at nine?" He listened, nodding into the phone. "Okay. Nine, then." He hung up and stared at the landman.

"What now?" J.D. asked.

Ethan sighed. "The sheriff wants me to talk about geology to some school kids."

Ethan saw J.D. studying him. "What?" he demanded.

"He's testin' you." J.D. nodded. "Yup, that's what he's doing. You gotta go."

"Oh, boy," Ethan mumbled. "That's all I need."

He kicked his shoes off, laid back, and locked his hands behind his head, watching the television but not seeing the ludicrous antics of Lucy's rapid-fire exchanges with Ricky. His mind clung to Emmett Brubeck.

Brubeck worried him. He knew he would not likely be able to work with possibly the wealthiest and most influential man in town. The guy's eyes had bored into him. His brief conversation with Brubeck seemed more like an interrogation laced with subtle accusations.

Ethan rolled to his side and laid his head on his elbow looking at the wall. The resemblance of Brubeck's facial features and his mannerisms unsettled him. A face from the past merged with Brubeck's—a menacing face with hair sheened and slicked, not a strand out of place. Major Donovan.

Ethan remembered, like Brubeck had done, how Donovan's head slowly swung toward him, the frigid eyes fixed like gunsights. When that head turned that slowly, coming around at you, hell was in store.

Donovan. If only he could forget him.

He counted the years in his head since he had last seen the bastard. More than ten now. Yet it was like yesterday. Would it ever go away? He grunted, sighed. Closed his eyes. Half asleep, he was barely aware when the television signed-off with the National Anthem, then died into blessed silence followed by the click of J.D. turning out the lights.

Sure, all of the fellows had been bitter about sitting out the war in Panama, guarding against an attack on the canal—one that never came. But Donovan took his frustration to horrid extremes.

The face appeared again, a map on the wall behind it. A hat with an emblem on it sat crushed down on the forehead, the bill hanging low over malicious, piercing eyes, the lips underneath them moving, cursing. "Bonner, I will not tolerate any more dry runs by you and any more intentional misses! You will fire this time, and you will hit! Do you understand?"

Ethan dipped his head—a half nod—a mumble. "Yes, sir."

He pushed the throttle, felt the acceleration, felt and heard the one-thousand horsepower Allison engine howl. He pulled the landing gear handle up and watched the brilliant beach flash underneath the wings, the blue Pacific with mottled green patches stretching to the horizon. He saw other P-40s around him, weaving, bobbling, so close he felt he could touch them, guns at the ready, Donovan out front searching. He hoped they wouldn't find what they were looking for. God, how he hoped.

The radio crackled with Donovan's inhospitable voice. "Targets nine o'clock low! Arm 'em up. Lead's in hot!" Then he saw Donovan's plane snap hard left, its nose pitching down as it rolled. The others followed. Ethan swallowed hard, armed his guns, and rolled-in behind them.

Tracer rounds raced out front of the planes ahead of him, the blue water breaking out in a rash of tiny white spots. The planes ahead pulled up. Now he could see the big gray oblong shapes gracefully weaving, breaking the surface, thrashing. Then Donovan's voice screaming on the radio: *Bonner, goddam you! You better shoot, you better hit!*"

He squeezed the trigger on the stick, heard the six .50 caliber guns bark, saw his own tracers racing down ahead, saw the hulks with their enormous tails and fins violently thrashing, saw the red in the water, felt the wet in his eyes, the retch in his gut.

He eyes snapped open. He heard J.D. snoring. He lay awake sweating.

6

LAURA

Corrine Buchanan's shrill voice yelled, her hands shoved at J.D.'s lapels, pushing him out onto the sidewalk. The landman stumbled backward into a passerby in front of the mercantile, knocking the man off-balance and sending his hat tumbling to the sidewalk. Other shoppers halted and watched as the woman concluded an angry tirade that had begun inside the store. "You crook. You thief. The nerve. Stay away. Stay out!" She spun and went back inside.

The rattled Whitley got out a handkerchief and dabbed his forehead. He heard the woman and her husband Ben exchanging loud words inside. He was turning to leave when Ben came out. "Mr. Whitley, I apologize for that. She had no call to be rude to you that way."

"It's okay. It's okay," Whitley said. "I sure didn't mean to insult anybody. I was only asking."

"I know," Ben said. "Look, come back another time when you get some money for leasing, and we'll talk. Next time I'll keep her out of it. I'm interested, Mr. Whitley, and I understand where you're coming from. But I just can't lease for free."

"I understand," Whitley said. "Will you just promise me one thing? Will you let me know before you lease to anybody else. That's all I ask."

Buchanan nodded and apologized again for his wife's rampage.

Laura's class, and those of two other teachers, was ready when the geologist came in carrying some boxes with him. He wasn't the handsomest thing she had ever seen, but she tried to look for other traits in people. She wondered if he would be as crass as those other oilmen she had met.

The minute he strode into the room, she eyed his sandy colored hair, high cheekbones, and tanned, weathered face. She watched his head movements as he arranged his articles on the table, hardly looking up at his audience. It took too long. Students coughed and whispered. Finally he looked up and formed a slight smile—a feigned one, it seemed to her. *If he is going to make a good impression,* she thought, *he'd better get on with it.*

Asking a real scientist to come and talk to your eighth graders is a good thing, she had told the other teachers. *Maybe it could inspire them.* But it appeared inspiration was slow coming. No doubt, some *were* inspired, she reflected after it was over. But it was the ideas they took home with them that started the trouble.

Every young eye in the room swung to the box and fixed on it. Laura's eyes stayed riveted on the bearer of the box. Impulsively, she fumbled for a brush from her purse and applied a couple of quick strokes to her hair while he poked through the box.

He wore khakis—both his shirt and trousers. She likened it to a uniform of some bizarre sort. He had on heavy, brown cowboy style construction boots, and his right pant leg was caught in the top of his boot. That bothered her. She didn't know why, but from the very beginning she wanted to walk up to him and reach down and jerk that damn pant leg out of the boot.

His voice sounded unusually soft for such an outdoorsy appearance. He spoke with a slight raspiness and seemed to prefer short, clipped sentences, sometimes pausing to let his listeners absorb the message. He introduced himself to the kids and told them he was born and reared in Duncan, Oklahoma, and lived in Shreveport, Louisiana. He started off simply.

"There are basically three types of rocks." His voice carried across the room, soft but firm, country but articulate. Laura began to feel hot and found something to fan her face with. "Sedimentary, igneous, and metamorphic." He explained that igneous rocks were the basic building blocks of the earth's crust. Granite and basalt were the most common. "Wind and water, and sometimes ice," he said, "breaks the igneous rocks down into tiny pieces—sand grains—that wash away and recollect in giant layered beds. Some of them form sandstones." He pulled out a piece of ochre colored rock and passed it around. He pulled out another one that was dark gray, smoother, and flat. "This is a shale," he said. "Shale forms when fine grains settle out of water to make layers of mud." He passed that one around.

"Then there's this one." He pulled out a blocky, gray rock with a bluish tint. "This is limestone. This forms in shallow seas where little organisms settle out of the water to form layers of calcium carbonate. Finally, there's the metamorphic rocks. I don't have any samples with me, but metamorphic rocks are sedimentary or igneous rocks that have undergone chemical alteration under the influence of extreme heat and pressure." He paused and wet his lips. Laura sensed he knew he had gotten too technical for his audience. "Marble, for instance. Marble is metamorphosed limestone." Laura glanced around the room and saw blank stares on the kids' faces. She figured Ethan must have also sensed that; he cleared his throat, and with an awkward smile, moved on to explain how sedimentary rocks piled up in many thick layers that were deposited by seas.

Danny McCleary put his hand up. "Miss Hamilton told us the sea was once here where we live!" Danny was the quiet, detached type. Laura was glad Ethan had captured his interest.

"Yes, Ethan said. "The sea was here where we are right now. Not once but many times."

Laura's star student Mary Jo, shot her hand up. "My daddy showed me some sharks' teeth and shells he found in the dirt on my uncle's farm. He said that was from the great flood of

Noah." She looked around at her peers with a gleeful grin. Laura wondered how Ethan was going to handle that.

"Well," Ethan began. He paused and looked down. His lips tightened and his right cheek contracted. His hand came up and scratched his face. "You know, I'm not saying your dad is wrong about this—he has a right to his opinion—but those fossils were deposited by a sea that covered this area a hundred thousand years ago. Maybe up to a million."

A dozen, "Wows," rose up from the kids. A freckled boy said, "A million? Wow!"

"But a million years is a drop in the bucket," Ethan explained. "Some of the rocks up in the northern part of the state are over three hundred million years old." Another round of wows and cackles arose. "And the earth itself is believed to be about four billion years old. That's four thousand million years." Ethan paused and grinned.

The freckled boy looked at his buddy and said, "Billion! Wow!"

Laura knew without a doubt her students had never heard these things. She nearly cringed thinking of the trouble that might arise if the kids carried this message home.

Ethan explained why he was in town, and that's when Laura got really interested—he was getting into new science, for her. He drew some diagrams on the chalkboard that intrigued her. He showed how the layers of rock bulged upward in some places, sometimes thousands of feet. He said the scientific term for it was "anticline."

"Fossil Rim," he continued, "is sittin' on a dome." He pointed down. Some kids looked down. Laura didn't take her gaze off him.

"We don't know why that dome of rocks is there or what caused it. But that's why I'm here. I'm an oil geologist. I look for oil trapped in the top of a dome like this." He pointed at the diagram he had drawn. "I intend to drill down to about 12,000 feet—that's almost two and a half miles—to try and find an oil-bearing sandstone draped over the dome."

Laura wondered how oil could exist in a rock—she never gave it much thought. She had always supposed there were big caves down there full of oil. She didn't have to wonder long.

"You see," Ethan said, "some rock layers are not as solid as you might think." His hand went into the cardboard box. and every eye in the room followed it.

He pulled out an unimpressive piece of brown rock. It was shaped unnaturally—like a soup can. He explained that the piece had been cut with a core bit in an oil well in Mississippi. He laid the core on the table and got out a cigarette and lit it. "I don't smoke," he said to the kids, coughing, "but I gotta make some smoke. I'm not inhaling this, by the way." The kids snickered. "Now watch this."

He took a draw from the cigarette and held it. He put the rock core to his lips and blew hard into it. His cheeks bulged and his face turned beet red. The kids giggled. After a few seconds tiny blue tendrils of smoke oozed out of the other side of the core. The kids applauded.

He put the core down and looked around for a place to extinguish the cigarette. Failing to find one he crushed it against his boot and dropped it into his box. "You see, this rock is very porous. You can't see it with the naked eye but it is full of tiny voids. And those voids hold fluids. Fluids like air, or water, or—" He paused and grinned, then whispered loudly, "Oil!"

His eyebrows arched, and he glanced playfully at the class. Laura figured he was a guy who was just slow to warm up, and now he was in his game. He gestured back at the core lying on the table. "That's what I'm here for." He pulled out another core that was stained black. "Maybe I'll find a layer of sandstone—like this one—underneath this town, that is full of oil."

He passed both cores around. When it got to Laura she saw that the black one was oily to the feel. She sniffed it and smelled a sweet, pungent odor, not unlike that of kerosene.

"But," he continued, holding out empty hands, "it might not be there. We'll never know unless we drill."

"Why?" a kid asked. The same question was on Laura's lips.

"Well, there might not be any rocks down there that are porous enough. In the oil business we call those kinds of rocks *tight*. Maybe porous rocks are just not there. Or maybe they are there and are filled with water, not oil."

Laura marveled over his ideas while he paused again in his curious way. "And that part of it is where luck comes in, I suppose."

Laura sat pondering Ethan and his words, feeling giddy and edgy at the same time.

As J.D. sat explaining to Ethan how he had gotten thrown out of the mercantile, the two of them saw Hub Tant come through the door of the Wagon Wheel.

Hub's eyes searched the room and finally fixed on them. The two oilmen braced for serious words. When the sheriff came over, smiling, and tipped his hat, they relaxed and invited him to sit at their table. "You stayin' sober?" he asked J.D.

"Oh, yeah," J.D. said. "I'm workin' hard. I'm sorry about how you found me, sheriff. I got me a little problem."

"Just make sure you don't become *my* problem."

J.D. nodded. "When Mr. Hull offered me a little nip of that mule kick I fell off the wagon. Fell hard, too."

"Victor used to run a still. He's too old for that now, but he's got friends out in the woods." The sheriff turned to Ethan. "Mr. Bonner, my niece called me and said you did a fine job with her school kids. She was mightily impressed. I confess I put a bug in her ear hoping she would invite you to the class. It was a way to find out if you were on the up 'n' up. A swindler wouldn't have wasted time doing that."

Ethan saw J.D. smiling behind his upturned cup.

"Would you both like to come over to the house tomorrow night for supper?"

"Much obliged, Sheriff, but I've got plans already," J.D. said, winking at Ethan.

Ethan glanced at the sheriff. "Casanova here, unlike me, makes friends of the female persuasion quickly. But I'll be happy to come."

Hub nodded toward J.D. "Miss Clairice, at the courthouse. I already know. You'd better be good to her. I'm watchin'."

J.D. put his cup down, nodded vigorously and assured the sheriff Clarice would be in gentlemanly hands.

Hub gave Ethan the directions to the house and got back to his work.

Ethan sat thinking. He wondered if enough good will had been sown to buy his exit. He needed to get back to oil country. There was much business to attend. He needed a drilling contractor and some money. J.D. assured him he would work hard on the leasing situation in his absence. He would continue to research the land ownership and would look for more free leases. "Well, so far we're batting 50 percent," Ethan said.

"Yeah, but gettin' your eyes nearly scratched out by a mad woman and then gettin' thrown out on your butt in the street is a hell of a price to pay."

Ethan chuckled as he got up. He slapped J.D. on the shoulder. "Keep asking."

Laura Hamilton also got an invitation for the Friday evening supper at the Tant residence. She was excited to be there with the geologist, but she hoped he would attire himself better for supper than he had when he visited the school. When he came in, she wished he still had the oilman uniform on. He wore a blue and gray plaid shirt with a tan tie. She wanted to tear the tie off his neck. The khaki pants were still there too, and the right pant leg was still stuck in the boot.

Edna, a rotund Holiness woman who wore her hair in a bun on the back of her head, put out a spread that could have fed a whole drilling crew: honey-cured ham sliced and piled high, candied yams, crowder peas, and snap beans. There was bowl of giant limas swimming in a thick beige broth and a platter of fried okra. Edna moved the dishes aside to make room for a huge steaming corn pone, bright yellow with brown crust on its edges. Among the heaps of vegetables, she edged in smaller saucers piled with tart, homemade pickles and fresh, sliced, Vidalia onions. Pouring Ethan's glass first, she started a huge tumbler of sweet lemon iced tea around the table. Then Edna sat down next to Ethan.

Hub gave Thanks. Laura watched Ethan to see if he bowed his head and closed his eyes. He did. He even locked his fingers together and said, "Amen," with Hub.

Hub fell right away to his supper and seemed to wait for someone to say something. Ethan spooned in the veggies, smiled and nodded approvingly at Edna.

"The kids loved your talk yesterday," Laura said.

He chewed, smiled, and nodded.

"They want to write thank-you notes. They need an address."

"Oh," he said with a mouthful. "Send them to the Do-Drop. That'll do. I'll be there for a while. Or at least I'll be in and out of there."

"Where do you live, Mr. Bonner?" she asked. "I mean permanently?"

"Not sure you can call me permanent anywhere. Right now I've got a place in Shreveport, Louisiana," he said, just before chasing down some pone with a slug of tea. "I'm originally from Oklahoma. By the way, call me Ethan."

"What did you do in the war?" Hub asked.

Laura rolled her eyes. She was so tired of hearing that stale question—not just from her uncle but from everybody it seemed, especially men. Why couldn't they let the war go?

"I was in the Air Corps," said Ethan, patting his mouth with a napkin. "Flew P-40s. I was down south in the Canal Zone the whole war. Never shot anything, except..." He didn't finish. Just shrugged.

Laura sensed he didn't want to get into details, so she pre-empted Hub with a new question.

"What got you into the oil business?"

He shrugged again and looked aside at her. She noticed his tongue seemed to be exploring some remote area in front of his gums searching for an errant crowder pea. "Nearly everybody where I lived worked in the oil business. I grew up working summers as a roustabout—"

"A what?" Hub interrupted.

"A roustabout. That's a laborer who works around drilling rigs and wells. I didn't care too much for that kind of work—it was a just a way to make some cash. But it taught me that heavy labor out in the sun was not what I wanted to see a whole lot of in my crystal ball."

He took a bite of pone and followed it with a sliver of onion. Edna shoved the bread plate closer to him then refilled his half-empty tea glass. She ate very little herself, preferring instead to tend Ethan's plate and glass.

"One day in college I was walking, and I saw these students getting into a bus, and they were dressed very differently. They all had on khakis and boots, and they carried a satchel on their belts. They had instruments in little leather cases attached to their belts and carried steel handpicks. They were throwing sleeping bags and tents onto the bus. I said, 'Where ya'll goin'?' They told me they were geology students heading out on a field trip to the mountains. I was flabbergasted. These kids were going on a camping field trip to the mountains, while I sat in a classroom studying annuities and insurance. Well—" Ethan shrugged and shoveled in some okra. "I wanted in on that."

"And you must have liked it," Laura said.

"Oh, I loved it. I excelled at it. Geology is the most wonderful science. Think about it—you can read the rocks and actually see millions of years into the past!"

"Millions?" Edna blurted, eyes abulge.

Laura noticed the perplexed look on Edna's face.

"Yeah," Ethan said. "Hundreds of millions! Billions, even!"

Laura knew she needed to change the subject, fast.

"Do you have a family, Ethan?" Laura tried to put on one of those coy smiles, but it felt odd and ridiculous. She had never been very adept at trying to charm a man.

"Yeah," he said, still chewing. "Just my mom back in Duncan." He swallowed and smiled. My daddy died in an oil field accident during the war."

"I sorry," she said. She glanced aside and saw that Edna was deep in thought, probably over the question of the age of the earth. She was afraid her deeply religious aunt would resurrect the subject. "No family of your own, then?"

"Oh, no," he blurted, laughing. "Not me. No woman would put up with my way of life." He cleaned the recesses of his gums with his tongue. "I'm married to the rocks." He winked at Hub.

"That was great, Mizz Edna," Ethan said, patting his stomach.

Laura recognized the universal male signal that the serious eating was finished. Apparently so did Edna. She began pulling Ethan's plundered plate away. Laura was grateful that Edna's attention was back on being a hostess. She knew what was coming next.

"I hope I chose something you like for desert," Edna said softly. "Lemon icebox pie?" Her eyebrows arched expectantly.

Ethan looked at her—eyes beaming, mouth open. Laura detected a performance in progress and hoped Edna didn't notice. Slowly, resolutely, he responded. "That is exactly my all-time favorite desert!"

Edna clapped her hands together and looked skyward. "I knew the Lord was in this!" She jumped up and rushed to the icebox. Ethan glanced at Hub and Laura and shrugged.

Hub stirred sugar into his coffee and eyed Ethan. "Have you taken any other mineral leases yet—other than Victor's?"

"No. we've been turned down at least once. But J.D. is still working at the courthouse records room, seeing who owns what. He'll start next week with some of the other owners."

Hub blew at the coffee then tested it with a gurgling sip. "You think there's oil under this house?"

Ethan thought for a minute. "We're about three miles north

of the Hull tract," he said, shaking his head, smiling. "Boy, if it went this far out, it would really be something!"

"What do you do now?"

Ethan stretched and put his hand to his mouth to cover a belch. "J.D. will go with me to Jackson to pick up his car and come back down here and continue leasing work. I'll get some estimates from drilling contractors and then go to Houston to see some folks who might want to buy into the deal. As soon as I get some commitments I can let J.D. start paying for leases instead of begging for them."

"But won't that be unfair to Mr. Hull?"

"I don't think so, because we gave him a generous royalty. Everybody who gets paid for their leases will get the standard one-eighth. Also, we gave him a six-month drilling commitment. If we don't spud in that time, he gets his lease back. Most paid-for leases will carry a five-year term on them."

"Okay. I remember that from our meeting in Mr. Brubeck's office. But what does *spud* mean?" Hub asked.

"That means the start of drilling operations. That's when the bit hits the ground turning."

Hub pushed back from the table, and the others followed suit. They carried their coffee to the parlor. Soon, Hub and Edna excused themselves and left Laura and Ethan.

Laura sat back and eyed Ethan as he looked down at his shoe laces and rocked his feet back and forth. She concluded he was good at small talk in the group around the table, but now the cat seemed to have his tongue. She studied him while she curled her hair around her index finger. He looked up at her and flashed an awkward smile but still didn't say anything.

"When you were at my class the other day, I saw a fire in you that I don't see much of in people around here. You love what you do." She paused. "And you said you just picked up on it because…because you saw somebody going on a field trip? I don't believe that kind of passion just leaps out and grabs a person. I think there was something already in you."

"In my genes?" Ethan said, playfully.

"Why not?"

"Couldn't a person just suddenly become passionate about something? Doesn't it happen all the time? Maybe you go half your life without knowing something exists, something that you were meant for. And all of a sudden you see it, and you know you want it."

"Sure," Laura said. "But I believe most people go through life never recognizing what they were meant for. And then others—like you—are destined for something, and you know it."

He studied his feet again. "Well, I guess there's more to it than what I told ya'll."

She waited for elaboration, not sure any would be forthcoming.

"I used to go out to drilling rigs with my mom to take dad's lunch to him. The big steel towers and their droning engines and men running around all over them made me think that something big was happening. Something you couldn't see happening was happening. Something you couldn't see coming was coming.

"When I saw my first drill bit I was actually scared of it. It looked like something from a science fiction movie. It looked like something alive." He held his hands together, making fists and shapes, but she couldn't make sense of it. "It had three inter-meshing rotating cones, each studded with dia-mond-cutting teeth.

"I stood on the drill floor and looked down the hole the bit made." He looked down and shook his head, smiling. "I couldn't see anything because the hole was full of drilling mud. But my imagination just took off like a prairie wildfire. I wanted to know what was down there!" He looked back at her and shrugged. "I guess I knew then what I wanted to be."

"Then why didn't you just tell us that?"

He shrugged again. "I just told you, didn't I?"

"But I had to pry it out of you."

He got up and started for the door. "I'll show you a bit when I get back from Houston, if you want."

"Will I be scared of it?"

"You'll be terrified."

After he left, Laura sat pondering possibilities. Did his parting glance at her linger a second or two longer than common politeness required? She shrugged and picked up her shawl. Her imagination churned as she strolled toward home.

7

ETHAN

It sounds like I'm on your staff. You forget. I'm just a hired leaser, remember? And working for nothin' at that."

Ethan shifted his toothpick in his mouth, looked at J.D. and nodded. "That's right. I guess you are on my staff, in a way. But will you do it? I'll make it worth your while when I can."

J.D. knew some of the landmen at Gulf. Ethan wanted him to write a letter to Gulf requesting a farmout on their remaining leases around Fossil Rim. They had about 200 acres still under lease which, if added to Hull's 420 acres, would give Ethan control over 620 acres—a handsome core block to build on.

"Yeah, I'll do it. What terms you want to offer them? The standard stuff?"

"Yes. Offer them thirty percent of their original position after we get payout. Go to forty percent if they press."

J.D. nodded.

"Okay," Ethan said, throwing his napkin onto his breakfast plate. "We'd better hit the road."

As they were about to get up three people came in and looked around, soon fixing their gaze on Ethan and J.D. One was carrying a black book that Ethan thought looked like a Bible. They walked to the table. Their apparent leader stood towering over the seated men. "I'm Red Pope. I'm the pastor at the New Hope Brethren Church. These people are elders."

Ethan sensed immediately that the three weren't there to evangelize him. Pope was tall, with a crop of hair that obviously spawned his name. Baleful eyes harbored by bushy brows peered out at him.

The woman on Pope's left held her piece but seemed about to burst in outrage. The man to Pope's right looked menacing. He was in his late twenties it seemed. A big loose lock of blonde hair hung low over his right eye. A thin stubble of bristly whiskers sprouted from his chin. He, too, beamed an icy stare at Ethan. He parted his lips, as if trying to intimidate with his missing and crooked teeth.

Ethan tried to smile as he got up. He offered his hand, but they didn't respond.

"You seem to come here to teach our children the Bible is wrong." Pope said.

Before Ethan could say anything the woman burst out. "My daughter said you said the ocean was here!" She pointed at the floor. "She said you said the Bible was wrong!"

Ethan shook his head. "No. No. I didn't—"

Pope broke in. "Another one of our kids said you said the earth was millions of years old. That's against the Bible. You're one of those people who think we came from apes."

"I didn't—"

"The devil sent you here!" the man with the bad teeth said.

Ethan saw Hub walk through the door. The sheriff approached the group but stopped at a distance.

"You've got this all wrong," Ethan pleaded. "Can you calm down a minute and let me explain it?"

Pope seemed the most reasonable of the three and waited for Ethan to elaborate, but Sheriff Tant put it all to a stop.

"I suggest you all either sit down or go outside. There's other people in here."

J.D. wasted no time getting out. The group followed him out to the sidewalk.

"Okay," Pope resolutely demanded. "What did you tell the children?"

"I told them the earth is about four billion years old. That's all. That's what modern science teaches us."

"Mister," the woman said, "we teach our young'uns what the Bible says about the world, and it says God created the world in six days and rested on the seventh. But you've probably never read the Bible, so you wouldn't know that!"

"I have read the Bible," Ethan said. It wasn't entirely true. He had not read it completely through. Just parts.

"Then you ought to know," Pope said, "according to Adam's family tree, which can be traced from him all the way up to Jesus, adding up the lifetimes of the people, it's four thousand years. And we know Jesus lived two thousand years ago. That makes this world six thousand years old."

Ethan tried to compose himself. He looked around and saw J.D. standing aside lighting up. Hub stood back with his arms folded.

"Look, maybe we can sit down and talk about this sometime. I really need to get to work."

"We know what you're here for, and we're not gonna let you do it," the bad-toothed man said.

"What? What are you not going to let me do?"

"You're tryin' to bring Scopes here," Pope said. "You want to corrupt our kids and our town. You're one of them—the Darwinists."

Pope looked around at his nodding associates. "We knew it would come here someday. We knew it!"

Ethan felt like the group was ganging up on him and stepped back. Hub stepped up and politely but sternly told them to leave him alone. They drifted back toward their car mumbling. The bad-toothed man shouted, "We won't let you do it!"

Hub shook his head and looked at Ethan. "You've stirred up a hornet's nest. They came to my office this morning asking where you were. I told them they'd likely find you here, and I followed them over just to make sure things stayed civil."

"Well," Ethan said, "if I could just talk to the pastor, maybe without those other people, I can convince him I'm not against the Bible."

Hub took off his hat and rubbed his scalp. "I doubt you'll be able to change his mind."

Ethan looked squarely at the sheriff. He felt as if he were shaking and hoped it wasn't noticeable. "Do you think I'm sent by the devil?"

"Oh, hell no."

"Okay, then. We've got to get on. J.D. will be back tomorrow, and I'll be back in a couple of weeks. I appreciate your help, Sheriff."

They loaded their bags and got into Ethan's car. "A lot of help you were," Ethan said.

"Help, my ass," J.D. blurted.

"You could have stepped up and supported me, somehow."

"I ain't got a dawg in that fight."

Ethan let out a disgusted sigh as he started the engine and eased on onto the highway.

"But the sheriff is right on the money," J.D. added. "You've stirred up a bee's nest. These people ain't likely to embrace the concepts of modern science when it conflicts with their beliefs, and here comes the whiz kid who says their Bible is wrong, and on top of that, wantin' to do business with them. Ho boy!" He shook his head.

"But I'm not saying the Bible is wrong."

"I don't want to get into no evolution debate," J.D. said. "I got me a big-enough problem with the here and now. But they think you're disputing the Bible, and there's where your problem is. And I'm the one who's got to deal with 'em."

J.D. took a last draw and flicked his butt out the window. He shook his head. "Damn! I wish I was back in awl country. I can't believe what trouble you've drug me into."

"If you were back in oil country you'd be sitting in your apartment feeling sorry for yourself." They glanced at each other. "I'm sorry. Shouldn't have said that," Ethan said.

"No," J.D. mumbled. "You're right."

J.D. took a deep breath, as if to get composed. "I hope that's the last we see of that bunch. The one on the left, Ethan—that guy with the bad teeth. That's the one that bothers me."

Ethan dropped J.D. off at his apartment in Jackson. "Can I depend on you to get back to Fossil Rim right away and pick up where you left off?"

J.D. nodded. "Tomorrow."

"When?" Ethan asked.

"When what?"

"What time will you leave here to start back? I want to know. I'm gonna hold you to it."

J.D. heaved his duffle bag and started up the steps. "Noon. Twelve o'clock."

"Nine," Ethan shouted. "I don't want you layin' around. Get started at nine."

"You ain't my momma!" J.D. mumbled as he climbed the steps.

"Nine!" Ethan yelled again as he got into his car.

His car and whatever pay telephone was nearby would be his office the next couple of weeks. He sat in it, found his address book, and jotted down the names and numbers of four local drilling contractors. He would visit them first, before calling out of town contractors. He needed to save long distance charges.

His first stop was at Adams Drilling, Inc. They told him all their rigs were currently booked at least six months ahead. He dropped in on another company and got a similar report. Both companies promised to work up a turnkey estimate for his well and mail it to him, but he knew he had to have a rig quicker than they offered. A call on another drilling company yielded more of the same.

Finally, there was only one left in town—Mercer Drilling. He had held that one for last because he had heard they were hard to deal with. He called ahead, and they told him they had a rig coming available in two months. Ethan rushed to Mercer's office.

He shook Mercer's hand and took the chair he was offered while the guy rummaged through his desk drawer for a match.

"Cigarette?"

Ethan waved him off. Glancing out the window from the 10th floor of the Standard Life Building, he could see for miles. The window was open, and an unseasonably warm spring breeze wafted through. Mercer lit up and waved the match out. Ethan recoiled.

"So, you need a rig?" Mercer asked, cigarette dancing from his lips.

"Yep." Ethan nodded, smiling.

"Where?"

"Mobile County, Alabama."

Mercer coughed, taking the cigarette from his lips, then chuckled. "Okay!" He eyed Ethan askance. "Think there's oil over there, huh?"

Ethan could pick out skeptics not so much by the questions they asked, but the way they asked them. He wanted to tell Mercer that was none of his business. The man drilled holes for hire. That's all. But he knew he had to be diplomatic.

"Mr. Bonner," Mercer said, as if about to dispense street wisdom to a greenhorn, "that's a long way to haul a rig. You know, we like to be able to keep our rigs in a particular area that's active with oil drilling. We'd have to charge you for transportation across that distance. And, for just one hole—" He chuckled condescendingly again. "You know, we'd have to haul it back."

Ethan pondered the veiled insult. "How do you know it won't be a hundred wells?"

Mercer chuckled again under his breath and sighed. "Ohh kay." He picked up a pencil. "How deep, sir?"

"Eleven, five."

Mercer's eyes glanced up as if appealing to his brain. His lips moved silently. Then he pulled a yellow legal pad from the edge of the desk and scribbled. He looked back at Ethan. He rotated the pad and shoved it toward him. "That's about what the turnkey will be."

Ethan looked at the paper and quickly shot a scornful gaze at Mercer, pointing at the figures. "What's this thirty thousand here for?"

"Transportation costs."

"Transportation penalty, you mean."

Mercer shrugged. "Like I said, we don't want to waste time drilling out of the oil patch."

"I can't afford that," Ethan said, rising from the chair.

"Good luck," Mercer mumbled. He turned away, as if to see to some other duty while Ethan found his way out of the office.

Suddenly Ethan felt hot. He paused to wipe his forehead with a handkerchief after walking out the door of the building, the tallest in Mississippi and a bastion of oil company haunts. He looked up at the hazy blue sky and put his hat on. He glanced behind him at the building, stepped off the curb and headed for the King Edward Hotel.

The waiter brought Ethan's coffee and left a lunch menu. He glanced through it looking for something cheap—a hamburger, maybe. He noticed a man approaching and looked up. Mercer. He started to rise.

"Don't get up," Mercer said, his hand waving him down. He dropped a piece of paper on the table. "You might want to check this out. A friend of mine told me about an old rig sitting out in the woods over near Ruston that hasn't moved in years. Don't know whose it is. Maybe you can get it, maybe you can't, but good luck."

"Thanks," Ethan muttered.

"Don't mention it," Mercer said, turning.

He looked at the scribbling and saw that the man had given him virtually nothing to hang his hat on. *10 miles southwest of Ruston, La* was all it said.

He watched Mercer rejoin his party at a table across the

room and recognized a few of them—oil men. One nodded toward him. Ethan smiled and told himself he didn't care that they didn't invite him over. He sipped his coffee and pretended to study the note Mercer gave him. He thought he heard them chuckling. He folded the piece of paper and put it in his wallet. Hiring a dilapidated a rig was a desperate idea. He discarded the thought, went back to his motel room and packed.

He stopped in Shreveport to check his mail and get his business suit at his apartment, then went to Noble's office with his lease map. He told Noble he had the Hull lease in hand, although it was on a short fuse. Noble nodded approvingly and congratulated him. He asked about the Gulf farmout, and Ethan told him he had asked for it, and he expected approval. Noble nodded again. "And this other acreage?" he asked, waving a hand over the map, sending cigar smoke swirling.

"We're working on getting more free leases on some of that."

"We?" Noble asked.

"Oh. Yeah. I've got J.D. Whitley working on that."

Noble cackled loudly. "Is he sober?"

Ethan shrugged. "No. Not all the time."

"Well, keep an eye on him."

"How can I do that when I'm here?"

"I don't know, Ethan." Noble puffed and grinned. "Okay. How much is a quarter gonna cost me?"

Ethan got out his prospectus and started to go through the details of the cost estimates. Noble puffed, watched, and appeared impatient. He interrupted. "Bottom line. How much?"

"Forty-five thousand."

He nodded. "I'll call over to the bank and have them prepare a draft for you." He reached out shook Ethan's hand. "Ethan—" He paused, swallowed, and brushed the back of his hand against his nose. He looked at Ethan as if wanting to finish his sentence but couldn't. He nodded, smiled and walked away.

Ethan's excitement over Noble's commitment waned as the days wore on in Houston, and the rejections piled up. He made the rounds to all the companies and energy investment institutions that he had dealt with in the past and those Noble had referred him to, with no success. He called and visited many more companies that he was familiar with and a few others he found in the Yellow Pages. Most of them politely refused to see him, but a few wanted a peek.

Two companies he visited were aware of the Fossil Rim structure. One staff geologist even showed him a map he had made from the same Gulf seismic data Ethan had examined. His boss had already rejected the prospect. He wished Ethan good luck. Finding someone else who agreed with him energized Ethan enough to keep him trying.

Late in his third week in Houston he thought he was on the verge of selling a quarter of his deal to a small company called Scatback Oil Explorers, Inc. The manager, a refined Englishman named Trevor Bentley, was interested in the idea and asked Ethan to sit down and show him the package.

Ethan knew better than to get excited. Others had looked and waved him off. He watched as Bentley sat down and spent what seemed an excessive amount of time arranging his notepad and pen. Ethan laid the maps in front of him. Then Bentley initiated a process that almost made Ethan cringe. He got out a pipe.

Ethan didn't oppose pipe smoking. Unlike cigarette smoke it had a pleasant fragrance. But he knew from past experience not to expect quick progress from pipe smokers. They were methodical, thorough, and entirely resistant to haste.

True to his ilk, Bentley carefully tamped tobacco into the bowl. Ethan felt it best not to begin talking until Bentley's eyes fell to the maps. The tamping went on.

Finally the pipe preparations were done, and the tip of Bentley's tongue emerged. It slid back and forth spreading wetness across the lips. Ethan leaned back and took in a breath. He needed patience. He knew better than to get started before the light-up.

The match flared and was promptly lowered into the bowl. Bentley's cheeks contracted. It was so quiet in the conference room Ethan heard the wind sucking into the pipe bowl.

"Oh!" Bentley blurted with a mouthful of smoke. "Sorry. Would you like some coffee or tea?"

Ethan waved a hand. "No, thank you."

Bentley puffed, getting a good fire going. His eyes still had not gone to the maps.

"Water; cola?"

"No," said Ethan. "Thank you."

Just as Ethan figured the light-up was successfully concluded, out came the tamper again. Bentley's eyes focused on the bowl and another minute was consumed with puffs and taps.

Finally the pipe came out of his mouth, and Bentley looked him in the eye. "Well?"

Ethan looked blankly at him.

"Are you going to show me what you've got?"

Ethan felt a quick flush of surprise and embarrassment over his silence and then quickly his hands began their familiar orchestration across the face of the maps. Bentley puffed as his eyes followed the movement of Ethan's hands. After a few minutes he took the pipe out and began tamping again. After re-kindling the fire, he took the bowl of the pipe in his hand. Ethan knew what was coming; pipe smokers always used their pipe stems as pointers. Bentley turned the stem toward the map and tapped it on the Soso Field in eastern Mississippi. "You're betting the farm that Lower Cretaceous oil sands extend such a long distance from here to," he moved the pipe stem to Fossil Rim, "here." His eyes shifted to Ethan's.

Here is was again. This was his Achilles' heel. This was the question fired at him from the beginning when he ran the idea past J.D. It came up again in showing after showing. And this was usually when the rejection was issued. He smiled and nodded. There was nothing more to say.

He expected Bentley to get up from his chair and offer a gentlemanly refusal. Instead he pushed away the geologic maps and said, "Let's see your leases."

Ethan perked. He usually didn't get this far along in his presentations. He showed Bentley the map that outlined the Hull lease, the Gulf farm-out, and the open acreage nearby.

Bentley coughed and puffed. His eyes slid aside to Ethan. "And the cost?"

Ethan slid an economic analysis in front of Bentley and began going over the details. When he got to drilling costs Bentley's eyes began shifting around the table as if looking for something. With the pipe clinched in his teeth he asked, "Do you have a drilling proposal?"

Ethan slumped back and shook his head. "No. I have not gotten a rig lined up yet. Rigs are hard to get these days. He tapped the estimated drilling cost with his index finger. That number is my best guess."

Bentley leaned back and puffed, his eyes focused on the number. "How much will a quarter interest cost us?"

Ethan moved his finger to the bottom line. "Forty-five thousand dollars."

Bentley puffed and pondered.

"How much time did you say was left on that big lease you opted?"

"Roughly four months," Ethan said.

"Hum," Bentley uttered. "You'd better move fast."

Bentley got up and offered his hand. "Thanks for taking the time to spend with me. Can I keep this package?"

"Sure. But you understand there are open leases here. I'll have to trust you."

Bentley nodded with clinched pipe. "You can count on it." He showed Ethan to the door. "I don't know if we want this, but we definitely don't want it unless you get a drilling obligation to spud in time to save that lease. When you get that, let me know, and I'll forward it to London with my recommendation that we join you."

He left feeling hopeful and encouraged about his time with Bentley but decided on a change of venue. He would head north.

Ethan's next stop was Fort Worth. He knew several oil people there, called on them, and showed them his deal. They were all cordial and seemed glad to see him but politely turned down the deal. The best he could get from them were referrals to others in Dallas.

But there he fared no better. Texas was booming with new and huge discoveries coming in, and a rank wildcat in Alabama held no romance for Lone Star oilmen. A couple of small investors like Trevor Bentley retained Ethan's prospectus for further consideration, but he sensed they were only collecting maps.

He asked to use one company's phone to call back to Alabama. J.D. didn't answer, but the motel clerk said he had seen him going in and out.

Ethan slept in his car that night.

8

A Worthless Piece of Dirt

Ethan had a lot to think about on the long drive back to Alabama. His entire future hinged on what would happen in a few busy months. But at least he now had some money and some breathing room. And he had a good man working for him, if only he stayed sober.

But then his mood turned somber. For all he knew J.D. could have been laid up stone drunk for days. He may not even be in Fossil Rim.

He passed a sign announcing Ruston, Louisiana, just ahead. Exhausted and tempted to stop for the night he pushed on, but then he remembered the slip of paper in his wallet that Mr. Mercer had given him. He pulled over and got it out. *10 miles SW of Ruston, La* was all it said. Was it worth a look? He looked that direction as if he might see it in the dark. He thought. He checked into the next motel.

The next day Ethan crisscrossed the county. He took every back road he could find and asked every person he saw. No one had a clue. Another day wasted. He started back toward town and stopped to gas up.

He watched the gas station attendant fill up his '47 Plymouth and handed him a ten-dollar bill. He pocketed the $2.27 change and drained his bottle of peach soda. He was sick of the idea of chasing the mysterious rig and had almost convinced himself that Mercer and his friends had pulled a hoax on him, but he figured might as well ask the attendant.

"I'm looking for a drilling rig that I've been told is around here somewhere. It's been sitting in the woods for about eight years. Know anything about that?"

The man spat a stream of brown slime onto the dirt and looked away. "They been drillin' around here for years," he mumbled. "Found oil ever damn where but under me."

"I know. Rigs come and go, but I'm looking for one that might be abandoned. I've asked a lot of people around here, and nobody seems to know anything."

"I don't know." Then the man cackled after a thoughtful moment. "If you find it, drag it over to my house and start diggin'! Ha!" Ethan got back in his car and headed back toward the main highway intending to waste no more time with it.

Shortly he passed a grass landing strip and saw a bi-winged crop duster—a Stearman. He slowed. The engineless plane sat derelict alongside a dilapidated shed. He suspected it was probably a war surplus plane converted for agricultural use. A tiny smile crept across his face. He pulled over and parked where he could see it better. He had logged—how many hours in those machines? A hundred, maybe. That was over ten years ago. A lifetime, it seemed.

He'd just turned nineteen when a place he'd never heard of, Pearl Harbor, had suddenly become a smoking hole in the ocean. They sat by the radio for what seemed like days before hearing President Roosevelt ask Congress to declare war on Japan. His mother stood looking into the radio nervously rolling her hands in her apron. His dad's gaze swung toward him. He asked Ethan what he was going to do. Ethan shrugged. He said he guessed he'd join up. "That's not what I asked!" James Bonner barked. Ethan's eyes widened. Mr. Bonner got up and turned the radio off. "I meant, son, what are you gonna do about them Japs?" Mrs. Bonner's brow wrinkled, and she had fled to the kitchen.

A heavy rumble from the southwest snatched Ethan's attention back. A man in grungy coveralls emerged from the shed wiping his hands with a rag and walked toward a cluster of steel drums. The rumble got louder, and a second Stearman rolled into view from behind the shed. It taxied to the drums and swung smartly around where the man in the coveralls threw chocks under its tires. Clad in similar grungy, stained coveralls, the pilot dismounted, turned away from the highway, and urinated while looking back at the plane. He hadn't bothered to shut down the engine. The Stearman sat idling while the two men pumped the wretched liquid pesticide into its empty hoppers, its big propeller swishing around in a menacing arc.

Ethan smiled at the sight of the idling plane and pondered why he never took his father flying while he had the chance. James Bonner was a Marine, had fought at Bellow Wood and the Argonne. "You goin' to the Marines?" he had asked after Pearl Harbor. Ethan didn't know what the hell he was going to do about the Japs. "They'll make a man out o' ya," he heard his father say, following him to the supper table. He heard his mother half crying, half shouting from the kitchen. "Jim, for God's sake he's our only child!" Jim ignored her, only looking intently at Ethan, as if Ethan would be his personal contribution to the war effort—his proxy. "Well?"

Ethan lied, told him he was thinking about the Air Corps. Jim stared at him and then fell to buttering his cornbread.

Six months later Ethan got off a bus, showed a guard his papers, walked through the gates of Lawton Army Air Field, and saw a hundred Stearmans. More droned overhead. Some moved slowly about on the tarmac, propellers swishing. He wrote his dad that night and told him he guessed he was about to become a man, the Air Corps way.

Ethan hadn't flown since he was called home on emergency leave to attend his dad's funeral. The war ended shortly after that, and he never flew again. He still thought about it sometimes, but he stayed too busy to miss it.

He studied the geometry of the biplane and listened to the

engine, wondering if he could still fly it. He watched the men tend the plane, suddenly realizing he was envying them. Their job was so simple. They fill it with chemicals and fuel. They fly it to wherever and dump the stuff and come back. Not a bad job—no worrying about trying to sell risky ideas to haughty men with fat wallets.

Excuse me sir, my name is Ethan Bonner, and I've got an oil prospect. If we can use your money I'll drill it for us.

What were they saying about him after he was shown the door? And after his string of dry holes?

He knew how to fly a Stearman; to hell with the oil business. Why not just go over and ask those guys if they needed another pilot? He could give the check back to Noble. And there was no reason to go back to that town. The lease option he had signed would simply expire, no harm done to anyone. The idea was dammed appealing. But J.D.?

J.D. wouldn't care. He'd just call him a quitter and go back to drinking.

He rubbed his stubbled chin, glanced at his watch, and started the car. A mile past the strip his eyebrows went up. He shouted to himself, "Yes!" He braked and turned around.

He got out and walked toward the idling plane. The pungent smell of the DDT burned his nose. The men were finishing and disconnecting the hose. In unison they wiped the grime off their faces. One of them yelled at him. "Whatchuneed?"

"I used to fly those things," Ethan shouted.

"We don't need no help."

"I'm not looking for a job. I'm looking for an abandoned drilling rig sitting out in the country about 10 miles southwest of town. Been there about eight years, they say. Have you seen it?"

"Yeah," the pilot said, throwing a nod over his shoulder toward the southwest.

Ethan's face broke into a gigantic grin.

"It's been there so damn long it's nothin' but a rust bucket. I use it for a landmark."

"Landmark?"

"When the visibility is low around here, and I'm trying to find my way back, I look for that derrick. I fly a headin' of fifty-five degrees off that derrick for six minutes, and I'm right back here at this miserable piece of dirt."

Ethan asked how to get to it, and the pilot thought for a minute. He bent down and drew a map in the miserable dirt. Ethan studied the motion of the man's oil-stained finger, no longer hearing the Stearman's harmonious rumbling. He thanked the pilot and didn't look back.

Ethan's heartbeat picked up noticeably as the pickup bucked across the rough farm road toward the steel spire jutting above the pines. The driver had talked very little since he had met him at the farmhouse doorstep. He had asked the farmer who the rig's owner was, and the man didn't know but said his $50 a month checks for renting the land the rig was sitting on came from the First Merchants and Farmers Bank of Shreveport.

The agreement by the farmer—to allow Ethan to go onto the property to see the rig—had been terse. Ethan sensed he was not the first stranger to inquire about the rig. If so, why had the others before him not attempted to get it? The notion that he was wasting his precious time and money in a wild goose chase troubled him.

They braked to a dusty stop beside the hulking tower. Ethan got out and looked up at it. The farmer stood by, hands in his overall pockets and spoke after a minute. "Ready to go now?"

"No," Ethan muttered as he looked up at the tower. It was bigger than he had imagined.

He pulled aside the thorny overgrowth and stepped toward the ladder leading up to the rig floor. He heard the farmer warn him from behind. "Watch for rat'lers. Whole nests of 'em. They're big as a man's leg around here. This warm weather is bringin' 'em out."

Ethan hated snakes. He slowly climbed the ladder and stepped onto the rig floor. The ubiquitous creeping green curse of the Deep South, kudzu, had encrusted the substructure and begun to climb the derrick. Ethan looked at the floor, astonished. The Kelly bar was sitting upright in its square hole in the rotary table. He looked up. The swivel was attached to the top of the bar. Over to the side a section of drill pipe sat in the mouse hole, awaiting its turn to be added to the drill string.

"How amazing!" Ethan whispered aloud, with a chuckle, as he slowly turned and surveyed the trappings of the drill floor. It was almost as if the crew had set the brake and simply walked away.

He shuffled through a thick mat of pine needles toward the driller's console. The glass on the big torque gauge was broken. His eyes searched the console for some form of equipment identification. He saw a data plate and brushed the crust of dirt from it. The rig was an Ideco model H-40, date of manufacture, 1942. He pulled out a pocket note pad and jotted down the serial number.

He wondered how deep the hole was. He wished there was a simple depth gauge to tell him, but he knew drillers kept track of depth by noting each joint of pipe that went into the hole and recording it in a pipe tally logbook. He studied the rig floor but saw nothing that looked like a pipe tally.

He stepped toward the dog house and peered inside. A whizzing clatter from the dark interior sent him scurrying back outside. He peered back in from a distance wondering if he had heard a snake or only imagined one.

He composed himself and turned to resume his survey of the rig. At the west side of the platform he peered down into the weeds and saw the mud tank and two mud pumps. He grinned. He turned back to the north side wondering if the drill pipe was any good after sitting in the hole all these years. Was there more pipe laying aside?

He walked to the north edge of the floor and peered down into the undergrowth. He saw pieces of equipment jutting through overgrown weeds. The reserve pit was barely noticeable. Trees had sprouted in it. He carefully walked to the side the pipe racks should be on and looked out seeing a swarm of scraggly cedar trees and scrub brush. Something was underneath the brush. He climbed down and made his way around toward the cedars.

"I wouldn't go in there," he heard the farmer yell. "Goddam snakes!"

Excited by the prospect of finding pipe, Ethan ignored the farmer's warning and slogged through the brush. He saw the racks first, then spotted the familiar open holes of the drill pipe with their marvelous upset screw threads. His heart leaped. The rig was whole—complete with drill pipe. He climbed across the racks of pipe slapping at bugs landing on his sweaty neck, counting almost one hundred pieces of the thirty-foot sections of pipe: three thousand feet—maybe more, plus whatever was in the hole. His grin widened. Drill pipe was in great demand. The pipe alone would go far in financing his well, even if the rig was worthless. But only if he could get it at a bargain. He waded out of the tangle of vegetation and rejoined the edgy farmer.

Ethan could hardly wait to get to the phone in his motel room. He placed a call to Ideco in Columbus, Ohio, and was connected with a salesman. He asked for some information on the H-40. His smile faded as he copied down the specifications. The rig's maximum depth capability was only 9,000 feet. He needed to go down to at least 11,000 and maybe 12,000. He asked if the H-40 could possibly make to 11,000. The man chuckled and said, "Possibly it could, if you want to run the risk of destroying the rig and getting somebody killed."

"But," Ethan asked, not knowing if the man was being sarcastic, "it can be done, right?"

The man hesitated and blew a breath into his phone. "Look, the maximum rated hook load on that rig is 250,000 pounds. If you can keep your string at or below that, it might can be done.

You'll probably have to use a smaller diameter drill pipe the deeper you go. With the right driller and pusher, yes, it might be possible, but I've never heard of it being done successfully."

The man offered to look up more specific information on the unit Ethan had found. He asked for the serial number. It took him a few minutes to find the file. Ethan waited, fidgeting over the long-distance charges.

"Oh, my God!" the Ideco man finally said. "This is that Lampasas rig!"

Ethan's spirits sank at the tone of the man's voice.

"Lampasas Drilling went out of business years ago. That particular rig is a hodge-podge of different parts and components. It's changed so much since it left our factory I couldn't tell you much about it. I'm sure most of the component list I've got here is out of date."

"Do you know why it's sitting abandoned in the woods?"

"Only rumors. We heard it went through the courts a time or two. You'd need to call—let's see here—Mr. Stanley Pickering. He was the last known tool-pusher we have on record. He worked for Lampasas."

Fending off the man's pitch to sell him a newer, bigger rig, Ethan copied Pickering's telephone number and thanked the man for his time.

He laid back on his bed, his enthusiasm spent. He stared at the ceiling and sighed. The rig was inadequate. He had wasted precious time. He drifted to sleep wondering if he was going to kill somebody trying to push it too deep.

After a breakfast in his room of Vienna sausages and crackers, he sat for several long minutes, not feeling good about the whole damn mess. He blew a breath of frustration and dialed the number for Mr. Pickering.

A woman answered and confirmed she was Stan Pickering's ex-wife. She said she hadn't seen him in eight years and didn't want to see him. He was down in Mexico somewhere drilling and whoring, she said. He thanked her.

He looked at his watch, as if it were a calendar, and thought about the coming deadline on his drilling option. He decided to give up this madness and head east, hoping he could yet find a willing contractor.

But he couldn't get the rig off his mind. The more he pondered it, the more he remembered his excitement when he first saw it with the farmer. One idea after another snapped through his visions. Could he spud with the rig, meeting his deadline, then switch it out for a deeper one? But where would he get another one with the funds he had available? Maybe more money would come in. Maybe not. He was only a few miles past Ruston, heading east, when he turned into a gas station and reversed back toward Shreveport. He began to wonder, with a smirk and a head shake, if his car was steering itself.

Ethan stopped by his apartment to freshen up. While washing his clothes he pondered visiting Noble. He wanted badly to pour out his worries to his old friend, but thought Noble might be cool to the idea of buying the rig. Chasing the rig might smack of weakness or desperation. Noble might even get mad at the idea that his money may be used to finance the crazy idea. *No, Ethan thought. Best to leave Noble alone.* He suddenly realized he might unexpectedly meet him on the street. Noble's office was only a few blocks from the bank. That thought chilled him.

He found a parking spot and walked into the bank. He was ushered from one bank officer to another, each time repeating his purpose for the visit, each time seeing eyebrows arched and watching momentary blank stares. Finally he heard sound advice. "Oh! You need to see Sam in the petroleum office." He was told to go up to the fifth floor.

Samuel Baumgarten was swinging a putter when he went in. Ethan was invited to sit and was asked if he played golf. *Golf?*

The idea that anyone had the time for that seemed ludicrous to him, but he politely smiled and shook his head. Baumgarten sat, and Ethan told him the purpose of the visit. As he talked he saw Baumgarten nod and stare pensively into the distance.

Finally Baumgarten spoke and told Ethan it had been several weeks since eight years of litigation over the rig had come to a close. The bank now had clear title. He said the bank had decided not to auction the rig but to sell it directly to one their oil clients, several of whom had expressed an interest over the years. Baumgarten seemed annoyed with the rig and had been putting off disposing of it. He said now that Ethan was here he might as well get on with it. Ethan was fourth in line. He told Ethan to come back in a few days after he had a chance to call down the list.

A few days! He didn't have a few days. He went back to his place and laid back on the sofa. On the television Ralph Cramden was holding a fat fist to Ed Norton's goofy face. He turned the TV off and fell into a fitful sleep, laced with visions of thrashing, dying whales.

He called the next day, about mid-afternoon, but Baumgarten still hadn't called anyone. He told Ethan to call back a couple of days.

Ethan found a café and sat sipping coffee wondering whether he should give up on this crazy idea of buying a creaky abandoned drilling rig. He shook his head. It was indeed a wild goose chase, robbing him of time and money. And the lack of communication from Whitley weighed heavily on him.

He decided to give Baumgarten the two days and then to leave for Jackson. He would revisit Mercer. Maybe he could get him to come off his steep price. And maybe he would get a better deal if he cut Mercer in for a quarter interest in the well. It was worth a try. He knew drilling contractors sometimes did that. As he sipped his coffee a man came alongside his table.

"Ethan?"

He looked up.

Noble.

His heart nearly stopped. He sprang up, spilling the coffee, grabbed Noble's hand and tried to compose himself.

Noble looked puzzled. He turned and introduced a man he was with. Ethan invited them to sit.

"How is the prospect going?" Noble asked. Ethan was hesitant to be candid with Noble with the other man listening. Noble must have realized it. He turned to his friend and politely asked if he could meet him later. The guy caught the hint and excused himself.

Ethan sighed and rubbed his hands through his hair. Noble stirred his coffee and waited. Ethan recounted his fruitless sweep in Houston and Dallas, except for the conditional promise from Scatback. Then he told Noble about the rig and the bank. Noble leaned back and listened, not offering a word or asking a question. Then he slid his chair back and got up. "Walk with me to my office," he said.

Noble was quiet as they walked for a couple of blocks and Ethan sensed he should be the same. As they waited at a noisy, busy intersection Noble spoke. "Your daddy taught me something. I don't think he gave it a bit of thought, but he taught me. When that fire caught hold of me—started bar-b-queing my hands, my feet, my arms and legs, and me with nowhere to go, all I could think of was, 'I want to die quick.'"

The light changed and they crossed. "But your daddy didn't give up on me. He hauled me into that harness and pushed me down that Geronimo line like he was walkin' in the park. He didn't give up on me."

They reached Noble's building and paused in front of the door. "I learned not to ever give up, not only on myself, but on other people. I'm not giving up on you, Ethan. And it's not just because your daddy saved my hide. It's because he didn't give up on me. I've committed my life to passing that forward, because if I don't, I'm not worth the sacrifice he made for me."

Ethan stood without words and waited. "Come on," Noble said.

They got into the office, and he told Ethan to sit. He picked up the phone and dialed. He swiveled his chair around to put Ethan at his back. Ethan got up and moved toward the opposite window to give his benefactor more privacy, but he heard mention of golf, a handicap or something, then a cackle. After a few minutes of muffled conversation Noble turned around and motioned Ethan over. "That crazy German said come on over and get your rig!"

"What?" Ethan asked, astounded. "What about those other people he was going to call?"

"Hell, I don't know, son. You go on over there and make a deal with him."

Ethan grinned, then frowned. "I may have to use your money for a down payment."

Noble waved him off. "You use it as you please. It's your deal. There's just one thing. If you don't drill the deal you sold me into, I get the rig and leases. Understood?"

Ethan nodded.

Noble slapped his arm and saw him to the door.

The next morning he went back to Baumgarten's office to open negotiations. The banker started at $100,000. Ethan countered with $25,000. The banker coughed and chuckled and came down to $75,000. Ethan offered $50,000. Baumgarten said, "Sir, I can't just give it away!"

Ethan said, "Mr. Baumgarten, that thing is a hunk of junk." He pulled out photographs he had taken. "Look at this. Kudzu is growing all over it and snakes are nesting in it. Rattlers as big as a man's leg!"

Baumgarten didn't touch the pictures, just winced at them.

"Ride out there with me and take a—"

"No!" Baumgarten blurted, with a vigorous head shake. "Not going out there!"

Ethan put the photos back in his satchel. "It'll probably take me $25,000, to get it going—if I can." He leaned back and pretended as best he could to be an immovable object.

Baumgarten tapped his pen on his doodle pad. He eyed the

clock and Ethan. He extended his hand and congratulated the new drilling contractor.

"There's just one thing," Ethan said.

"What?"

"I don't have all the money yet. Can you give me the rig and a few weeks to pay?"

"Oh, hell, man. No! You're tryin' to get me canned. Don't you have any money?"

Ethan only had Noble's $45,000. "I'll give you $25,000 now and the other half later."

"How much later?"

"A year?"

Baumgarten sighed and looked out his window. "If you weren't sent over here by Abrams, who I've got to face on the golf course every week, I'd throw you out. Six months!"

Ethan grinned. They shook hands.

"Leave those photographs here," Baumgarten said. "I may need them to defend myself when the bank's auditor comes snooping around."

Ethan arranged for an insurance policy on the rig, and the bank gave him the deed the next day. Ethan asked Baumgarten's secretary if he could borrow the phone. He called Trevor Bentley in Houston and told him he had a rig. After a short pause Bentley said he had already gotten London's approval pending a drilling contract. He would send a letter of agreement right away committing to a quarter interest, and within a week, a check.

Ethan grinned. Then he called the Do-Drop Inn and left a message for J.D. "Sold another quarter and bought drilling rig."

He left the bank feeling as if he were selling his soul a piece at a time. The burden was piling up. He had less than three months left on the Hull lease and still he needed to find a drilling crew, possibly his biggest challenge yet, and a trucking company to take the rig to Alabama. He could only hope J.D. was making progress with the leasing operations and staying away from the bottle.

$\mathcal{9}$

PLUNKET

Ethan wasted no time looking for men. He asked around
Ruston, found some Mexican men who needed work and escorted them out to the site. He set them to cutting brush and kudzu
from around the rig and then went back into town. He inquired
at a small oil field service company about sending a mechanic
out to get the engine started on his rig. They didn't have one,
but they told him to call a retired oil field mechanic they knew
about. The guy laughed when Ethan told him what he wanted,
but he referred Ethan to his nephew, who laughed too, but said
he would look at it Saturday, two days away. Ethan knew this
was the best he would likely get. He accepted.

Saturday morning he met the mechanic, a bespectacled
beaver-toothed man named Marlin, and they drove out to the
location. The laborers had done a fair job of clearing the brush
out and now he could see his rig clearer. He and Marlin moved
carefully around it, examining each component, but Marlin made
it clear he was a mechanic. He had worked as a roughneck years
ago, but he didn't know much about anything other than engines.

The two examined the blowout preventers. Together they
grabbed the main valve wheel for the pipe rams and strained to
turn it. After a fitful moment of huffing and grunting it turned.
That part was serviceable.

They looked over the Caterpillar diesel. Marlin got under it and unscrewed the oil drain. A molasses-like fluid oozed out. He went back to the car and brought back his tools and a case of oil. He disconnected the battery and put on a new one. Two hours later, after changing the oil, cleaning the injectors, and adding five fresh new gallons of fuel Marlin yelled at Ethan.

"I'm gonna try to start it!"

Ethan hurried over. He had been sweeping the drilling floor.

Marlin primed the engine and pushed the starter button. It revolved slowly, with a heavy heaving sound. The two men cringed. It sounded like metal grinding against metal. After a minute of hard cranking Marlin released the button. The engine didn't hit a lick. The mechanic shook his head. Ethan stood watching.

Marlin disconnected two injectors and pumped raw fuel into the cylinders. He hit the starter again. The engine belched a mushroom cloud of black smoke and died. Marlin smiled, showing his appalling teeth. "We'll get this thing alive, yet." He grabbed a handful of tools and climbed onto the engine. Ethan looked up at the derrick and decided to go aloft.

He carefully climbed the ninety feet to the platform called the monkey board where a derrick man normally worked manhandling stands of drill pipe. Higher still sat the crown block, the main overhead pulley, and sheave complex. He looked around at the flat Louisiana farmland. From above the trees, he could see many miles.

To one side he saw the Geronimo line, a cable descending at an angle to a point out in the brush where it was anchored in the ground. This, he knew, was an escape route for the derrick man if a blowout occurred. A cable-mounted carriage with a T-bar attached sat at the top, waiting to take the derrick man to safety if hell broke loose down below.

Ethan thought about Noble and his father. Through Noble's stories he had reconstructed what had happened. An upward rushing flash of flame from below had burned and stunned Noble who was working the monkey board. James Bonner, working the driller's console heard the screams from above. He had set the brake and scurried up the derrick to help. As he climbed, the floor crew had fled the rig when the fire re-ignited and grew upward.

James had reached Noble just as the inferno hit them both. With flames lashing at his legs he picked Noble off the monkey board floor, heaved him into the escape harness, grabbed hold and pushed. Noble felt them both descend, body to body, with Jim Bonner clinging to the T-bar with his bare oily hands.

"Hang on!" Noble had heard him yell. "Don't let go!" He remembered looking into Jim's face, only inches from his own, at the moment Jim lost his hand-hold.

They found the body in the reserve pit, burned and drowned, his lungs filled with drilling fluid.

Ethan's knees weakened. He swept his eyes from the escape line and swallowed hard, suddenly realizing he was hearing a rumble below. He looked down and saw smoke belching from his engine and felt the derrick vibrate.

"Let's try and pull the pipe!" Ethan yelled as he clamored to the ground. Marlin shook his head violently. "Uh uh. You better get somebody out here who knows what they're doin'."

Ethan went up to the draw works and looked over the controls. None were labeled. He knew Marlin was right. They shut the engine down and went to town. Ethan had to find a crew. Fast.

Three more fruitless days passed, and Ethan grew more worried about his thinning wallet and the ticking clock, not to mention Whitley.

He had promised himself not to go into Noble's money for his own sustenance. He would need every penny of that for leases and drilling operations. And more—reminding himself that half his deal was still unsold.

His search for a crew came up dry, but he found a driller who said he might be able round up a couple of roughnecks and a roustabout or two. The guy heaved with laughter and shook his head when Ethan told him about the derelict rig. As Ethan turned to leave, the driller suggested he go to the Journey's Inn in Bossier City. He said oil people hung out there, and he might find some willing men. That meant another drive to Shreveport, or nearly so. Ethan had just spent three frustrating days there hunting helpers. He started the Plymouth and headed west again trying not to dwell on his mounting troubles.

He opened the door at the inn's tavern and stepped in, coughing in the smoky gloom. He looked around at the small groups of men sitting around sipping beer, mumbling and laughing. A big man wearing a hard hat and coveralls, the back of which read, *Western Oilfield Equipment*, stood feeding coins to a jukebox. The man turned and eyed him. Some of the others swung their heads around. The jukebox began spewing the sound of snapping fingers, then Tennessee Ernie Ford's powerful, crisp voice began drawling out *Sixteen Tons*.

Ethan stepped to the bar and ordered a Pabst. The bartender pulled a dripping can from the cooler, picked up his opener tool, and punched a triangular hole in the top. With a flip of his practiced wrist he spun the can and punched another hole on the opposite rim. Ethan sucked the foam off the top and listened to the Ernie drone about being older and deeper in debt. Looking down at the bar he shook his head and squelched a cynical chuckle. Tennessee Ernie knew who was listening.

Ethan watched the busy bartender, and when the man swept past him, he asked if there were any rig crews in the bar. The bartender cackled and flung his arm in a wide sweeping arch, almost hitting Ethan in the face. "Take your pick, fella!"

Ethan turned and surveyed the room. He went from table to table offering his proposition, hating it, feeling like a beggar, feeling like a fish out of water, wanting to be out of there, even if it meant failure. A knot of menacing looking men in a dim corner were watching him. His senses told him to avoid that table.

Except for the juke box, most noise in the room had ebbed

as all eyes watched him go around pitching his appeal. At table after table, heads shook. Some chuckled at his rejections. He felt he was entertaining them.

He swallowed hard and looked toward the men in the dim corner. They were the only ones left now—and his final shot.

They watched him approach.

"Are you fellows roughnecks?" He asked.

"Yeah," a burly, red-skinned drinker retorted, "just like about everybody else in here."

"Except you," another man said. A round of chuckles arose.

Ethan sized the big guy up. Bushy rust-colored hair grew everywhere on him except the top of his head. Shiny bulging eyes shifted about as if out of control in their sockets. The meaty cheeks almost matched the color of the beard. The buttons on his undersized shirt appeared to be cocked and ready to explode in Ethan's face.

Ethan had made the error at an earlier table of telling them he was a geologist. The *college boy* slurs came at him like arrows. He wouldn't commit that mistake again.

"I'm a company man," he said.

"What comp'ny?"

Ethan thought up a name. "Bonner Operating Company."

"Never heard of it."

The other men shook their heads.

"We operate back East," Ethan said. "I need some experienced men. Y'all available?"

"Maybe," the big one drawled. "Did you say 'back East'?" he asked with deep wrinkles in his huge forehead.

"Yeah. Alabama."

A roar of guffaws broke out around the table. The big guy cackled so hard he spilled his beer. "Ala-where?"

Across the table a thin weed of a man with wide lips that looked like a pair of string beans butted in with a duck-like voice. "Mister, I'll drink all the oil in Alabama!" More guffaws broke out, including at the neighboring tables.

"Tell him, Harvey!" a tall, earthy youngster blurted, almost spewing his Dr. Pepper.

Ethan looked at the thin Harvey and wondered how anyone so frail looking could work a drill floor. He saw the man focus his eyes on something behind him. He yelled. "Grady, come here! You gotta hear this!"

Ethan turned to see a tall, broad-shouldered man emerging from the men's room zipping up his trousers. He stepped by Ethan and took the empty chair. "What?" he asked, picking up his Pabst.

"This here's a comp'ny man from Ala-fuckin-bama! Says he needs a drilling crew!" More laughter erupted across the room.

The one they called Grady took a swig from the can and eyed Ethan, who was still standing. "Sit down," he said.

Ethan sensed adult leadership was speaking when the others stopped their banter. The big one obligingly reached for a chair at a nearby table and swung it behind Ethan's butt. The tall guy reached across the table and extended a huge calloused hand. "Grady Plunket."

Ethan took the hand and damned near winced at the squeeze. "Ethan Bonner."

The big red guy suddenly turned more civil. "I'm Cuz."

Harvey, the thin one, didn't offer a hand but nodded and mumbled his name, "Harvey Lee."

"An' that 'air's my nephew, Skeeter," Plunket said, cocking his head toward the stout kid who sat behind a cluster of empty Dr. Pepper bottles.

"Skeeter's the derrick man," Harvey said, nodding. Skeeter's face turned to a goofy grin.

Plunket sat eying Ethan in a weird way, head slightly turned as if using only one eye. He was tall and brawny—even while sitting. His lower jaw jutted out. The forehead towered over a beaked nose, and the face reminded Ethan of the *National Geographic Magazine* photos he had seen of the mysterious stone carvings on Easter Island.

"Alabama?" Grady asked, singing the word. "I ain't heard of anything going on over there." He looked aside thoughtfully.

Finally, Ethan thought, sensible conversation. "Nobody's found anything there yet. I aim to. I couldn't find a rig to hire, so I bought one. Now I need a crew."

Grady peered at him suspiciously. "Where'd you get a rig?"

"Found it near Rustin. A bank repo."

Grady's eyes narrowed. He turned somber. Said nothing.

Ethan glanced at the other men, sensing their restiveness. Cuz's bulging eyeballs were riveted on his beer can. Harvey looked intently aside at Grady. Skeeter swung his head from Grady to Ethan, back and forth, his jaw hanging askew.

Ethan grew unsettled. "What's the matter?" he asked, swinging his head side to side, appealing to someone to answer.

Grady broke silence in a low, menacing tone. "You bought the Lampasas rig?"

Ethan nodded.

Grady leaned forward and looked squarely at Ethan. "They didn't tell you?"

"They who?"

"Whoever you bought the rig from."

"Tell me what?"

Grady took a pack of cigarettes out of his shirt pocket and lit up. "Well," he muttered thoughtfully, smoke streaming from his gaping nostrils, "of course they wouldn't tell you. They wanted to get rid of that thing."

Ethan waited for the explanation that seemed slow coming.

"That rig's snake bit," he said out of the side of his mouth, the cigarette jumping in his lips as he spoke. "It's got bad luck. I ought'a know."

The others nodded.

Ethan looked away and sighed.

"That damn thing's never drilled a single producer," Grady added.

"You're kidding?" Ethan said.

Grady shook his head. "Every company that owned that rig has gone out of business. Every hole it drilled was a duster." He tapped the ashes off the end of his cigarette. "It had problems. Lots of 'em." He paused for a pull from the Pabst. The other men watched him and waited. "Fishin' jobs—hot-a-mighty!" He shook his head. "That damn thing stayed stuck more'n it drilled. I think it might have left more junked holes behind it than dry ones. Mechanical problems, too—mud pumps always breaking down. I know they went through three or four engines and put in a new draw-works."

He sniffed. "One time the cable snapped while they were raising the derrick. The whole shebang slammed down so hard it rattled windows for ten miles."

The men shook their heads. Ethan wondered if it was all a big joke.

"And that's not all." He paused while they all stared at him. "A man got kilt on it. Derrick man. Fell. He hit right there on the drill floor in front of the driller and roughnecks. Splat!"

He took his time and peered menacingly at everyone around the table. "Cracked his skull wide open."

Cuz and Harvey instantly recoiled, swearing silently.

He paused. Ethan sensed he was allowing them all to form a picture in their minds of the ghastly scene.

"They had just tripped out to change the bit. All the pipe was stacked, so the hole was open." He paused again. "The poor bastard's brains spilled into the hole."

Skeeter stared ahead for a few seconds with a contorted face, then asked, "What about his safety harness?"

"It was on him when he hit. Like I said, that thing is snake bit."

He fell silent and leaned closer to Ethan favoring his right eye, a big coal-tinted orb that seemed to be growing and targeting Ethan. The others fidgeted. After an eternity of seconds Grady leaned back.

"You gonna tell him, Grady?" Cuz asked.

Grady slowly shook his head.

"Tell me what?" Ethan barked. "What?"

No one answered. They just sat until Grady spoke in a low solemn tone. "Another man lost an eye on that rig."

Ethan had heard enough. He figured he was being cleverly played for a fool. He finished his beer and got up.

"Where you goin'?" Grady demanded.

Ethan shrugged. "Anywhere but here."

"Sit down."

Ethan slowly reseated himself.

Grady wiped his lower jaw and looked aside at the wall.

Harvey began a question. "You ain't thinkin' of—"

"I'll go out and look at it," Grady interrupted. And—"he paused and nodded toward the other men. "If these smelly snake eaters will go with me, maybe we can get that thing running. We'll see."

A cautious grin grew on Ethan's face.

"But first, what you willin' to pay?"

"Standard rates. Two-fifty an hour. Three for the driller." He looked around then back at Grady. You're the driller?"

Grady nodded, grunted and got up to leave, prompting the whole table to rise.

Ethan had spent most of the morning on the phone trying to track down additional men and getting estimates from trucking companies. When he pulled up to the rig the engine was humming. Grady and Marlin were working on one of the mud pumps. Cuz was busy lubricating the draw works.

"Glad you could make it," Grady called out when he saw him. Ethan walked up and looked over their shoulders at the pump. Grady had sent Skeeter into town to get an electrical relay. As soon as they got that he would test the pump.

When Skeeter arrived with the relay Grady set it aside. "First let's go up and try to pull this pipe out and see how much you've got!" He sent Skeeter aloft to the monkey board. The floor crew pulled on their heavy gloves. Ethan grinned.

Grady took his place at the control console while Cuz and Harvey stood aside, ready. Grady lifted the brake and stepped on the accelerator pedal. The engine roared. Smoke belched. Metal components in the derrick clinked and clanked under the strain, but the drill pipe didn't budge. Grady looked at Ethan and yelled the word Ethan already feared. "Stuck!"

He applied more power. Nothing happened. He engaged the rotary clutch and tried to rotate the pipe clockwise, the normal direction for drilling. The pipe twisted a few degrees and stopped. Grady tried a few more times and then reversed direction, hoping the pipe would unscrew somewhere downhole. It wouldn't turn that way either. After fifteen minutes of struggling he motioned for Marlin to shut down the engine.

Wiping his hands on a rag, he walked over to Ethan. "We're good 'n stuck."

Ethan nodded. "What now?"

"We've got to shoot it. You know who to call?" Ethan shook his head. Grady gave him a name and phone number.

Two hours later a truck showed up with a hefty Cajun, whom Grady introduced as Gator. Ethan watched for a long time, becoming impatient with the two men's back-slapping bantering over old stories. Finally Gator turned to Ethan and told him the cost of the service would be $100 per shot, cash money. No checks. Grady kicked at the dirt while Ethan looked in his wallet. He had $229. He looked at Grady.

"Do you think two shots will do it?"

"Hell if I know. Maybe just one. Maybe ten. Maybe we'll never get it unstuck."

He put the wallet in his pocket and put up two fingers. Gator nodded, got out two primacord cartridges, and took them to the rig floor. Cuz and Harvey helped him rig the first explosive on a wireline down the inside of the drill pipe. The descent through the thick mud took about fifteen minutes. The crew backed away and Gator pushed the ignition button. They all heard a muffled "whump" issue from the pipe and felt the drill floor shake. Mud spewed out the drill pipe into a ten foot geyser. The flow subsided in a few seconds and Gator nodded.

Grady shoved the brake handle and revved the engine. The pipe lifted an inch, no more. He tried several more pulls. Then he engaged the clutch and tried rotation. Nothing worked.

They pulled the wireline and attached the second cartridge. After its descent Gator fired it and Grady tried more pulls and twists. The pipe remained stuck. They pulled the wireline.

Ethan paid Gator and thanked him. Gator slapped Grady's shoulder and waved to Cuz and the crew, then headed for his truck. Ethan turned to Grady. "Leave it in the hole. Let's rig-down and get this thing ready to move."

Grady shook his head, looking down at the pipe. "Mr. Bonner, there might be a few thousand feet of drill pipe down there. That's worth a lot of money if it's in decent shape. Try one more time."

"I've got twenty-nine bucks," Ethan said.

Grady watched Gator get in his truck. He yelled at the crew. "How much cash ya'll got?"

"About forty bucks," Harvey said.

"Twenty or so," said Cuz.

Skeeter was counting his cash. He looked up. "Seventy five."

"Dollars?" Grady yelled.

"Cents."

Grady pulled a twenty from his wallet. He yelled down to Gator asking him to bring another shot up.

Ethan looked at them like an astonished child. He needed to say something, but the words were as stuck in his throat as the drill pipe was in the hole. Grady held a hand up, blocking any forthcoming expression of gratitude. The men went back to work.

Following the third shot the pipe lurched a few inches upward and shuddered to a stop. Grady engaged the clutch. The pipe strained, jerked and started rotating. He continued rotation until he thought the stuck joints were loose enough, then pulled. The pipe came out. They all cheered.

Hours later 3,420 feet of drill pipe stood in ninety foot tri-ple-joint sections. Grady declared it to be in good enough shape to put back into service. They slapped each other and cackled.

He turned to the beaming Ethan. "With the pipe that's layin' down there in the racks, that makes about 6,600 feet. How deep you plannin' on goin' boss man?"

Ethan drew a deep breath. He had dreaded this question. He paused and looked into the driller's eyes, noticing again the odd way one eye looked askance. "Eleven thousand, five hundred."

Cuz and Harvey suddenly stopped bantering and looked his way. Grady's left eye bored into Ethan. "Do you know this here rig you bought is only rated to seven or eight thousand feet?"

"Nine thousand," Ethan said. "I called Ideco about it."

"So you knew when you conned us in to coming out here that you were gonna ask us to do something stupid?"

"I don't think it's stupid," Ethan said. "The Ideco man said it might could be done with the right crew." He looked aside at the roughnecks.

Grady turned and walked to the rail. He peered over and spat. He turned about. "What the hell else you holdin' back from us?"

Ethan heard the roughnecks utter, "Yeah!" He stood with his hands in his pockets, pondering what to say.

"You are holding somethin' else back, ain't you?" Grady growled.

Ethan swallowed hard and took a deep breath. He felt flushed—even a bit scared. Tough, hardened men stood around him, not happy. "I don't have all the money I need yet to get the job done. I've got to raise more."

Grady grimaced and looked at his crew.

Harvey shrugged. "Long as I get paid, I don't care."

"I ain't got nuthin' else to do," Cuz said. "But, can we take this thing that deep without bustin' our asses?"

Grady just shook his head slowly. He turned to Ethan. "All right. We'll drill. But we're not guaranteein' we'll get as deep as you want. And we'll walk off this piece of shit quicker 'n you can blink if you miss a pay period."

Ethan nodded and smiled. He held out a hand. "No more secrets. Promise."

Grady slapped Ethan's hand away with a quirky smile. "I can't believe I'm doin' this." He sighed and turned to the men. "Let's start layin' this pipe down."

Ethan went to the side rail and turned away from the men. He felt his eyes water up. He wiped them. He turned to the men, as they were putting on their hard hats and gloves. "I'll buy the beer tonight!" He thought that might cheer them up, but they ignored him.

As he opened the door to his dirty Plymouth Ethan heard a rumble overhead. He looked up and saw a Stearman pass over the derrick heading northeast to its miserable piece of dirt. He smiled and nodded.

10

A Resourceful Man

J.D. got right to the point when Ethan met him at breakfast. "Did you come up with anything by which you might get yourself into the awl business, like money, namely?"

Ethan studied him while sipping his coffee. "You didn't get the message, did you?"

"Naw, I guess I didn't."

"Yeah. I found some money."

"Good! And a rig?"

"Rig, too."

"Okay, here's what we got," J.D. said, before giving Ethan a chance to explain that he had actually bought a drilling rig. He slid paperwork in front of Ethan and explained what his research had fetched.

There were no more free leases, but several others were almost in the bag. J.D. needed money to secure them. One of the choicest was Ben and Corrine Buchanan's tract, which they allowed a farmer to sharecrop. J.D. found Ben to be an affable man, easy to talk to and reasonable to deal with. But Corrine, as he had discovered early on, was contentious and mean. She wanted more. "She's the woman who threw me out of the store that day. Remember?"

Ethan nodded and snickered.

"You wouldn't laugh if you had that mad hen jump on you like she did me. And that's not all. Two people have sent me away empty-handed because they heard you were sent by the Devil."

Ethan rolled his eyes. "Aw, come on! Are you kidding?"

"No. I am not! The Reverend Pope and his friends are causing us to miss out on some good acreage because of this non-sense. We took Mr. Hull's lease in your name. I suggest you form a company that does not include your name, so that the folks won't get suspicious."

Ethan sighed heavily. This would be another time and money consuming chore.

"Ain't got time, J.D. Just do your best."

J.D. shrugged his shoulders and smashed out a butt. "There's more," he warned.

Ethan became even more troubled when J.D. told him he had seen Emmett Brubeck in the records room. Ethan took a deep breath and long pull at his water glass then asked what Brubeck was up to.

"Busting your block!" It'll be easy to do by going to the people who refuse to lease to us because we're demons."

Ethan stared through J.D., thinking.

"And there's more still."

"What?"

"Benny Hull raised hell for a while. He threatened to sue us. Says we tricked his daddy."

"How'd you handle that?"

"We shared a little bottle of who-hit-john, and he mellowed out, for now."

Ethan snapped at him. "J.D., you—"

"I never gave you any promises. Remember? Anyway, we have to watch out for that guy."

Ethan nodded and sighed. Then he told J.D. how he had found the rig and bought it and how he had advanced Grady a thousand bucks cash so that he and his crew could dismantle the rig. Ethan would pay the trucking company, and Grady would pay the crew. He would also try to find more men. One crew wasn't enough. After telling J.D. about finding the crew and reviving the rig, Ethan sat back and grinned.

"Well, I'll be damned," J.D. mumbled. "So you're in the drilling business, too, now?"

As they finished breakfast a waitress told Ethan the motel had called. He needed to return a long distance call. J.D. headed up the street to talk anew to the Buchanans, now that he had spending authority. Ethan split toward the Do-Drop Inn.

As he had hoped, the call was from Grady. Good. That meant Grady had located a trucking company to haul the rig to Fossil Rim. He got Grady on the line.

"Mr. Bonner, I don't have good news."

Ethan's head slumped.

"The trucking business over here is booked up with local runs. I couldn't find but one that would even talk about hauling a rig to Alabama, and they've only got two trucks available. It's gonna take six to move this beast. That means three round trips with two trucks. That's about ten days to two weeks to make the move if—and that's a damn big if—everything goes well. They want a dollar a mile."

Ethan did some quick mental math. Almost $5,000. He put his hand to his head.

"Well, sir?" the voice in Louisiana said.

Ethan thought about the expiring Hull option and all the expenses to come.

"Well?"

"What about putting it on a freight train?"

"We'll still need trucks to get it to a rail head here and get it off the train there and out to the location. That don't make sense to me."

"Okay. Get the trucks started."

"All right, boss. You get the location ready, and we'll get it comin' your way, piece by piece."

Ethan sat and worked the trucking fee into his calculations. He remembered what Noble had once told him about cost estimates in doing business: Carefully consider all aspects; evaluate all options; double-check everything; when you arrive at your final cost estimate, double it.

Now he knew Noble was wrong. Triple it.

A knock at the door shattered Ethan's concentration. It was the drilling fluids specialist, better known as the *mud man*. He invited the guy in and thanked him for coming. "Wow!" the mud man, said. "Alabama! I never thought I'd be working this far east." He looked, to Ethan, to be fresh out of college. "I'm excited about this!" The two went over Ethan's drilling plans and discussed the expected geology. The mud man said he would calculate the number of gel sacks needed and send them over with a recommended mixing program to control viscosity and density at various depths. Ethan saw him to the door and went back to his work table.

Next on his agenda was site preparation. He figured he could save some money by getting a local construction company to prepare his location. Bringing an oil field construction company in from Mississippi would probably be another blow to his account. Several companies in Mobile gave him estimates but they floored him. *No, Noble*, he told himself; *you need to multiply by four.*

Finally he found a guy named Floyd Peavy who had a D-8 Caterpillar and lived just down the road a piece. He operated out of his home and would do it for only three times what Ethan thought it was worth.

The guy wasn't familiar with oil field work. Ethan told him he needed him to clear and level a roughly one-acre site, then excavate two rectangular pits, one to hold excess drilling mud and a larger one to stand by as a reserve pit. When the rig arrived he would use the D-8 to drag the heavy components into position. Peavy said he would be on site next morning.

When he hung up with Peavy, Ethan realized he had not yet gotten a state permit or staked the location. He rubbed his hair and shook his head. Other people had always done these things. On all his past deals, the actual operations had been assumed by one of the companies that bought into the deals. They did all the leg work. He had only needed to concentrate on his next prospect.

He stared at the calendar on the wall. Less than two weeks left. If he didn't make this happen, there would be no next prospect.

The afternoon heat was ebbing as Laura graded papers her summer school students had worked on. She liked to sit sideways in her porch swing with her bare feet propped over the far armrest of the swing. The green Plymouth pulling into the driveway surprised her. *Ethan Bonner. My God, Why didn't the man call before he came?*

He was out of the car and on the porch before she could even think of getting herself ready to receive a visitor. He took his hat off and handed her a half-dozen roses, diverted his eyes away from her legs, then stepped back as if she might throw the flowers at him.

She shifted upright, pulled her dress lower, sniffed the flowers and muttered thanks. On the excuse of getting a vase for the roses, she went in, combed her hair, and got on her shoes. She came back out more composed.

He was still standing, hat in hand. "I got something for you to see," he said. He nodded toward the car. She followed him. He opened the trunk and looked at her, grinning. "My bits!"

Her mouth opened, but nothing came out for a while. Then, "Oh." She looked at him. "They don't scare me. They are interesting, though."

He told her he had bought the bits from the Hughes Oilfield Supply store in Laurel, Mississippi. They were heavy. His car sat low on its rear wheels. "I've been running around like a tornado," he told her as he slammed the trunk down. "Had to go up to Tuscaloosa to get a drilling permit. They approved it while I waited. Then I swung over to Laurel to get the bits. Saved the delivery charges that way."

He invited her to dinner—said he hoped he wasn't imposing on her, asking at such a late hour, and she pretended to mentally canvass her evening's agenda before saying she could work it in.

While he waited on the porch for her to get ready, a car slowed down in front of the house. It passed, then reversed and stopped. A man's face scanned the porch and yard, then settled on Ethan. While Laura was getting ready she heard the man in the car yell, "Is Laura all right?"

Ethan answered. "Yes! She's dressing for supper."

"Who are you?" the man asked.

"Who are you?" Ethan countered.

Laura parted the curtains and peeped outside.

The man switched off the engine, got out, leaned back against the car and lit a cigarette. "Benny Hull. You're that oil man. Ain't cha?"

Ethan nodded. "Your Victor Hull's boy. Ain't cha?"

"Yeah. He ain't doin' too good, ya know? He ain't his self."

Giving her hair a last few strokes with the brush while watching, Laura noticed Ethan didn't hesitate to get into the pissing match with Benny.

Benny puffed, blew a cloud and raised his chin. "Laura and me are pretty tight, you know."

"Is that so?" Ethan asked.

"Me and her got plans."

"That makes three of us."

After powdering her face, and with a final flourish of her hair brush, she opened the door and went out, purse in hand. She saw Benny out by his car, sighed, and looked at Ethan. "I take it you two have met?"

"In a way," Ethan said. Then he yelled out to Benny. "See ya, buddy."

Benny's tires squealed as he lurched away.

Ethan took her out to the location before dinner and showed

her the stake the surveyor had driven. "This is where the bit will hit the ground turning," he said. "We call that spudding-in."

"Spudding?" she said. "Where did that term come from?"

Ethan laughed and shrugged.

She looked to the east and pointed. "That other oil company drilled over there, about a quarter mile." She held her hair against the evening breeze, remembering her visit to that drill site five years ago when the crew teased her. "So, if you are only going to go deeper than they did, why didn't you put the stake over there where they did?"

He studied her face and smiled. "Good question. The structure under here is so broad you can choose about anywhere within a square mile and be very close to the top of it. Actually the main answer to your question is not very scientific. I couldn't get that lease over there from Buchanan for free. This one here—the Hull farm—I could. But it came with a six-month commitment to drill. I'll lose this big Hull lease if I don't spud by next Thursday at midnight. Ready to get some supper? How about Susie Q's?"

She smiled and nodded. In the car Ethan explained that the Wagon Wheel would be crowded on a Friday evening with too many people who knew him by now, and he didn't want any questions. She said she was tired of that place anyway. They drove down to Chunchula to the little cafe he had discovered there.

They ordered ribeyes and baked potatoes.

"There's been talk, Ethan," she said, softly. "Some people are calling around telling others not to lease their land to you."

"I know. J.D. told me."

"So. Am I dining with the Devil's agent?"

He cracked a devious smile and chuckled like a wicked evil-doer. "What do you think?"

She gleamed. "I think you're just a big, oafish Boy Scout."

"That's about right." He looked uneasy for a while then composed his words carefully.

"I've been under a lot of stress. Problems are coming at me from every direction. Oh boy, the stakes are high." He looked deep into her eyes. "I'm keeping from coming apart at the seams by thinking about you. You have a gentle way that settles me." He looked away and ran his hand across his chin. "You know, I've never been very close to anybody. I can't slow down long enough."

She said nothing. Just smiled and touched his hand.

Ethan was sifting through some small tract leases J.D. had taken when he heard commotion, loud voices, cackling and hammering on the door. He opened it and found his drilling crew swarming around him, Cuz towering, Harvey smoking, Skeeter clutching a Dr. Pepper, and Grady behind them leaning against the hood of his 1952 Buick Roadster four-holer convertible.

Cuz bellowed, pointing toward the street, "Boss Man, where you want us to put these pieces of shit?"

Ethan looked. Two large tractor-trailers sat idling on the street side, the drivers huddled by, smoking. The low-boy trailers behind them were piled high with equipment. Ethan recognized the rig's substructure, dismantled into four pieces occupying both trailers. Already townspeople were coming to examine the caravan and its curious cargo.

Sheriff Tant pulled up and got out. He took off his hat and scratched his scalp, surveying the trucks. "I didn't know you were bringing in the Barnum-Bailey Circus!"

"You hit that one right," Grady spouted. "And it ain't all here yet. Not by a long shot."

Ethan introduced the two.

"Man, I'm glad to see you," he said to Grady.

The driller shrugged and stamped out his cigarette. "Show us the stake. We need to get these trucks unloaded and start 'em back to Ruston. You got the location ready, I hope."

"Yes, said Ethan. "Except for the pits. They'll be finished by the time we need them. I've got a trailer coming, too. Tomorrow." He needed a rented house trailer to serve as an onsite office. As a bonus Ethan planned to move into it to get away from J.D.'s abominable snoring. "Did you find a second crew?"

"Yup. They're loadin' your rig. They'll be here with the last truck load. I need to get a check back to them today. That thousand you gave me is long gone."

Ethan turned to go in for his checkbook.

"I'm still short for worms," Grady yelled. "Need one or two for the night shift. We'll have to recruit 'em from around here. That's up to you."

"Worms?" Sheriff Tant asked. "What's that?"

"Roustabouts. Laborers. People who do general work around the rig."

Ethan came out and handed the check to Grady, then turned to the sheriff. "Can you put the word out that we need a couple of stout men?"

Hub wrinkled his eyebrows and then nodded.

Ethan started handing out motel room keys to the men as Hub got in his cruiser, turned on his red rotating light and led the convoy to the drill site. A line of local cars and pickups followed, accumulating more as it went.

From his third-floor window at the bank building Norman Brubeck looked toward the drill site, watching the dust kick up as the trucks wheeled onto the location. His secretary knocked and peeped in. "Mr. Hull is here."

"Send him in."

As Benny came in, Emmett said, "Over here." Benny went to the window and looked where Emmett pointed. "They've got about a week left before your Daddy's lease runs out." He puffed on his cigar, took it out and studied the tip.

"Benny, do you want that lease back?"

"Huh?"

Emmett's eyes lifted. "I said, do you want that lease of your daddy's?"

"Well, I don't want it back. I just want 'em to pay for it."

Emmett studied Benny for a moment. "You and I have done a little bit of business before, haven't we, ole buddy?" He gave Benny a chummy slap on his back. "And it worked out pretty good, I'd say, wouldn't you?"

Benny grinned. "Oh, yeah! That land deal we brokered." He cackled loud. "That ole colored fella, Rufus, still thinks he got a good price for that! Ha ha."

"Yeah, well," Emmett quickly added, "let's don't be talking too much about that." He took out his cigar and wet his lips. "Oh." He reached for a box on his desk. "Sorry, Benny. Cigar?"

Benny's smile broadened. His eyebrows arched up. "Sure, Emmett."

Emmett cleared his throat as Benny fumbled for his lighter with the cigar clenched in his teeth. "You gotta lick it first, Benny. Lick it good. Make your spit soak into the wrapper. That's it. No. Don't light it yet. Bite off the end. The other end, Benny."

Emmett rolled his eyes as Benny finally completed the cigar preparation as instructed. He struck a match and held it to the end of the log as Benny's cheeks contracted and bulged.

"Do you want to do business again, Benny?"

Benny's head nodded ponderously with the tobacco log still in his mouth. "Sure, Emmett."

"Good." He turned back toward the window and gestured out with his cigar. "I'll help you get that lease back. We could force them to delay drilling until the lease expires. It then reverts to your family." He paused to let the implications sink in.

"I could sell it back to 'em!" Benny said, as if he'd just had his first original thought.

"Sure, you could. And for my part of the deal I get half of what you make."

Benny frowned. "Half? Ain't that a little steep, Emmett?"

Emmett leered at him. "It wasn't too steep in the deal we did with ole Rufus. Besides, if it comes to needin' outside help, I've got connections. Do you, Benny?"

Benny looked back out the window and puffed superficially at the cigar. "How do we do it?"

"We stop those men from drilling before midnight next Friday."

Benny glared at Emmett in wonderment. "How do *we* do that, Emmett?"

Emmett stared into the distance beyond the window. "They've got a lot of equipment out there. It would be too bad if something important broke down or disappeared just before they needed it." He turned aside to Benny. "Wouldn't it now, Benny?"

Benny's eyes moved back and forth.

Emmett could see the few wheels in Benny's brain turning furiously. "You're a resourceful man, Benny. You'll figure out something."

Benny's face suddenly flicked into a frown. "But what about Daddy?"

"What about him?"

"He wouldn't like going back on his word to them men."

Brubeck looked back out the window and puffed. "Let me take care of your daddy. I've known him a long time. You stop those men from starting drilling before midnight Thursday night."

Ethan parked beside Grady and the two walked out onto the location while the crews began to unload the trucks. "There," Ethan said, pointing at the stake in the ground that the surveyors had driven.

They walked to it. Grady took off his hat and scratched his head, looking around. "This is it?"

Puzzled, Ethan nodded. *Where else would it be?* "Here!" He pointed down at the stake.

Grady looked askance at him. "You're supposed to have a conductor hole drilled and cased before we got here."

Ethan froze. "Oh."

"And a rat hole and a mouse hole," Grady added.

He knew what a conductor hole was. It was basically a *starter* hole drilled about twenty-four inches wide, sometimes wider, and about thirty feet deep. A section of steel casing would then be set down into it and be driven in with a pile driver, and that would be the starting point for deep drilling operations. The rat hole was a shallow hole to park the Kelly bar in, and the mouse hole was where the next pipe joint in drill sequence would be stored.

But someone else had always seen to these kinds of details before. He never got involved in operations. He felt flushed with embarrassment. How could he let vital details like that escape him?

Grady kicked at the dirt and spat. "I thought you needed to get this thing going before this lease expires?"

"I do. Just forgot about the conductor hole and the others. I'm new to drilling operations, you know."

"No shit," Grady grumbled as he put his hat back on. "Well, I was plannin' to build up the substructure today over this spot, but I can't do it till you get that conductor put in."

"How?" Ethan asked, realizing how badly needed Grady's guidance.

Grady, shaking his head, spewed a long rush of air. "It's usually done with an auger truck."

"I'd better get on it now." He turned for the trailer but stopped, seeing a truck driver walking toward him. Skeeter and one of the roustabouts they had brought with them from Louisiana were unloading and stacking the two hundred sacks of bentonite gel Ethan had ordered from Hattiesburg. The driver asked for a check. "Won't they bill me?" Ethan asked.

He shook his head. "They told me to get a check."

Ethan wrote it and handed it to the man then went back into the trailer. A Southern Bell technician was finishing installing a phone. He began thumbing through his oil directory and as soon as the man left he placed his first calls to every oil field construction company in Mississippi he could find. After hours of calling he came up dry. None could get an auger truck over to him in less than a week.

He sat dumbfounded for several minutes. It looked as if his entire project would crumble because he had overlooked important details. He went back out to tell Grady.

He found the driller perched atop a section of substructure, standing up there like a human derrick, hands shrouded in gigantic gloves. Ethan yelled up at him, telling him the bad news.

Grady looked around, then climbed down. "All right, Mr. Bonner. We might can do without conductor. If the surface formation stays firm and don't cave on us as we spud in, than we can start out with the 13-inch surface hole. I've seen it done."

"Then let's do it!" Ethan said, relieved.

"I said we *might* can do it. If the hole caves in we'll have problems. You might have to hire somebody to drill a conductor hole over there to the side and case it, and we'll have to skid this rig over to it. That's the worst case situation."

Ethan nodded, holding up his hand. "Got my fingers crossed."

Ethan heard Grady mumble at his back side as he headed toward the trailer. "Forgot the conductor hole! Damned fool office-boy geologist. Shit-a-mighty."

Ethan called the trucking company in Louisiana to check on the progress of loading the rig. They gave him more bad news. Due to heavy rains and mud they were having delays loading the derrick, which had been dismantled into two pieces, one for each truck. But they hoped to get it out in a day or two. And, could he send a check for that last round trip? He said it was on the way back with one of the truckers.

Ethan hung up and looked down at the linoleum floor, rocking his feet. Rains in Louisiana coming his way. He looked out at the freshly graded location. It wouldn't take much to turn it into a quagmire. That meant more delays. The hours were now down in double digits till lease expiration. His dusty boots rocked, toes to heel, 180 degrees out of phase.

11

Lucky Lucy

Grady stood atop the assembled substructure, peering down through the open Kelly bushing hole at the ground. Cuz and the others stood on the ground near the mass of steel girders and beams. Grady's arm beckoned eastward. "Come on! Three more feet."

Cuz relayed the shout to Peavy.

Ethan saw black smoke blossom from the exhaust stack of the D-8 and heard the metallic substructure clank and creak as the dozer shoved it on its skids across the ground.

"Whoah!" Grady shouted.

"Hoah!" Cuz and Harvey shouted.

Ethan joined Cuz and Harvey under the floor and stood by the stake. They looked up through the open Kelly hole, seeing Grady standing up there dangling a plumb bob, peering down at them. He yelled. "Looks like we're pret' near right on top of it!"

Ethan nodded. The bob hung only a couple of inches from the stake at his feet. It was a good spot. The spud bit would hit the ground at the stake.

"Let's get to work!" Grady called down to the crew. They scrambled.

He heard Grady yell. "Mr. Bonner!" He turned and approached the substructure. Grady looked down at him. "Boss, where are we gonna get water?"

Ethan had not thought of it. *More expense!* He would have to rent water tanks and a pump. The water would have to be hauled in to mix with the mud and to supply the never-ending job of cleaning the rig. What would that cost him?

He saw Grady looking out in the distance, pointing. "Is there a creek in that tree line?"

Ethan shrugged and walked toward it. After about 100 yards he came upon a small brook. He smiled. It would do, he hoped. And it was on Hull's property, too. He would dispatch one of the roustabouts to Laurel tomorrow to rent a pump and some hose.

Ethan returned to the trailer and set up his paraphernalia. He placed his centerpiece—the stereo-microscope—on the middle of the table. He put the fluoroscope and a bottle of acetone on the left. On the right he placed a tray containing sample slides, and an array of dentist tools for probing and breaking minute rock fragments. He pulled out a tablet, took a straight edge and drew a vertical line. He labeled the left column DEPTH and the right column DESCRIPTION. At the top he wrote, *No. 1 HULL, Bonner Operating Company.* He pushed the pad aside. He wouldn't need any of the stuff until drilling was well underway. He smiled, thinking of showcasing his *lab* to Laura.

He swiveled his chair to the opposite table and looked over his finances again. Suddenly he froze, staring at the spread sheet. He had forgotten something—his promise to the crew to find some small diameter drill pipe. That was his offer to persuade them to take the rig below its rated depth. He shook his head and sighed. He needed to get on it, now.

He called every supplier he knew of in Mississippi. Drill pipe smaller than 4½ inches outer diameter was rare. None was available. He called supply yards in Louisiana. That, too, was a dead end. Frustrated, he knew he had to shove that problem on the back burner. There were more even more pressing phone calls to make.

He sat thinking, knowing his next move was the hardest job a wildcatter ever faced, and he had known it was coming. He got out an old oil company directory book and spent the rest of the morning cold-calling. New Orleans, Houston, Dallas, Fort Worth, Oklahoma City. He even made a call to New Mexico and another to Colorado. He tried not to think about the toll charges.

Some of the companies he called were ones he had visited on his money-finding tour back in the spring. He hoped they would reconsider now that spud-in was imminent. Many numbers had been disconnected. He didn't get past the receptionist of most of the ones that did answer. They told him their exploration manager was away or in a meeting. He left messages and requests for a return call, knowing few would do so.

When he was lucky enough to actually speak to a boss, he told them he was about to spud an 11,000-foot wildcat on top of a tremendous structure. He tried not to sound desperate as he pitched the opportunity for the company to participate. And of course he would be happy to air-mail copies of his maps and economic analysis for their evaluation. When they asked where the prospect was, and he told them, they chuckled and wished him luck. One man even said, "You're about to spud a rank wildcat, and you still have half the deal unsold? I wouldn't touch that with a triple joint drill collar!"

At mid-afternoon he gave up. No return calls were coming in, but maybe tomorrow they would. He would need to stay close by the phone.

He found J.D. in the motel room working on leases. "How's it looking?" he asked the landman.

J.D. took off the reading spectacles and rubbed the bare part of his scalp. "Well, there it is—so far." He motioned to his map. The Hull lease was shaded with a red pencil. Other small tracts surrounding the Hull lease, which J.D. had secured, were shaded green.

"We've got a little over two thousand acres so far. A fourth of that is Mr. Hull, and half the rest is the Gulf farmout. Accordin' to your outline, we need about a thousand more to protect the prospect.

Ethan looked at him. "Well?"

"Well what? There's just so much one man can do, especially as tight as you are with money. You know, Ethan, if you haul off and get a discovery here, vultures are gonna swoop in on this place and grab up what we didn't get but should have, and you're gonna end up provin' up a lotta good oil property for somebody else."

"I know. I know!" Ethan said. "I'm not new to this game. Just keep leasing as best you can while we drill."

"Drill?!" J.D. shouted. "You ain't got nuthin' to drill with yet. Just a few pieces of shit laying out there while the clock is ticking." J.D. got up, calmed down, and lit a butt. "Listen, Ethan. I've stayed with you longer than I thought I would. Even after you finally started payin' me, I still thought every day about dragging up. I'm tellin' you, boy, this seems more and more hopeless every day that goes by. About the only thing keeping me right now is—well, forget it."

"I know what's keeping you, and I'm glad for it."

J.D. smiled, saying, "You're glad. I'm glad. I don't know about her!"

Ethan laughed. He patted J.D.'s shoulder. "I promised you I'd stick with you through your good and bad spells. Now I need you to stick with me. I don't just need you to lease for me. I've found you to be more than that. I need your counsel."

J.D. nodded and gathered the papers. "I'm off to see some more owners. I'll do my best."

The trucks with the derrick arrived along with the rains. Grady and crew, with Peavy and his heavy machine, set about dragging the sections off the trucks. The dozer's treads churned the muck into brown pudding but managed to align the sections close enough for the rain-pelted crew to insert the pins and mate the two sections together. With a final mud-slinging lurch Grady yelled, "Hoah!" when the derrick lie in the correct position next to the superstructure.

Peavy then rumbled over to the trucks and pushed them out of the muck. Following Ethan's instructions, they wasted no time pulling out for Ruston. The mud pumps, the engine, the blow-out preventer, the ramp and catwalk, and the drill pipe all needed to be brought over.

Ethan felt the tension mount as he watched them leave, worrying they'd need still another run to fetch it all. He looked back seeing his crew busy with the prone derrick. If all went well, they would be ready to raise it at sun-up. He hoped his spirits would rise with it. He needed a break. He knew where there was a refuge. He went in to wash up.

"I honestly don't know how I'm going to make it," he said, studying his toes going back and forth. Laura sat next to him in the porch swing. He looked over at her. "The pressure just gets heavier every day."

She watched his feet rock. "Will you stop that?"

"Stop what?"

She pointed.

"Oh." He stopped. "I review my accounts every morning. Then I recalculate my expected expenses. It would be a miracle if I can stretch the money to the logging."

"What's that," she asked.

"When we reach our target depth—11,000 feet, more or less—I'll get a contractor out to evaluate the hole electronically. Then we should know if we've got a well. I've set aside the money for that. I cannot go into that account. Logging is a must-do."

He looked aside at her. "I've never felt so far out on a thin limb in my life."

She took his hand.

"It seems I've always been left behind," he said, staring into the night. "Discoveries are made while I'm watching somebody else make them." He shook his head.

"Sometimes, I wonder what the heck I'm doing. I could be

safe somewhere. I could be on a company staff." He got up and paced to the porch rail. "Heck, I could be—flying crop dusters or airliners, just going out and flying and collecting that pay check and—" His voice trailed off into a heavy sigh.

"Ethan, what on earth are you talking about?"

"I flew in the war, you know. Haven't flown since, though."

She got up and went to his side. "This crop dusting talk is nonsense."

He looked aside at her and smiled. He suggested a walk. They headed down the sidewalk past oak trees tinseled in Spanish Moss. "I've never told anyone this before—not a soul."

She walked on, holding his hand, waiting for whatever revelation was forthcoming. "I couldn't even kill whales without crying like a baby."

She stopped, dumbfounded.

"I sat out the war at a fighter strip in Panama. My squadron shot whales in the ocean for gunnery practice."

"Oh, God, that's horrible!" she cried, hands on her face.

"I killed those gentle giants. Pumped fifty-caliber rounds into them. Watched the water turn red."

She stepped back.

"I didn't want to, Laura. I dreaded every time we took off to go out there. He forced us to do it."

"Who?"

"Donovan, our squadron commander. Most of the guys didn't care; they were so bored they thought it was good sport. I laid awake at nights worrying about it, feeling rotten." Ethan stared past her. "I knew it was wrong. I knew somebody should have reported it to the inspector general. I was scared of Donovan. Had no guts." He turned away from her. "I still have nightmares about it."

He nudged her along.

"I hoped I'd get over the whales, but I never have. In fact I'm thinking about it more and more." He looked aside at her. "I know what you're thinking. Millions of humans died in that war, and I'm sorry for a few whales?"

She shook her head vigorously. "That's not what I'm thinking."

"What then?"

"I'm wondering what the whales have to do with what's worrying you."

Fair enough, Ethan thought. "Day after day the bills pile up. Day after day the problems mount. I get laughed at for trying to do this. I'm chasing the biggest, riskiest drilling prospect any fool has concocted in years. This time I'm *hoping* there's a whale down there. It looks like it's just a big empty ocean. But I'm pulling the trigger. Sometimes it feels like I'm pulling a trigger to my own head. Certainly to my career." They arrived back at her driveway, and he started for his car.

"There's somebody you should talk to," she said. "My preacher, Brother Billy."

Ethan let out a disgusted sigh. "I've had enough of preachers in this town."

"Billy is easy to talk to. Why don't you show him the rig. Ask him to bless it."

Ethan froze, mouth hanging. "I can't do that. That's... that's...I've never heard of anyone doing that. That's silly."

"I just thought it would be a good idea."

He watched her close the door. He sat in the car for a long while before heading back to the trailer.

When he got there he called her and apologized for being insensitive. He said he would welcome Brother Billy if he wanted to come out to tour the rig.

At sunrise the derrick was ready to go up. Ethan's restless legs trembled as Grady's men prepared to raise the derrick from the horizontal position. Ethan had seen this only a few times, but each time it had stirred his emotions. The raising of the derrick had become almost a ritual in the oil field. It was a visual signal for miles around that the talking was done—the race downward for the prize was at hand.

"Boy, you've done it!" J.D. said. "I can't believe you've done it. The Hull lease expires at midnight tomorrow night."

"That depends on those trucks getting here soon with the rest of the stuff."

"They will," J.D. said, lighting up with a puff.

Ethan turned to look at the crowd who stood at a distance despite the early hour. Word had gotten out. He noticed Laura standing with Edna and others.

He took off his hat and greeted the ladies.

"Well," Laura said, "it looks like you're going to get your chance."

Ethan smiled. "Yeah. I'll finally get my chance to find oil here."

"No. That's not what I meant. You still don't get it."

"Huh?"

"Look!" Harry Little shouted, pointing. They all turned. The rig's diesel engine roared, black smoke belched. The drawworks began turning. Slowly the tip of the derrick lifted and began arching toward the sky as the drawworks spooled in the big cables attached to it. Ethan had waited for this moment for six months. He wanted to savor it.

Under a growing drizzle the derrick reached vertical, and the crew pinned it. He saw Skeeter scurry up the ladder to the crown block and attach an American flag—an oil field tradition. Cheers went up from the crowd. Ethan opened Laura's umbrella and led her up the steps. She looked around, eyes beaming. Grady stepped over, took off his hardhat and bowed. "Grady Plunket, driller. At your service, Ma'am."

Ethan introduced her to the rest of the crew. She looked around and upward in astonishment. "My, oh my, what a machine! It's so big!"

"Ma'am," Grady said, "this thing is a toy compared to some I've worked on. Why, out in west Texas we had one that was so tall we had to lay it down every night to let the moon go by."

She giggled.

Behind them they heard pounding. They turned. Cuz lowered a hammer and turned, grinning. He motioned to the sign he had just attached with bailing wire to the doghouse door. It read *Lucky Lucy* in coarse hand lettering.

"We were watchin' *I Love Lucy* back at the motel," Cuz said, grinning. "Lucy's always gettin' into trouble, but she always comes through it." Harvey, Marlin, and Skeeter began clapping. Ethan looked over at Grady. He leaned against the console grinning and shaking his head.

"Well, hell, we might as well put this up there, too," Grady growled. He reached into his tool bag and got out a horseshoe. Another cheer went up as Cuz wired the horseshoe over the sign.

"How long you been carrying that?" Ethan asked the driller.

"Went out 'n' found one first thing, after I met you."

Cuz let out a heavy belly cackle.

Ethan looked around at the men's faces, grinned, and savored the moment. He had never felt so happy in his life.

The rumble of truck engines roused Ethan out of his sleep. He checked his watch: 2:10 a.m.

He got up and shook Peavy. They dressed and went out. The crew was already swarming on the trucks, their flashlights swinging beams. Ethan heard Peavy fire up the D-8 as he slogged through the mud toward the trucks. He heard many new voices and saw unfamiliar faces scurrying about in the dim light.

Grady, directing the work, turned and saw him. "Here, cap'n. Over here!"

"Meet Jerome Thibodeaux here."

Ethan looked up at a monster of a man towering over him. A big, bushy, black beard framed a hard face with thick, alligator lips parting to show a wide bank of white teeth.

"Everybody calls him *Tiny.*"

"I see why," Ethan said, shaking the massive hand.

"Tiny's the driller on your new night crew."

"Glad you're here," Ethan said. "Did you have any trouble breaking the rig down over there in Rustin?"

"Trouble?" Tiny thundered. "I ain't had nothin' *but* trouble since I got cajoled into this deal," he turned his face to Grady, "by a slick-talkin' Texas son-of-a-beech who said I couldn't do it!"

Ethan saw Grady's smile under the glow of his cigarette. "I told this big coonass galoot and his crew of screw-ups you would buy all the beer they could drink if they helped us get spudded on time."

"I don't think there's that much beer in the county," Ethan said.

Peavy's D-8 rumbled out of the darkness.

"Over there!" Grady shouted, arms stretched. "Get the mud pumps off first!"

Peavy backed away slinging mud on the three men and swung the dozer toward the second truck.

Nobody saw the figure kneeling in the brush, watching from the drill site's dark perimeter.

"Congratulations, my friend." J.D. said as they finished their morning coffee. "A hearty congratulations. I didn't think you could do it. I didn't." He sat smiling and shaking his head. Ethan looked at his watch.

"We should be ready to spud by about 9 p.m.," Ethan said, beaming. "We'll beat it by at least three hours."

Skeeter suddenly burst through the door of the cafe. "Mr. Ethan, Uncle Grady wants you out to the location right now. We got trouble!"

Other diners looked around.

Ethan said, "Shh. What trouble?"

Skeeter didn't answer. He had already turned and headed back out to his uncle's Buick. Ethan and J.D. looked at each other and hurried out.

When they got to the rig they found the crew huddled around the mud pumps. Grady looked grim. "Both pumps are down."

"What's the matter?"

He held up a gallon paint can. It contained a small amount

of a dark, caustic-smelling liquid. "Somebody put acetone in the oil. The engines are trashed."

Ethan stared speechless at the can.

"Somebody don't want us to spud," J.D. muttered. "And furthermore, they don't care that we know that."

"Huh?" Grady said.

J.D. nodded at the can. "They didn't leave that here by mistake."

"Maybe they forgot it," Grady blurted. "Maybe they're just stupid as hell."

J.D.'s eyes narrowed at the driller.

They all stood silently, thinking, eyes shifting. Then Ethan said, "When did ya'll get the pumps set up?"

"When we got them off the truck this morning—about four a.m.," Skeeter said. "I fueled them, checked the oil, started them up, and let 'em run for a while just to make sure they were okay. I turned the mud back to the pit. Then I went back up to the floor to help rig the block and Kelly."

"It must have happened right there in that hour or two before sun-up," J.D. muttered.

Ethan looked around. "Did anybody see anybody?"

The crew all shook their heads.

Ethan glanced at his watch, then at Grady. "Can we get another pump, quickly?"

Grady shook his head. "Don't look at me. I'm a Texas man. I don't know anybody in the oil business around here. Hell, there ain't no oil business around here." He took off his hat, sat down on a pump and yawned. He looked at the ground and shook his head. "I told you folks. I did. This damn rig is snake-bit."

"Yeah? Well, maybe you're snake-bit," J.D. retorted.

Grady looked up at him and slowly got up. "What are you doin' out here anyway? Maybe you ought to get off your ass and go do whatever it is you do."

J.D. put up his fists. "I'll whup your ass right here and now."

Ethan jumped between the two—a move he knew saved J.D. serious bodily injury.

"Shut up, both of you. You're acting like kids."

Grady started to leave.

"Hold it," Ethan said. "I need you. Help me figure this out. We can't just walk away."

Grady stopped and lit up.

"You got any ideas?" Ethan asked.

He let out a long plume of smoke and flashed an intimidating glance at J.D. "As I said, you can make some calls back to Mississippi, but I'd say the chances of gettin' a pump here in the next"—he paused.

"Eight and a half hours," Harvey said, holding his arm up and pointing to his watch.

Grady sniffed and wiped his mouth. "Eight hours. The chances are slim to none."

Ethan turned to J.D., also smoking, but with a shaky hand. "You're a lawyer. What do we need to do to satisfy a spud deadline?"

J.D. blew out a plume. "I'm a half-assed lawyer. You need to talk to a real one." He thumped the butt to the ground. "But I doubt even that would do you any good."

"Why?" Ethan asked.

"The state oil and gas rules in Alabama don't define what the official spud point is. I checked it. It'll be up to a judge if it gets challenged and good luck finding one in this state who will side with us. If you've got a driller who's worth a shit, he'll start that surface hole, which only needs water—not mud—which you can dump in with a regular hose pipe, and he'll make it look to anybody watchin' like he's spudding the well."

Grady frowned, then nodded.

J.D. mashed out the butt. "Get started on that surface hole before midnight, or you're sure to get an injunction slapped on you."

Ethan looked at Grady, expecting a response.

"We'll do it." He looked at the crew. "All right, let's get after it."

Ethan started away with J.D. at his side and stopped when they were a distance from the crew. "I told you I'd stick with you through your drinkin' problem, but I won't put up with you agitating the driller. Understand?"

"I'm sorry, Ethan," J.D. muttered, kicking at the dirt. "Tryin' to stay sober is takin' its toll on me. I'm jumpy. You know what I mean?"

Ethan nodded and slapped his shoulder.

"I've got to go see the sheriff about those pumps."

Hub took his feet down from his desk and walked to the coffee pot. Over his shoulder he said, "Got any ideas who it might have been?"

"Yes," Ethan said. "Somebody related to Mr. Hull."

Hub turned and stared at Ethan. "That would be Benny."

Ethan shrugged. "I've got no proof, but who else would want us to lose the drilling option? You see, if we don't spud before midnight, that lease will become null and—"

"I know that," Hub interjected. "You explained it two or three times to me already."

"Well," Ethan continued, "Mr. Hull could kick us off his land or renegotiate a very stiff deal with us. He'd be in a powerful position."

Hub drank his coffee and sat down. He got out a form and slid it to Ethan. "Fill out this report, but with no eye witness there's not much we can do. Obviously there are folks who don't want you here. I'll start night patrols out there."

12

Brother Billy

Ethan glanced at his watch. 11:47 p.m. Grady eased up on the brake handle and lowered the big spud bit to the ground, then stepped on the throttle peddle. At once the rotary table began turning clockwise. Cuz let out a rebel yell. Ethan raised a fist. J.D. clapped.

Ethan turned to Sheriff Tant, grinning. "Thirteen minutes to spare!"

"Noted," Hub said. He nodded and smiled.

Suddenly Ethan felt the sturdy pressure of something like a mop against the small of his back. He tried to turn, but big hands grabbed him at the shoulders. Loud whoops went up behind him. The swab worked its way up his backside to his neck, and he smelled the soapy odor of pipe dope. He broke away and put his hand on the back of his neck, pulled it away and saw the puke yellow slimy dope that the crews used on pipe threads before they mated them together. Harvey stood back holding the dripping swab, laughing like a hyena. Ethan grinned at them all.

The sheriff laughed.

"Thanks for coming out," Ethan told the lawman as he wiped the back of his neck. "I just wanted a neutral witness."

"Mind if I stick around a while?" Hub said. "Just want to watch. But I better not get that stuff put on me."

Grady, satisfied that the revolutions-per-minute and weight-on-bit were correctly set, lit a cigarette and stepped near Ethan. They watched the Kelly bar spin. "What are we gonna do for a tool pusher?"

Ethan dreaded that question. "I'm working on that."

He descended the ladder wondering how he would honor that promise. A pusher was needed to over-see the operation on a twenty-four hour basis.

As he walked over to the trailer, he glanced toward the main road and saw several cars parked. Here and there people huddled near the cars. He was certain someone was watching with more than just a casual interest. He paused at the trailer door and scanned them, knowing the one who trashed their pumps could be there.

He yawned and eyed the bunk beds in the back of the trailer, but he knew his mud pump crises had to be solved before he slept.

Emmett Brubeck's cigar glowed in the dark as he puffed. He took it out and turned to Benny. "Gimmee them binoculars."

Benny lowered them and handed the set to Emmett. He put his cigar back into his mouth and raised the binocs over it. In the dark he could make out bright lights and men walking back and forth against them. He saw the pipe rotating. He lowered the binocs and took out his pocket watch. "Damn," he muttered. They've done it. He looked around to insure no one was within earshot and turned back to Benny. "Whatever you did, it didn't work."

"What do you mean, *whatever I did*?" Benny asked, puzzled.

Emmett glared at him. "I thought we had an understanding," he uttered, straining to keep his voice low. "You were going to arrange for something to break down out there so that they would get delayed."

Benny jammed his hands into his pockets and kicked at the dirt. "Emmett, I couldn't think of anything. And anyway—you know—you could go to jail for that." He looked at Emmett and shrugged. "I didn't want to take the chance. I was just hoping they wouldn't make the deadline."

Emmett moaned. "Well, hell. If you don't want to do it yourself, man, you get somebody else to that that kind of work. Tells me how reliable you are." He resumed looking through the binoculars.

"Well, what do we do now?"

"Now that they've beat us to the draw, we want them to succeed." He turned to Benny. "We want oil! Understand? Let them find it for us."

He took out the cigar and wet his lips with his tongue. "Now we file papers. In the meantime your job will be to find out as much information you can about what they're doing out there. If they find one speck of oil, I want to know it right away. Understand?"

"Yeah, but how? You want me to sit in a tree and spy on 'em?"

Emmett sucked in his jaws and sneered, then formed his words carefully. "No, Benny. Use your head. Maybe they need extra help. Send somebody—hopefully somebody smarter that you—down there to ask for a laborer job, or whatever. Get it?"

Benny perked. "I know just the man!"

Ethan checked his phone number list and called oil field suppliers in Mississippi, finally finding one that answered at 2 a.m. but they didn't have a pump available. They gave him the number of another company that might have one, but there was no answer there.

He tried to nap, but the worrying about the pumps kept him awake. At seven he heard the crews talking outside as they switched tours. He went out and asked how much hole they had made.

Grady grunted. "Sixteen feet. We just got through the topsoil and then some. You know we can't drill ahead without a pump.

The other crew is headed up there now, and they'll just pretend to be drilling. You best get them pumps fixed, or get another."

"Do we really need them both?" Ethan asked.

Grady shook his head. "No, we only need one. The other one is a backup. You got to have a backup pump when you get down deep. If one quits you may not have enough time to fix it or replace it before the mud properties go to hell in a hand basket, and you lose your well. But we can get started with just one if that's all you can come up with."

Ethan went back in and tried a number again. Success! He was promised a truck to bring him one pump to be delivered around noon. But as usual the price staggered him. He arranged to send the wrecked pumps back on the truck for repairs and resolved to make do with one for now. He closed his ledger, grabbed a couple hours of shut-eye, and headed into town for breakfast.

He breakfasted alone, wondering where J.D. was. They usually ate together in the mornings and went over the leasehold situation. Ethan finished and went to the motel. After several knocks with no answer he cracked the door open and peered in. The smell stiffened him. He went to J.D.'s bedside. Empty beer cans lie on their sides on the bedside table and were strewn about on the floor.

J.D. lie in a contorted position making sucking, grunting sounds. Ethan shook him, then shook him harder. J.D. moaned, cursed and rolled away. Ethan paused in the doorway and looked back. A feeling of aloneness overcame him as he returned to the trailer and began the now familiar morning ritual, crunching numbers and fighting off despair when again realizing the money would not stretch.

The door burst open—Skeeter. "The pump's here, Mr. Bonner."

He walked out and watched the crew unload and set the pump. The driver wanted a check. As he came out of the trailer with the check in hand he heard Grady yell, "Skeeter, get your ass out there and start mixin' mud." Skeeter scampered toward the mud hopper and grabbed a sack of gel, tore it open, and poured it into the hopper.

Ethan paid the truck driver, and soon the pump was humming. A yell erupted from the floor. Ethan looked up and saw Cuz looking down at him. "We're turnin' to the right with mud, bossman."

Ethan grinned. "Turning to the right" was the universal oil field phrase that meant all is well. They were making hole.

He stood back, arms folded, and watched the Kelly bushing rotate. He saw the little rag tied to it go round and round. Drillers often mistrusted their tachometers and calculated rpm by counting rag revolutions.

He noticed an object in Grady's belt. He looked closer. A revolver. Grady saw him looking at it. He yelled from his console, "That's in case the bastards come back." The excitement of finally drilling ahead had made him forget about the sabotaged mud pumps. He needed to get back to work.

Ethan went back to the trailer and resumed his calculations. His account just took a $2,225 hit with the pump. He could pay these men three weeks on what he had left. That would leave just enough to pay the fuel and mud bills. If he found oil he should be able to secure quick bank loans to finish the job and start other wells. He rubbed his scalp and pondered.

He figured it would take five weeks to reach 11,000 feet. That would be more than 300 feet per day. That sounded doable. But that didn't include frequent trips out of the hole to change bits. Those usually took six to eight hours, maybe more. If he factored that in, he figured he needed to make 350 to 400 feet per day. *That's pushing it*, he thought. And that didn't take into account any more mechanical problems that might come up—or more attacks against his equipment. Then he remembered his promise to find some small diameter drill pipe. His previous efforts at that had all come up dry. And how would he pay for it when he found it? He would need all the luck he could get.

He slammed his pencil down. *Impossible!* He stared out the window at the rig and shook his head. Had he actually thought about luck as if it were a part of his planning?

He remembered what Abrams had said back when he was considering going independent. He had visited with Noble and asked him for his counsel. "Don't figure on gettin' lucky," Noble had said. "Idle people mistake luck for hard work and a willingness to take risk. In the end, when the work pays off, the idle people look at it and call it luck."

Luck or not, based on what he had spent of Noble's and Scat-back's money, and projecting expenses to come, Ethan realized anew he didn't have enough. He circled a number. *$73,250.* Beside it he wrote: *Need this to make it!*

Soon he would have to decide between payroll and services. If he continued to pay the crews he wouldn't have the money to evaluate the hole once it reached target depth. Schlumberger charged dearly for their wireline logging services. And there were the on-going costs: mud supplies, diesel fuel, fresh bits, and the additional leases J.D. was signing almost daily.

Several banks had already turned him down for loans against the rig. They were ready to give him one, but when they asked him if he owned it free and clear, he had to tell them about Noble Abrams's lien against it. That was a deal breaker. But he had to tell them, even if his deal with Noble was only on a handshake. That's the way Noble did business. Not to tell them might get the loan, but it would invite trouble and dishonor Noble. He ran his hand through his hair, and put the pencil down when he heard the footsteps and a knock.

A slender man of about thirty asked to see the boss. Ethan invited him in. He asked for a job.

He looked to have weak eyesight—the spectacles were thick, but he saw clear eyes behind them. The guy looked around and chuckled. "Looks like a mad scientist lab here." His grin spanned wide into deep crescent creases, covered with a week's stubble. But he looked stout enough. He said his name was Buford Kidd. He didn't know anything about oil rigs, but he was willing to learn

The trailer door opened, and Skeeter came in. "Here's the

latest sample bags, Mr. Bonner." He heaved the batch of little white bags onto the floor, paused, and nodded at Kidd.

"Hey, Skeeter," Ethan said. "Escort the gentleman up to the floor, and let him talk to Mr. Plunket about hiring on."

Skeeter nodded and left with Kidd. He watched Kidd head for the drill floor and went back to his work. Good. That would round out his night tour.

Minutes later Grady came through the door with Kidd in tow. "Mr. Bonner would you put this man on the payroll? I think we can use him."

"Okay. I guess you're on the payroll," Ethan told Kidd.

"I don't need to sign anything?" Kidd asked.

"No. We do things simple around here. I'll give you a dollar an hour, payable every Friday. Come back at 6 p.m. tonight ready to work to sun-up."

He slipped away whenever he could to the refuge of Laura's porch where he spent as much time as he dared sitting at her side, sipping iced tea and sifting through her fossil collection, telling her as much as he knew about paleontology—which wasn't much. He told her oil field stories, and she laughed. He told her more about his dad saving Noble at the cost of his own life. She teared-up and grew quiet.

She finally got up and leaned against the porch rail. "Ethan, I don't have a colorful life, like you do. I'm as dull as a dish rag. But you—you've brought so much hope and excitement to this town. I'm so glad."

He stood and shook his head vigorously. "You are certainly not dull. You're interested in things. You are always seeking knowledge, asking questions. And listening. I value that. I've never met anyone like you." He moved closer to her. "You can never know how important it is to me to come here and share those things with you. You're my escape from that rat-race."

Her smile faded.

"Did I say something?"

She looked away from him. "I'm an escape for you? Is that it? If you need an escape, you could go to a movie. The library. Fly a kite. No, you come to Laura. She's a good *escape* for you! Lucky me. I'm an escape place for poor over-worked Ethan. And all this time I thought I was a mere friend."

He stood dumbfounded. "I used a bad choice of words. I'm a klutz. I'm sorry."

Her eyes shot to him and then back into the night. "It's okay. I quite get it, Ethan. I'm glad you like to be with me. But when that hole is done, you'll be makin' tracks for somewhere else, and I'll be sitting here on this porch wondering what hit me and where it went."

He didn't know how to reply to that because he suspected it was true. He would be gone in a flash if the hole was dry. And even if he hit a bonanza of oil, he would stay only a little while longer. He jammed his hands into his pockets and looked out toward a street light.

Still leaning against the rail facing the other way, she asked so low he almost didn't hear her, "Ethan, what is it you want out of life?"

He pondered it a long time before offering an answer that seemed hollow. "Happiness, I guess. Just like anybody else."

"And where do you expect to find that?" she muttered.

He shrugged and looked at her. He risked a small smile. "I prospect for happiness, and when I see a possibility of it I drill."

"So, am I a prospect, Ethan?"

He had painted himself into a corner, and he knew it was critical he not blow it with another foolish selection of words. He smiled. "You are the finest prospect I have ever seen." He took her hands. "In fact, you are more than a prospect. You are proven reserves!"

His ejection from her porch had been a swift one, almost as if she had kicked him in the ass as he beat a hasty retreat, and for all practical purposes she had done exactly that. His efforts at damage control took days. Finally she began to talk to him again. Each time he called her to apologize, she warmed to him a little more. Her insatiable curiosity for the progress of his well was his ticket. Yet his worries over the well mounted.

Daily he looked at the samples under his microscope, recording the characteristics of the grinded-up grains on his sample log. The samples looked chalky: *The Selma Chalk*, he thought. He looked at the depth on the bag: 4,020 feet. He subtracted the elevation of the drill site to get depth below sea level: 3,750 feet. He pulled the log from the Gulf No. 1 Buchanan and found where he had identified the top of the Selma: 3,780 feet. He grinned. Now he had his first indication of how his well was *running* against Gulf's dry hole. So far he was 30 feet high. There might be hope yet that he would find the shallow oil Gulf missed when he reached the Eutaw and the Lower Tuscaloosa after that.

He sat back chewing his pencil eraser and stared out the window at Lucky Lucy. Two weeks now into the drilling he had begun to notice Grady was tiring. Daily now, he was asking Ethan, "When are you going to get a pusher out here? I can't keep this up."

Ethan would like to have hired another driller and promoted Grady to pusher full time. But the oil fields were booming across Texas, Louisiana, and Mississippi, and he couldn't pay a candidate even if he could find one. He had to offer Grady an incentive.

When he saw the driller coming toward the trailer he made a decision he had been pondering for days. Grady came in, grabbed a banana and coffee and started back out.

"Wait," Ethan said. "Sit for a while."

"Ain't got time to sit around. We're drillin' ahead up there."

"Couple of minutes."

Grady sat.

Ethan leaned forward, elbows on his knees, looking at the floor. "I've got barely enough funds left to cover the services we need—mud, fuel, logging, you know." Ethan knew this was probably not the first time Grady worked for an outfit that went broke in the middle of operations. "Grady, if you'll hang with me, be my tool pusher, work the console when you have to, and convince the crews to stay, I'll assign you half ownership in the rig."

Grady stared, eyes focused beyond him, mouth open. Ethan waited for his offer to sink in, knowing the wheels were turning in the driller's head. Grady took in a deep breath and spewed it out. "Whew!" He scratched his head and walked to the window turning his back. "I damn sure didn't see that comin'." He turned, facing Ethan. "You sure 'bout that?"

"Yes."

Grady turned back again to stare out at the rig. "Gettin' the others to stay without full pay is gonna be tough." He turned back to Ethan. "I think my tour will stay a while longer. They don't have families to support. But that night tour—they just might walk."

"I'll take care of their motel and meals," Ethan said. "And I'll make sure everybody gets their pay before it's over."

Grady nodded. "I'll see what I can do."

He looked back at the rig and rubbed his nose. "I've always wanted to get into the drillin' business. Never figured it would happen though." He turned back to Ethan. "I'll take your offer, but I feel like this is a one-hole deal. If we miss oil here that rig will go back to the bank quicker 'n I can spit. Ain't that right?"

Ethan nodded. "That's right, unless we can get it contracted out to somebody else real quick."

Grady looked back out the window at Lucky Lucy and stared a long time. Ethan let him think. He turned.

"Did you know I've got a glass eye?"

"Huh? Well, I always thought it was weird the way you looked at me sometimes, but I figured you were just tryin' to intimidate me."

"Ha! Ha!" Grady cackled. "That's exactly what I was doing."

He eyed Ethan and pointed over his shoulder. "I lost my eye right up there on that drill floor. Right there! I was holding a chain while another man swung a sledge hammer driving a pin into the chain stop. A shard flew off the pin and hit me in the left eye. The doc couldn't save it. It happened on that damn rig out there."

"Why didn't you tell me this?" Ethan asked.

"I did. Remember? That first day, back at the tavern where you met us. I told you a man lost his eye on it. Didn't say who."

Ethan nodded and smiled, remembering that weird conversation.

"Okay, partner. I don't know how I'm gonna live without sleep, but I'll give it a shot." Grady dipped his head and swept out the door.

As night fell Ethan heard a knock at the trailer door. "I'm William Colby, Miss Laura's pastor."

Ethan greeted him and asked him in. He was surprised. Colby wasn't what he had envisioned—no black neck band; no Bible in hand. He was an agreeable looking guy, wearing an open-collar plaid shirt and jeans, about forty. He instantly disarmed Ethan with smiling eyes.

The preacher looked around and asked to look in the microscope. Ethan let him examine some cuttings and explained how the crew collected a bag of cuttings every ten feet, washed them and brought them to the trailer for him to examine. Billy seemed fascinated with the concept of finding oil in the tiny voids between the sand grains.

"Mr. Bonner," Billy said. "I've been hearing about your problem."

"What?" Ethan asked.

"Your differences with Red Pope—and others."

Ethan raised his eyebrows. "Oh. Yeah. I've been too busy to think much about that, but I'm troubled with it."

"Are you really an evolutionist? I've never met one before."

"In a way, I am, Pastor."

"I'm Billy."

Ethan sat down, gesturing Billy to sit. He reverted to his old stance, elbows on his knees, looking at the floor between his legs. His feet began their rock. "I appreciate you coming out here. I know Laura asked you to come. So, I guess this is a good opportunity to explain what that other guy didn't want to hear. Since you brought it up I want to make it clear that I did not come here to this town to start a religious debate with anybody. I regret that I said something to the school kids that would have been best left unsaid. I've got too much work to do, and I'm not good at that sort of thing anyway. So, just let me say what I might have said to Pope, if he had let me." He looked up from his stare at the floor. "Why did Jesus use parables?"

"To illustrate a point that might not otherwise be understood."

Ethan nodded. "When Jesus commanded us to pluck out our eye if it offends us, did he mean it literally?"

Billy smiled. "I see where you're going."

"Why, then, do we want to say one part of the Bible is symbolic and another part is literal? Who's to judge?"

Billy waited for more.

"If God was inspiring some ancient writer to record creation, would He use the language of modern science, or would He write in ways ancient people could understand?"

"That's a point I've often considered," Billy said.

"Do you preach that?"

Billy shook his head vigorously. "I don't preach my opinion. I preach the Word."

"And, let me ask you another question," Ethan said. He looked at Billy's smile and saw an invitation to go on. "Did God have the power to zap the universe into place, just like that?" He snapped his fingers in front of Billy's face.

"Of course. He is omnipotent. He's all powerful. Yes, He could have."

"But, according to the Genesis account, He took six days."

"Yes," Billy said. "And some people think that a Genesis day may not be twenty-four hours."

Ethan nodded. "Symbolic, then?"

Billy shrugged. "I'm not a Hebrew language scholar."

"Consider this. The first day in the creation story God makes light. The second day he makes water. The third day he creates the land, then plant life. Then comes the stars, which was a little out of sequence, it seems to me. And on the fifth day He makes birds and fish, and on the sixth, animals and man." He thought for a moment. "It was a progression. It started simple, and got complex. The work of one day built on the results of the previous one. See? The science of how our world came into being is like that. You could say science tells the same story in more technical language."

He got up, paced and turned. "Brother Billy, I don't see any conflict. Genesis is a symbolic account of what science tells us."

"There are a lot of people who think evolution isn't science; that it's just a theory because it is not proven."

"But it's what I choose to believe. I've seen it in the rocks. I'm not an atheist. I think God used natural processes to create the universe, and us."

Billy got up and walked to the sample table. He touched a small pile of drill cuttings and stirred his finger in them. He grinned and shook his head. "Hard to believe. Oil can hide in these tiny little grains."

He looked back at Ethan. "There's a major problem with what you believe."

Ethan watched him.

"And it's what's so disturbing to Pope and the others. And me. I'm troubled by it also."

"What?"

"If we evolved from apes, what keeps us from behaving like apes?"

Ethan looked at Billy's finger swirling the cuttings, not knowing how to respond.

Billy smiled and nodded. "Did you say this is not what you intended to talk about?"

Ethan nodded. "Brother Billy—" He paused. He had rehearsed what he would say to the preacher, but it seemed trite now. He just sat down and shrugged.

"Something else troubling you?"

"Oh, yeah," Ethan said without delay. "I'm over my head in debt. My crews are fighting with each other and threatening to walk off because I'm late paying them. I've got expenses up to my neck, and this old rig's always breaking down, needing repair and parts."

Ethan got up and looked out the window at the rig, watching as the night crew switched on the flood lights turning the derrick into a brilliant tower seen for miles around. "I've got to hit oil here, or I'm finished. I need success."

Billy stood beside him. "So, let me guess. You want me to pray for oil?"

Ethan looked aside at him and nodded. "Oil and—and a money tree, or something, to pay my bills until I find the oil."

"Why don't you do it?"

"I'm not much at praying. I think the Lord will understand if I want you to do it for me. Don't you think?"

Billy pursed his lips and shook his head. His eyes scanned the room. "You got a horseshoe nailed up around here somewhere?"

Ethan's eyebrows arched.

"How about a rabbit's foot?" He paused again. "Do you want my prayer to get added to your collection of good luck charms?"

"Huh?" Ethan felt flushed. The preacher had read him like a book. He was always looking for a stroke of good luck, the law of averages, serendipity—anything to supplement his geology. And now he had asked this preacher to invite the God he served into his own bucket of lucky charms. He couldn't remember ever feeling so unworthy of another man's caring. He looked at the floor.

Billy stood staring at him, and when Ethan finally looked up at him he saw no condemnation in the preacher's face.

"Let's go out there and have a look at your rig."

Ethan gave the pastor a tour of the rig floor, introducing him to the crew. He saw Billy look askance at him when he saw the horseshoe over the doghouse door—saw the grin, too. He showed Billy the draw works and the driller's console. Then they went down and looked around the pumps, engine, and pipe racks. Finally they moved into the shadows near the reserve pit, listening to the distant conversation on the rig floor and an occasional shout or cackle over the diesel's throb. Standing in a shaft of moonlight breaking through the steel framework, they looked up and saw the derrick man preparing to receive the top end of a pipe joint.

Billy stood, saying nothing, taking in the sight. Ethan wondered if he was praying silently.

He swallowed hard and looked at Billy. "Well, sir."

Billy glanced at him, then got down on one knee. Ethan did likewise. Billy put his hand on Ethan's shoulder and prayed, but Ethan noticed he didn't pray for oil or success. Only for discovery.

They walked back to the trailer and went in. Inside, he heard a familiar gruff voice. "Hello, Partner!"

Grady sat with his feet propped on the waste basket. He got up when Ethan introduced him to the pastor.

"I've been talkin' with the boys," Grady said. "My crew and also them misfits up there on the night tour."

Ethan leaned against the wall, arms folded. "And?"

Grady glanced at Billy.

"It's okay," Ethan said. "He's a friend."

"And, my crew agreed to stay on if you'll buy the meals, beds, and beer, just like you said. Of course they want to be paid soon as you—ah, *we*—can come up with the money. Two men in the night tour dragged up and left the minute I told them what we wanted. Skeeter and Harvey are up there now taking their place. I've got to find replacements tomorrow. I think I'll take your suggestion of using local men. I've had a few more asking about work."

Ethan looked at Billy. Billy grinned. Ethan felt a lump in crawl up his throat.

13

KIDD

With a painful grunt, Buford Kidd pulled another sack of gel off the pallet and heaved it to his shoulder. Sweat dripped from his brow as he turned and carried it toward the hopper. Every bone in his body ached. He had never worked so hard in his life. To make things worse, since starting on the night tour three days ago he had been constantly yelled at and badgered by Tiny and the night crew.

"Get me that," he muttered as he trudged under the weight of the sack, mocking Tiny. "Bring me this." *Big oafish bastard.*

Whenever they ran out of stuff for him to do, they put him to washing, cleaning, and chipping paint. Never a minute to rest. For all he cared, these oilmen could pack up and go back to Texas or wherever the hell they came from. He kneeled and let the sack crash to the ground. It burst open.

"Hey, kidd!" came the reprimand from the derrick man, who was responsible for mixing the mud when he wasn't aloft handling pipe joints. "Don't spill that stuff, dammit!"

Kidd nodded, mumbled an insult under his breath, and started back for another sack. He reached the pallet and paused, looking toward Bonner's trailer. He saw the geologist come out and get in his car. He snickered. *Must be goin' to see the teacher, Miss Laura.* Not that he blamed him. Buford had a crush on Laura since the ninth grade, but Benny always seemed to be in the way of him cottoning up to her. He chuckled. And now Bonner was elbowing in on Benny.

He looked at the stack of gel sacks and sighed. A dollar an hour wouldn't be near worth it if Benny hadn't also paid him two dollars a day on the side. That reminded him of why he was really here. He was really working for Benny. And it was about time to deliver some goods.

Then he saw Mr. Plunket come out and go to his Buick. *Wonder where he's going? A late supper, maybe.* Buford watched him drive away, wondering if he had bothered to lock the trailer. He looked up at the rig and squinted at the brilliant flood lights. The floor crew was busy. He looked around then headed for the trailer, keeping in the shadows. Reaching the door, he knocked—just in case. It was quiet inside. He looked around and behind him again, then quickly opened the door and slipped in.

He closed the blinds and took out his flashlight. He looked around, touching and fiddling with this and that piece of paper. He wished he knew what the hell he was supposed to be looking for. He saw the microscope and the logs. He examined the logs and Ethan's notes. He shook his head. *A bunch of gobbledygook!* He would like to simply take some of the stuff; he really didn't care what. He didn't understand any of it; he just needed to deliver Benny some information. *Let him and whoever he's in cahoots with sort it out.* But he knew it might be missed if he stole it. Still, he had to take something to Benny to earn his keep.

He saw the large pile of sample bags. Yeah! If Bonner misses one or two of those, he'll figure they just got lost. He stuffed them into his pocket. He was about to leave when he noticed writing on a legal pad. The dollar signs by the numbers got his attention. He sat down and read.

Now this, here, makes some sense. Bonner was figuring his finances. Wow! Look what he wrote here, and where he circled that number! "$73,250—NEED THIS TO MAKE IT!" *So, Mr. Bonner is running short of money. Benny surely would like to know that.*

He smiled. He looked back out the window. He needed to

get back out there before they missed him. He slowly opened the door. He put his head out first. Not a foot from his face, a pair of eyes peered back at him.

Buford gasped and recoiled. His heart jumped and the breath left him. The wild eyes in front of him instantly grew as big as half dollars, then fell away. The other man stumbled backward. Something fell to the ground with a metallic thump. Buford heard fluid bubbling out and smelled gasoline.

"Who are you?" Buford yelled. "What are you doin' here? Hey! Don't I know you?"

The man scrambled backward, crab-like, on his hands and feet, then turned, got to his feet and scurried into the night.

His heart pounding, Buford turned on his flashlight and saw the gasoline can lying on its side. He looked up again and shined his light in the direction the man ran. He looked around, breathing heavily, shaking. It wasn't only the encounter that had him frightened. Someone had spotted him from the rig floor. They were yelling at him. Now he had to explain what he was doing here.

"Over here!" He yelled, waving his arms. "Hurry! Come here!"

Tiny's massive form trotted up.

"I saw somebody messing around the trailer, so I came over to have a look. A guy was trying to burn it. Look at this stuff!"

Tiny looked at the can and then spotted a box of matches lying near it. Buford tried not to shake. He knew he had to divert attention from himself. "I saw him. I can describe him. Let's get the sheriff!"

The rotating light atop Hub's cruiser bathed the group of men in red every few seconds as they stood in front of the trailer. Hub carefully picked up the can and the match box to protect the fingerprints. "You say you saw him?" Hub asked Buford.

Buford nodded. "I know the guy. Seen him around. Don't know his name."

"Describe him."

"He had crooked teeth—one or two missing—and a short beard on his chin. Had a big lock of hair hanging down over his right eye."

Ethan's eyes shot up to Buford. "What color was the hair?"

Buford shrugged. "Light colored, I think. Blond, maybe. It was pretty dark."

"You know who he's talkin' about, Mr. Bonner," Hub asked.

Ethan shook his head. "No. Just sounds familiar. Can't recall where I saw him though."

The lawmen departed to start a man-hunt. Ethan went into the trailer. He sat and rubbed his hands through his hair and looked around. Losing the trailer in a fire with all his notes, logs, and equipment would jeopardize the whole project. He would have to rig flood lights around it and keep it locked.

He sat and wondered why this had happened. He had met his spud deadline obligation. Why would anyone now try to stop him now?

The next day, Sunday, Ethan went to Brother Billy's service, as he had promised the preacher he would do. He hadn't been in a church in quite a while and felt out of place, but having Laura sitting beside him felt very right.

After the hymns, Billy launched his sermon from the book of Ecclesiastes. "Follow with me, brothers and sisters, beginning with chapter one, verse nine: *'The thing that hath been, it is that which shall be; and that which is done is that which shall be done: and there is no new thing under the sun. Is there anything whereof it may be said, See, this is new? It hath been already of old time, which was before us.'*"

He put the Bible down and took off his glasses. "This question has been asked since the beginning of time. Think about this, my friends. Generations of people come and go. The sun rises and sets day after day. Rivers flow, oceans churn and swirl.

Mountains slowly rise up and wind, water, ice and rain tears them down again, and their remnants wash down into the valleys and build up new land—" He paused and looked in Ethan's direction, smiling and lowering his voice—"as a friend of mine explained to me the other day."

Ethan returned the smile.

"But, friends," Billy continued, his voice echoing off the church walls, "one thing never changes, and it's the question we have asked ourselves since King Solomon's time. Like the slowly changing Earth, we toil and build and work our hearts out, and at the end of the road, when we look back over our lives, we ask, What was this all about? I know what I have accomplished, but what have I discovered—about myself, about the world I live in, and about the God I serve? Has my life been just surviving? Just being entertained? Just getting more stuff? Always looking inward to the self and never outward to people in need? When will we ever understand that all the things that charm us, all the work that challenges us, and all the accomplishments that honor us are only empty vanities lying at the foot of the Cross?"

Footsteps coming up the aisle broke Ethan's intense focus on Billy. Heads turned.

Skeeter took off his hard hat, kneeled and whispered loudly across the laps of several people between Ethan and the aisle. "Uncle Grady said we just got into a heck of a drilling break. Says you need to get out there."

Ethan looked at Laura, then at Brother Billy, who had continued to speak but with a broken and disturbed rhythm. Skeeter's disturbance rippled across the sanctuary.

Ethan whispered to Laura. "Got to go." He got up and shuffled toward the aisle, stepping on people's feet, excusing himself. Brother Billy paused and watched him.

He looked back at Laura, J.D., and Clarice, lifting his eyebrows in embarrassment, realizing he was causing a ruckus. People were mumbling and murmuring. He dipped his head toward the pulpit and apologized in a loud whisper. All heads turned, following him. Several people in the back got up and followed him out. Then others got up. The murmuring got louder. The pews began to empty. Brother Billy stood clutching his pulpit, his mouth hanging open with astonishment.

"Get back on out there," he told Skeeter as he got into his Plymouth. "Take samples every five feet."

Several men crowded alongside his window and wanted to know what was going on. "Did you hit oil out there?" one asked.

Ethan shook his head. "I don't know yet. We just hit a big drilling break, that's all. I've got to go!" As he backed out he yelled, "Ya'll go on back inside. Brother Billy's got a good message today." Some drifted back inside, and a few got in their cars and followed him.

Before going up to the floor he went into the trailer and pulled out the Gulf well log. He saw they had penetrated the Lower Tuscaloosa Massive sand at 6,601 feet subsea in that well. He jotted the number down and grabbed his hard hat.

"The crew was bantering so loudly he could hear them from the bottom of the stairs. "Look at her go!" Cuz yelled.

Grady stood at the console adjusting the weight-on-bit, cigarette in his teeth, grinning. He stepped back and looked at Ethan. "Feels like we poked into Hell's whorehouse," he yelled above the din of machinery screeching and rumbling.

Ethan grinned. By carefully watching the rotating Kelly bar where it went into the spinning bushing he could actually see the bar sinking deeper—a rare sight.

"Penetration rate is about a foot a minute!" Grady yelled to Ethan.

"That would be the Massive. Where'd you get it?"

Grady looked at his log. Ethan could hardly hear him mumbling over the racket. "Let's see. About 6,796."

Ethan made a quick mental calculation, subtracting Kelly bushing elevation. He smiled and yelled, "Sixteen feet high to Gulf!"

"Mr. Brubeck, Mr. Hull and Mr. Kidd are here."

Brubeck looked up from his *Mobile Press Register* and punched the button. "Send them in."

"Buford came up with some interestin' information," Benny said, grinning. "Listen to this." Buford was looking around in admiration of Brubeck's office trappings.

"Well?" Brubeck said.

"I found this note that said, *$73,250*. And right beside it read, *'Need this to make it.'*" He handed the piece of paper to Emmett.

Benny grinned. "He's broke, Emmett. He's runnin' out of money."

Emmett got up and paced to the window and back. The other men knew better than interrupt his thoughts. He turned. "Kidd, did you take that piece of paper."

"No sir! I was afraid he would miss it. I just copied it."

Emmett nodded approval.

"Good work. Keep your eyes peeled."

Buford yawned and stretched. "This all night work is killin' me. I might have to quit."

Emmett and Benny studied him. Emmett took a key out of his pocket and unlocked a drawer. He pulled out two twenty dollar bills and slid them across the desk. Kidd looked at them, but didn't take them. His eyes went back toward the drawer. "Don't push it, Buford," Emmett warned.

"You might want to put out some more when you hear what else, Emmett." Benny said, grinning. "Listen to this!" He gestured toward Buford.

"I caught an arsonist out there last night," said Buford.

Emmett froze.

"What?"

"Yeah! He was trying to get in the trailer as I was coming out. He ran away and left a can of gas and matches."

"What did you do?"

"Right about then the crew saw me at the trailer. I told them

I saw him snooping around and went over to investigate. Now they think I'm a hero."

Emmett opened the cash drawer again, got out a couple more twenties, and handed them to Buford. He stood pensively for a few seconds, then said, "Kidd, get out." The command was terse enough that Buford wasted no time clearing the room.

"I don't know what's going on out there," he said to Benny. "But somebody wants to stop Bonner." He paused to gather more thoughts. He whirled and looked at Benny. "Who?"

Benny shrugged. They both retreated into their own thoughts for a long while.

"Well," Emmett said, "this news about him getting low on money is good. That'll make him weaker if we're forced to make a deal with him. But it could work against us, too."

Benny looked puzzled.

"He might go broke too soon and have to shut down. Then we've got nothing."

J.D. walked into the trailer and mashed a butt out in the ash tray. "I heard we're in the Massive?"

"Yup," said Ethan, looking up from the scope. He let out a deep breath. "But we got no shows."

"Well, hell," said the landman. "You didn't expect shows there did you?"

Ethan shook his head. "No. But since we're running high to Gulf's dry hole, I'd hoped there might be a chance we'd get something in the Massive or in the thin sand lenses above it."

J.D. nodded and sat. "I'm ready to get some more leases when you give me some more money."

Ethan's chin fell. "I know. I know we're risking losing leases if we're successful. But like we've discussed before, success will bring money, and we just have to be ready to move fast."

J.D. looked at the floor and shook his head. "Bass ackwards! This is all bass ackwards, the way you're doin' it."

"I know, J.D. I know. It's tearing me up inside. Just make good notes and be ready to spring. See if you can get people at least to come back to us if they get another offer." J.D. nodded and left.

The following week, drilling was erratic as they got through the Massive and entered new and unknown depths. He was now below Gulf's hole. He had to try and correlate his sample log with wells back in Mississippi. He guessed he had penetrated the alternating sands and shales of the Washita-Fredericksburg formation—all with no shows. The unpredictable sands were hard to correlate causing Ethan to suffer through days of not knowing what geological neighborhood his bit was passing through. Then came the day he was dreading.

He saw Grady approaching the trailer. The door opened. He came in, sat and lit up. "What's our next target?"

Ethan opened his eyes widely, as if recovering from a slumber. "Paluxy. The Paluxy sands are next. At about 9,500."

Grady nodded and sat quietly for a minute. "I guess you know we went through 9,000 feet this mornin'."

"I know. It's the design max depth, according to Ideco," he said, remembering the scary fracas he had with the crew back in Louisiana over the rig's depth limit.

"From here on out, we don't know what to expect from the rig. Some of the boys are gettin' nervous." He took a deep draw, exhaled long and heavy, then mashed it out. "You got some three and a half inch drill pipe comin'?"

"Still working on it, Grady."

Grady got up and paused at the door. "Like I said, the boys are gettin' nervous, and I don't blame 'em. We're countin' on you to come through with that pipe. I'm your pusher, but I'm also your day driller. I can't do it all."

Ethan nodded. "I know."

Ethan came in to the Wagon Wheel and sat across from J.D.

He yawned and smiled at the waitress as she poured his coffee. "Your usual breakfast, Mr. Bonner?" she asked.

He nodded. "The usual, Abbey."

J.D. was engrossed in the *Press Register*. He put it down and reached for his coffee. "Anything good happening?"

Ethan shook his head, reaching for the cream. "No shows in the Paluxy." He stirred, sniffed, and sipped. "Our opportunities are running out, J.D." They sat in silence for a while. "And there's something else. I can't find any three and one-half inch drill pipe at any of the supply yards. Grady says the crew is nervous about going below 9,000 without it."

"Why don't you call some of the other drilling contractors over in Mississippi?" J.D. asked. "See if they've got some they'll sell or rent to you."

Ethan shrugged. "Well, I suppose that's an idea. I'll—"

"Mr. Bonner," a deep voice called from the door. It was Sheriff Tant. "Can you come out here?" Ethan got up and went to the door. Tant told him to accompany him to the jail. "We've got a man that fits the description Buford Kidd gave us. I remember you also said you recalled his features. I want you to take a look."

They went to the jail, stopped in front of the cell and saw the man sitting on his bed. Ethan recognized him right off. He was stunned at how the man had changed since seeing his menacing face those months ago when they met at the cafe. Now he was a pitiful sight, weeping and praying.

"Now I remember," Ethan said. "He was with Red Pope that day at the restaurant."

"I remember that, too," Hub said. "He says his name is Cain. That's all. Got no other names of record."

Cain looked up with eye sockets crusted with what Ethan thought were dried tears. Ethan expected a tirade, but the man stayed silent.

They went back out to the office and sat. "Okay," Hub said, "we'll book him for vandalism and attempted arson. He'll get a few years in state prison. Enough time to keep him out of your hair."

Ethan studied the floor and his rocking feet for a minute. "Wait. Can you just hold him for a while. I'm not sure I want to press charges."

Hub frowned. "Mr. Bonner, this is the most cut 'n' dried case of criminal activity I've seen around here in a long time. Are you sure?"

"No, I'm not," Ethan said. "I just want to think about it."

"Okay," Hub said, sighing. "I can hold him for a few days. But make up your mind."

Ethan walked back to the restaurant and saw that J.D. was still there studying his courthouse notes. "They caught him, J.D.—the arsonist. He was one of the guys that came in here with Red Pope that day and called us demons. He's the one with the bad teeth. Remember?"

"Yeah. I do remember that guy. Well, good. Glad we got that mystery solved. Do you think he's the same one that sabotaged the mud pump?"

Ethan nodded. "He confessed to it."

"Well, I'll be damned. I thought it was Benny Hull or one of his friends trying to stop us from spuddin' before the Hull option ran out. I'll be damned."

They sat for a few more minutes, both of them thinking more than talking.

"J.D.," Ethan said, "I'm thinking of not pressing charges."

"What? Are you crazy? He could try somethin' else on us."

"I don't think so, now that he's been fingered. Don't you think a little forgiveness would go a long way mending these bad relations we've had with some people in this town?"

J.D. pondered, then shrugged.

Abbey came back to the table. "There's a call for you, Mr. Bonner. They want you back out to the oil rig. I'll sack your breakfast to go."

Ethan looked at J.D. as he got up. "What now?"

Ethan got out of his car and saw right away the rig was in trouble. The engine was idling. As he trotted toward it he saw the bent girt bar above the swivel. The crew was standing well away from the derrick. He passed them heading to the steps.

"Don't go up there, Ethan," Grady shouted.

He backed off and looked high into the structure. He saw more damage—a brace hung dangling high in the rigging.

"We're too deep for this rig," shouted Harvey.

"What happened?"

"The drill string got too heavy," Grady said. "When we started trippin' out to change the bit we 'bout caved the derrick in trying to pull it." He pointed up into the derrick. "That brace snapped and that girt bent. And that's just what we can see. We'll have to lay the derrick down and take a good look at it to see if that's all."

"Can we fix it?"

"Ain't none of us got experience doing fabrication work." You've got to find somebody who knows what they're doin'."

"How long?"

"A day or two—at the least. Maybe a week." He shrugged. "Hell, maybe it's totaled. I don't know."

"And there's another problem. When we pull off the Kelly and swivel assembly we won't be able to circulate mud. The mud will just sit in the hole."

Ethan nodded. He knew what that meant. The mud could lose its properties. It might become too thick. That would complicate their attempts to pull the pipe out and to evaluate the hole properly once it is complete.

"Start laying it down," Ethan said. "I'll get on it."

"Not so fast, Mr. Bonner. That thing groaned and moaned and then snapped and clunked. We're damned lucky it didn't cave in and kill us all. It's happened before, you know." He paused, lit up and gestured to the crew. "Them boys say they ain't goin' back up there."

"Is that so?" Ethan asked them.

They nodded. "Scared the hell out of us, Mr. Bonner," Cuz said.

Harvey nodded. "Told ya. Did so, now."

"Okay," Ethan said. "What'll it take to get ya'll to lay that derrick down so we can inspect and repair it?"

They stood shuffling their feet, looking up at it. Then Grady offered a solution. "If we do get it fixed, we ain't gonna drill another foot unless we get some skinnier drill pipe." He looked at his crew. "That will reduce the weight of the string. We don't have that much farther to go. I think we can do it if we baby it and don't twist off. It'll be slow though."

Ethan felt immensely relieved, and exceedingly glad he had offered Grady half ownership in the rig. Otherwise he might have been making tracks west by now.

Ethan looked at each of them. One spat. Another kicked dust and sighed.

"I'm going to wake up Tiny's crew," Grady said. "We'll need all of 'em out here for this."

Ethan went to the trailer and got out his Yellow Pages. He spent the afternoon calling steel fabricators. They all turned him down. None were familiar with the oil industry and didn't want to tackle such a job. As he was calling yet another one, Laura walked in.

"Oh, Lord am I glad to see you," Ethan said. He got up and hugged her a long time. Finally she pulled away, flustered. Neither said anything for what seemed a long time.

She had heard there was an accident at the rig and rushed out, but was relieved when she saw it, expecting it to be shattered and piled. He explained what happened.

"So, I'm calling all these guys in Mobile, and none of them will touch it with a ten-foot pole."

"Have you checked with the shipyards," she asked.

"Shipyards?"

"Yes. When I worked there during the war I saw lots of heavy duty steel work going on. They've probably got the material you need, too. Why don't you call the shipyard office and see who they use for that kind of work?"

Ethan smiled, leaned over and kissed her cheek. Then he attacked the phone book.

The crew set the slips that held the drill string in place and then disconnected the Kelly and swivel and held their breath as they removed the hinge pins from the A-frame. All except Grady backed a safe distance away

Grady carefully let out the draw until the derrick lay flat on its racks. It was nightfall by then, and they all drifted back to the motel to wait.

The fabrication truck arrived next morning in a light drizzle. Two workers got out and walked around looking at the rig asking questions. Grady pointed out the needed work. They found several more deformed girts. One man started setting up equipment while the other called back to his shop ordering new steel to be brought up to replace the broken and bent pieces.

Ethan was too busy to worry about the cost. Now he had the task of locating the rare small-diameter drill pipe. More headaches, more money. He shook his head and dialed.

The calls to the drilling contractors netted nothing. A few companies had the pipe he needed, but they were either using it or weren't willing to let him rent it. The only company left to call was Mercer Drilling. He ran his hands through his hair for the thousandth time since he got to this town. He swallowed hard and dialed, whispering, "Okay, Mr. Mercer. You're my last shot."

The steel workers plied their magic quicker that Ethan imagined. By nightfall they were loading up their truck and asking for a check. The phone rang as Ethan was writing it out.

"Mr. Mercer! Thanks for calling back. Did you get the message about the pipe I need?"

"I did. Sorry to hear you're having problems out there. Just so happens I've got about five thousand feet of three and one half at my Laurel yard, plus a few subs and collars. I'll need that pipe before the end of the year—if you can be done with it by then."

Ignoring the subtle insult, Ethan grinned at his phone. "How much will I be charged?"

Mercer cackled. "Hell, son. Don't you know if you have to ask, you can't afford it?"

Ethan's heart sank.

"Naw, just kiddin'. Nothing. No charge. Just get it back to the yard as soon as you can. There's just one thing. If you twist off and leave it in the hole, I'm comin' after you."

Ethan slumped in his chair, let out a huge lung-full, and rested his head in his hands. Then he smiled, looked up through the ceiling of the trailer and held his arms aloft.

He went out and dismissed both crews to the motel, not wanting to risk rigging back up in the dark. Besides they needed a break.

The new pipe arrived the next morning, just as Ethan was watching the derrick raise. By noon they were rigged back up. He climbed the steps and stood beside Grady, wanting to show the crew he had confidence in the repairs. Grady carefully pushed the engine pedal and lifted the brake. The pipe was slow to move upward. All hands kept looking up into the derrick with shifty, nervous eyes—looking for signs of more failures. Suddenly a metallic thump reverberated from above and the drill floor shook. The men instantly jumped backward. Skeeter made for the steps, then stopped and stared upward with the others. Grady set the brake then climbed into the derrick searching for signs of more failures.

In a few minutes he came down. "Didn't see anything," he mumbled to no one in particular. "Guess it's just adjusting." He wiped sweat, stepped to the console and resumed pulling pipe. The jittery men took their positions and disconnected and stacked as Grady brought the pipe up one stand at a time until the worn bit reached the surface. They quickly spun it off. Then they laid 3,000 feet of drill pipe in 30-foot sections down the slide and hoisted it onto the racks.

They wasted no time lifting the new 3½ inch pipe up into the derrick racks, attaching the new collars and bit, and going back into the hole. Ethan went to the trailer and fell into the bunk. The first sleep in thirty-six hours came quickly.

14

The Shows

Grady babied the rig, keeping only as much weight-on-bit as he dared to keep from buckling the smaller pipe with excessive compression. That slowed him down, but finally the crews enjoyed steady progress. As Ethan expected, they went through 700 feet of almost solid shale. His next target was the Rodessa Sands. It was now a nervous waiting game.

He visited Laura every day now, enjoying moderate success at relating to her without affronting her in some fashion. He was with her on the evening of the fifth day since they resumed drilling after repairing the derrick. Laura's phone rang.

She sat her teacup down and answered. Ethan heard her listen, then giggle. "Mr. Plunket, you are such a charmer!" He heard Grady's tiny electronic voice issuing from the receiver ten feet from him but couldn't make out the words. Laura responded to another of Grady's now familiar overcooked swagger. "Now, I know better than that." She giggled again. Ethan wished he could make her laugh like that.

"I know how beautiful those Texas women are." She cut eyes back to Ethan and listened to more of the tool pusher's banter. Ethan sipped his tea and shook his head with a resigned smile.

"Okay, well, here he is." She held the phone toward him.

"What's up?" Ethan asked the pusher.

"Mr. Bonner, I know it would be a challenge for you to break away from that fair maiden and come back to this noisy, smelly rig and join us snake-eaters, but I think you'd best come down here and see what we've got."

"What?" Ethan asked, rising from his chair.

Grady paused. Ethan could hear him picking his teeth with a toothpick.

"What? What?!"

"Just a few little ole shows, that's all."

Ethan's face broke into a wide grin. "Shows?" He looked at Laura, eyes beaming. "Shows!"

"What's that?" she asked.

Ethan turned back to the phone. "What shows? How deep?"

"Just come out here," Grady said.

Ethan hung up. He stared at the wall momentarily, then turned toward Laura. "Shows! I've got to go."

"What are shows?" she demanded.

"Later," he yelled heading for the door. Then he turned about. "Wait. I need to tell J.D." He used Laura's telephone to call the landman. As he started for the door again he motioned to her. "Come on, come on, go with me."

They pulled up to the rig near 10 p.m., and Ethan saw that Grady had ordered Tiny to halt the drilling. The drill string was standing idly in the hole. The mud pump hummed, circulating the mud. Grady stood at the base of the stairs smoking. Ethan trotted up with Laura in tow.

"Show me," he said.

Grady ignored him and took off his hard hat, bowing slightly toward Laura.

"Miss Hamilton, you are so easy on my eyes, but you shouldn't be in this nasty place. Can I get you some coffee?"

"Where?" Ethan demanded.

Grady looked askance at him. "In the trailer with the other samples. Where else?"

Ethan strode straight for the trailer. Grady offered his elbow to Laura, and they followed.

Ethan quickly poured a small pile of the still wet cuttings onto the table and pulled out his hand lens. He put it to his eye and leaned close to the table, examining the bits of rock while probing them with a dentist's prong.

"Stain," he mumbled. He looked up at Grady and grinned. "Oil stain!"

"Tellin' me somethin' I don't already know?" Grady uttered, winking at Laura. He gestured to the ultraviolet box. "Now, look in that damned thing and get ready to have your socks blown off!"

Ethan looked with a smile at Grady as he pulled the box over. He picked up a dropper and reached for the acetone bottle, intending to let a few drops of it fall on the cuttings so they could be examined under ultraviolet light.

"I've already done that," Grady growled. "Just look in the box."

Ethan grinned at the pusher before looking in the box. This was a geologist's job, but Grady's years in the oil patch had made him more than a rig hand. He leaned down and looked in the viewport. The cuttings glowed with a magnificent bluish-green brilliance.

"Bingo," Ethan shouted.

The trailer door opened behind them and J.D. stepped in. "We got good shows," Ethan announced to him.

J.D. nodded, lit a cigarette and offered one to Grady. Grady nodded and took it.

Ethan got up from the chair and let Laura have a look. He turned to his pusher. "How many feet?"

"Hell, I don't know," Grady uttered, toothpick wobbling at one corner of his mouth while the cigarette jutted from the other corner. "You're the geologist! What are we in, anyway?"

Ethan pulled a stack of electronic logs from Mississippi wells that sat at the corner of the counter and slipped two of them against the hand-written sample log he had been working up. The others leaned over his shoulder and watched Ethan ply his wizardry. "I don't know for sure," he mumbled, "but I think it's the Rodessa."

"What's that?" Laura asked.

Ethan looked up. "That's what produces oil over in Mississippi at Soso."

"Humph!" Grady uttered, turning for the coffee urn. "That's almost a hun'ert miles from here. It might be Rodessa and it might be sump'n you never heard of."

"He's right, Ethan," J.D. added, nodding.

Ethan swung his swivel chair around to Laura. "The Rodessa is a sandstone of Lower Cretaceous age—about 130 million years old—that produces oil in parts of Mississippi and further west.

"There you go again," J.D. scolded. "Keep throwin' them millions of years around this town and the deeper in trouble you get."

Ethan ignored him as he arranged the sample bags in order of depth. Grady's crews had dutifully collected them every five feet since the shows came up and marked the depths on the bags. The three watched as he separated the samples and examined them, looking back at them with an occasional smile of satisfaction. Finally he pronounced that he thought they had at least forty feet of good show and possibly as much as sixty.

Laura's face lit up. "Forty feet? Is that good?" The oilmen assured her it was, but Ethan offered caution.

"Keep in mind that you can get shows even in wet sands."

J.D. nodded agreement.

"In fact I have seen shows this good in water saturated sands."

"How will we know?" Laura asked.

"We won't until we log."

"And maybe not even after that," Grady interjected.

Ethan frowned at him and nodded reluctantly.

"When will you do that?" Laura asked.

Ethan looked at Grady, his eyes soliciting counsel.

"How much deeper we goin'?" Grady asked.

Ethan thought about the payroll and the mud bills. "How much longer are the crews willing to stick with us?"

"I've told you before, the boys'll work as long as we buy 'em beans and beer while they're waitin' for their pay. It's the other stuff we gotta worry about."

Ethan stared, thinking.

"You got to think about the bills," Grady continued. "We got mud and bits to pay for yet. And diesel fuel, too. Remember, I got my reputation on the line here. I promised all of the suppliers you'd pay."

Ethan pondered the lower formations. If he made a well in the Rodessa he could drill the next one deeper to probe the Sligo and maybe even the Hosston. All those produced oil at one place or another back west. But that would take another week, at the rate they were drilling. Maybe more. If he was going to go deeper, he had to do it now. But the bills.

He looked back into the box and again admired the fluorescing rock fragments. He remembered how he was already far below the rig manufacturer's maximum recommended depth. He decided it was now or never.

"Let's log."

Grady slowly nodded, turning for the door.

"Wait a minute, Ethan," J.D. said. "We got something to talk about."

Laura took the hint and started out the door. She looked back and smiled at the two men, then went out.

"Ethan," J.D. said, "Don't get me wrong. I love her, but—can we trust her with all this stuff she's hearing?"

"Of course," Ethan said, visibly miffed.

J.D. put up defensive hands. "Okay, okay. I just need to know what I can say in front of her and what I can't."

"I trust her. Say anything."

"Okay. I need to talk to you about the Buchanan lease." You want me to go to the car and get the lease map?"

"No. Not unless you've updated it since we last went over it."

"Mr. Buchanan is one of the nicest men I have ever met. Humble, dignified and bright. I wish I could say the same for his wife. That woman is a first class b—" He stopped short of his description when Ethan put a hand up and shook his head. "Anyway, Buchanan is driving a hard bargain. He'll lease the whole package only—all 1,800 and something acres, not just a piece of it like you want. That's about $90,000."

Ethan stared at the samples and shook his head. "Can't do it."

J.D. got up and sighed. "Okay. At least I think he'll give us the first shot if we get oil. But we have to be ready." He pointed down. "I know we've been over this time and again, but it bears repeating, if you get oil here you're gonna have to get some money fast, or you'll lose him to somebody with deep pockets."

Buford Kidd walked toward his truck in the dawning light and threw his lunch pail in it. He started up while watching the day crew begin their tours. He rubbed tired eyes and backed away. He passed a phone booth on the edge of town near the Greyhound station and pulled over to make a call.

"Benny. This is Buford. Sorry to wake you up, but somethin' happened last night. I don't understand it much, but they got mighty excited. I heard them talking somethin' about *shows*, whatever that is. I guess it means oil—hell, I don't know. Hey, buddy, this work is killin' my ass. When will you—" He paused for Benny. "Okay, that sounds good. I need it. Let me get some sleep and I'll come by and get it."

Laura got out of her car, put on her sunglasses, and folded her arms. She stood for a moment surveying the drill site. She saw a strange truck backed up to the rig. Busy men were scurrying around everywhere.

"Laura!" Ethan yelled. He beckoned her over to the side of the big blue truck. "I'm glad you came," he gasped as if out of breath. "This is a big day! In a couple of hours—" He paused and glanced at the rig, then dipped his head at her. "We'll know."

They looked at the blue Schlumberger truck and its accouterments. "That's French," he said. "It's pronounced *Slum-ber-jay*."

She saw a big spool of cable on the rear of the truck. The

Schlumberger hands had rigged the cable over a pulley in the derrick and lowered it into the hole. Ethan explained that a long thin tool called a sonde was attached to the end of the cable. The operator was at that moment lowering the sonde to the bottom. After that he would slowly bring it up, measuring critical rock properties as it came up.

"Will it tell you if there's oil?" she asked.

"No. Unfortunately it won't. It'll only tell us if the rock properties are favorable for oil. Let's go inside."

Inside where? she wondered. He led her to a door on the side of the Schlumberger truck. It was dim inside. They heard Hank William's voice twanging from a radio. They saw a wide-bodied man with a flat top haircut sitting at a console of blinking and steady lights, his back to them, bent over a pile of paperwork, a half-eaten sandwich sitting aside. "He's probably working on my invoice," Ethan cracked.

"As a matter of fact, I am," the guy said, turning. "Oh," he exclaimed, seeing Laura. He got up.

"Laura, this is Vergil, the Schlumberger engineer assigned to this truck. He's a Yankee." She smiled and offered her hand.

"Is this your first time in a logging truck?" he eagerly asked Laura, ignoring Ethan's remark. She nodded. Without asking her, he set about giving her a tour his lair. Ethan noticed an old Bluetick hound curled in a corner and petted it. The hound began sniffing Ethan's pantlegs.

"That's Rocky!" Vergil said. "Watch him when we log your zone." He winked to Laura. "If he looks up and raises his ears, you've got a well! If he just lays there..." Vergil's voice trailed off. He shrugged and cackled. Ethan didn't appear to share the humor.

"Oh!" Vergil shouted, noticing his depth gauge. "We're on bottom. He sat down back at the console and began twisting knobs and punching buttons.

Laura sat on a chair and watched Ethan staring into the console. She began to feel emptiness, then dread. *In about an hour this may all come to an end*, she thought. *Then, in a day or two, these machines will be gone. And all the men. And him, too.*

In a strange way her life, too, seemed to be at a turning point. She had absolutely no stake in the oil venture. Ethan had been kind to her and interested in her. He had sat with her. Listened to her. Had taught her exciting things about his science. He was rough around his edges and sometimes insensitive, even when he didn't realize it, but he had brought hope, excitement, and a keen sense of anticipation to the whole town. And especially to her.

Oh, how she needed this well to hit—not a cent at stake, and she needed it more, she imagined, than anyone else. Except, of course, Ethan. She saw him petting the Bluetick, then slowly turning his head toward the television-like screen where, Vergil had explained, the truth of the rocks would soon be told. *Funny,* she thought. I *haven't a thread of ambition to participate in the oil wealth, not even if Ethan and I were to*— She stopped that thought.

Still, she had never known such a profound moment, and a foreboding feeling overcame her. She suddenly felt terribly out of place. She wanted to burst out the door and run—to get back to what was familiar and secure, where the gap between success and failure was wide enough to dwell in with a measure of contentment.

"I'll just log a little bit of the rat hole here," Vergil mumbled, "to calibrate the tools, then we'll be in business." A few minutes later he announced he was beginning the logging process. Ethan huddled near the console watching the bright squiggly lines dance back and forth as the depth marks crawled down the bright green screen in increments of two feet. Soon a printer beside the screen came to life, and a seemingly endless flow of folded paper began to issue from it. The trailer filled with the pungent stench of the paper's ammonium hydroxide-based ink.

She saw Ethan take the paper as it came out, accepting it like a baby from the womb. He examined the squiggly lines on it, his eyes moving quickly from feature to feature. In the background Fats Domino sang *Ain't that a Shame* on Vergil's radio.

Ethan looked at Laura. "Not the song I want to be hearing right now."

Laura cocked her head aside, cheeks wrinkled in a smile.

Vergil cackled. "What you want me to do, turn off the radio and whistle *Dixie* for you?"

"No," Ethan said, sighing. "I don't need any lost causes right now, either."

"Okay," Vergil said, exhaling. Here we come."

Laura flashed an expression of confusion at Ethan. He said, "The sonde is about to come up through the Rodessa." He hovered over the printer.

Ethan glanced over his shoulder at Rocky. The dog lie asleep. Not a whisker moved.

"I saw his nose twitch," Vergil said. He nodded first to Ethan then to Laura. "It definitely flicked."

Laura got the hint. She nodded to Ethan. "I saw it, too. It definitely twitched."

"You said he would look up, and his ears would come up. That's what you said," Ethan blurted.

"Yeah, but sometimes he twitches his nose, too," Vergil said, arching his eyebrows at Ethan. Laura sat still and swallowed hard. She felt Ethan's tension. She wasn't sure the dog talk eased it for him. She saw him suddenly jerk upright, grabbing the out-scrolling printout with both hands. For the next two minutes he cradled it as it came out, drinking in the squiggles and twitches of the traces. She watched his eyes for a clue but found none. Presently, he sighed and got up. He let the continuously printing paper drop in a big pile on the floor.

"It looks like great porosity!" Vergil said in a consoling tone.

"Yeah, but I only saw half an ohm on the induction curve," Ethan muttered. Laura felt his dejection.

"What does it mean," she asked.

Ethan blew out a heavy sigh. "It means we're probably water saturated. We needed at least one ohm for oil."

"We don't really know that, do we?" Vergil asked, rhetorically.

"Ya know, we're a long way from the fields in Mississippi," he said with a nervous chuckle. Resistance properties in the formation fluids over here could be different." He looked up at Ethan. "It's a new ball game over here."

Ethan shrugged. "I know that. But I wanted a definitive conclusion. All I've got is a probable water saturated hole, with a slight *maybe* that it's not."

"Call Halliburton," Vergil suggested.

"I had hoped that wouldn't be necessary," Ethan said, sitting back down to watch the rest of the log come out as the sonde inched its way upward. Ethan looked at Laura and shook his head slowly.

Laura became nauseated with the ammonia smell and excused herself. She waited in her car. An hour later Ethan came out with the folded logs in his hand. Laura saw him pause in the door and thank Vergil. He stepped toward her with a meek smile and a slowly shaking head. Virgil appeared in the door. "Uh, Mr. Bonner." Ethan turned. Vergil looked embarrassed. "Back at the office, they asked me to get a check from you, if I could."

Laura saw Ethan nod subtly. "I'll bring you one."

As they were walking to the trailer Ethan told her, shaking his head, "They don't trust me. Normally they let you mail in your check with the invoice, but..." His voice trailed off and he shook his head more.

As they stepped into the trailer Laura asked, "What does he mean by Halliburton?"

"Halliburton is one of the companies that run drill stem tests—DSTs, we call them. It's an expensive, dangerous test that I don't want to do, but it looks like I'll have to, to find out for sure if we've got an oil well. This log is not telling me what I wanted to know. If anything, it's telling me we've got a dry hole." He laid the log on the table and sat to examine it closer.

"What if it is dry, Ethan," she asked. "What will you do then?"

"We'll plug this hole and leave," he said dispassionately, not looking up.

Laura got up and went to the door. She looked back at him. He didn't seem to even notice she was leaving.

15

OVERDUE

The news swept through the town's streets. Something was happening at the drill site.

Harry Little quickly finished cutting his customer's hair and closed the shop. He hurried across the street, stepped across the railroad track, and strode past the used car lot. He passed Grover Shine getting out of his truck. They joined others flowing toward the rig from shops, offices, and parked cars. Corrine Buchanan hurried along ahead of them.

"Where's Ben?" Harry shouted to her.

Corrine yelled over her shoulder, "He said he's too busy to watch the circus."

"Ha!" Grover blurted. "He'll change his tune if he sees that black gold coming out of the ground."

"Don't hold your breath about oil, Grover," Harry muttered. "And quit walking so fast! We ain't going to no fire."

The group rounded the corner of the Sinclair station and saw the derrick standing tall against the pale blue sky.

"Oh, my Lord," Corrine cried. "Look at all those cars!"

"Looks like everybody in the county is out here," said Grover. "Ben's missing out on this."

"Oh, I suppose he'll be along," Corrine muttered. "You know him. He wouldn't get excited if the Russians were a-comin'."

"He just don't want to get disappointed," Harry said. "That's all."

"Humph!" Corrine snorted. "What about me? I've been disappointed all my life. I'm ready for my luck to change."

"I'm with you on that," said Grover. "I feel like my luck *is* gonna change."

The three walked to the edge of the rig site where most of the vehicles were parked. They nodded to Emmett Brubeck and Benny Hull, who leaned against Brubeck's Chrysler Newport. "You better put that cigar out, Emmett," Harry said, grinning. "It might get oily around here."

Emmett glanced toward Harry and raised his cigar-studded jaw, grinning back. Benny tipped his hat to Corrine. The men resumed their private conversation.

Harry, Grover, and Corrine stopped alongside Brother Billy and the town's doctor, Doctor Maven. "What's happening, Doc?" Grover asked.

"The geologist fellow told us they were about to run a test." He took out his pipe and pointed the stem. "See that truck over there?"

Corrine read the name on the truck. "Hal-ah—" She paused, squinting.

"Halliburton," the doctor said. "He said it came in from Mississippi. There's some specialists with it who are going to run the test."

"A while ago they put a tool in the hole," Billy said. "We saw it go down."

The group watched as Cuz and the crew lowered the tool, sequentially adding joints of drill pipe to the string. The test tool had been attached to the bottom of the drill pipe, replacing the bit. The rig's big diesel chugged and hummed as Grady lowered the swivel with its heavy load and raised it again and again to latch onto more pipe lengths.

The doctor turned to the pastor. "Brother Billy, do you agree with Red Pope? You think the oilman is poisoning the town with his theories?"

Billy stared toward the drilling rig for a moment. "I think the man is sincere in what he believes about science. That doesn't mean I agree with him completely. But you know something? We sometimes forget that the Lord didn't just create us, He also created science. He created more stuff than we'll ever know. But the same God that made the natural world gave us His holy Word. I don't think He ever meant to confound us by creating confusion between the two. We do a pretty good job of confounding ourselves."

"That point being that science and faith are harmonious?" Doc Maven asked, removing his pipe to press the point.

Billy looked back at the doctor. "To tell you the truth, I just don't know, Doc. But I trust the Word."

Up on the rig floor Ethan looked at his watch, then at Grady. "It's two o'clock. We've got about five hours before dark."

Grady nodded and set the brake to allow the roughnecks to screw another pipe length onto the string. "We'll be on bottom in fifteen minutes," he said, wiping sweat. "That'll give us four hours to test. The state won't let us test after dark. Too dangerous."

Ethan stared at the driller and nodded.

"Don't worry, Cap'n," Grady assured. "We'll get it done."

Ethan descended the rig steps, walked to the trailer, and glanced at the crowd of people standing at the edge of the street. Some sat on the ground, others on the fenders of vehicles. A few were sharing a basket of fried chicken. Many fanned in the afternoon heat. Ethan tipped his hat at them, and they waved. "When's the oil comin' out?" someone yelled. Ethan shrugged, smiled, and stepped into the trailer.

Laura looked up from the microscope as he came in. J.D. was hovering closely over her. "Mr. Whitley is showing me how to use your microscope," she said.

"Uh huh," Ethan uttered, cutting eyes to the landman.

J.D. ignored him and continued explaining the cuttings to her. "See the grains? They're little pieces of sand stuck together. You can see their corners and crevasses."

"Yeah," she whispered, smiling as she peered into the scope.

"Oil hides out in the spaces between those grains," he explained.

"There's oil here?" she asked abruptly, looking up.

Ethan stole the initiative from J.D. "We don't know that yet. All we see there is shows. That's where oil is—or *was*."

She looked befuddled. "But where did it go if it was there?"

"Poof!" J.D. blurted, his hands going upward.

Ethan explained that the oil moves upward through porous rocks until it reaches a barrier of some sort, a trap. If the trap is not there, it will flow right on through and just leave a footprint.

She put her eyes back to the lens tubes. "It's fascinatin'," she sang. "I can see the tiny grains." She turned slightly toward Ethan with that little lopsided smile that warmed him. "Seeing the little grains makes me feel so small."

"I'd think it would make you feel big."

"No. I'm a grain. I'm a little grain in a big world."

"Is a big eye looking at you?"

J.D. rolled his eyes. "I'm goin' up the drill floor where sane people are."

She giggled. "I hope a big eye isn't watching me all the time! Thanks Mr. Whitley!"

"Oh, by the way," Whitley said, "you got a call a little while ago from Noble Abrams's office. She didn't say what it was about. Just wants a call back."

Ethan sat and looked out the small window toward the rig, watching Whitley mosey toward it. He decided he could wait until after the test to return the call."

"How does that work?" she asked.

"What?"

"That thing they put in the hole? You only said they were running a test for oil."

He drew a diagram in the margin of a newspaper. "They take the bit off and put a packer on and run it down to where we want to test, which is the Rodessa Sand at 10,950 feet."

"A packer? What's that?"

"A thing that swells out against the hole and blocks off the area above it, but still lets liquids flow through the pipe. They put the packer just above the Rodessa and set it. By that I mean they make the packer expand against the side of the hole to seal off the Rodessa from the two miles of mud weighing down on it.

"At the same time a valve opens at the bottom of the tool that will let oil, gas, or water enter the drill pipe. Whatever. We'll see the pressure that it creates in the form of gas bubbles coming out of a tube in a bucket of water."

"That's it? Just a few bubbles?"

"Yup, until we get the tool back out. It will bring fluid samples up with it. But if there are no bubbles on top, it usually means nothing at the bottom."

She slowly shook her head. He watched tiny strands of hair crawl across her shoulder. "I thought it would blow out like in the pictures."

"No. It shouldn't do that. If that happens, we've done something wrong."

"All those people out there will be disappointed at a few bubbles."

"Well, I didn't invite them out."

Laura turned squarely at him. "What are you going to do if it's dry?"

"You asked me that before. What I always do," he said, still looking out the window. "Keep hunting."

"And what will you do if it hits?"

He chuckled and looked at her. "Keep hunting."

She propped her head against her arm, elbow on the table, looking at him. She turned and looked back out at the rig. "Mister Plunket's coming," she said.

Ethan looked up as the driller came in. "Well, Boss. It's time for the blow." He grabbed the coffee pot and poured.

"That stuff's pretty stiff," Laura said. She got up to make a fresh pot for the driller.

Ethan jumped up. "They've opened the valve already?"

"Yessir," said Grady, grimacing at the vile liquid.

Ethan rushed out and headed for the rig floor.

"I pray he gets it," Laura mumbled, watching him through the window.

"Well, I ain't much for prayin', but I believe when it comes to oil, the Lord works in mighty funny ways," Grady said.

She looked at him. "How so?"

He poured the awful stuff in his cup into the sink. "I've seen some of 'em find oil by throwing a dart at a map. Others work their hearts out tryin' to use science to figure out where to drill and then still come up a duster. It seems like they work hard as hell trying to get the geology right—all for nothin'." He paused while she poured him a fresh cup. He studied her over a sip. "But findin' oil don't mean you're gonna find what you're lookin' for."

She looked squarely at him. "What does that mean?"

Grady looked out the window at the rig then back at Laura. He pointed to her heart. "The real discovery, I reckon, is what you find in here." He winked and grinned.

"Mister Plunket, you are so wise. Can I go see the bubbles now?"

"Well, that is not one of the safest things we do. But you can come if it's all right with Ethan."

He presented his elbow. She took it, and they went to the rig.

Corrine saw Laura coming out of the trailer with Grady. She shook her head. "That woman would sell her soul to get some of that oil money. Look at her."

Ben, who had finally showed up, looked aside at her and shook his head. "Corrine, we've known her since she was a child. She's not like that, and you know it." Corinne looked on, lip curled, arms folded. "Sim was a good friend of mine," Ben added. "He raised her right."

"If he raised her right," Corrinne mocked, "then why is she hanging out with them oil people all the time? Something's goin' on, I tell you. She spends too much time in that trailer of theirs." She rolled her head toward the barber and Mr. Shine and cracked a smirk. "If you know what I mean."

Grover chuckled. Harry raised a brow, as if imagining what Corrine had suggested.

"I don't want you talking about Sim's girl like that," Ben said, raising his voice. "Now stop it. You're spreadin' poison."

"I'm spreadin' poison, you say? What about him? That oilman? He's going around tellin' our children we came from apes, and you're tellin' me *I'm* spreadin' poison?"

Grover spat a stream of brown juice and changed the subject. "I don't care if we came from doodlebugs as long as we get oil."

Harry slapped his hands and cackled, "Doodlebugs!" Then he asked Grover, "Have you leased yet?"

Grover wiped his mouth with his sleeve and looked back at the barber. "Not yet."

"Have they been out talkin' to you about your minerals?"

"Nope. Not yet. It don't matter. I'm gonna put my farm up to lease to the highest bidder. I guarantee you that."

Harry thought for a while. "That's strange. I'd a thought since your farm is right beside Hull's they'd of leased you already."

"Ha!" Grover blurted. "They know I ain't givin' away my lease, like old Hull did. They'll have to pay and pay big time."

When Laura and Grady reached the rig floor Ethan was down on one knee peering into the bucket. J.D. stood behind him, hands in his pockets.

The Halliburton crew chief knelt on the other side of the bucket, chewing gum and eyeing the crowd of people out by the road. "It's gonna be hard to keep this one tight," he remarked to Ethan.

Ethan looked up at him. "We gave up on that weeks ago. When you drill this close to people, they're going to find out."

"What does *tight* mean?" Laura whispered to J.D.

"Means *secret*."

Ethan studied his watch. Grady stared at the floor. Cuz and the crew reclined in the shade of the dog house and slapped at gnats. Ethan looked up toward the crown block at the top of the derrick. The American flag at the top hung listless, signaling no hint of breeze. The idling diesel's throb permeated the stillness.

J.D. and Ethan leaned over the Halliburton man's shoulder, peering at the pressure gauge. It read zero. Ethan looked back into the bucket. Laura appeared beside him and stared down. Ethan saw their faces reflected in the water.

He remembered the DSTs he had been involved in before. But those times he was working for other people. The appearance of the bubbles meant corporate success. No bubbles meant just another dry hole.

Not so, now. The weight of the past eight-months' work and worry rested on his shoulders now as never before. To lift the burden, he only needed to see some simple bubbles. The behemoth drilling rig rising around him like a stairway to the heavens was only a big, surreal tool; the people along the road just faces come briefly into his life to help him watch for the bubbles.

If the bubbles didn't come, it would all be over in a matter of hours. Tomorrow morning he would rise to the heart-piercing daylight of another failure. A rancid, sickening paste formed in his mouth. The bubbles were overdue.

The shadows of the steel infrastructure slowly moved across the floor. The Halliburton man looked at his watch yet again. "Mr. Bonner, I don't think we're going to get anything. Dark's comin' on."

A clap of distant thunder rolled in almost the same time as the wind picked up. It sounded to Ethan like a tolling—like the final buzzer at a losing basketball game. His time was done.

Ethan looked up and around. His eyes met Grady's. Grady's head slowly shook. He turned to J.D. The landman sighed heavily with slumping shoulders. "Okay," said Ethan, as if about to shoot a lame horse. "Let's end it."

Grady signaled Cuz and the crew with a tilt of his head, and they put on their gloves and hardhats and got up. The Halliburton men made preparations to recover their DST tool.

The long wait shrank the crowd, but those with the most to gain stuck it out.

"Look," Corinne said. Something's happening!"

The men rose from their squats in the grass and looked toward the rig. Dr. Maven and Brother Billy drew nearer to it. Emmett and Benny stopped chatting and turned toward the oilmen. Dozens of others began walking toward the rig. Mothers stayed behind holding back their children while their husbands moved closer. Ethan saw them coming.

Dr. Maven yelled up to the floor. "We got anything?"

The word, *we,* struck Ethan. It worsened his awful feeling that he had let down the entire town. He walked to the edge of the platform and put his hands on the rails. He looked down at them. He shook his head.

The doctor nodded, lips pursed. He turned with others and went back toward his neighbors shaking his head. A low murmur rose from the watchers as they all turned and flowed away.

Ethan watched as the engine roared and belched smoke as Grady lifted stand after stand of pipe, the floor crew manhandling each 90-foot section into the racks. Laura came out of the doghouse and joined him.

"That Halliburton guy is nervous about you being up here," he said.

"Want me to leave?"

He looked at her, shook his head, and looked back out toward the people. "I let them down," Ethan said.

"What?" she yelled above the din of engine and screeching pipe tongs.

"I let 'em down," he said louder.

"You didn't let anybody down. You showed them how to dream.

You showed them how to hope. Most of them have never even done that before. Their lives will be better for it."

"And you?" he asked. "Will you be better for it?"

She held a hand against her blowing hair. "I already am."

Ethan heard the engine roar again as it pulled up a length of pipe; then he smelled something. He turned and saw the roughnecks drenched in brown steaming drilling mud. "Get into the dog house!" he yelled to Laura. He grabbed her by her shoulders and ushered her out of the raining mud.

The mud rain stopped momentarily as the pipe section was brought to the top. Ethan looked high up and saw Skeeter grab the top of the section. He looked back down and watched the roughnecks attach the tongs to bottom of the joint. Grady pushed the lever that turned the Kelly, and gunned the throttle. The lower drill string rotated while the upper joint remained stationary—held back by the tongs.

"Watch out!" Grady yelled. "Here it comes again!"

When they unscrewed the upper joint and separated it, another spray of mud erupted from the drill string. The roughnecks threw the elevator clamp onto the string and immediately Grady shoved the lever and sent it skyward toward Skeeter. This time hot steaming mud spewed out the top, dousing Skeeter and raining back down on the floor.

"What's happening?" Ethan yelled, as the mud-drenched Grady worked at the console.

"Sump'in's pushin' it out!"

Ethan went into the doghouse, took a machine rag and tossed it to Grady. He took another and began wiping his own face. Laura had already wiped her face and arms with her skirt. He looked at the brown slime oozing from her hair and smiled. "It looks good on you." She didn't appear amused.

"What's happening?"

"Something has gotten into the drill pipe and is causing the mud to blow out. It could be salt water under abnormal pressure, or it could be a gas bubble."

"Or—" she asked, anticipating another possibility.

"Or—" He paused, as if he didn't want to say the word. "We'll see soon enough."

"But why weren't there bubbles?"

"I don't know."

After Grady and the crew pulled a few more stands of drill pipe with the mud raining down from each one, something in the air changed. They all smelled it. Grady and Ethan looked at each other and grinned. It was sweet, pungent, and very familiar.

"Look at that!" Cuz yelled.

Ethan whirled and saw them looking at the open drill pipe. Shiny, slimy, blackish brown fluid laced with tendrils of tan-colored mud welled-up and poured over the sides of the pipe.

"Ha haaa, ha ha ha!" Grady cackled. "Look! Look! Look! Ha haaa, ha ha!"

Ethan saw J.D. surge out of the doghouse and make a break for the steps. He slipped and fell backward on his ass, lips spewing curses. Ethan trotted over to help him up but slammed down on his own butt. Still laughing, he carefully got to his feet while J.D. recovered his footing and clambered down the steps.

Ethan turned back and watched Grady orchestrate the controls. He engaged the draw works and hauled the pipe out, lifting it as fast as he could toward the top of the derrick, cackling above the noise. "Ha haaa, ha ha ha!"

The upward motion of the pipe set the oil inside it on an upward vector. When Grady stopped the pipe the oil continued upward, spewing through the crown block. It sprang into the sky like a sinister geyser and sprayed out into the wind blowing off the thunderstorm.

Cuz and the floor crew, drenched in slime, continued to unscrew the stands, laughing and bantering as they worked. Skeeter, at his station at the top, manhandled them, setting them into the rack, while Cuz and Harvey swung them at the bottom end. Men and pipe alike dripped with shiny, bronze ooze. Again Grady hauled the pipe toward the top and again the oil erupted through the crown and into the wind. It wafted toward Main Street.

Grover Shine had opened the door to his pick-up when he heard the commotion. Harry waited for a Southern freight to pass before stepping across to his shop. The engines rumbled past in front of him. He heard Corrine yelling. He turned and saw her running toward him, her face speckled with brownish-black spots. He trotted to meet her and touched the oil. His mouth fell wide open. They broke into a trot back to the rig site.

Along the way people ran and yelled, breathing the odd sweet smell that fell in a mist along the street front. Cars and pick-ups passed with black slimy runs on their hoods, doors, and windshields. Harry trotted past some people who were pointing toward the track. The engines were barely moving, their wheels slipping and spinning on the oil covered rails.

Ethan looked toward the distant thundercloud. He saw lightning. He looked upward at the tall steel tower above him. He turned toward Grady and pointed toward the lightning.

"I see it," Grady yelled. "We're hurrying!"

Laura came alongside Ethan and watched the people scurrying about, laughing, cheering.

They turned and grinned at each other. Ethan looked at Laura's oily face, her messy hair, and felt a wild compulsion. He grabbed her, pulled her to him, and kissed her long and hard, half expecting her to pull away and slap him. But she didn't. He tasted the oil on her lips. He pressed hard into her face, hearing the roar of Grady's engine, the screech of the pipe threads, shouts of the crew, the cat-calls, taunting him—they saw the kiss. Still she didn't pull away. He squeezed her harder, pressed tighter against her, put his hand in her slimy hair, and drilled her face with his lips. He had never before kissed a woman like that.

Finally she disconnected and backed away, grinning, heaving for breath. He saw her smile. To his delight she wasn't miffed or horrified. She grinned and giggled. Ethan tilted his head back and laughed as hard as he had ever laughed in his life.

The oil continued to fall, the engine roared, and Ethan heard Grady's jubilant shouts but couldn't understand them through the din. He didn't care. He stayed riveted on Laura's flashing eyes and her broad smile, the taste of her kiss lingering on his lips. For a blissful moment he didn't think about the oil or the rig. It could all vanish in a dream; he didn't care, as long as that kiss, so unplanned, so unpracticed, and so long in coming, was real, was here, and was now.

When Grady's crew pulled the last stand of pipe out the oil rain stopped. The Halliburton men swarmed on the DST tool and began breaking it down. Grady and Ethan approached the crew chief, still wiping their faces.

The crew chief looked at them and answered their question before they could ask. "I'm sorry, fellas. We've got a new kid on the crew," he said, jerking a thumb toward an oily lad carrying a load of equipment to the trucks. "He forgot to open the valve at the top of the drill string for the bubble tube."

"It's all right," Ethan said, grinning. He hit Grady in the arm and nodded.

The driller cracked a smile. "Let's clean this place up before we get a lightning strike. Then we'll condition this hole and go do some celebratin'!"

Ethan chuckled and flashed the driller two dripping, oily thumbs-up then carefully led Laura to the steps, both of them slipping and giggling as they grabbed the handrail. People standing near the rig cheered and waved. Ethan waved back.

"Come on to the trailer and clean up," he told Laura.

J.D. was washing up at the kitchen sink when they went in. Laura went straight to the bathroom. Ethan grabbed a towel and wiped his eyes and hands, then sat and started dialing a number.

"You're calling old Abrams, I bet," J.D. said.

Ethan grinned broadly. "Yes sir. I am. I am indeed placing a long distance call to Noble Abrams." His grin lasted as he waited for an answer.

"Hello, Millie," Ethan barked. "This is Ethan Bonner. I've got some great news for Noble!" He covered the mouthpiece and whispered to J.D. "Millie is Noble's secretary." His grin faded. "What?"

J.D. stopped wiping himself and stared at Ethan.

Laura came out saying something but paused when she saw Ethan's expression.

Ethan listened longer. "Will—will you let me know when the arrangements are made? I'm sorry, Millie. I'm so sorry." He put the phone down and stared at the wall.

Laura and J.D. glanced and each other and waited.

"He's dead," Ethan mumbled. He looked at J.D., then Laura. "He collapsed on the golf course this morning. He died in the hospital."

J.D. squeezed Ethan's shoulder and went out. Laura leaned over and put her arms around him. Ethan's head went down, his shoulders shuddered.

"Darlene, call Mobile. Get Matt Chambers on the phone, now!"

"Okay, Mr. Brubeck," the secretary said. "What's that on your face and clothes?"

"Oil!" he blurted. He burst through his office door and trotted straight for his desk, moving as fast as he had in twenty years. He grabbed the phone and wiped oil specks from his forehead while he waited for the call to go through.

"Matt. This is Emmett. They hit oil!—I'm not kidding. We need to move fast. Oil shot up through the derrick and landed on the street. I've got it on my car. Hell, I've got it on myself," he cackled. "This suit's ruined. Matt, we've got to get started. Sure, Matt. I'll see you in the morning."

16

CHAMBERS

Ethan woke up in the bunkroom of the trailer, splashed water on his face, and rubbed his eyes. His whole sleep, it seemed, was beset with dreaming. He recalled seeing Noble standing beside him on the rig floor as the oil fell; had felt Noble slap him on the back; had heard him say, "Ethan, look!" He had turned and seen his dad at the console.

He rubbed his eyes again and saw the pile of oil-soaked clothes he had kicked off in the bathroom. The oil was no dream. But Noble was. He felt robbed. His dad was long gone and now Noble, too. There was no one to tell.

The party had broken out in Grady's room as soon as his crew got off their tour. He had made a brief appearance. He knew they wondered why he was so somber. J.D. had whispered to him, "You want me to tell them?" He had nodded, smiled at the bunch, and excused himself.

He got dressed, went up on the floor, and found the hung-over crew quietly cleaning up the rig while the mud pump hummed. While he had lain dreaming in the trailer, the evening crew had re-entered the hole and begun circulating mud while waiting on the production casing to arrive. Ordering the casing—a happy telephone call for any oilman to make—was bittersweet. Grady had done it while Ethan slept.

He went to the Wagon Wheel for breakfast and passed a

newspaper rack near the door. He dropped a nickel into the honor box and picked up a copy of the *Mobile Press Register*. The big bold headline read, *OIL!!!*

He went in and found his usual table without looking up from the paper. Abbey set his coffee down and congratulated him. Before he finished the article, other people came up to him wanting to shake his hand. One man laid down a plat of his land and asked him to lease it. He referred the man to J.D.

Finishing the article he slowly shook his head in astonishment. He didn't remember talking to a newsman. And judging from the gross inaccuracies in the story, *no* oilman had talked to the newsman.

He hoped J.D. or some of the crew might have shown up to join him, but none did. He had his breakfast and went back to the rig.

The pipe arrived that afternoon from a supply yard in Laurel, and the crew began running it into the hole. Grady had already alerted Halliburton that he would need their services again, this time to cement the pipe in place.

Ethan sat at the dining table in the trailer. He pulled a notepad from the heap of logs, files, and coffee-stained newspapers, and hovered his pencil above the paper. He had never given much thought to this part of the process. He had found oil. What now? He had a ton of bills to pay and not enough cash. He needed a loan, but that shouldn't be a problem now, he figured. He started to list his needs, but then paused and thought about Noble, then the oily kiss in front of the whole town. It all seemed a dream. He laid the pencil aside, changed clothes, and went to the car.

Laura met him on the porch and planted a smack on his lips, but it didn't match the indulgence of the day before when oil rained. He wondered if that might have been only a result of a passion of the moment. "I came to ask you to go to Noble's funeral with me. In Shreveport. Will you?"

She looked far off, pondering the invitation. "Okay," she said. "When?"

"Tonight. It'll be a quick trip. I have to get back here." He looked at his feet. "I need you."

Emmett Brubeck's car came to a stop just outside of town beside the railroad with himself in the front right passenger seat. The driver, Benny Hull, shifted the Lincoln into park and shut off the engine. They had driven up from Chunchula where the two men in back had left their Cadillac Seville parked. That car would have captured unwanted attention had they driven it to Fossil Rim. Emmett rolled his window down and peered eastward toward the drilling rig in the distance.

The rear window came down. A wisp of cigar smoke wafted upward from the window and another face stared toward the rig, this one with eyes as ebony as the thin mustache and slicked back hair. The men inside the car talked in low tones, as if concerned they might be overheard.

Brubeck twisted back to see the rear seat occupants and hung his elbow over the seat back. "Matt, this is the biggest thing to ever hit this state. History is being made right here under our noses."

Matt Chambers's head slowly rotated toward Brubeck. His question came out soft and sharp, with the cold threat of an unsheathed blade. "And what makes you think I'm interested in history?"

Brubeck saw the reflected light playing across the smooth waves of Chambers's slickened, black hair. The wide thin lips sat underneath an equally wide thin black mustache that tapered to sharp points. In a past deal, Chambers's aide and lawyer, Finch, had confided to Brubeck over whiskey that his boss fancied himself a Clark Gable look-alike. And he was, Brubeck agreed, but without the actor's cocky, engaging smile. Chambers's face was a handsome one, no doubt. Handsome like a stainless steel Colt 45.

Brubeck retrenched. He managed a grin and tipped his head.

"Money, too, Matt. There's money about to be made. More than anybody in this state ever dreamed of."

Benny, seated behind the wheel, let out a lustful, "Oh, yeah!"

Chambers glanced at Benny, but the glance showed no respect. He looked back at the drilling rig and mumbled. "Okay, what's your idea, Brubeck?"

"Pretty simple. Benny, here, will file a complaint charging that Bonner tricked his daddy into signing the lease. He'll ask that the lease be declared null and void due to Mr. Hull being without full mental faculties."

"Go on," Chambers said, still gazing toward the rig.

Brubeck started to continue, but cleared his throat and ran his finger inside of his collar. "You, uh—you and Judge Bundy—ya'll are—friends."

Chambers' icy stare swung from the rig back to Brubeck.

Brubeck continued, uncomfortably. "Judge Bundy will see it our way, will he not?"

Chambers stared a hole in Brubeck's face. Benny saw it and turned his gaze to the front of the car, slumping in the seat.

"Suppose he does?" Chambers uttered, so terse he was ominous.

Emmett cleared his throat. "As soon as the judge nullifies the lease we file a motion to declare Victor Hull's only offspring, Benny here, to be the administrator of the estate with power-of-attorney to lease the minerals to whoever he chooses." He paused to grin. "Benny lets us have the lease, and we can either set up our own oil company, or shop it back to Bonner. He'll have no choice but to rebuy it from us at far, far better terms for us than poor old Mr. Hull got."

Chambers took a puff. "And so, my friendship with *His Honor*, is what buys me in?" He dragged out the word, *friendship*.

Emmett nodded.

Chambers leaned forward, his face contorted and menacing. "Look, you two." Benny turned, eyes wide and scared. "My relationship with the judge will not be discussed again—ever—by either of you. Understand?"

They both nodded, Brubeck pensively, Benny with frightened eyes.

"Now," Chambers said, relaxing in his seat. What are the cuts?"

Emmett looked at Benny. "He'll get a third." He looked back at Chambers and nodded, "You're in for a third, Matt. And I get the other third."

"No." Chambers immediately and resolutely uttered. I get 50 percent, and you two split the rest."

Brubeck's eyes widened; his mouth dropped open, as if wanting to say something, but knowing he shouldn't. He swallowed and glanced at Benny. Benny kept his head straight toward the steering wheel but cast his eyes toward Brubeck. He dipped his head twice.

Brubeck forced a smile. "Okay, Matt. Sure."

Chambers took another puff and looked at the man sitting beside him, eyes arched. "Well, Finch?"

Chambers's assistant, his attorney, seemed to be still thinking. "Well?"

"It might work. But you will have to have Mr. Hull declared incompetent by an expert."

"And how long will that take," Chambers asked.

"A few weeks," Finch guessed. "Those academic types are slow. The longer they take, the more they charge you."

"Humph," Chambers grunted.

"But," Finch blurted, for emphasis, "it is quite possible that we can file a petition for an injunction while the competency evaluation is being done. The injunction would halt all operations by Bonner. But this will work only if we convince the judge."

Chambers's lips formed a smile around the cigar. "Arrange it," he said, his words garbled by the cigar.

Finch smiled and nodded. "But what if Bonner can't pay the price you want?"

"This oil strike will attract others," Brubeck interjected. "Somebody will buy it."

"Bonner will appeal it," Finch added. "It could go to the state Supreme Court. It may drag out for years."

Chambers slowly nodded. He turned back to Emmett. "And if that happens?"

Emmett shrugged. "I don't think Bonner has the staying power for years of litigation. I think he'll play ball."

"Humph," Chambers huffed yet again. "So you don't have a backup plan, do you, Brubeck?"

"I think I'll take a walk," Finch suddenly said, reaching for his door handle.

Chambers nodded toward Benny. "Take him with you."

The two got out of the car and walked away lighting cigarettes. Emmett ran his handkerchief inside his collar again.

Chambers took a long drag at his cigar then examined the tip. He let it flow out his nostrils. "Brubeck, you don't see the big picture. You may be the big shot here in this one-mule town, but you don't know jack squat about bi'ness."

Brubeck knew to stay quite.

Chambers motioned toward Bonner's drilling rig. "What's standing between us and that oil? What?"

Brubeck shrugged. "Bonner's lease."

Chambers slowly shook his head. "No." He looked back at the drilling rig and repeated, "No!"

He looked back at Brubeck and leaned closer to him. He grabbed Brubeck's sleeve and pulled it to him. "Bonner. Bonner is what's between us and the oil. Do you understand now?"

Brubeck swallowed hard. His face turned pale. "But, Matt, how will—will eliminating Bonner get us the deal?"

Chambers studied Brubeck for what seemed an eternity. "Bonner is a piss ant. He's not a real oil company. With him gone there's only a group of heirs and investors left that won't know what to do, and they will be anxious to deal with us on our terms. They won't have the patience to wait out the litigation."

Brubeck nodded.

"Now," Chambers continued, forming his words carefully, "you will file your motion in circuit court. I'll ask my friend on the bench to find a way to preside. But we won't wait for Bonner to fight us in appellate court, which he will. You will find a way to persuade Mr. Bonner that he ought to go back to wherever he came from and get out of our way." He paused and let Brubeck absorb the words. "And if he won't, you will make him go away. Do you understand?" He emphasized the word *make.*

Emmett wiped the torrent pouring from his forehead. "Matt, you're the one who is, ah, better equipped to *persuade* people to, ah, go away, you know? Perhaps you would—"

"If I have to do it, Brubeck, why do I need you in this deal? I didn't come up here to play legal cat and mouse."

Brubeck squirmed and mopped his face again, then nodded. "I'll think on it. Matt. I will."

"You do that."

Ethan mumbled something as they walked across the grass to the graveside service.

"What?" Laura asked.

"I was thinking how happy it would have been to give Noble the news about the discovery." She squeezed his hand.

Ethan and five others hauled Noble Abrams's casket out of the hearse and placed it on the lowering device over the grave. He noticed other oilmen from around the area standing aside as the minister said the final prayers. Many of them eyed him.

Afterward Mr. Baumgarten, of the bank, came up to him. "He talked about you a lot on the golf course," he said, wiping his eyes.

"He did?" Ethan asked, surprised.

"Yes. He told that story about your dad saving him to everybody he met. And he said you would hit big someday." Baumgarten managed a smile and slapped Ethan's arm as he turned away.

Ethan called after him. "I did!"

Baumgarten turned. "I know." He nodded toward the casket. "He knows, too."

Ethan and Laura were the last to leave. He waited for the

attendants to lower the casket into the hole, then he uncapped a small jar of black fluid and sprinkled it onto Noble's box.

The all-night drive back from Shreveport sapped his energy, but having Laura to spell him at the wheel saved him. His mind kept going back to Baumgarten's remark.

"What did Mr. Baumgarten mean, Laura?"

"Huh?" she answered, her head leaning against his shoulder.

"When Baumgarten said Noble knew about my strike. How could he have known?"

She raised up and rubbed her eyes. She looked at him. "Ethan, everything happens for a reason. Noble came in to your life. He helped you, and he went out. His purpose in your life was served. I think that's what Baumgarten was trying to say—that Noble knew he had a role in the direction your life went." She snuggled closer. "Yes. He knew. He knew who you were, who you are, and who you can be. Be thankful for him and quit exasperating yourself. Be free from trying prove yourself to other people." She laid her head back on his shoulder.

He smiled. "Do I have to prove anything to you?"

"No."

He loved the gentle feel of her head against his shoulder. It made him realize what a lonely life he had been living and how badly he needed her. But other, darker thoughts clawed their way into his mind, and he resented their intrusion. He tried to blot them out. But they wouldn't go away. Was she at his side because of the oil? Wasn't he just a convenient escape from Fossil Rim for her? What if she were just a skillful actress? Where would that leave him if he found out too late?

He drove on in the dark early morning hours across the Mississippi River at Vicksburg, eastbound to Fossil Rim pondering the seeming miracles that had gotten him this far, and the one he hoped was sleeping at his shoulder.

At 4:15 a.m. he stopped in front of Laura's house to drop her off.

"Why are you stopping?" she asked.

"To let you off!"

"You said they were about to bring oil up. I'm not going to miss this."

He grinned and they drove on to the well, arriving just in time in to see the Halliburton crew rigging up their perforation truck.

"Glad you could make it, boss man," Grady yelled as he lowered the tool. Ethan poured a cup of strong coffee and went over to stand beside the Halliburton engineer's console, watching him adjust knobs and switches. The hard-hatted man turned to him. "You ready?"

"Shoot it," Ethan said, then turned his head up to the rig floor, grinning at Grady. He made a motion with his hand as if firing an imaginary pistol. Grady nodded and grinned.

The Halliburton man punched a button, watched his instrument needles dance and proclaimed, "Good shoot!"

The crew began tripping out of the hole.

"What are they doing now?" Laura asked.

"They're bringing the perforating tool out of the hole." He saw the next question forming on her face. "The tool is a long pipe with little guns spaced up and down it. When he pushed that button, the guns all fired bullets that went through the pipe wall, through the cement and out into the rock formation. That's the way the oil will come through. If it's got enough pressure it'll come straight on up as they pull the gun out. If it doesn't follow the gun up we will have to go back in with a swab cup and get the oil started out by sucking it. That's called swabbing. We'll see in a few hours."

"First I've got to meet with J.D. Then I have to go to Jackson right away," he told her. "Got to get a loan."

"Why can't you do that here?"

He sighed, thinking of the small community bank. "Not even in Mobile. I need a bank that does business with the oil business. Jackson is the nearest. I'll get some sleep and leave tonight."

At lunch time the perforating tool reached the surface and following it up, a long slug of rich brown crude. It sprayed all over the rig floor, messing it up again. Tiny's crew had toiled after the DST cleaning the rig. Now it was oil soaked again, but this time they quickly turned the oil flow through valves and pipes out to the reserve pit. After a couple of hundred barrels flowed through, free of mud, Ethan was satisfied. He ordered Grady to shut in and start rigging down. He hurried to the trailer and made a couple of calls.

The first went to a supply company in Laurel. He rented three 1,000 barrel stock tanks, to be delivered. The next call went to another company who would come and run tests to determine the flow rate and pressures. He needed that data to take to the bank, but knew he couldn't wait that long. He decided to take what information he had about his well and head to Jackson. If they needed more he would forward it later.

Ethan woke up feeling beaten and spent. Bringing Grady on as tool pusher and roommate in the trailer had hidden consequences. Grady's snoring was worse than J.D.'s. He hurried to the restaurant and sat down with J.D. at their usual corner table, which they preferred because it was mostly out of earshot of the other tables. The restaurant rarely let anyone else use it, and they kept the adjacent tables empty when they could. Ethan rubbed tired eyes.

"Did you get Ole Abrams buried?" J.D. said as he shuffled through his papers. Ethan glared at him. J.D. looked up. "I'm sorry, man. That sounded insensitive. I know he meant a lot to you."

Ethan nodded. He ordered coffee while J.D. peered at a legal pad through his reading lenses, stabbing at it with a pencil. Before getting into the leases Ethan decided it was time to solve a mystery.

"Are you ready to tell me now?"

"Tell you what?" J.D. muttered without looking up.

"Why you didn't tell me you were an engineer—and a lawyer, for Pete's sake!"

"I don't remember ever promisin' you I'd talk about that."

"Yes, you did. You said, *later.* Remember? Our first day here."

"I must've been drunk."

"No you weren't. Dammit, now tell me."

The rare curse from Ethan brought J.D.'s eyes from the legal pad to Ethan's face. He sipped coffee and coughed. "Okay. I don't really think it's any business of yours, but I got a petroleum engineerin' degree at Mississippi State University and went to work for Gulf Oil, which kept me out of the war, which displeased me very much. I wanted to kill Japs and Nazis. But they said they needed oilmen, so they wouldn't let me enlist. I worked for Gulf and a couple of small companies for a few years, doing reservoir estimates and designing completion plans and such."

Ethan stared at him, waiting for elaboration.

"That's it." J.D. said as if hoping to put the subject to an end.

Ethan's stare remained riveted on the landman. "And a lawyer, too, huh?"

J.D. finished his coffee, threw a quarter on the table, grabbed the papers and started to rise.

"Sit down," Ethan commanded. J.D. looked to see if anyone heard the rebuke, then slowly lowered himself back into the chair. He put both hands on the table, palms down and studied the back of his hands. Ethan became strangely uneasy, seeing J.D. without a cigarette or a cup in his hands.

"I decided I might have a go at lawyerin'. Oil lawyers were making big money." He heaved a deep breath and let it out. He stared at his hands for several heavy breaths before continuing. "I never took the Bar exam." He swallowed and paused. Ethan wanted to swab it out of him but knew he needed to let J.D. say it at his pace.

"My wife died just as I finished law school."

Ethan's jaw dropped.

"Cancer," J.D. muttered, nodding at the table top. "I watched it murder her." He sighed, still staring at the tablecloth. "I took to drinkin'. I became a beer-drunk—the worst kind of alcoholic there is." He turned to Ethan. "I'm not trying to offer any excuses. So now you know. Let's talk about these leases."

"Wait," Ethan said, but J.D. interrupted.

"Now you're gonna ask why I never took the Bar, never engineered again. Well, I'll tell you. Because I just didn't give a damn anymore. Eventually I had to do something to buy groceries and beer and pay my rent, so I started doing land work. I had a course in mineral law, and that helped me get into the land leasing game. I never had any interest whatsoever in going back to engineering, and nobody would have me anyway. Now let's talk about these leases."

"Children?" Ethan asked.

J.D. looked down. He shook his head.

"I'm sorry about your wife."

J.D. nodded at the table.

"Okay," Ethan said, after a long thoughtful pause. "What have you got?"

J.D. looked to make sure no one was sitting or standing nearby and unfolded his lease map. His finger tapped a green shaded block. "The Buchanan family leases. Are you finally ready to make a play for them? I know for a fact that Sunrise Oil is talking to him, as well as possibly others."

Ethan straightened, alarmed. "Already?"

"Already—yes!" J.D. snapped. "Hell, they were talkin' to them before we got our results. Word gets out fast, you know. And we got to act fast, or we'll lose leases that we ought to have done got."

Ethan nodded pensively. The need to get to Jackson quickly pressed in on him. He needed more money, now. He realized he had been spending too much time the last few days overseeing the completion work on the hole. He needed to let Grady take care of that. He straightened and started to get up. "Okay. Keep working on it. I've got to go find a banker who'll lend to us."

"Wait a minute. Sit down. I'm not finished."

Ethan complied. J.D. pointed at another tract on the map east of the Hull acreage. "How bad do you want this?"

Ethan studied the map. "We've got to have it. The field may extend that far."

"Well, there's a little problem. Those minerals are severed. I found the owner, one Mrs. Margaret Hogan of Avenal, California. She agreed to $50 an acre and 1/8th."

"That's all right," Ethan said. "And, out of good will, let's give the surface owner of that tract a generous damages settlement."

J.D. nodded. "I was gonna do just that."

Ethan rose. "I've got to get to the bank."

"Wait." J.D. commanded. "We've got another decision to make."

Ethan sat again.

J.D.'s hand swept across the map. "Look here at all these town lots. Half acres. Third acres. An acre here and there. Hundreds of 'em. They are all in your buy box. You want 'em?"

Ethan let out a heavy sigh. He had long been aware that the town lot problem would sooner or later challenge him. "If we don't get them others will."

"I can't do that myself, Ethan, and it would cost you a fortune to hire a team of landmen to do it. But I've got an idea, if you want to try it."

"Let's hear it."

"Let one of the local men do it. Insurance salesmen are no strangers to legal documents, and they know their local territory. I already know one. Had coffee with him a few times here. I'll give him some quick pointers and turn him loose. We can offer him ten dollars for every lot he leases."

"Sounds doable," Ethan muttered. "And it would free you up to do this other stuff. Who is he?"

"Name's Winfred Sweeney."

Ethan nodded and got up.

"Wait," J.D. said. "Would you please sit down? You ain't thinkin' things through."

Ethan lowered himself, wondering what else.

"You do know that you can't just start selling oil without the state's permission, don't you?"

"Damn," Ethan uttered, slapping a hand on the table. "Forgot about that." He ran his hand through his hair, then looked at his landman. You take care of that."

"Huh? Ethan you hired me to lease minerals, not to—"

"Maybe Miss Clarice will want to take a nice trip to Tuscaloosa with you," Ethan interjected. "And I'll pay you your normal day rate."

J.D. pondered, nodded, and smiled. "Okay."

Ethan smiled over how easily the landman warmed to the idea of the trip. "Visit the state offices and get us a temporary order to produce. Can you do that yourself without getting a lawyer up there?"

"I doubt that, but I'll try."

"Also, while you're there you might as well walk a permit through for the next location, the Hull No. 2. Before I leave for Jackson tonight I'll fill out the form and leave it in the trailer. Get it and take it with you."

J.D. nodded, gathered his papers, and they headed out. A man met them at the door holding a land deed wanting to offer his lease. Ethan told the man J.D. would have a look to see if it was in the buy box. He slapped J.D.'s back and took off. "I'm going back out to the location to see what's happening."

Ethan chose the Jackson Guaranty Bank, the biggest bank in the state, to apply for his loan—a bank he knew did regular business with the oil community. J.D. had given him the name of the bank's petroleum department manager. He hauled a briefcase with him containing the engineering and geologic data he hoped would convince the bank to give him a loan.

"I'm glad you came to us, Mr. Bonner," the banker said, vigorously shaking Ethan's hand. "You know, we are the major bank here in the Deep South for petroleum financing. And congratulations on your discovery!"

Ethan sat, speechless. He put his brief case on the floor. Apparently it wouldn't be needed.

The banker started without waiting for Ethan's requests. "I can approve $250,000 right away. We can perhaps approve more later, after we do an engineering assessment of your discovery. The monthly installments will be $10,000 plus 5 percent interest on the balance. Would that work for you, sir?" Before Ethan could answer, the banker asked, smiling, "And how long before you get some oil flowing?"

Ethan wanted to tell the man to slow down. This was all too fast. A quarter million bucks? He couldn't imagine having such cash. But he knew he might need much more. "Ah, we hope to start selling the product right away—say in two weeks or less."

The banker grinned then turned business-like. "Now, we can't release the funds without security. We need copies of all your leases and we will execute a lien on all of them." He dipped his head and peered at Ethan over his glasses rims.

Ethan nodded. He had expected that. He had copies with him. "Sure."

They shook hands and the banker escorted him to another department where the loan papers were prepared on the spot. In thirty minutes Ethan walked out into the hot Jackson sun tucking his new checkbook into his coat pocket, smiling. It was lunchtime.

He sat at a table in the King Edward hotel, ordered a hamburger and a Coke and did some quick mental calculations. He already owed almost half of that $250,000. He needed to get the crude flowing quickly. He ate fast.

A man approached, and he looked up. Robert Mercer held out his hand. "Nice discovery, Mr. Bonner. Nice indeed! We can help you if you need another rig."

"Thank you," Ethan managed, swallowing a big bite, and getting up. "Thank you, but we're okay for now." He picked up a napkin and wiped his lips.

"Well, well!" Both men turned at the approach of two more suit-clad men. "Bob, is this Ethan Bonner?" one of them asked.

"Yes, it is," Mercer said. He introduced the men to Ethan. They were two of Jackson's most successful independent oilmen. They congratulated him and asked questions about his well. He gave vague answers and they smiled—the smiles of men knowing they would have done the same. The three politely excused themselves and wished him well.

He paid his bill, found a phone booth, followed the operator's instructions, dropped the requisite number of quarters in the slot, and dialed J.D.'s room number. When the landman answered he said, "I've got a loan. I'll be in tonight. Get ready to hit the leasing trail!"

17

BUCHANAN

Laura slowly pushed her grocery cart past the fresh vegetables at the Piggly Wiggly and paused to examine a head of lettuce. Suddenly a pair of hands closed on her eyes from behind.

"Guess who?"

She peeled the hands away and turned.

"Let me push this for ya, Sweetheart," Benny said, chomping gum.

"I can manage, Benny." She couldn't help cracking a smile.

He ignored her and grabbed the cart. She put the lettuce in and walked ahead, pausing to select a bundle of celery.

"Ya know," he said between chomps, "I've been real busy lately. Ain't had much time to spend with you."

"Is that so?" she said softly, walking on toward the meat cooler. "I haven't even noticed."

"We need to get together, like old times, you know?"

She looked over the chicken and selected a frier.

"You gonna cook that for me?"

"No, Benny. It's just for little ole me."

He followed her, still pushing the cart, to the dairy area. She picked up a carton of eggs and put it in.

"How'd you like to have a servant cook that for you?"

She turned and looked at him. He raised his eyebrows and grinned.

"And one to clean house for you too? A big house!" He chomped some more, still grinning.

"What on earth are you taking about?"

He grinned bigger than ever. "I'm gonna be the richest man in town, I'm tellin ya. We won't have to worry about nothin'."

She saw him shift his gaze. "Oh, hi there, Miss Clarice!" he said.

She turned and saw Clarice holding a hand basket, looking as chipper as ever, cocking her head, smiling. "Hi, Benny. Hi, Laura."

Laura started to explain. "Benny and I just—"

Benny cut her off. "Ah, we were just discussin' how were are goin' to spend the oil money."

Laura saw that Clarice's smile was animated. Clarice waved a hand.

"Ahm, got to go! Ta ta!" She turned and hurried up another aisle.

"Benny, quit it! It's not old times. Now go and let me shop."

"Okay," he said, turning more serious. "But I meant that. We could travel all over the world. Anywhere you want. Live anywhere you want."

She pushed her cart faster. "That oil man is just gonna go from dirty old well to dirty old well the rest of his life. Rags to riches and rags again. That's the way it is with those people." She stopped abruptly, pretending to examine the cheeses. "We're not getting any younger, Laura," he called from behind.

Something—she didn't know what—compelled her to turn. He was gone.

After arriving back from Jackson, Ethan went to the motel and found J.D. going over the lease map. "Give me the map," he said, as they sat down with their coffee. J.D. slid it to him. Ethan took a straight edge and a red pencil and tripled the size of the buy box.

J.D.'s jaw dropped. "Ethan, we don't even have all the leases in your original buy box yet. I'm going to have to—"

"It's okay," Ethan said. "I know. You need help. Hire some more landmen. We've got to get moving. And we've got some money. Not enough to buy that whole box." He tapped the map. "But more will come."

J.D. let out a big sigh. "Man, it's about time. I'll make some calls. I'll get a couple of people down here to help us. But why such a big area?"

"Wait," Ethan said. "It's time you see something. I'll be right back." He went out to his car and lifted the trunk. He grabbed his geological structure map—the one he had made in Gulf's office and carried to Texas to help sell his deal. He took it back in. "This is confidential, you understand? I don't want you talking about it."

J.D nodded. Ethan unrolled it. J.D. stood to get a broader view. He looked back at Ethan. "Do you think it's really that big?"

Ethan grinned and shrugged. "Who knows? What if we've got oil down to the lowest closed contour?"

"What if?" J.D. said. "I'll tell you *what if*. If the oil-water contact is even half way down to the lowest closed contour you've discovered a giant oil field, my friend—a 100 million barrel field, at the least. Very few giants have ever been found, Ethan. Especially east of the Mississippi."

Ethan gathered up the map. "Well, it's too early to be talking about slaying giants. Much can happen. Besides, I suspect there are dozens of scattered oil sands down there, not just one big one. Anyway, we need to drill, drill, drill, and analyze the pressure data. We'll find out soon enough."

"Oh, did you get everything done we needed to do in Tuscaloosa?" Ethan asked.

"Yup. Not a problem. The new permit and the temporary production order is over there in that folder. I looked around for a lawyer who does oil-and-gas work and came up dry. But we'll figure somethin' out.

"Good job."

"Clarice and I had a good time up there," J.D. said while

lighting up. We took in a John Wayne picture. A really good one, man. You ought to go see it—*The Searchers.*

Ethan sighed. "Were they searching for oil, too?"

"Nope. Just a girl."

"I wish I had time for movies."

"Yeah, it was a good trip." J.D chuckled. "They're all excited up there about a new football coach who came down from Kentucky to take over at the University."

"Haven't got time for sports either," Ethan uttered. "By the way, has your man, Sweeny, gotten started on the town lots?"

J.D. picked up a pile of lease forms and dropped them in front of Ethan. "He's been doing some quick work."

Ethan's eyes widened as he looked at the pile. "Already?"

"Yup." Of course they're all one-half acre and one-third acre lots. They don't amount to much. But remember, we owe him ten dollars for each one."

Ethan picked up the top lease and studied it closely, then looked at the next one, and the next. He frowned. "It seems we're paying him more than that."

"What?" J.D. said.

Ethan looked at him. "Did you promise him an override?"

"Hell no!"

"Well, what's that?" He pointed to Sweeney's hand-written words on the lease forms: *Subject to a 1/64th overriding royalty interest payable to Winfred L. Sweeney.*

J.D. studied the entry. "Well, that little rat bastard. I didn't tell him he could do that." J.D. started to get up. "That's not a legal entry. Any court will throw that out. I'll straighten this out."

"Wait," Ethan said. "Let it be. It'll keep him motivated. There are a ton of lots out there to lease. And we've got bigger fish to fry."

J.D. nodded and sat. "And speakin' of bigger fish, we've got more competition. I've already seen strangers in the courthouse. This place is about to start poppin'."

"What about Buchanan? Is he still holding out?"

"Oh, almost forgot to tell you. "I've got a dinner invitation from Ben, believe it or not, tonight."

Ethan's brow lifted. "Tremendous! Why don't you take Clarice? She might keep Corrine occupied while you and Ben talk."

"Yup. Done thought of that."

Ethan hugged Edna that evening after another gigantic feed. "Halliburton is putting on a crawfish boil out at the new well location Friday afternoon," he told Laura, Edna, and Hub. "Y'all are invited. Please come out."

"Well, that'd be good," said Hub. "I haven't eaten crawfish in a long spell. Can my deputies come? The mayor, too?"

"Sure," Ethan said.

"That's right nice of them to do that," Hub said.

Ethan chuckled. "After all I've paid them, I'm sure somehow I'm paying for it."

Ethan said goodbye to Hub and Edna and walked out patting his stomach. He and Laura walked toward her house, and he told her about J.D. and Clarice going on the Tuscaloosa trip together.

Laura giggled. "She's good for him."

"That's exactly what he said."

They walked in silence for a while. Ethan wondered if she was thinking what he was thinking. Was Laura good for him? Was he good for her? Every day he had begun to think about her more often, although there had been no more kisses like the one that day the oil rained on them. And no more talk of love, either. She had been the first to broach that subject. He wondered if she were waiting on him to use that word. He didn't know if he could say it. Hell, he had *never* said it, except in reference to food or to the fragrance of warm crude oil.

They sat on the porch swing listening to the cicadas serenade them. Laura mentioned that she had bumped into Benny Hull at the grocery market.

"Did you, now?" Ethan asked, trying to sound casual.

She nodded. "I'm not trying to play games with you. The only reason I mentioned that is, he said something that was very curious to me."

"What did he say?"

"He said he was coming into some big money."

Ethan didn't like the sound of that, but dismissed it as hollow bragging. "Well, I guess he expects his daddy will share some of that royalty with him."

She shook her head. "I don't know about that. Benny has always been an exaggerator, but he wasn't talking about a few thousand dollars. He was talking about millions of dollars. Or so he said."

Ethan frowned. "Where did he come up with that?"

Laura shrugged again.

He wondered in silence what Benny might have been talking about.

J.D. felt Clarice's shoulder cuddling against his as they drove slowly down one of Fossil Rim's stateliest streets. Spanish moss hung like old disheveled gray beards from gigantic oak trees on either side of the street. Between the strands he saw glimpses of antebellum style homes with tall, floodlit columns. Here and there he saw Victorian houses, most in need of upkeep.

A petite, neat-as-a-pin woman of about 55 years, Clarice was a fixture at the courthouse. She knew it front and back and knew everybody in town. J.D. remembered when she had told him she was aware that people around town couldn't quite understand what she saw in him. He had shrugged and cackled, but his insides didn't fell too good about hearing that. Yet she had also told him she thought he was an honest man, if a bit earthy. He had been up-front with her about his alcohol problem, and she had told him that even with his faults he was a huge improvement over the previous unmentionable man in her life. He had not promised her anything, but had not had a drink in a long spell.

"Next house on the left," Clarice said. J.D. parked. He leaned over and kissed her on the cheek. "Hope I have better luck gettin' that lease tonight."

They went to the door and rang the bell. Corrine opened it. She greeted them and hugged Clarice. The Buchannans had known Clarice for decades. Corrine flashed a strained smile at J.D. and invited them in.

J.D. had met with Ben several times already at the mercantile to discuss leasing the rest of the Buchanan family's vast acreage, most of which was cut-over timberland. Ben didn't own it all by himself, but his brothers and sisters wanted him to negotiate on their behalf. Yet Ben was in no hurry to lease, and he didn't hesitate to let J.D. know he had talked to other companies.

Ben greeted them, and they all sat at the supper table. They dined on pork tenderloin smothered in gravy, mashed potatoes, succotash, and hot buttered biscuits. They chased it all with sweet lemon-laced iced tea. J.D. savored every bite and began coveting a cigarette but, knowing the Buchannans didn't smoke, managed to hold his compulsion at bay.

Clarice did a fair job of engaging Corrine in chit-chat, but every time J.D. steered the conversation between himself and Ben to the topic of oil Corinne stopped in mid-sentence with whatever she was saying to Clarice and bore in on the men.

When supper was over the women cleared the table. J.D. went out on the porch and burned a cigarette then came back in and saw Ben spreading maps of his family's lands on the table. J.D. opened his briefcase and pulled out his own maps. They both studied each other's maps for a while to determine that they showed the same thing, a procedure they had already been through twice. Ben's map was slightly different, but J.D. was confident that his—constructed from his own courthouse research—was the most accurate.

The Buchanan family owned 1,828 acres across the county, most of it concentrated south and down-dip of the Hull well. Ben asked what *down-dip* meant, and J.D. explained that was the direction the rock strata was inclined downward. Since oil wanted to move upward, any lands deemed down-dip were less probable to hold oil. Been nodded, as if comprehending. Because of the probability of the lands being down-dip, J.D. told Ben that Mr. Bonner estimated that only about a fourth of the entire tract was prospective of oil. But Ben was shrewd. He had insisted that he would lease all or none.

Ben knew the acreage was getting more valuable each day as oil speculators flowed into town. J.D. had opened the offer at the first meeting with $25 per acre plus a 1/8th royalty. Ben had let silence speak, and it spoke well. J.D. was a skilled negotiator, but his one weakness was silence. He abhorred a vacuum and the more he talked, the closer he had moved into Ben's camp.

Finally J.D. thought he might be getting close to a deal. Being invited to Ben's home seemed a breakthrough. J.D. had gotten Ethan's approval to pay $75 an acre—a huge piece of change for Ethan—plus 3/16th royalty.

With the numbers being batted around between J.D. and Ben, Clarice was not able to keep Corrine corralled. Corrinne sat down and stared at the men as they talked, her eyes bulging, hands nervously darting to various parts of her attire. With each offer J.D. made, Corrine urged Ben to go higher. Ben would only flash an annoyed glance at her then look back at the maps while J.D. squirmed. Clarice sat back, sipped her coffee and studied Corrine's dining room furnishings.

J.D. finally shook his head. "Seventy-five dollars is all I can offer, Ben. And three-sixteenths. That's generous, sir. That is!"

Ben yawned, got up from the table, and thanked the couple for coming to supper. As they walked to the door J.D. felt the sinking notion that the deal was escaping him.

At the door Corrine hugged Clarice, limply shook J.D.'s hand and excused herself. Ben watched her retire and turned to J.D. "Mr. Whitley, you've got a deal!"

J.D.'s eyebrows arched. He broke into a grin, then laughed.

"Okay!" He grabbed Ben's hand again. "Let me write out the lease and a bank draft."

"No. No. We can do that tomorrow. Come by the store in the morning."

"Swell," J.D. said. "I'll see you in the morning."

When he closed the door, Ben turned and saw Corrine behind him, her arms straight down, hands curled in a fist. "You could've gotten more!"

He waved her off, heading for the bedroom. "I got him up a bunch. Enough is enough, Corrine."

She followed him. "But what about that other company that talked to you? Who was it? Sunrise Oil? Won't they offer more?"

"Yeah, I suppose I could get them to top it by a few dollars an acre, or so. But I'm tired of this haggling. Besides, I'd rather them boys who came in here first and made all this happen get the lease. Sunrise Oil and the others just came running here when they saw Mr. Bonner strike oil. If he hadn't been here first, them others wouldn't give us the time of day."

"Well, I don't care who was here first, top dollar is top dollar!"

"I know what your saying, Corrine. It's just that I'm tired of playin' them against each other. I don't enjoy it. Besides, it's done. We shook hands on it."

The next morning, as the sun broke through a misty cloud layer, Ethan looked out his trailer window and saw Halliburton's cooks rigging up their boilers for that afternoon's scheduled crawfish boil. He finished writing a check, the size of which would have broken him a few weeks before. He ripped it from his book and handed it to the test crew foreman. The service company from Mississippi had finished installing the necessary equipment to begin production: a valve assembly—called a *Christmas tree* because of its abundance of appendages: gauges, handles and knobs—and the three 1,000 barrel stock tanks.

"We tested the flow," the man said. "Here is the pressure data."

He handed Ethan the papers. "As you can see, your well flowed 305 barrels into the tank in less than six hours with no pressure decline." Then the man grinned. "You'll be needin' a big tanker here about every week, Mr. Bonner." Ethan matched the grin, shook the man's hand and walked to his car. "Don't pull her too hard!" the man advised as he got into his truck.

Ethan didn't intend to take any chances. He would comply with the state's temporary production order which allowed him to flow at a maximum of 200 hundred barrels per day. To increase the flow higher could pre-maturely deplete the pressure and draw up water. The well would be ruined. He had seen it happen.

As the men drove away, he saw Lucky Lucy's derrick being raised beyond a tree line over at the location he had staked for the Hull No. 2. He looked around. Other than the Christmas tree, the tanks, and the boilers being set up, the Hull No. 1 location was now just a big scuff on the land, with some scattered pieces of debris and equipment lying around between massive ruts and puddles. The reserve pits were still there, but he would have them pumped out and then bring Peavy and his dozer back to level the site.

Ethan began thinking about hiring a pumper to manage the well—and those to come, hopefully. He thought Peavy might be a good choice and was thinking of asking him. Then he looked around to the sound of Sheriff Tant's cruiser braking to a stop.

"Morning Hub," Ethan said, greeting the lawman as he unfolded his big frame from the car.

Hub spat tobacco and surveyed the site. He shook his head. "You people sure do know how to get that machinery in and out quick. But I hope you'll be cleaning this mess up."

"I've already arranged to have the mud pumped out of the pits and have them bulldozed over. We'll smooth this area out, plant rye grass and get it back as close to the way it was as we can."

Hub stared for a few more seconds and looked at Ethan. He held out an envelope.

"What's this," Ethan asked.
"It's an injunction."

Ben Buchanan had hardly gotten the door to the mercantile unlocked when he saw J.D. Whitley coming.

"Good morning, Mr. Buchanan," Whitley yelled.

"Good morning. Come in and have some coffee."

Ben filled a cup for J.D. and they sat at the round table the old timers usually gathered round about 10 a.m. to chew, spit, and tell lies. They were the only two people in the store. Corrine usually didn't come in until about nine, and J.D. was glad of it.

J.D. opened the briefcase and got out the lease, pointing to the essential features. "It's all filled out. Here's your three-sixteenths royalty. Here's the term, three years. One dollar-a-year rentals. And here's the bonus, $75 an acre." He reached back into his briefcase and got an envelope. "And here's the bank draft for $137,100. A nice sum."

Ben looked at the draft, and then studied the lease. J.D. asked permission to smoke and lit up.

There was a knock at the door. Both men turned. A man in a gray suit stood outside peering in. Buchanan got up and let him in. "Hello, Mr. Buchanan," he said, smiling. He nodded to J.D.

J.D. looked but didn't smile or get up. He looked back at Buchanan. The man walked to the table and laid down a lease. "Mr. Buchanan," he said, "I don't know what this gentleman has offered you, but Sunrise Oil Company wants your lease and this will prove it. He placed a draft in front of Buchanan.

Buchanan's lips moved as he read it, whispering. "Two hundred thousand dollars!"

"Yes sir," the Sunrise man said. "Two hundred thousand dollars. Ah, is that more than this gentleman's check?" He stepped back and grinned.

J.D. coughed and looked up at his competitor. Ben looked at them both, then stared out toward the street. Finally he said,

"Excuse me." He slowly got up and went back to his small desk the in store's back room. He sat and rubbed his jaw, listening to the murmurs of the men talking out front. Occasionally one of them raised a voice, but Ben didn't care what they were saying to each other.

He swiveled his chair around and looked out the tiny window, seeing only the aged brickwork of the drug store next door. After a while he turned back to his desk and studied the photographs of his children and grandchildren. Below the pictures he saw the old Bible, tattered and frayed, that he read every morning. His lips moved silently for a minute, then stopped. He leaned over the desk, put his forehead in his hands and closed his eyes.

He didn't know how much time had passed but he realized the talk out front had ebbed after a crescendo of shouts and curses. He got up and walked back out to the round table. The two men stopped arguing and watched him.

Ethan stood staring at the envelope, his mouth hanging open. His hand began to tremble.

"They're stopping you from selling oil, Mr. Bonner," Sherriff Tant said.

"Who?"

"The Hulls."

"What?" Ethan cried, opening the envelope.

"I'm not supposed to open that envelope, and I didn't, but I know what is says. Benny says you tricked his daddy into leasing for nothing. He says you took advantage of him being old and senile. That's probably not the exact words them lawyers use, but I know what goes on around here. They've petitioned Judge Bundy to nullify your lease, and he has ordered you not to produce any oil until after the hearing he has set for September 16."

Ethan looked up from the papers, realizing that in one hand he had the technical data proving he had a great oil well and in the other a challenge to take that well away from him. He breathed through an open mouth and stared afar. Hub shook his head and got into the cruiser.

"You let me know if I can help. Good luck."

Ethan nodded. September 16 was almost a month away. The money in his loan from the Jackson Guaranty Bank would be gone by then if he didn't sell oil. He leaned against the hood of the car and dropped his head.

"What's the matter, Boss?" Grady asked from behind. Ethan had not even heard the Buick arrive while talking with the sheriff. He turned and looked at Grady, anger welling, eyes tearing.

Grady dropped his cigarette butt, stepped on it and studied Ethan, waiting. "You okay?"

Ethan handed him the injunction. Grady put on glasses and looked it over. He looked up. "What'll you do?"

"Get a lawyer."

"Whew!" Grady said, shaking his head. He looked at the distant sight of the raised derrick. "You want us to shut down?"

"No!" Ethan blurted. "The injunction doesn't say we can't drill. It says we can't produce. Keep drilling."

"Yeah," Grady said. "They would want that. They want us to drill 'em more wells at our expense. You got other leases, ain't ya? Let's move to one of them."

"Spud in where you are," Ethan commanded. "I don't want to step out and drill an outpost. Too risky. I've got to develop what I've found."

Grady nodded slowly and kicked at the dirt.

Ethan glanced toward the east, seeing the derrick's crown, now vertical, over the line of pines. If he made a well there, too, it would also be stolen from him. That same rotten feeling that he had suffered from so often in Panama, welled up and sickened him.

Ben sat down at the round table and looked at the two leases.

The Sunrise man leaned forward expectantly, grinning, nodding. J.D. held back, eyes shifting from papers to Ben and back again.

Ben swallowed hard and picked up the pen. He looked at the Sunrise Oil draft, then at the Bonner Oil draft. He leaned back and looked around slowly at the store and all its shelves and items. He gazed long toward the door and out the windows at the street while the two oilmen fidgeted.

He pulled J.D.'s lease form and signed it.

J.D. let out a huge sigh of relief. The Sunrise man began cursing. Ben interrupted him and asked him to leave. He grabbed his papers and draft and started for the door as Corrine came in. He yelled at her as he swept out, waving the $200,000 check in her face. "Your husband just turned down an extra $63,000!"

Stunned, she turned and looked at Ben and J.D. "What?" She trotted over to the table. "What's he talking about, Ben? What?"

J.D. quickly gathered his copy of the lease and hurried for the door.

She looked at the draft. "What did that man offer you? What?"

Ben picked up J.D.'s draft and got up. "Two hundred thousand dollars, Corrine. That's what he offered."

"And you didn't take it?!"

He shook his head. "No. I didn't. Last night I gave my word to Mr. Whitley. I shook hands on it."

"You idiot!" She slapped him.

Ben stood still, making no move toward her. He put his hand to his face. "I'm going to the bank, Corrine. I've got to deposit this." He got his hat and started out.

She slammed her purse to the floor and began sobbing.

He looked back at her. "I'm sorry, Corrinne. There was nothing else I could do."

She sat at the table and buried her head in her hands. "You, on your high horse," she moaned. She looked up as he went through the door and yelled. "To hell with you!"

He froze momentarily but didn't look back, then turned toward the bank.

"Mr. Chambers wants you to call," Darlene said, as Emmett came in the door, coffee in hand.

"Okay. Dial him." He went into his office, stood at the window facing south and waited. Now that the derrick had moved he couldn't make out any features at the first Hull location. Darlene stuck her head in and announced Chambers was on the phone, then shut the door.

Emmett tried some start-up talk, but Chambers got right to his point. "Yes, Matt," Emmett said, still standing. "They served him the injunction this morning."

Chambers wanted to know how long before the lease could be transferred to Benny.

"Oh, we've already done it, Matt." Emmett grinned. We recorded it at the courthouse yesterday. That's a done deal."

Chambers wanted to know when Benny's lease would be subdivided the three ways agreed upon.

"We'll do that as soon as you and I can set up holding companies—one for each of us." He lowered his voice. "We wouldn't want our names on the leases, at least not right away."

Emmett listened, nodded. "Sure, Matt. Sure. Okay. Goodb—" He didn't need to finish his goodbye. Chambers had hung up. He mumbled an unflattering reference to Chambers' character as he hung up the phone.

Ethan drove to Laura's place and told her about the injunction. They sat for a long time on the porch, not saying much. "How does a man defend himself when every cannon in the world is shooting at him?" Ethan asked.

Laura let out an exasperated laugh. "I'm not shootin' at you, Ethan." She took his hand.

He smiled. "Come on. Let's go to this silly crawfish boil and try to look happy."

They pulled into the location and saw a collection of unfamiliar vehicles parked about. Oil field service companies, drilling contractors, suppliers, and consultants from the oil regions to the west had found their way to south Alabama. Even Mr. Mercer and some of his staff were milling about.

Word of an oil field crawfish boil always spread quickly. Some local people were there as well, invited probably by J.D., Ethan reckoned.

"It looks like the whole county is out here," he remarked to Laura. He shut the engine off and looked at her. "This should be happy time for me. But it's not. The injunction—"

"I know," she said softly. She touched his shoulder. "Don't think about that. It'll work out."

He leaned over and kissed her.

They heard loud laughter as they walked up to join the crowd. Folks parted for them. A voice yelled, "And here comes the man who did it!"

People applauded. Grady forced a Falstaff into Ethan's hand. A cheer went up and cans were raised.

Ethan shook hands with the Halliburton men who had brought out the boilers and provided the drinks and crawfish. He made rounds greeting the crews and the salespeople. He held Laura's hand, towing her along.

A stranger approached and grabbed Ethan's hand, shaking it vigorously. "Mr. Bonner," he said. "I've been looking forward to meeting you. I'm Dr. Walter B. Jones, the Alabama State Geologist. I have known for many years this was coming for our state. Nobody believed me, but I knew it."

Ethan flashed a big grin. Finally, a co-believer. They chatted for a while and Ethan shuffled on.

He saw J.D. arm-in-arm with Clarice. He congratulated him again on landing the Buchanan lease. "Oh," he said nearly forgetting something as they started to part. "We're drilling the Hogan lease next. Isn't that the one with the severed minerals?"

J.D. confirmed it.

"Have you gotten out to that farmer yet and settled for damages?"

"Tomorrow," J.D. said. "First thing in the morning."

Ethan nodded approval and strolled to old man Hull, who was seated in a wheelchair, eyes shooting back and forth, round and about. Ethan doubted the old man knew anything about the injunction. He stopped and tried to chat with him but couldn't make out many words the man said. Benny walked up with a drink in hand. "So Mr. Bonner, I heard you can't sell any oil. That's too bad. Sounds like we need to do some business."

Mr. Hull looked up at the two, his lips moving, gibberish coming out. Benny ignored him.

"What business?" Ethan asked Benny, forcing a smile. "We've already done business." He waved his arm toward Lucky Lucy, now erected and waiting to spud the second well on the Hull property. "I'd say we've done y'all a pretty good job."

Benny chuckled and shook his head. "Yeah, but what you did ain't right. We'll see you in court."

Suddenly a loud burst of laughter roared behind them. Ethan turned. Grady was beckoning him to come to the boiler. Ethan saw Benny wink at Laura as they turned away.

Over by the gargantuan boiler stood his day and night crews, the off-duty ones tipping Schlitz and Falstaff cans and cackling.

"Oh, my," Laura said when she peered into the steaming cauldron. Crawfish—red as the setting sun and big as a man's hand—floated among pieces of corn on the cob, potatoes and links of sausages, their big pinchers bobbing, twisting, intertwining with each other like a big crustacean orgy. At first she thought they were actually alive, the way they writhed and wiggled, but then she realized the boiling water only made it appear so.

"Are they ready?" a voice boomed.

The Halliburton cook stirring the hotchpotch yelled, "Not quite."

Cuz emerged and peered into the boiling, steaming cauldron. "I'll test it. Let me at them mudbugs." Everybody stepped back. He reached in to the bobbling critters with his bare fingers and selected a large crawfish. He lifted it high so everyone could see it. He snapped the crawfish's body in two just behind the crustacean's hard head. With steam spewing from the head cavity, he pursed his lips and pulled the head to his mouth. He sucked the contents of the crawfish's head, cleaned out the cavity with his tongue, and smacked his lips. Then he shook his head slowly while grinning. "Mighty, mighty good, but not quite done yet."

Another roar of laughter and cheers rolled in.

Then a shadow moved over the 285-pound Cuz. "Child's play," Tiny said. Stand aside." Cuz did as told.

Tiny reached into the cauldron and extracted a glowing crimson crawfish with claws the size of clothes pins. As he stared Cuz in the face he stuffed the steaming mudbug into his mouth, tucking the head, whiskers, claws and tail in with his fingers, then chomped, crunched and smacked his lips.

A roar went up.

Laura grabbed her throat and said, "Oh, my God." She turned away.

Ethan saw one of the local men retching. He chuckled and looked around grinning at the men who had stuck with him.

"Mr. Mercer stepped up on a pile of heavy timbers and shouted, "Well folks, I guess now the oil field has officially arrived in Alabama!"

18

SHINE

Emma Shine came in from the front porch drying her hands on her apron, yelling for Grover. He emerged from the bathroom, pulling the straps of his overalls over his bare shoulders. "What the hell you yellin' 'bout, woman?"

"One of 'em's here. He's drivin' up."

"I been 'spectin' it. Git on back in, now."

The woman did as told but stayed back in the shadows, peering out toward the long dirt drive leading from the highway to their place. Dust curled and wafted behind the black Nash as it made its way past green cotton rows, the bolls not yet open. Grover lowered himself into the rocker on the porch, pulled his pocket knife out and began whittling. As the car approached he kept his gaze on his knifework.

For weeks he had practiced this moment over and over in his mind. He would play this oilman for all he was worth, never tipping his hand, never letting on like he was eager. This man was about to find out he wouldn't be dealing with an old man like Hull or a damn fool like Buchanan. He would make the oilman earn his pay. He would be cordial, but cool to the man. That would show him who was in charge. Above all, he would not make any quick decisions. He would let the oilman make an opening offer on his eighty acres. He would whittle on, then chuckle, shaking his head, not looking up. The oilman would know he had to go way higher. The times for people to talk down to Grover Shine were over.

People had looked down on him all his life. He was just a dirt farmer, like his daddy before him. Didn't have no education, never been further away than Biloxi. He went there for his induction physical. Hell, even the Army didn't want him in the middle of a war—flat feet, they said. Yeah, been nothin' but looked down on, all his days. His kids now, most of 'em grown. All but one of them moved off and got piddly-assed jobs. The youngest boy was the most promising. He was about to graduate high school and was talking college.

Son, how do you think I can pay for college? he remembered asking the boy. Even if the kid had sense enough to go, there was no way on God's green earth he could afford it. The boy left, and they didn't see him for hours. Emma scolded him, said he ought to have encouraged the boy, helped him. "Help him with what?" he had thundered at her. "How the hell am I gonna help him?" He had taken a bottle and went to the creek bank to drink it. But now. Now he really *could* help the boy. Now there was going to be money. Lots of it, most likely. His farm was right next to old Hull's. The oil couldn't just stop at the property line, could it? He shook his head and smirked. It'd be his lousy luck.

But he wasn't gonna think like that. The oil was down there right below his feet. Yeah, the money was coming. Now he would be able to call the boy in and sit him down and smile at him, and ask him which college he wanted to go to. And after that college bill was paid, he suspected there'd be plenty left to fix up this damned place and replace the old Farmall that he kept running with tape and baling wire. Oh yeah, that oilman comin' up the drive was what he'd waited for all his life.

But he wouldn't bow down to that man. No sir. He had some pride. He was in charge now. It was his eighty acres—his oil. And now after weeks of waiting, here they come to lease it. Man, how he had waited for this, and it would be worth the wait. He kept looking at his whittling, heard the car stop, the door open and slam, and voice of that oilman he had seen around town.

"Mr. Shine?"

He nodded but kept looking down at his whittling. He heard the man coming up the steps, heard him sigh.

"Shew! It's a hot one today."

He glanced up and saw a hand being extended. "J.D. Whitley. Bonner Oil Comp'ny."

Grover nodded, then jerked his head toward a stool he had placed on the porch for this occasion, a small stool. Whoever sat on it would not be comfortable and would be below his eye level.

J.D. paused to pull in a breath of humid air, then pointed west, back over his shoulder. "That's our rig over yonder." He sat on the stool wiping his forehead with a handkerchief, looking out at the fields. "Looks like you gonna have a good crop of white stuff, Mr. Shine."

Grover nodded, glanced up. "How's that well on the Hull place doin'?"

"It tested-out good," J.D. said. "But we've got it shut in for now. Got some paperwork to file, you know."

Grover looked at the oil man, then shifted his gaze to the west. "I been sittin' here on this porch watchin' that oil rig of you'rn."

Whitley careened around again and saw Lucky Lucy's derrick jutting above a distant tree line. "Yeah, boy! It's makin' hole real good!"

"Whose that other'n down south o' here." He jerked his knife in that direction.

Whitley looked. "That would be Mercer Drilling Company. They're puttin' in a hole for Sunrise Oil Compn'y down on the Morris farm. My man says that'll likely be a dry hole."

Grover stole a glance at him. Who did he think he was dealin' with, a child? So, the oilman thinks he can drop a hint that there ain't no oil south of here. That might make old Grover nervous and cause him to lease cheap. He nodded and cut at the stick. Time now to wait for the man's first offer.

"We'll be movin' the rig here next. We'll send a survey crew out toward the end of the week. They're gonna drive the stake in the southwest corner of your west forty." He pointed.

Grover looked out that way, and nodded. "Ain't you gettin' a little ahead of yourself?"

"Huh?" Whitley muttered. "Oh. I come here to settle with you."

Grover let out a muffled humph and a subtle chuckle. If this oilman thought he was going to get a deal on his minerals in one quick afternoon, he was in for a big disappointment. Nossiree. There were other oil companies in town now looking for leases. None had been to see him yet, but they would. He would take the highest bidder. Oh, yeah. This was going to take a while.

"Mr. Shine, I know cotton sold for forty cents a pound last year. As you know it's been goin' down steady since the war. But we're willin' to give you the benefit of the doubt and pay forty-five cents a pound. I'm guessin' you'll make about 300 pounds an acre, so forty-five cents a pound, that's $135 per acre."

Grover kept whittling. He glanced briefly at Whitley. What was the oilman up to? How come he was talking about paying for cotton, anyway?

"We'll need two acres for our rig, and our road going in to the rig will probably take out another acre's worth. So that's three acres of crop we will destroy. Whitley hesitated and looked at his notes. "That comes to total damages of $405. But, under the circumstances, we'll bump that up to $500." He sat back and smiled.

Grover saw the smile was a put-on. The man looked nervous. He was wiping his forehead again. He stopped whittling. "You talkin' about damages to my crops?"

The oilman nodded.

"Hmph!" His gaze froze on the stick. "To hell with that. Let's talk about the big money. Let me borrow that pencil 'n' paper of yorn." Whitley gave them to him. Shine looked up at him while wetting the pencil tip with his spit. It was a show; he had made the calculation a hundred times already. "Now, I'll

do some cipherin', and it ain't gonna be about cotton damages."
He began scribbling.

His lips moved in whispers as he figured. "Eighty acres times
two hunnert dollars is…is." He let out a chuckle. "Is sixteen
thousand dollars. That's what I want, Mister Oilman. Two hunnert Yankee dollars a acre. Sixteen thousand total." He looked
at Whitley and found him with a puzzled expression.

Mr. Shine, I don't think—"

Grover cut him off. "And what kind of give-back you gonna
give me?"

Whitley's face became more distorted. "I don't understand,
Mr. Shine. What do you mean, *give back*?"

Shine felt his forehead heat up. Here he was being talked down
to again, just because he couldn't remember some fancy word.

"You know! The part I get from the oil! How much? Ben
Buchannan got three-sixteenths. I don't care what you offer. I'm
not takin' a bit less than one-quarter!"

Whitley's mouth fell open. "Are you talkin' about royalty?"

Shine let out a deep breath, nodding. "Yessir, hellfire, that's
what I mean, goddamn royalty! Whatever the hell you call it."

Whitely swallowed and wiped his forehead again. "Mr. Shine,
you don't understand. You—"

Grover jumped up, letting the stick fall to the floor. "I don't
want to hear any more o' that talk. Quit talkin' down to me,
mister! Just make me a offer on my lease and go yer way."

Whitley swallowed again. Grover saw him look around, as if
to evaluate escape routes. He got up. "Mr. Shine, you don't own
your mineral rights."

Grover froze.

"I'm sorry to have to tell you this, but I thought you
already knew."

"Knew what?"

"Your daddy sold the minerals under this property back in
the Depression; 1930, I think. I've got a copy of the courthouse
records right here." He began to fumble in his briefcase, glancing

alertly back at Shine as he searched. "Here it is." He pulled out the transmittal form and pointed at the key sentences. "He sold all the mineral rights under this eighty-acre tract to the Gulf States Investment Company, Mobile, in 1930." He glanced at Grover. "That company's gone out of business, but I traced the ownership back to the wife of the man who founded the company. He died a few years ago. Her name is Margaret Hogan. She lives in Arcata, California." He paused.

Grover pondered words that weren't making any sense.

"I called her last month and signed her up. She leased to us, Mr. Shine."

Grover couldn't move.

"Mr. Shine, by law you have to let us on your land to drill because Mrs. Hogan has a right to her minerals. And by law we have to pay you fair and reasonable damages we cause to your property. And we have to do it every year as long as we have a well here."

Grover's bottom lip hung open, quivered. His eyes bore into the landman, the pocket knife in his hand hanging at his side. Whitley began a retreat toward his car.

"Here. I'll leave this with you." He laid the paper down on the porch rail, but it blew off onto the floor. "I guess you need time to think about this," he said while picking it up. He folded it and stuck it into a crack in the rail, keeping his distance. "I'll come back in a few days. Mr. Shine, I think I can get some more money than the $500. A thousand, maybe. That's more than fair. Mr. Bonner's a good man. He'll understand. We'll bump it up good for you." He put on his hat and, noticing Mrs. Shine in the shadows, tipped it.

Grover watched the dust kick up behind the Nash.

"What did he mean, Grover?" Emma asked from the opened living room window.

"He don't know nuthin'." He turned to the woman. "Nuthin'! He's jist tryin' to scare us, that's all." He ran his hand across his scalp and looked around, teeth gnashing. "He's a lyin' sack of shit."

He picked up the paper and looked at it for a few seconds, eyes bulging. He breathed through his mouth, felt a fuse burning behind his eyes. He ripped the paper apart, put the pieces together and ripped it again, then wadded it and threw it toward the yard, but the breeze blew it back at his feet. He sat back in the chair, heaving for breath, his hands shaking, rubbing his mouth and nose. The woman hurried out and gathered the pieces of the paper.

"I'll find out 'bout this," he mumbled. "I'll get to the bottom of this. And there'll be hell to pay, there will."

Emma stood at the top of the steps holding the papers, tears welling. "Grover. Oh, Grover."

"Shut up! Git in the house."

She hurried in, sobbing.

He sat trembling, breathing, eyes flashing left and right across his property. He went in and took the bottle above the pantry. He heard Emma weeping behind him. He headed out back and toward the tree line where the creek was, holding the bottle by its neck. He sat on the sandy bank and gazed at the pod of sand his shoe had pushed up. He saw a shark's tooth tumble from its sandy tomb and slide toward the water. He uncorked the bottle and raised it.

After moving the trailer to the Hull No. 2 location Ethan went over his ledger again and slammed it shut. It wasn't supposed to work this way. He had discovered oil. He was supposed to have cash flow by now. He was supposed to be paying off loans. Yet he was pondering what to say to the Guaranty Bank in Jackson. He needed them again.

He heard a knock, and the door opened before he could say anything. J.D. stepped in and sat. He let out a deep breath. He told Ethan about the encounter with Shine.

Ethan got up and paced. "That poor man. Lord!"

"I was afraid he was goin' to come at me with his whittlin'

knife." J.D. sighed. "I guess I'll have to go back out there in a couple of days and hope he's cooled off."

"J.D., up the damages to one thousand dollars," Ethan said.

"I've already promised him that."

"What will we do if he keeps rejecting us?"

"Well," J.D. said, "again we find ourselves in a state where there may not be any case law on this situation. But in the oil states we could file an injunction on him, let the judge decide damages and force him to let us on."

"God, I hope we don't have to do that," Ethan muttered in a worried tone.

J.D. sighed. "I got to admit, that broadsided me. It rattled me."

"I can understand." Ethan said. "Hey, changing the subject, did you find a lawyer in Mobile?"

"Yes, that's the other reason I came here to see you." He pulled a business card from his shirt pocket. "I found an attorney in Mobile who will work with us—Melvin Posey. It took all day. Most of them didn't want to touch it. Seemed scared, almost."

"What makes you think that?"

J.D. pulled out a stale donut from a box on the cabinet and took a bite. "The way those lawyers responded to me—all of them except the one we got—said they'd get back to me on it. I think they made some calls, found out something, and decided to pass."

"Do you think they're scared of Brubeck and Hull?"

"Oh, hell no. I think they're scared of Matt Chambers."

"That's a sobering thought. Do you think he's involved?"

"I don't know, Ethan. I'm just guessing. Anyway, this lawyer guy, Posey, is working on it now. He'll try to get the injunction thrown out, and if he can't he'll try to get permission to sell enough oil to pay our bills and put the rest in escrow."

"Do you think this—this Judge Bundy will go for that?"

"If he's really in Chambers's pocket, no. He won't. They want to squeeze you, Ethan. If you can't get your hands on your own revenue to pay the bills, they figure you'll have to play ball with them. We'll have to take it to appellate court. Chambers will try to pull some strings there too, probably. They could run this out for years."

Ethan stared at the floor and nodded. He looked back up at J.D. and ran his fingers through his hair. "That's what they want, isn't it?"

"Yup," J.D. said, munching. "They'll be coming to you with a deal. But they'll wait for you to bleed money for a while."

Ethan walked to the window and sighed. "Do you think the bank will give me another loan."

J.D. shrugged. "Don't know. Just don't know."

Ethan stood pondering the situation, then J.D. changed the subject. "There's something else, Ethan." Ethan looked up. "The Gulf farmout is beginning to press us. We've only got a couple of weeks to save it."

Ethan looked aside at the land map. "We'd have to move a mile west. That would mean skipping over Buchanan and drilling an outpost."

J.D. nodded. "What we need, Ethan, is another drilling rig."

Ethan let out a big blow, then chuckled. "With what we've discovered, I ought to be able to place a call and get a rig heading out to that lease. But I can't because I don't have the money! J.D. it's fallin' apart on me." He gathered his thoughts. "Can you get Gulf to give us an extension?"

"I knew you were gonna ask that. If you were them and somebody had just made a good discovery a mile off your leases, would you give them an extension?"

"Maybe I would. Depends on what else is on my plate. Let's give it a try."

J.D. nodded and got up. "All right. I'll do what I can."

Ethan turned back to his financial papers. He ran his hand through his hair again. He put the pencil down and gazed out at Lucky Lucy. It seemed his success was becoming just another form of bondage.

19

BENNY

Ethan, J.D., and their attorney, Posey, stepped down from the Mobile County courthouse. "I'm sorry we couldn't get the injunction lifted," the lawyer told Ethan. "Judge Bundy is—" He looked at the ground. "Well, let's just say that I wish we could have gotten a different judge. I tried."

Ethan asked to retain him. Posey scratched his chin and stared away for a second, then asked, "You're going to be able to pay me, right?"

Ethan nodded. The two shook hands.

The judge's decision to let stand the injunction took less than fifteen minutes. He set a date of December 1, sixty days away, to hear arguments on the nullification of the Hull lease due to Mr. Hull's alleged incompetence. That, he reasoned, would give the plaintiff ample time to have Mr. Hull clinically evaluated. Judge Bundy had approved the sales of oil from the lease, but it had to be placed in an escrow account until the disposition of the lease could be determined. Posey requested approval to draw monies from the account to pay for Ethan's operations but was summarily denied.

Ethan and J.D. got in the car. Ethan tilted his head back, closed his eyes and sighed. "What am I going to do, J.D.?"

J.D. cranked down his side window and lit up. "Ethan, you've got to get some oil from another lease, quickly."

"I know. I also know I've made a mistake going ahead with the Hull number two." He started the engine. "I should have sent the rig over to the Buchanan or the Hogan lease. But those are both step-outs. You don't confirm a discovery by drilling a mile away from it. Do that and you're back to wild-catting."

"Nobody's denying you did the safe thing."

"Let's get back to Fossil Rim and see where we are. We've got to finish this well quickly and, if we find pay here, we'll get to the Hogan lease." J.D. nodded and blew a lungful of smoke out the window.

Ethan dropped J.D. at the motel and headed for the location. He grabbed his hardhat and went up to the floor. The Kelly was spinning to the right. Grady saw him and came out of the dog house. "Well?"

Ethan shook his head. "It's a no-go, Grady. They'll let us sell oil, but we can't use the money until another hearing in December. And the lawyer says maybe not after that either."

Grady looked up into the derrick, drew a deep breath and blew it out. "What do we do?"

"We wrap up this job as quick as we can, and, if we find oil here, we move yonder." He pointed east. "The Shine farm is next. That oil is unencumbered. J.D. was able to get that farmer to accept a damages check, so we are cleared to move onto it."

Grady rubbed his chin. "Why don't we just stop?"

"Stop this hole?"

"Yeah. You can always come back and re-enter it."

"I've thought about that. But if we get a dry hole here, we may not want to move east. We might want to move another direction."

"Okay, Boss," Grady said. "It's your call. If you can get the money to finish out here, that'll work."

"What's our depth?"

Grady checked the pipe tally. "About to go through 7,700 feet. I've let up on the weight because we just started in with the three and a half inch again. Don't want to risk twistin' off."

"Risk it! We've got to finish this hole fast."

"All right. It's your ball game."

Ethan drove back to the trailer and called his banker. The banker listened quietly as he explained the situation with the injunction. He assured the banker he would soon be getting at marketable oil if only he could get a $100,000 advance. He was told they would make a decision and call the next day.

Ethan hung up and slumped back, staring at the ledger. If the bank didn't ante up what he needed, he could only keep drilling by calling J.D. and his leasers off. That meant allowing prime oil leases to fall to his competitors.

Brubeck dialed a familiar number in Mobile. "Matt? Emmett. We won a stay of the injunction. He can produce, but he can't spend. It goes into escrow." He paused to listen.

"I don't know how long he can hold out Matt. I don't know how much he's got. It was a gamble, you know. We want him to keep drilling as long as he drills Hull land, but we want to pressure him to the point he's willing to make a deal." He listened.

"That's right, Matt. Good point. If he moves onto somebody else's lease, he'll start making money, and he might not need us too much." He paused a long time and began to fidget.

"What? Say that again?" He ran his finger inside his collar. "I understand—don't let him drill on another lease. But how will we do that, Matt?" He wet his lips and looked toward the window.

"Okay, Matt. I think that that might work." He relieved his pasty mouth with a drink of water while he listened. "I will, Matt. In case that happens, I've got a plan already. Okay. Good bye, Ma—"

He heard a click before he finished. He lowered the handset and looked into it as if he could see Chambers. He made a gesture into the phone with his other hand.

Ethan found J.D. in his room going over maps with the two men from Jackson he had hired to help with leasing operations. He exchanged pleasantries with them and waited, sipping a Coke, until the meeting was over. The two left, and J.D. lit up and looked at Ethan.

"For a man who not too long ago discovered a good—and maybe a gigantic—oil field, you don't look too radiant, Ethan."

Ethan upended the bottle and set it aside. "I don't feel too bright and beamy, either. J.D., I'm desperate. I'm running out of money again."

"I know. But what about the bank?"

"They're thinkin' about it, but they're not too enthusiastic about loaning me any more money on oil reserves that might not really be mine." He looked at the floor and let out a blow. "They're supposed to call me with a decision tomorrow."

"There's other banks."

"I've already called the banks in Mobile. They don't want to play—don't know anything about the oil business. And," he paused and flashed a smirk toward J.D., "they might be in Chambers's ah, let's call it, *sphere of influence.*"

J.D. mashed out the butt. "You got a Plan B?"

Ethan looked up. "Yep. Plan B is to sell the Buchanan lease."

J.D. sprang up. "Sell it? We just got it!"

"I know. We'll sell it to Sunrise for what they offered Buchanan. We'll keep a small override, and we'll use the money to drill the Hogan lease.

"But what about your partners? Scatback and Noble's associates?"

"They've each got a quarter of the lease already. They'll keep it. I will only be selling my half to Sunrise to raise the money I need to keep running. Trevor and Noble's guys can do whatever they want. Sell, ride, or participate with Sunrise."

J.D. sat back down, leaned back and stared at the wall. "Ethan, if you do that, you'll be losing the most prime oil lands on this discovery."

"Do you know another way?"

After a minute of thought J.D. shook his head. "When are you going to make that decision?"

"After I hear from the bank tomorrow."

J.D. got up and walked to the door. He opened it and leaned against the jam. "Look at 'em out there, Ethan." He nodded toward the street. "Half the cars out there are out of state. The courthouse is so busy they're only allowing six people at a time in the records room and limiting them to two hours." He looked around at the activity on the street. "Ethan it's slippin' away from you."

Ethan jerked his head up. The feelings suddenly returned—the demon of hopelessness and the specter of failure. He swallowed hard. "Boy, I feel alone, J.D."

J.D. nodded. "You are. And you will be. It's the nature of what you do."

They didn't say much for a while, just listened to the traffic noise through the open door. J.D. came back in. "Ethan, there's somethin' else." He looked aside.

"There's not much that goes on around here that Clarice doesn't know about. Ethan, Laura's been seeing Benny. Clarice overheard him promisin' her anything she wanted." He shook his head and reached for his pack. "Ethan, don't take this wrong, please. But is she hedging her bet?"

Ethan glared at him.

J.D. threw his hand toward Ethan. "Forget I said that. It's just that I've come to know you pretty good. I mean—you've come to be my friend, Lord knows why, and I don't have many." He turned back into the room, as if retreating. "Hell, I don't know if there's anything to it, Ethan. Just thought I needed to tell you."

Laura parked her car in her Uncle Hub's driveway where he normally parked the police cruiser. The sun was just getting high enough to bring the bugs out. She grabbed her basket and made her way around the side of the house fanning gnats away from her face. It was the hottest late fall she could remember.

Around back she saw Edna already in the garden stooping among the cabbage plants. Laura joined her. They hugged and Edna placed two cabbages in Laura's basket. "We've got to get the last of these," she said, "before they rot. Then they moved to the row of collard greens.

"Look there," Edna said, pointing. "These cucumbers are starting to rot."

"You're just too good a gardener, Aunt Edna," Laura said. "You grow stuff so fast you can't harvest it all."

Edna smiled and began cutting some cauliflower. After a few minutes of not saying anything—unusual for Edna—she dropped a bomb. "There's been talk."

Laura looked aside at her. "What talk?"

Edna rose up. She let out a whoosh of breath and looked around as if they had an audience. "Oh, these people! You know what I mean." She bent back toward the plants.

Laura put her hand on Edna's shoulder and nudged her back up. "No. I don't know, Aunt Edna. Who are *they*, and what are *they* saying?"

"Oh, the ladies in the quilting club. And, and Mrs. Hambright—your neighbor lady across the street. She and I are on the benevolence committee at the church, you know."

Laura waited for more with her eyes broad and focused on Edna, but her mind was already out front of Edna's slow drawl. "It's about me and Ethan, right?"

Edna nodded and adjusted her bonnet.

"What are they saying, Aunt Edna?"

Edna started to bend to the plants again, but Laura stopped her. "Aunt Edna, what are they saying?"

"Oh," Edna uttered, looking about again. "I should never have brought this up, but I thought you needed to know." She squirmed. "They think you're chasing Ethan because he struck oil." She picked up the basket and started toward the house. Laura followed. "I know it's not true," Edna said over her shoulder, "but that's what they think."

"I think he's a good man," Edna said as she washed the vegetables at the kitchen sink. But I'd rather you marry somebody from around here so you wouldn't go away."

"Marry!" Laura blurted. "Aunt Edna, I'm not considering marrying anybody, and I'm certainly not chasing anybody, so stop talking like that, please."

As she watched Edna place the washed vegetables in her basket, she pondered what her aunt had said. She felt like banging her head against a wall. She was probably the last person in town to realize was going on—or seemed to be going on.

The more she thought about it, the more it became apparent. Of course it appeared she was chasing oil money. Then an icy thought struck her making her want to shiver. Did Ethan think that as well? She had not seen or heard much from him lately. She just figured he was very busy, but—*But what?*

She sighed. "I just don't know, Aunt Edna."

"What?" Edna asked, turning.

"I said I just don't know what's going on. I'm confused. I'm angry. I'm afraid."

Edna looked at her with a bewildered expression. "Afraid? Oh, Honey." She hugged Laura. "Afraid of what?"

Laura teared up. "I'm afraid life is going to pass me by. That's all."

Edna hugged her tighter and patted her back. "Oh, it won't. It won't."

Ethan emerged from the Schlumberger truck with a broad smile. He showed the freshly run logs to Grady. "Two new pay sands, Partner!" Grady pushed his hardhat back and put on his glasses. He pulled the logs closer. Ethan pointed at the two Rodessa sands that had good porosity and resistivity.

"Well, I'll be damned!" Grady uttered. "Congratulations. You've done it again."

"Yeah, but what have I got to show for it except for bills?"

Ethan said, folding the logs. "We found more oil, but it can't do us any good because someone else is claiming it."

"I know," Grady said. "So what do you want to do now?"

"Order the casing and set it, then rig down right away. We'll come back later and perforate. We've got to get this rig on to a lease we can make money on."

Grady nodded. "Okay. Have you got the next one staked and permitted?"

"Yes. Peavy is already over on the Shine place preparing it. Get the rig over there as quickly as you can."

Ethan spent the rest of the morning going over his finances—a drill he was sick to the core of doing. Yet, he did it daily now, sometimes twice a day, hoping he might find a breakthrough of some sort: an angle he had not considered; an economy measure he had not recognized; an opportunity not seized. He leaned his head into his chin and felt whiskers. He realized he had not shaved in days. Nor had he washed clothes in days. He felt stiff and earthy. He had drunk so much coffee he felt poisoned. At times he felt his chest thumping.

He thought about Laura—about the settling and peaceful talks and walks and the oily kiss. It was all over now, it seemed. Where was she? She didn't come to the trailer any more. Had she decided Benny was the better bet?

He sighed. It didn't matter. His life was a captive of the rock cuttings in his sample bags and the numbers in his ledger. He figured he was simply living day-to-day now—just trying to keep the dream alive, just one more day. He had no time for—for what? He rubbed his eyes and lowered his head into a cradle of arms on the work table.

What would he do now? Where was the next prospect? He had a few ideas, a few hunches—but nothing solid. They were filed away somewhere. Could he generate another deal that anyone would buy into? He had found oil—had found it for somebody else, not himself, it seemed.

The ringing phone jolted him. He reached for it like a man

grabbing a lifeline. It was the petroleum man at the Jackson Guaranty Bank.

"Mr. Bonner, we've discussed your request for further funding, and I'm sorry to say that we can't do it at this time due to the encumbrances on your Hull lease which is of course your main lease, and so far the only one you've proven productive."

"But I've just made another well," Ethan said. "A good one. We found two new pay sands."

The banker asked if it was on a new lease, or on the Hull lands, and learning that it was still encumbered oil that Ethan had found he apologized again and said there was nothing he could do.

"Ah, one other thing, Mr. Bonner," the banker said. "Your first installment on your original loan is due next week. Let's see, here. Oh yes. Ten thousand dollars." The man cleared his throat. "Can we expect that to be honored?"

"Yes, sir," Ethan uttered, weakly. "I'll make that payment."

He hung up and rested his chin in his palms for a long time. Finally he got up. There was much to do now that they were moving Lucky Lucy to new hunting grounds. But first, he had to know if the gossip was true. He would ask Laura outright, and if being honest about it poisoned their relationship then he guessed it was not meant to be.

Laura sat at her kitchen table and thumbed through her students' work, but was utterly unable to concentrate on it. The visits with Edna in the garden and the things Edna said continued to trouble her. She couldn't get her thoughts off of the coolness she had felt from people she thought were her friends. Did they think she was selling out to oil money? Their stares told her they did. And the rumors of her and Benny getting back together again made it all the worse, since he had also come into oil money. She rested her chin in her hand and looked away from the school work. She had a hard time accepting how the happy times of only a few weeks ago had given way to this confusion and emptiness.

She had not heard from him now in two weeks. Several times she had started to drive out to the trailer but stopped short of going. The appearance of chasing the oil money was more than she could stand at the moment. She turned back to her papers. She heard footsteps and a knock. Could it be him?

She hurried quickly to the mirror and made three swift passes with her brush then on to the front door. Her smile faded. Benny stood with a dozen roses in one arm and several wrapped gifts in the other, each with brightly colored, swirling bows. He grinned and winked. "Hi, Sweetheart."

As he moved forcefully past her into the living room she glanced across the street toward Mrs. Hambright's house, then followed him in. He deposited the roses on an end table and the presents on a chair. She promptly picked up the flowers and moved them to the dining room table. "Benny, you shouldn't have," she said dispassionately.

He shoved one of the gifts at her, smiling. "Go ahead and open it. Go ahead."

She stared at it and shook her head.

"Okay," Benny said. "Let me." He glanced up at her a time or two as he unwrapped it, smiling hugely. "I got these in New Orleans." He pulled back the lacy white paper and lifted a stunning silk scarf in blue, pink, green, and yellow. He chuckled. "This came from London!" He put it around her neck. "This will look mighty good on you in Rome." He stepped back. "Hell, it looks mighty good on you now." He cackled and reached for another gift.

She felt a fleeting smile appear on her face, and quickly squelched it. "Benny. No, Benny. Please. I appreciate these things, but I can't accept them—Benny!"

He tore open a smaller package and pulled out two tickets. "Look here, Laura. Look, right here." He pointed gleefully. "Rome! These are our tickets to Rome. And after that, wherever you want!" His arms shot out to the side. "How about Greece? Where else? I don't know. Anywhere you want. Laura, you and me, we been sweethearts a long time, Laura. It's time to leave here and go out and see the world together. I'm gonna have the means to do it now."

He took her shoulders in his hands and looked her closely in the face. That charming, dimpled smile that had captured her when they were in high school resurrected warm memories, good times.

"Laura," he whispered, "me and your daddy were like father and son. He would smile right now if he knew we were together, like he always wanted. Laura, let's get away from this place. Let's go, Darlin'." He put his arms around her but she pulled away. His grin faded, then came back. "Let's open these others," he said, undeterred by her coolness. When he turned his back to get the presents she retreated into her bedroom and closed the door.

20

The Associates

Ethan drove to a clearing on the southeast side of town where he had a view of the countryside. It had become a favorite spot for him to think. He stopped and sat at the wheel for a long time pondering Laura and Benny. It certainly seemed true—that Laura was staking her hopes on the most probable winner.

A lump grew in his craw. He thought it best to try and forget her, and concentrate on salvaging what was left of the mess he had gotten in to. Then he would get out of this place.

The thought of getting some Oklahoma air in his lungs seemed a refreshing idea. He would get back to the old homestead his uncle had been farming and maybe get in some hunting. A little time out there in the country he grew up in would help him get over her. After that, he'd get a plan together—a prospect somewhere—or a job. Lots of small companies were looking for experienced oil hunters. With this discovery on his resume he could find a position. Somehow he'd get back in the game.

But she wouldn't be with him as he once imagined she might. The thought of the oily kiss that day on the rig floor and that feeling of being on top of the world seemed like a dream that happened in another life. Where did it all go? Why was he being excluded? He remembered what J.D. had said a week ago. "Ethan, it's slippin' away from you."

The daylight waned as Norman Brubeck eased off the paved highway and took a dirt road that went down a slight hill and curved back under a bridge over Chickasaw Creek. Two cars sat under the dark bridge. Three figures stood nearby smoking. Brubeck reached into his glove box and got out his .38 Special. He wedged it under his belt and pulled his coat tails down over it. He didn't plan on using it, but it seemed a good idea to have it for this meeting. As he approached the men, he recognized Benny in the dim light.

"Hi, Norman," Benny called in a low voice. Benny took a last drag on his cigarette and thumped it into the creek. He gestured to the two figures nearby. "These are our new associates. This here is Raymond." Brubeck didn't offer a hand, just nodded. The man dipped his head. "And that's Gerrard." Gerrard nodded.

In the dim light Brubeck couldn't make out many features of the men—and that was a good thing, he thought—but he could see their forms. Raymond was a giant man, barrel-chested, square-shouldered, and menacing. The other fellow was smaller but stout. They both wore street hats and heavy jackets.

"These fellas are interested in helping us, Norman." Benny's voice sounded wobbly and uncertain.

Brubeck looked at the men, not getting too close. In a very low tone he asked, "What will you charge to help us?"

The two looked at each other and chuckled. The smaller of the two dropped his butt and mashed it out, then said, "Depends on what kind of help you need." They both laughed again.

"All I need is for you to persuade a man that he needs to make a deal with me. If that means you just talk to him in a persuasive way, fine. That's what we want. If that doesn't work and you have to use other means, then I guess that's up to you. I'm not going to tell you what to do."

The big man spoke up. "What are you willin' to pay?"

"Five hundred dollars each."

Raymond, stepped toward Brubeck. Alarmed, Brubeck stepped back and put his hand inside his coat near the .38, but Raymond, moving with a surprising swiftness, caught his arm, and held it so tightly Emmett winced. "What are you reaching for, Mister? Your li'l willy?"

Gerrard laughed.

Raymond continued to hold Emmett's arm tightly, forcing his face so close Emmett could smell the brute's garlicky breath. "Now you listen to me. We don't work cheap. The price is five *thousand* dollars apiece, not five hundred. You got that?"

Emmett nodded.

"And we want half of it up front, see? Got that, too?"

Emmett pulled away, stunned and flustered. "Okay. Got it. I'll set it up with Benny. He'll get you the money and tell you what to do next. But I'm the boss. You'll do what I tell you. Got it?"

Raymond looked back at Gerrard and laughed. "Ha ha. Got it, Gerrard?" He jerked his thumb back toward Brubeck. "This here is the boss man." They laughed again.

Emmett and Benny walked briskly to their vehicles. All Emmett said was, "Call me tomorrow morning." The two sent dirt spurting from under their tires.

Ethan awoke the next morning to a racket of diesel noise, men's shouts and metal objects jolting and clanking. He opened the trailer door just in time to see Lucky Lucy's derrick being slowly lowered. Grady stepped up with coffee and a cigarette. "We're headed to the Shine place, partner. We'll spud tomorrow."

Ethan nodded. "Okay. Get this trailer over there today if you can."

Grady nodded, turned and passed J.D. coming in. "I got the money from Sunrise for the Buchanan lease," J.D. said, nodding to Grady. He handed Ethan a check. "Here is $137,100—exactly what you paid Buchanan for it. And here—" He paused and sighed, holding another check—"is the $62,900 profit I made on the deal. Are you absolutely sure you want me to give that to Buchanan?"

Ethan looked at it, swallowed hard, then nodded. "J.D., we've got no right to profit on him after he was so good to us. He kept his word. I've never known anybody in my life who was so honest. Go give it to him and explain what happened."

J.D. stared at the check and nodded. "Okay," he said sadly. "Now we've got to talk about other matters," he said, brushing past Ethan to the coffee pot. He poured and sat. His tone gave Ethan that sick-to-his-stomach feeling again. More bad news coming.

"Ethan, Gulf declined our request to extend the farm-out terms. They want their acreage back so they can drill it themselves. It expires in ten days. You got to get this rig over there in a hurry."

"But J.D., that's a step-out of a mile," Ethan said. "We'll be back to exploring again. The Hogan lease is only 1,800 feet from these good sands we just drilled here. I need cash flow. I need it now."

J.D. shook his head and sighed. "Boy, I just don't understand you. I don't. The very act of comin' here to drill that first well was a risk so big hardly anybody wanted to join you. "And now—" he got up and paced. "Now, you've turned so cautious you're lettin' things get away that you need to keep." He turned to Ethan and put up a hand. "I know. I know. It's your decision, your money. But we're losin' yet another piece of prime acreage."

Ethan got up. "There's a difference, man, between taking a big risk to get something you want and being cautious not to lose it."

J.D. stared at him. "Is there? Figure your luck could run out, huh?"

"I'm not feeling like I'm lucky. I'm feeling like I'm in a foxhole with bullets hittin' all around me. That's what I'm feeling like."

J.D. stood staring at the floor with a despondent look on his face.

"Look," Ethan said. "The Hogan lease is eighty acres. If we can get two good wells on it, we're back in business. J.D., I've got to go for the best shot. I can't risk a dry hole right now. It would kill us."

"Okay, Ethan. I understand. But, you know, I'm basically done here. Without money I can't lease. You'll just be paying me to sit on my ass, and you can't afford that. I'm headin' back to Jackson tomorrow. You can call me back if things go good for you, but I doubt there'll be much acreage left around here to get."

Again Ethan felt helpless and alone. "J.D., I need you more than you know. I need you to keep me going. I need your counsel. I feel like you're more of a partner than a hired landman." He let out a lung full of breath and walked to the window, running his hand through his hair. "If you go back home, what'll you do?" He turned to the landman.

J.D. looked at the floor and shook his head.

"Look," Ethan said, "You might as well stay. You know what will happen if you go back. You've got something here, J.D. You've got friends who'll support you. If you go back, you'll turn back into that guy I saw at your apartment that first day we talked. Don't go back to that."

J.D. nodded at the window. "Maybe I'll stick around a while longer." He turned back toward Ethan. "But I might have to sign on with somebody else. I got bills to pay, too."

"Hold off on that for now," Ethan said. "I'll keep paying you as long as I can."

J.D. rinsed out his coffee cup and set it in the sink. "Did you know that Sunrise is already moving in a rig on the Buchanan lease?"

Ethan's eyes bulged. "Already? No. I didn't."

"They're not wastin' any time. They'll have oil flowing from that lease in a month or less."

"Emmett, why is it you always want me to drive your car when you and me go somewhere in it? It's like I'm your chauffeur, or something."

Emmett's gaze remained straight ahead. "Benny, shut up. I'm thinking." For hours now, dread had crawled up his spine like a snake looking for a spot to sink its fangs. He had gotten no sleep last night and even felt nauseated at breakfast. He had considered calling Chambers and telling him he was too sick to come, but he knew that would likely worsen things. This whole business with Bonner had turned ugly and sour. He regretted getting Chambers involved. Hell, he probably would have gotten the injunction on his own without Chambers and Bundy. But there was no turning back on that now. He wiped his forehead with a handkerchief. They came upon a sign: *Polecat Bay Next Right*.

They turned onto the dirt road and drove through a half mile of marshlands that opened up to what appeared to Emmett to be an abandoned barge terminal—just a couple of shacks, some razed foundations and concrete barge mooring structures out in the river. They parked and cut off the engine. Benny got out and walked the shoreline, smoking. Emmett sat. In the distance to the southwest he saw the buildings of downtown Mobile sprouting above the low profile of stands of privet and alder.

Matt Chambers's black Cadillac Seville rolled to a stop beside him. Finch, the lawyer, was driving. The two got out. Emmett got out of his car and joined them. "Let's take a nice walk, Brubeck," Chambers said. Finch dropped back to trail the two out of hearing range. Benny stayed a great distance away.

"Brubeck, it seems I've got to get more involved in this than I wanted to, and that grieves me. You don't seem to be making anything happen."

"But I am, Matt. I am."

"Oh? How so?"

"Matt, I've got two men who will do anything I tell them. Good men. They can persuade Bonner to sign the agreement. I just haven't chosen the time and place yet. I've got to keep our tracks covered, you know."

Chambers looked aside and mocked Brubeck. "*I know?*" He let out an exasperated breath of cigar smoke. "Okay. That's what I pulled you out here for. I've already figured that out." He stopped and turned. "Finch did some research. He found out that Bonner is about to drill on the farm of one Mister Grover Shine."

Brubeck nodded. "I know him."

"And this Shine fellow doesn't own his minerals. Seems his granddaddy sold them long ago."

Brubeck nodded. "Yes, Matt. I heard that."

"*You heard that?*" Chambers mocked again. He shook his head. "The state oversees mineral rights. Did you know that Brubeck?"

He nodded.

"Not the county or the city. So our circuit judge friend can't help. Here's what we do. On behalf of poor Mr. Shine, you will tell the attorney general in Montgomery that Bonner has stolen Shine's minerals. You don't have to get technical. You don't need to go into detail. Just do it. The attorney general is planning a run for governor. Any publicity that lets him look like a champion of the little man works to his advantage. It doesn't matter if he has any legal jurisdiction in Mr. Shine's troubles or not. He'll jump on this opportunity."

Chambers looked aside at Brubeck. "You see, I was a big supporter of the attorney general in his election. I'll nudge him, and he'll listen to you. On behalf of Mr. Shine you will ask him to issue an order to cease and desist drilling operations on that well until an investigation can be made into Mr. Shine's being bullied and bamboozled by Bonner's big bad oil company."

Brubeck nodded.

"So, Bonner will again be delayed from gettin' oil," Chambers said. "Then you can press him to settle on our terms on the Hull lands."

Emmett grinned. "Oh, yeah, Matt. Excellent. Then he will think seriously about playing ball with us."

"Yeah, and he might not," Chambers added. He stopped walking and turned to face Brubeck. "Brubeck, like I told you before, you got to have a back-up plan. Now listen to me. You will create an opportunity to get Bonner alone. And when you do, he will either agree to our deal or he will have an accident of some sort. Like we discussed when I was up there a few weeks ago, with him gone it'll be easier to deal with whoever takes his operation over, if anybody. It'll be ripe for a fire sale." He pushed his cigar so close to Emmett's chest it singed his shirt. "You will see to it. Understand?"

They completed a big circle that ended at the cars. Just before getting in Chambers tapped the ashes off his cigar tip and watched them fall. "It might help things out if Mr. Shine got some publicity that would get the attorney general's sympathy for his unfortunate situation."

Emmett looked puzzled. "How so, Matt?"

"You figure something out."

Grover Shine heard something. "They're here," he told Emma. He put down his cup and arose from the breakfast table. They stepped to the front porch. The sun was rising behind them and the activity in the west was still cloaked in dim light. Headlights moved through his field. Engines roared and ebbed as gears were shifted. Flashlight beams swung from side to side, and he could make out shouting voices in the distance. He wiped his mouth with the back side of his hand.

Emma turned toward him and studied his face. "Grover, let's take a trip. Why not go up to Miller's Ferry? You was talkin'bout that last year. Remember? You said we would stay with your brother for a while. You and him fish and hunt." She looked out at the activity in the field, then back at her husband. His face was contorted, pained, broken. "Grover, let's go. We don't need to watch this."

It was as if he didn't hear her. He stepped to his rocker, sat and stared out at the preparations being made to take his oil.

Ethan sat down to check his spreadsheet. The money from the

sale of the Buchanan lease was already getting low. In short order he would be against the ropes again. A gentle rap at the trailer door annoyed him. Who now? "Come in," he yelled.

Laura stepped in.

His mouth dropped open. "Laura!" He got up. He ran his hands across his hair and mumbled. "I'm sorry. I—I'm not too presentable." He pulled her a chair.

She sat and looked around, then studied him.

"Coffee?" he asked, looking back at the pot. She shook her head.

"Ethan, why on earth haven't you called me?"

His mouth and throat felt extraordinarily dry. He wet his lips with his tongue. He was as glad as a love sick school kid that she had come to see him, yet something in him held back. Was she two-timing him? Was she working him against Benny? That way she could choose the winner.

He looked out the window and shrugged. "I've been really busy."

After studying him for a while she said, "Ethan, you look terrible. Why don't you clean up? We'll go down to Susie Q's and get something to eat."

He kept staring at the rig.

"Ethan?" she pleaded.

He snapped his gaze to her. "Have you been seeing Benny Hull?" He immediately regretted raising his voice and sounding demanding. He saw her expression turn chary. Who was he to accuse her, anyway? Was she ever his? Before he could apologize she jumped up from her chair and started for the door. "Whatever you say about Benny, you could take a lesson from him in manners!"

She stepped through the door and turned back. "At least he's got feelings." She slammed the door behind her. Stunned, he slowly began to sit down. The door burst open again. She stuck her head in. "And he's clean. You're a pig!" She slammed it again. He watched her hurry by the window, saw the tears.

The door opened again. Grady came in, pausing to look toward Laura retreating to her car. He pushed his hard hat back. "Damn! What got into her?"

Ethan leaned closer to the window to watch her leave and shook his head. He looked back at the pusher. He didn't want to discuss her. "What's going on up there on the floor?"

Grady walked slowly by him toward the pot, eyeing him suspiciously. "Nothin's going on up there, 'cept we're drillin' ahead. Hey, you all right?"

Ethan felt jumpy. He got up and rubbed his head. "Am I all right?" He tapped the spread sheet. "Am I all right?" He turned back to Grady. "I'm running out of money—again! After cannibalizing my own leases. And I'm being sued. They're trying to steal the oil I've found. On top of that, other companies are coming in here getting leases that ought to be mine." He looked back toward the direction Laura departed and gestured toward her. "And she—" He stopped and shook his head like a horse shooing off flies.

"She—what?" Grady said looking over the rim of his cup.

Ethan looked menacingly at him. "She comes in here and—" He looked aside again.

"And?"

Ethan raised his voice. "And she comes in here and says I'm a pig!"

Grady sat. "Well, you are. Lately, that is. Been wantin' to tell you myself, seeing as how I got to share this trailer with you."

Ethan shot a scornful glance at him.

"Look," Grady said. "It ain't none of my business, but I ain't seen you with her in weeks now. Ya'll used to be *like that*." He held two fingers up side by side. "You were a damn sight easier to get along with back then. I'll say that."

Ethan sat and regained some composure. "Grady, let's just concentrate on our business. Okay? How deep are we?"

"About fifty feet deeper 'n' that last time you asked me, which was after breakfast."

Ethan leaned back and let out a big sigh. "When do you say we'll reach Rodessa?"

Grady shook the last drops of the cup into the sink, rinsed

it and set it aside. "Hell, how many times do I have to say it? You're the geologist. You can guess it better than me. But I'd guess by Thanksgivin' day."

Ethan looked at the calendar above the sink. Two and a half weeks.

Grady left to go back up to the floor, leaving Ethan staring with a blank expression at the calendar.

Mornings, Grover Shine would drive out and ask how deep they were, and the men would tell him and offer him coffee, but he knew they were keeping a watchful eye on him.

Days, as he worked his fields, he lived with the steel tower's invasive presence in his west forty. When the damned Farmall's generator belt snapped off he kneeled with a groan to loosen the idler pulley and reroute the belt, glancing over his shoulder at the rig, hearing its engine whine, seeing the crew manhandle another section of drill pipe into place.

Evenings, he sat on the porch and whittled cedar chunks into heaps of pink shavings on the floor, eyeing the spire, seeing it come alit with a vertical row of brilliant lights, watching the night crew take over, watching the headlights of vehicles come and go through the dusty road they had built into his cotton, hearing the engines throb, sometimes hearing men shout, smelling the hot pungent mud, knowing that with every hour those people got closer to his oil, thinking that soon the thing and its noise, its smells, its human doings would be gone, replaced with only a valve head, a tank and some pieces of equipment, leaving him with a useless road through his eighty acres of dirt. An empty reminder.

Whole meals would go by without him saying anything, Emma just looking at him and worrying, watching him glance out the door toward the rig between bites. Trying to start a conversation, she would ask how deep they were, but he would grunt and shake his head at his plate.

Nights, he lie in bed watching the wall glow with the bright lights from the drill site, listening to the incessant rumble riding the breeze in through the window past swaying curtains. Knowing it would end, and soon. Oil passing him by.

Early in the day during the third week of drilling he went out to the rig in his pick-up, as he usually did most mornings, to ask how deep they were. The tool pusher-man, Mr. Plunkett, chatted with him a few minutes, and then he started back out to the main road.

Passing a small cluster of privet, a man wearing a hard hat came out and flagged him. Grover stopped to see what he wanted. Then another man appeared on the other side of his truck. Grover got spooked and hit his accelerator, but it was too late. Before the truck jerked forward, he felt strong hands gripping his arm and shoulders.

21

Despair

Laura pulled into her driveway and shut the engine off. She sat for a while nursing the lump in her throat. The trip to see him had been a disaster—far worse than she feared it might be. She sniffed and wiped her eyes. Maybe it was for the best. If she had seen him as he truly was—an insensitive, jealous slob—then it was a blessing. She didn't need to be involved with someone like that.

She took a deep breath and got out. As she opened her door, she took pause. But what about all the other times? Sweet times, there on the porch. Times when they had shared their dreams and hearts. He had inspired her and given her hope. Had he been pretending? Which Ethan would he be after they—they what? Married?

She went in, set down her purse, and hung up her sweater, pondering what had happened at the trailer. She leaned into her palms. She had found him smelly, dirty, unshaven, and cranky. But then, he *was* an oilman. They were like that, Benny had warned her. But what about when he raised his voice so sharply to her, asking about Benny? So what if he was jealous? Why would that be bad? She leaned back into the sofa and pondered. Was she upset over nothing?

She looked aside at the picture of her dad and remembered what Benny had said about him approving, if he were living, of Benny and her getting together. He would have. He loved Benny like a son. She sighed and slumped. At least with Benny you knew what you were getting.

She shook her head as if to clear it. She couldn't believe she was actually considering Benny as a mate. They were as different as night and day. He was shallow and garish. He was pushy, pretentious, and presumptive. And beyond that, he just wasn't very bright.

She kicked off her shoes and picked up a newspaper, looking at it but not seeing it. She sighed again. Neither one of them was worth her tears. She didn't need them.

She looked around at the house. She could sell it and get enough to maybe go around the world. That was a thought. London, Paris, and Rome. Athens, Jerusalem, and Baghdad. She'd put it up for sale tomorrow! No. After this semester. The school board would need time to hire a replacement. She would need a passport. And a Realtor to sell the place. Oh, if she could do it all tomorrow, she would. If she could sneak out of Fossil Rim undetected and take a boat out of Mobile or New Orleans, wouldn't that be sublime? She giggled. What would they say? She'd leave a letter posted on the church bulletin board. *Bye Ya'll! I'm going around the world! Love, Laura. P.S. Ain't no one going with me! Ha!*

She opened a drawer in the end table and pulled out a stack of dog-eared travel brochures. She felt a chill and pulled an afghan over her. She sank back into a rounded corner of the sofa, pulled the afghan farther up around her neck and stared at pictures of the Egyptian pyramids. She mopped the corners of her eyes and tried to purge thoughts of everything except her sipping tea at a table near that pyramid, happily alone.

Ethan was walking from the post office toward the diner when Hub slowed and called out to him from his cruiser, "Mr. Bonner, would you kindly get in?" Ethan joined the sheriff, and they went to Dr. Maven's office, a few blocks away. Grover Shine lie on a gurney, his cheeks and eye sockets swollen, purple and blue. He stared at the ceiling as if no one else was in the room.

Benny Hull, sitting at Grover's side, got up and glared at Ethan.

"Benny, here, found Mr. Shine lying in a ditch not far from your drilling rig," Hub said. "You know anything about that, Mr. Bonner?"

Ethan looked Shine over and shook his head. "Is he going to be all right?"

"I'm sending him down to Mobile to get him x-rayed," said Dr. Maven. "But I think he'll be all right."

"Your men did this," Benny shouted.

Hub held up a hand. "Cut that out. I'll do the accusin' around here after I get the facts." He turned to Ethan. "Mr. Shine says the men who jumped him were wearing oil hard hats and oil field clothes. He said one was big-framed and the other one was smaller but strong. You got anybody that fits that?"

Ethan thought of Cuz and Tiny. Cuz was working the floor, so he had an alibi. Tiny should have been sleeping at the motel. "Yes I have a couple that would fit that, but they got no reason to do this. You know there are oil crews all around here now. If whoever did this are oilmen, they could be from anywhere."

"Yes," said Hub, "but this happened almost within sight of your rig, Mr. Bonner. And they robbed him. That makes your people somewhat suspect now, doesn't it?"

Ethan shook his head vigorously. "No, it doesn't. Like I said, they've got no reason to do this."

"Oh they don't, don't they?" Benny shouted. "I heard you ain't even payin' them!"

"Benny, lower your voice please," Dr. Maven said.

Benny glared again at Ethan while directing his words to the Sheriff. "They stole his minerals, Sheriff. The ones who stole his minerals beat the hell out of him 'cause he was trying to make them give him his oil rights back. That was their way of getting him to shut up. It was!"

"That's ridiculous," Ethan shouted. "And what were you doing on Grover Shine's property anyway? You just happened to be out for a leisurely drive, eh?"

Hub held his hand up to stop Ethan but seemed not to pay much attention to the men's allegations against each other. "Well," he said, "all the same, I think I'll have a talk with your night crew. Maybe let Mr. Shine get a look at them. At least we'll be able to eliminate them."

They walked back to the police cruiser in silence. When they got in Hub said, "Mr. Bonner this isn't going to look good for you in the public eye. Everybody in town knows Shine ain't getting any oil out of his farm, and they don't think it's right."

Ethan chuckled sadly. "Sherriff I haven't been popular here since the first week. Remember? I'm the devil."

Hub spat out the window and snickered.

Ethan opened the Mobile paper the next morning. A picture of Grover's bruised face appeared under the headline, *Farmer Claiming Oil Is Stolen From Him Found Beaten Up*. Ethan folded the paper and slammed it down on the table. "Did Mr. Shine ever accuse us of stealing his oil?"

J.D. took a big bite out of a biscuit and shook his head. "Not exactly," he said still chewing, "He didn't trust us at first, but he understood after he read the deed. He's not dumb."

"Then the paper made this up?"

J.D. swallowed and wiped his mouth. "I doubt they made it up, but they probably took the story and ran with it on a tip."

"And who might have given them that tip?"

J.D. shrugged. "Somebody who is trying to make you look bad."

"Why would they want to do that?"

"A hundred reasons. Could be to persuade people not to lease to you. Maybe to cause the injunction to go against you. Judges and juries read papers, too. And of course, you're the devil who came here to tell everybody their grand-pappies were apes."

"Not funny," Ethan mumbled.

Abbey stepped up to refill their coffee.

"Abbey, you don't think we evolved from apes, do you?" J.D. asked.

"Oh, for Pete's sake, J.D.," Ethan protested.

Abbey's face became contorted. She looked at them both. "Sometimes when I'm with my boyfriend, I think he came from an ape."

They burst out cackling. Abbey left looking over her shoulder with a bewildered gawk.

"Well," J.D. added, looking around the table as if to spot something he had missed for breakfast, "we've just got to get oil flowing. Got to. This other stuff is the sheriff's business."

Emmett had stepped into his reception room when his secretary informed him, "Mr. Brubeck, Mr. Chambers is on the line." He hurried into his office and shut the door.

"Yeah, Matt. I just saw it," he said while unfolding the paper. "I'll make sure the attorney general sees it. Matt— What? You've already done it? Great— Okay— Understood— Ha! Yeah, Matt. I'm ready— Okay, goodbye, Matt…Matt?" He slammed down the phone and sneered at it.

Ethan got out of his car and started for the trailer but heard shouts from the floor. Grady was yelling at him with cupped hands around his mouth. He beckoned to come up. Ethan cut toward the rig and clambered up the steps.

The Kelly bar was sitting still and the crew was huddled around a bucket. "Look here, Mr. Bonner," Skeeter said, holding a handful of grainy, sandy cuttings. "Smell!"

Ethan took a pinch with his fingers and sniffed. He grinned. "Wow! I've never smelled it that strong before! Depth?"

Grady put on his glasses, looked at his pipe tally and

scribbled some calculations. "Ten thousand, two hundred and forty-six feet."

Ethan got up from his squat. "That sounds high. Could be Paluxy."

"No matter what it is, if it's got oil," Grady uttered, lighting up a cigarette.

"It matters," Ethan said, staring into the distance. He turned back to the crew. "Drill ahead. Take five foot samples and bring every one of them to me as you get 'em." He headed down the steps and toward the trailer.

He paused before entering. A strange car had pulled up. Two men and a woman got out and came toward the trailer. He recognized one man. It was the State Geologist, Dr. Walter B. Jones, whom he had met at the crawfish boil on the Hull number 1. He liked Dr. Jones but wished he had chosen a different time to visit. He greeted him with a handshake. "Hello, Dr. Jones. Nice of you to pay us a visit."

Dr. Jones introduced the other man, a photographer, and the woman, Mrs. Gloria Ackerman, a journalist for *Lifetime Magazine*. "We heard about your success all the way up in New York," she said, "and my editor asked me to come down and get your story. If you have time, that is?"

Well dressed and attractive, he found her powerfully charming. "Dr. Jones was kind enough to drive us down. We needed an introduction," she said with a radiant smile.

"Sure," Ethan mumbled. He invited them inside, apologizing for the unkempt trailer. He got them coffee and gave them a tour of his work table. "As a matter of fact," he said, "I'll show you the new shows we just got."

The inevitable question popped out, and he was glad Dr. Jones intervened and explained what *shows* meant. It gave him time to prep the samples he had gotten from Skeeter and get them under the scope. Then he put them in his bluelight box, and they gazed at the magnificent fluorescence.

"Looks like you've got another good well," Dr. Jones said.

Mrs. Ackerman got out her notebook and began asking questions.

Ethan wondered how much of, and what, he should tell her. He wished he had consulted with J.D. first.

She said her mission was to report on how the big discovery had impacted the town and its people, but her main interest at the moment was the science and engineering.

He felt that was a safe enough subject, so he canvassed his thoughts and got ready to do a bit of teaching.

Like all lay people, she wanted to know what was down there. Was it a big cave full of oil? A river of it?

Ethan said, "Imagine we have a large round table here in front of us." He gestured to the floor with his hands, as if it sat in front of them. "Now, this is no ordinary table. It's not only round around the edges, it is also round on top."

He saw her forehead wrinkle. That must not have gotten across too well. "Imagine the table has a hump on top of it—a big rounded dome like the top of a scoop of ice cream, or a mushroom."

He saw her smile. He smiled, as well. He had not seen a woman so pretty in a very long time. Maybe never.

"It's just a big wooden table that bulges upward. You wouldn't be able to put any magazines or cups, or whatever on it because they would slide right off."

Dr. Jones chuckled with approval, grinned, sat back and nursed his pipe.

"Now we start throwing a bunch of pancakes on that rounded table. We're actually talking about sandstone bodies that are very porous, but by way of illustration we'll make them pancakes. We toss 'em all over it. Big ones. Little ones. Fat ones, thin ones. Some would be oval, some round. Some would even be long and snake-like."

Mrs. Ackerman crossed her legs, which momentarily drew both men's eyes, and leaned forward as if to examine the imaginary table. She smiled enchantingly and peeked at Ethan over her glasses.

"So," Ethan continued, "we've got this tabletop piled with weird shaped pancakes and many of them are saturated with syrup."

She burst out laughing and turned to Dr. Jones. "They should have sent the food editor!"

They all chuckled. "So you see we drill down to the table top and we get to enjoy sucking up the syrup. One well may go through one pancake and the well next to it through another. Other wells may go through two or more pancakes. They are not all connected."

"Gotcha!" the writer said, winking at him. "Okay, now tell me about this strange table top though. How did it get there?"

Ethan leaned back and drew a breath. "That's not so easy to explain. I have talked to people who have studied this. More ideas are being developed constantly, and I'm not a researcher. But it is generally thought that there is a big salt dome down there—rounded on top, like our imaginary table—and it is, in effect, pushing up against our pancakes.

"Salt?" she blurted. "You mean the stuff we put on our fried eggs?"

He nodded.

She turned back to Dr. Jones. "Yes, the food editor should have come."

Again they all had a laugh, and Ethan realized he was enjoying this. The door burst open, and Skeeter brought in another sample bag, and Ethan knew it needed his attention. Mrs. Ackerman asked him to continue his story over dinner, and without a second's hesitation he said, "Sure."

After a shower and a fresh change of clothes he met Mrs. Ackerman at the Wagon Wheel, and they took his usual table.

They had finished their course of meatloaf, potatoes, and carrots and were talking about his upbringing in Oklahoma, when an annoyingly familiar voice interrupted.

"Well, well."

He looked up at Benny Hull. Benny immediately un-hatted. "Mr. Bonner, you gonna introduce me to your friend here?"

Ethan held from telling him to get lost, but decided to keep his composure. "This is Mrs. Ackerman. She's a magazine writer, Benny."

Benny didn't take his eye off of the woman. "Mind if I sit and join you for a while?"

"Benny, we're—"

Benny pulled out a chair and planted himself in it, ignoring Ethan. Within a few minutes, Mrs. Ackerman had gotten out her tablet and was jotting notes. He was riled that Benny's rambling prattle about the goings-on around Fossil Rim seemed to interest her more than Ethan's engineering and science. But then he remembered, by her own admission, she came to do a story on the townspeople, and Benny must obviously be an interesting subject. Ethan crossed his legs, sat back, and listened to Benny try to charm the New Yorker. At times she cut a glance and a smile toward him as if she were humored by Benny's swagger.

"Well, hey," Benny said, looking at his watch. "I got to go."

He hurried to Laura's house.

"Benny?" Laura said, surprised.

"Hey, Laura. You had supper yet?" She shook her head.

"Sorry I popped in on you like this, but come on down to the diner with me. They've got meat loaf tonight."

"Benny, I can't. I'm just going to have some leftovers at home."

He grinned hugely. "Come on, Laura. You look great. Just get your coat."

She stared beyond him, as if looking for someone else.

"Laura, you've been spending too much time in the house. You need to get out, okay? Com'on, don't make your ole Benny eat alone tonight. Please, sweetheart? Pretty please?"

"Okay, Benny. Let me run a comb through my hair and paint my lips."

A few minutes later Benny and Laura entered the Wagon Wheel and selected a table opposite the side of the room with

Ethan and his interviewer. She didn't notice them at first. Benny ran his mouth, checking occasionally that Ethan and his guest were still there and monitoring Laura's head movements. Finally he saw her fix her gaze toward them. He stopped his prattle. He said, "Laura, what is it? You look like you've seen a ghost?" He looked. "Oh, It's Mr. Bonner and—and, who's that? Want to go over and talk to them?"

She shook her head vigorously. She glared at him. "You brought me here to see that, didn't you?"

Benny was caught off guard. He hadn't thought his scheme through. He decided to confess. "Laura, if I had told you he was seeing her, you wouldn't have believed me. Laura, I did it for your own good. I don't want him to hurt you."

She got her purse and sweater and got up. Benny jumped up. They started for the door.

Mrs. Ackerman interrupted Ethan. "Look there's Benny and, I suppose, his wife."

Ethan turned. His eyes met Laura's as she swept out with Benny in close trail. Benny waved and smiled.

His beating at the hands of the brutes did not deter Grover Shine from his usual morning drive out to the rig. Grady came down from the rig floor to greet him and noticed the muzzle of a shotgun occupying the truck's passenger seat. The pusher was appalled at Grover's bruises.

Ethan looked out of the window of the trailer and saw the two. He went out and joined them. Mr. Shine seemed to be in no mood for small talk. He looked up at the towering derrick. "How deep today?" They could hardly hear him.

"Ten thousand, four hundred and forty-six feet, Mr. Shine," Grady said.

Grover nodded feebly. "Are you in the oil yet?"

"Yes, Mr. Shine," Ethan said. We've been drilling through good oil sands all night. This may be our best well yet."

Grady frowned at him. Ethan immediately regretted saying that. He knew he should have played it down. Why torment the man?

Grover sighed and looked around, then back toward his house. He nodded to them and got back in the truck. Ethan felt a strange impulse to follow him to the truck. The farmer looked at him with a blank stare, then said, "I don't suppose you'd use some of that oil money to take care of my people, would ya?"

"What do you mean, Mr. Shine?" Ethan asked.

Ethan felt Grover was staring through him at some object very far away. Grover shook his head. "Forget it." He started his truck.

Grover drove slowly back to the house, grabbed the Long Tom, got out, stepped up onto the porch and went inside. He leaned the gun against the kitchen cabinet and looked for Emma. She was in a closet picking things out of a cabinet, getting ready to start her sewing. He paused and thought about going in there and touching her on the shoulder. He used to do that while she worked, and she would reach back and put her hand on his. He turned away.

He stepped to Buddy's door and glanced in, making sure he was off to school, stared at the bed, remembered the beatings— the ones he got as a boy and gave as a father. It was far too late to set things right with the boy now. His mouth turned pasty.

He stepped back into the kitchen and picked up the Long Tom, opened the breach and checked that the single round of twelve-gauge buck was still there. He started to close it up but halted. He didn't want Emma to hear the breach being closed. He hooked the gun over one arm and with the other took a bottle from under the sink and went out back. He walked behind the shed and out past the scum pond. He sat on an old pine stump, facing the drill rig. He heard its engine running. Smelt the drilling mud. He took a long deep pull from the bottle, drained it, and set it down. He closed the breach and cocked the hammer. He took off his right shoe. He swung the gun's butt to the ground, put his big toe into the trigger guard and grabbed the end of the barrel with both fists. He pulled it to his mouth.

_22_

The Order

Ethan stood, hat in hand, looking down at his feet, his tie fluttering in the breeze. He heard only a few scattered words of Reverend Pope's long-winded eulogy. The wind carried the preacher's voice away, along with the weeps, groans, and sniffles emanating from the sizeable crowd gathered around the homestead grave.

Periodically he looked around searching for Laura, but couldn't find her. At times he glanced toward an assemblage of state troopers standing a short distance away, holding their hats to their sides. Beside them sat vans with the letters of television stations on them—one from Mobile and another from Montgomery. Cameras on tripods aimed toward the preacher and a well-dressed stranger with his arm around Mrs. Shine's shoulder at the front of the crowd

Finally he heard a solemn, "Amen." Men began to put their hats back on.

The camera men and a couple of microphone-toting reporters then wedged into the crowd and converged on the well-dressed man who seemed to be fervently orating for the news people and whomever else gathered around him.

Ethan saw Dr. Maven a short distance away and moved toward him to ask about the man.

"He's the attorney general, down from Montgomery," the doctor said.

"Why is he here," Ethan asked.

Doc Maven shrugged. "Maybe he knows the family."

The crowd around the attorney general made it hard for Ethan to make sense of the man's words, so he joined the consolation line for Mrs. Shine. When his turn came he gently took her hand, worried she might draw back, but she didn't. He whispered that he was sorry for her loss. He moved to her son, wondering if the boy would reject him. Buddy seemed to be staring toward the horizon showing no emotion. Ethan patted his shoulder and started toward his car.

While walking he turned his gaze toward Lucky Lucy, standing like a distant steeple over the man's grave. He heard the pumps gently humming. Tiny and the night crew had agreed to tend the rig while the day tour, who knew Mr. Shine from his daily visits, went with Ethan to the funeral. Ethan had ordered Tiny not drill but just circulate mud during the service, so as to keep the noise level down.

Ethan turned and looked at his crew. None of them had brought any dressy duds from their homes back in Texas and so had changed into their cleanest work clothes. They stood out like sore thumbs among the mourners, and he could see they were anxious to be gone. They drifted back toward their cars.

As he neared his car, he felt a hand on his shoulder. It was the preacher, Red Pope. "You caused this," the preacher muttered, obviously trying to keep his indignation under control. "You and your ways. Are you satisfied you drove this poor man to his grave? He had no hope of the Hereafter because you told him he came from apes. He had no Creator. You spread your false doctrine in the most wicked and shameful way you could—through our children!"

Ethan's face turned red. He needed to say something, wanted to debate this man. His gut told him he needed to defend himself or else he would fret over it for days, weeks. He needed to settle it. He fought the urge, looked away from the man, and got into his car.

On his way back to the rig, with his thoughts laboring over

Pope's assault, Ethan noticed the state troopers following. He parked in front of the trailer and got out. He stripped his tie off as Sheriff Tant's car came to a stop. The troopers' cars had stopped out by the highway. The lawman got out with a manila envelope in his hand.

"What's that, Sherriff?"

Tant took his hat off. "Ethan, I'm tired of having to give you these things."

Ethan realized that was the first time he remembered the sheriff using his given name.

Tant looked at the envelope and sighed. "This time the order comes from the state police." He handed it over.

Ethan swallowed hard and opened it. The sheriff stood staring at his toes. Ethan shook his head. "They can't do this to me! They can't!" He looked at Tant. "They're shutting me down." Ethan finished scanning the document then stared into the distance, his mouth hanging open.

Tant fidgeted.

"I've got to finish this hole first." Ethan muttered.

Hub gestured toward the cars parked alongside the highway. "Those are the state troopers who brought me this order. They're the same ones that escorted the attorney general down from Montgomery."

The two men saw the television vans arrive and park behind the state troopers.

"They're waitin' to see that I enforce it, Ethan," Hub said. "If I don't, they will. You'll have to order your crew to stop whatever they're doing and leave."

"Leave?" Ethan blurted. "We can't just walk away! This hole needs to be watched. Even if we stop drilling, the mud needs to keep circulating and its chemical properties monitored." He stared intently at the lawman. "Sheriff, this can cause me to lose this well."

Tant shook his head. "This order is clear. You can't work any longer."

"But how long, Sheriff?" Ethan pleaded.

Tant shrugged. "I don't know, and I don't know of anything you've done wrong. Now go tell your crew to shut everything off, gather up their belongings and leave. You and Mr. Plunkett will have to sleep somewhere else. I've got to put a lock on your trailer. Please get your stuff and let me see it before you go. And I'm gonna put a sign up over there by the road saying it's off limits by police order."

Ethan stood a few moments longer.

"Ethan, please," the sheriff said.

Ethan turned and slowly walked toward the rig, seeing that both crews were up on the floor and in the process of changing shifts. He climbed the steps. The lawman stayed at the bottom. Ethan looked at Tiny and made a throat-cutting motion. Tiny stopped the Kelly and set the brake. Grady walked to Ethan. "What's up with all them lawmen?"

Ethan looked around at the crews and motioned them over. "Boys, they've shut us down. We have to secure this rig as best we can and leave the location."

"What?" Tiny thundered. He swung his massive arm around. "We can't just leave!"

"I know," Ethan said. "But we have to. They don't understand. They think we can just shut down and come back later and pick up where we left off."

"We might could do that if we had just got started," Grady said. "But we're in too deep now." He turned to Tiny. "Tell him what you just told me."

"We took a kick while ya'll were at the funeral," Tiny said.

"Oh, no!" Ethan uttered.

Grady said. "If only we were in Texas where people knew some shit about this business." He shook his head in disgust.

Ethan looked down at the Kelly bushing as if it were invisible, and he could see through it to the restless earth below.

"Can't we at least leave somebody out here to watch it?" Grady asked.

Ethan shook his head. "Sheriff Tant's got nothing to do with this, fellas. This order came from Montgomery."

"But why?" Grady asked. "We ain't on the Hull lease anymore."

"This is different. It's got nothing to do with Hull. They are shutting us down because of what happened to Mr. Shine. They want to investigate."

"Humph," Grady said. "Investigate hell! They just thought of another way to get us. We treated that man good when he came here. We didn't have nothin' to do with him killin' himself."

"I know," Ethan said. "It's not about that. They are using the excuse that we stole his minerals and saying they need time to investigate."

They heard the sheriff's voice calling for them to come down. They grabbed their stuff.

At the base of the steps Grady paused to look under the substructure toward the blow-out preventer stack. He looked aside at Ethan. "What do you want to do, Ethan?"

"Let's close the pipe rams," Ethan said. "At least that will protect the annulus."

Grady sighed and started toward the stack. He turned. "You sure you don't want to shear it?"

Ethan shook his head. "Too much damage. We might be able to beat this and get back out here pretty soon. Just close the pipe rams."

"What are you doing?" the sheriff asked?

"We are closing off the annulus," Ethan said. "That's the open part of the hole. The hole diameter is bigger than the drill pipe diameter. That will stop a blow-out from coming up outside the pipe."

"But it won't stop a blow coming up the inside of the pipe!" Grady blurted. He pointed to a higher valve. "That's the shear ram. That cuts off the whole shebang." He turned again to Ethan.

"Let's save that," said Ethan.

Grady took a deep breath. "Okay, you're the boss. But the accumulator pressure will eventually bleed off without our engines running, and you won't have the shear rams if you need them." He grabbed the manual shut-off wheel on the pipe rams and turned it until it would turn no farther—the rams fitting tightly against the drill pipe.

Ethan and Grady took their personal possessions from the trailer. Ethan picked up his sample log. Tant shook his head. "Nothing technical can leave, Mr. Bonner. I'm sorry. That's what they told me."

They went to the motel. Ethan put his stuff in J.D.'s room and sat down at the phone. He called Posey, the lawyer in Mobile, and explained his predicament. Posey was appalled. He said he didn't think the shut down order was legal, and he would appeal it right-away. He thought the chances were good that he could get them back drilling within 48 hours. He figured the attorney general was just strutting around on a show of support for the local land owners and, of course, voters.

"Is somebody pushing him to do this?" Ethan asked.

"I think somebody is urging him on," Posey said, "But that's only my opinion. Let me see what I can do. I'll get back with you quick as I can."

J.D. came into the room as Ethan was calling his partners at Scatback Oil Explorers and Abrams Energy. He turned on the TV and laid back on his bed while Ethan made other calls to his vendors and suppliers. Suddenly J.D. sat upright, then rushed to the TV to turn up the volume.

Ethan, still on the phone and annoyed, motioned for him to turn it down. "No!" J.D. shouted. "Listen!"

Ethan cut his call short and hung up the phone, his eyes riveted on the TV. He got up and moved closer. It was the evening news out of Mobile. They were interviewing the attorney general after Mr. Shine's funeral.

"I saw that when I was there," Ethan said, "but I wasn't close enough to hear him."

"Shh! Listen."

"Mr. Shine," the attorney general told the reporter, "was a

good, hard-working son of the Confederacy who was taken advantage of by a big out-of-state company. My office, at this moment, is taking measures to stop the taking of the Shine family's oil until a thorough investigation can be made of this situation, and we don't care if it takes months. The people of Alabama deserve to be protected from outside poachers and to enjoy their God-given rights."

Ethan let out a cynical chuckle.

"Now my friends," the attorney general went on, "I am here today, at poor Mr. Shine's funeral, who was driven to take his own life in despair, to declare that we are not going to rest until we get to the bottom of this shameful and tragic situation that has befell a man and his family who did not deserve this treatment."

J.D. shook his head in disgust. "Maybe Dr. Jones up in Tuscaloosa can do something about this bullshit. The State Geologist ought to be able to carry some sway."

Ethan shook his head. "Done called him. He said we had not violated any of the oil and gas statutes—as far as he knew—and he would call the attorney general and tell him that. But he said he doubted the guy would listen."

"Well, where do we go from here?"

Ethan sighed and stretched. "I don't know about you, but I know where I'm going."

Laura sat in her bathrobe at her kitchen table stirring tea and leafing through a new travel magazine. She spent only a few seconds on each page, sniffling and coughing from a cold. Her hair hung in long ungainly strands. After the encounter at the restaurant she had not left the house, changed, or bathed.

She had heard about Grover Shine. The news didn't totally surprise her, but the method he used made her nauseous. She had tried not to think about it, but couldn't help wondering how bad the depression must be to drive a man to blow the back of his head off.

She lifted her gaze to the window. Brown leaves rocked and swirled as they drifted down. Winter would soon to set in and she hated it. She had never felt so lonely.

Her eyes widened when she heard a knock at the door. She frowned. *Damn you Benny! It's over? Thick headed numbskull!*

The knock kept up.

She got up and stepped in front of the mirror. Alright, it would serve him right to see her like this. Maybe that would scare him away for good. She marched to the front door and jerked it open.

"Ethan!"

Ethan stood, hat in hand. He looked aghast. "Laura, are you sick?"

"Don't you know how to call first?" She began moving strands of hair out of her face.

He chuckled.

She stood dumbfounded. "What's so damned funny?"

He grinned, pointing at her. "Gotcha! You did it to me. Remember?"

She stood with her mouth open, then started to giggle. Then they both burst out laughing.

"You crazy bum," she cried, shaking her head. "Go away. Come back in an hour."

Ethan did as instructed, thinking that all was well because of the mutual laugh, but again he had misjudged. His second reception at her door was cooler than he expected.

He sat on the opposite end of her sofa. She sat with folded arms, as if symbolically keeping her distance and having nothing to say.

"You look good," he said. "I mean, you look great, Laura. You do." His words felt awkward and failed to jump-start a conversation.

He looked around remembering the sweet evenings they had spent there. He saw a stack of travel brochures lying on the coffee table and picked one up. On its cover was the Acropolis in Athens. He looked at her. "Going to see it?" he asked playfully.

She glanced at the brochure, then looked away. More long heavy silence ensued.

"You know, the Greeks started it all," he said.

She raised her eyebrows as if to ask what he meant, but said nothing.

"They started drilling technology—ole Archimedes, you know?" He snickered but felt self-conscious about it.

She nodded, and finally spoke, without looking at him. "Ah, yes he invented the screw, didn't he? And you perfected it."

He let out a nervous chuckle, then turned somber. "She was just a magazine writer, Laura. She came down from New York. I was busy at the rig. She asked to interview me over supper. Sounded okay, so I met her and answered her questions. After that she called a taxi to come up from Mobile and pick her up. That's all."

Laura continued to look away and shrugged. "I didn't bring her up. Why did you? Why do you think I care?"

"Laura, I didn't come here to talk about her anyway. She's nothing. I've got a lot of other stuff pressing me down." He sighed. "I came to talk about us."

She looked at him.

He tried to speak, but his voice sounded shaky and uncertain. "I..."

She relaxed her frown.

It came out as a whisper. "Laura, I need you."

Emmett's buzzer sounded. Darlene said, "Mr. Brubeck, Mr. Hull is here.

He closed the door behind Benny. "Hello there, Benny, my boy. What you up to?"

"Hi, Emmett. Nothin' much. Just thinkin' about things. I get scared sometimes, you know."

"Well, Benny, don't worry about it. Things are gonna work out good for us and your daddy. Is he doin' all right?"

"Seems like he's gettin' worse. He can't remember anything now. I was over there this morning, and he told me, *Benny was coming*."

"Hmm. Too bad. Say, Benny. Let's go coon huntin' tomorrow night. I ain't been in a long time. You up?"

"Well, sure Emmett. But with all that's going on around here now, I don't know if I've got much of a cravin' for it."

"Benny, we're going on a make-believe coon hunt."

Benny's eyes arched. "A what?"

"If, after tomorrow night, anybody asks you—you and I were on a coon hunt down at my cabin. Understand?"

Benny nodded weakly, but looked puzzled and worried. "Are we gonna hunt? Really?"

Emmett got closer into Benny's face. "Benny, you *do* understand, don't you? I was with you coon huntin' if anybody asks—tomorrow night."

Benny's lights seemed to finally come on. "What are you gonna do, Emmett?"

"Benny, you and I are going to meet with Bonner and ask him to sign our agreement. If anything goes wrong, we will both need to prove we were somewhere else. So, we were coon huntin'."

"Go wrong? What might go wrong?"

"Come on, Benny. You just told me you've been thinkin' about things. Raymond and Gerrard are going with us. You know what could go wrong."

Benny backed toward the door. "Emmett, I ain't goin'. There's nothin' I can do out there."

"Oh, hell yes, you are going! I've got to have you there for my own insurance. If you don't go, you might go back on your word about me and you off coon huntin'."

Benny's face turned pale and panicky.

"There ain't no backing out of this, Benny. Chambers expects it. If we don't go through with the plan, we'll both get found floatin' belly down in the Tensaw." He paused to let that sink in. "And if you don't go with me, Raymond and Gerrard might not like it if I told them you made off with the rest of their money."

Ethan got out of his car and made his way toward his room. Across the way, his crews, both daylight and night tours, stood huddled under a streetlight by a parked car. He heard them talking but couldn't make out the words. The smooth harmonics of the Flamingos flowed from the car's radio and echoed across the parking lot. *I Only Have Eyes for You.* He heard Skeeter try to sing the refrain, "Sha-bop, sha-bop." They laughed. He saw cans being lifted to their lips. He kept to the shadows.

He opened the hotel room door and tip-toed in the dark toward his bed. "I'm awake," came a gruff voice from the dark. Ethan saw a point of amber light from the direction of the voice. It glowed brighter for a second and then went dim again.

"You know you shouldn't smoke in bed," Ethan said as he felt for the bathroom door. J.D. switched on his night stand lamp.

"Well, here we go again," J.D. lamented, exhaling a lungful of blue vapor. "Got my roomie back."

"Yeah. Again," Ethan called from the bathroom.

J.D. took another drag. "Ethan, the lawyer, Posey, called a little while ago."

Ethan came out of the bathroom and looked at him expectantly.

"He's resigning."

"What?" Ethan asked, stunned. "Why would he? We're paying him."

"He said he had his family to think about. I think Matt Chambers got to him. I tried to get it out of him, but he wouldn't say anything except his concern about his family."

Ethan sat on the bed and stared at the floor. "What are we going to do without counsel?"

J.D. didn't answer. He sat silently for a while leaning back against the bed's head board. "There's more, Ethan."

Ethan looked up. J.D.'s tone boded more bad news.

"Emmett Brubeck just called here."

"What did he want?"

J.D. shrugged. "Wouldn't tell me. I ain't on the best of terms with him."

"I'd say that reflects positively on you."

"Anyway, he wants you to call him tonight."

Ethan glanced at his watch. It was near midnight. He turned to J.D. "Are you sure?"

J.D. mashed out the butt and nodded.

Ethan sat on the bed and eyed the phone. "Should I?"

J.D. shrugged again.

Ethan rubbed his face then laid back on the bed with his arms locked behind his head. "J.D., after this is over I'm going to head back to Oklahoma as soon as I can get away. I need a break."

"She goin' with you?"

"I don't know."

"So, you gonna leave this bucket of worms with ole Grady and me?"

"If there were any worms left in the bucket I'd stay and fish. I know when I'm beaten. Grady can contract the rig out to another operator. He'll keep it drilling. There's plenty of work for you around here, too."

"That's loser's talk," J.D. muttered.

"Loser, hell!" Ethan said, jumping to his feet.

J.D.'s eyes skewed aside toward Ethan.

"I have worked like a mad man to make all this work out. Risked everything I had." He began to pace. "I worked night and day. Round the clock, sometimes. Nobody worked harder than me to make this—" he waved his arm as if toward his wells, "—this whole ridiculous FUBAR work out!"

He paused to get his breath and rub his hand across his scalp. He looked back at J.D. with a menacing stare. "Don't you call me a loser."

"Sorry, Ethan," J.D. mumbled. He stared at the ceiling. "I had no call to say that. 'Specially a loser like me."

Ethan sat down on his bed and softened his voice. "Hey."

J.D. turned.

"Remember when you said I wouldn't be able to depend on you? Well, I have depended on you. And you came through for me. I don't call that a loser. I call that a winner. And a friend."

J.D. smiled and laid back in his pillow. His eyes cut back toward Ethan. He chuckled. So did Ethan.

Ethan eyed the phone and sighed. "Well, I'm going to call him."

He dialed the number J.D. had jotted down and waited for the answer. "Emmett, this is Ethan Bonner. You wanted me to call you tonight?"

J.D. listened to the tiny voice and strained to hear Brubeck's words.

"Okay," Ethan said. He paused to listen. "Tomorrow night? At the rig?" Ethan looked at J.D. with wide eyes. "Why there?"

J.D. raised up on his elbow, mouth agape, eyes alarmed.

"You're kidding?" Ethan said into the phone.

J.D. began shaking his head.

Ethan eyed J.D. and frowned.

"Why the rig, Emmett?" Ethan pressed. "I could meet you anywhere." He paused to listen.

"You never seen the rig up close, you say?" repeating Brubeck's words for J.D.'s benefit.

"You want to get a tour in the dark, eh? ... You hold the cards, huh? ... Well, maybe you do and maybe you don't."

J.D.'s head shook more forcefully. His lips formed a, *No.*

"You're telling me, the sheriff won't have anybody out there guarding it? How you gonna make that happen, Emmett?" Ethan listened but didn't respond.

"Yeah, Emmett, I'm still here." He listened again. "Okay, Emmett. I'll be there." He hung up.

J.D. swung his legs over the side of the bed and sat up. "Ethan, don't even think about doin' that."

"What choice do I have, J.D.? He said he holds all the cards, and he does. I've got to hear his deal."

J.D. leaned forward and pressed an urgent plea. "But not there, Ethan. Not there alone at night. He'll eat you alive!"

"J.D., he's just a timber broker. What can he do?"

"Somebody sicced those thugs on poor old Mr. Shine. Who do you think did that? I'll tell you who. It was that harmless *timber broker* you just talked to."

"They took his money. J.D. It was a robbery."

"My ass, it was."

"I'll be careful, J.D."

J.D. got up and pulled his duffle bag out from under the bed. He took out his Colt 1911, dropped the clip out, glanced at its stack of .45 slugs, then slammed it back in. He pulled the slide back and released it. Ethan nearly flinched at the metallic snap of the slide slamming back into the receiver. "You ever used one of these?"

Ethan shook his head. "Just Army revolvers."

"Ethan, do you even own a firearm?"

Ethan smiled and shook his head again. "Did once. A shotgun. Had to hock it, though." He looked aside and chuckled. "Needed money."

J.D. checked that the safety lever was engaged and carefully handed the pistol to Ethan.

Ethan sat on his bed and stared at the offer.

"Take it," J.D. said. "For my sake, take it. Otherwise I won't sleep tonight. I might not anyway."

Ethan nodded and took the pistol. He turned it over in his hands. The light went out and he heard J.D. lay down. He laid the pistol on his bed stand and leaned back against his pillow. An hour ago he was in Laura's arms and finally feeling whole again—finally making some sense of his world again. Making plans to finish here and move on.

But now. Now his troubles were back, and it made him sick to his stomach.

23

CHECKMATE

Hub Tant's phone rang as he sat down to the supper table. His dispatcher told him she had gotten a call from somebody who said that shots were being fired at a farm, near New Hope Church. A house and barn were reportedly on fire. "Who's on patrol?" Hub barked into the phone.

"Other than Jerry, who's already headed out there, there's Floyd out at that oil rig," the dispatcher told him.

"You say there were shots?" Hub asked.

She said that's all the caller told her.

"Radio Floyd," Hub commanded, "and tell him to leave the drilling rig and get out there to back-up Jerry!" Hub grabbed his gun belt and hat and rushed out.

Daylight languished as Ethan slowly turned into the rig road, looking around and wondering where the lawman was who was supposed to be watching the rig. Arriving at the base of the rig, he got out and carefully scanned all around him. As Brubeck had prophesized no lawman was in sight. Lucky Lucy's shadowy derrick loomed above him, standing eerily quiet. He heard nothing, not even a bird. The stillness unsettled him more than the quiet. He had never felt so tense.

He sat for a moment eyeing the glove box where he had

stashed J.D.'s Colt. He took it out and stared at it, then looked down and around his belt line to evaluate where he might put it, not wanting it to be visible. He tried jamming it behind his belt—first on the left side, then the right. He felt like a tin horn cowboy. He imagined himself emptying the magazine into someone's belly. The thought revolted him, and he put it back in the glove box, reasoning that he might still be able to get to it if the need arose.

He glanced at his watch. He had arrived precisely at seven p.m. Brubeck was late. He stood a while longer debating whether to go onto the rig for a quick inspection before it got too dark. Suddenly he felt a thump under his feet and heard a rattle in the derrick. Then the rig fell quiet again. A rancid paste developed in his mouth.

He began breathing heavily. He looked back out at the road and saw no one parked or approaching. He turned toward the hydraulic control panel that operated the shear rams on the blow-out preventer. He peered into the darkness underneath the substructure. There was a button on the control panel that opened the accumulator valve that would slam the shear rams inward and pinch the pipe completely closed—if there was still sufficient pressure in it. He stepped closer to the dark underbelly of the rig but felt bumps crawl up the back of his neck. Someone could be waiting for him under there. As he stood evaluating the risk, he heard a car. With a strange feeling of relief he turned and watched it.

Emmett Brubeck's Lincoln rolled to a stop beside Ethan's car. Ethan stayed put. Brubeck sat in the car for a couple of minutes. Someone else was with him, but he couldn't tell who. The two sat for a while, then Brubeck got out and approached him. He stopped and turned back to the car. "Roll your window down and say hi to Mr. Bonner, Benny."

Ethan saw the window go down. Saw Benny wave. He felt something was terribly odd about that. "Hello, Ethan," Brubeck said, taking out a cigar from a jacket pocket.

Ethan nodded toward the car. "What's up with him?"

Emmett laughed. "He's turned bashful, I guess." He offered a cigar, but Ethan waved it off. He put one back in his inside jacket pocket and proceeded to light the other. His cheeks contracted and rebounded like a fish's gills as he puffed to get the fire going.

"Smoking is not a good idea around here right now," Ethan said.

"Humph!" Brubeck uttered. He looked around and up at the derrick. "Damn," he said with a mouthful of cigar. "I've never been this close. This thing is big!" He took the cigar out, inspected the tip, and looked at Ethan. "Ethan, I like you. You're an honest, hard-working man. Smart, too." He puffed again. "Do you play chess, Ethan?"

He shook his head. "No time for it."

"I don't play either. Used to. But you know, Ethan, all this stuff we do around here," he gestured the cigar toward Ethan, "you and me, and the others—it's all like a chess game. I make a move. You make a move. Pretty soon one of us gets trapped and can't move anymore." He lowered his cigar down to his side, exhaled a cloud, and shook his head, as if in pity. "Ethan, you can't move anymore. It's checkmate, my friend."

He reached into another jacket pocket and pulled out a stapled assemblage of papers. "This agreement here—"

"Why did you insist on meeting me out here?" Ethan interrupted.

Brubeck snorted. "There are a lot of prying eyes in my building, and you're not popular with some of my associates. They don't need to know we've talked. Besides, I like to get out of the office."

"Do you realize this hole is in oil sand right now," Ethan warned, "with no crew here to control the pressure if it gets out of hand?"

Brubeck looked up again at the silent derrick. "Looks like it's sleeping like a baby to me. It probably needs a rest, the way you been working it. Besides, this won't take long, if you're as smart as I hope you are."

"What's your proposal?"

"Ethan, you know the Hull lease litigation is going to get

strung out for a long time. And I don't care if you get the best damned lawyer in the country, the judge is gonna rule in our favor. In the end—if you can last that long—you'll lose."

"Maybe I won't lose. Maybe I can get an honest judge to hear the appeal."

Brubeck chuckled.

"I don't need the Hull oil to keep going," Ethan said. "I can use the oil right here under our feet to keep me operating."

Brubeck smirked. "Oh, yeah? Well, here's the deal. You assign us half the Hull interest and half all your other leases as well—including this one we're standing on—and I call off the lawyers, and I tell the attorney general that everything down here is hunky-dory, and you can start drillin' again." Brubeck broke into a huge grin. "We'll be partners, Ethan."

"Us? I assume that means you and Matt Chambers?"

"Never heard of 'im."

"So, let me get this straight," Ethan said in a mocking tone. "I give you half of all my leases, not just the ones under litigation."

Brubeck nodded, smiling.

"And, of course you agree to pay your half of all your expenses for drilling and operating, right?"

"Oh, no!" Brubeck blurted, chuckling and shaking his head with the cigar in his teeth swinging back and forth. "You're still payin' it all! But we'll let you recover your expenses from production before we come in."

"The answer is no."

"Look, Ethan, I personally don't have anything against you, like some of them around here do. Like I said, I even like you. I don't want to see anything happen to you. So let's make this easy."

Little hairs bristled on the back of Ethan's neck. His eyes shot side to side. He looked behind him. He swallowed hard, wishing he had belted the Colt. "What do you mean?"

"I mean this is your last chance to settle. Now I'm offering you a good deal—half interest. If you stay stubborn you'll lose everything. Do you understand what I'm saying—everything!"

Ethan saw Brubeck was getting worked up, sweating more, and breathing hard. He seemed edgy. Ethan sensed the man was not just determined but maybe even desperate.

Brubeck looked aside in the direction of the dark substructure and nodded. Ethan's eyes shot in that direction. A figure stepped from the shadows, a hulking, looming man, walking straight from the direction Ethan had considered taking to the blow-out preventer. "These gentlemen will help you change your mind."

Ethan quickly looked around but saw only the one man. He took a step to gain some separation from Brubeck and his gorilla, but then the other *gentleman* appeared. They had him blocked on three sides. He whirled around and darted in the only escape direction—straight into the steps to the rig floor.

He clambered up, hearing the steel steps clanking loud under his feet, then hearing them clanking louder under heavier steps below him. Reaching the floor he sprinted toward the doghouse and stopped short of it. There was a back door to it, but the door opened to a fifteen foot drop. He turned to see the two thugs reach the floor and stop. Brubeck arrived at the floor a few seconds later.

Brubeck stopped and took out a handkerchief. Wiping his forehead, he said, "Now you tell me one last time, are you going to cooperate with us or not?"

Suddenly mud erupted through the Kelly bushing and began to flood around their feet. Brubeck and the thugs ignored it, but Ethan looked at the mud and pointed. "We've got to do something about that right now!"

"What?" Brubeck shouted.

"This well is about to take a kick! Maybe a big one."

Knowing Brubeck knew nothing about oil drilling, he pointed again at the mud, now welling far out onto the drill floor with increasing volume, and looked at the big thug. The guy ignored the oozy flood and stepped toward him.

Ethan turned and started to make a break for the catwalk, but the other brute blocked him.

Brubeck yelled from behind him. "Ethan, a man could break his neck falling off this thing. You really ought to cooperate with me!"

The two men stood still to let Ethan consider Brubeck's appeal. That gave Ethan the seconds he needed to evaluate his only escape route—the derrick ladder. But that would take him exactly where they wanted him. It would be a long, perfect, *accidental* fall.

He thought quickly. The escape from the derrick was the Geronimo line. If he could reach it in time he could use it to get away. He lunged for the ladder and scrambled up, his feet barely escaping the big man's grasp.

His fingers clawed for the rungs, one over the other while he kicked his feet, hoping his boot would smash his pursuer in the face and slow him down. He could hear the man's feet kicking at the steel rungs, his heavy grunts and hissing breath a few feet below him. From the bottom he heard Brubeck's shouts. "Give it up, Ethan! Deal with me, now! We can still make this easy!"

He felt the derrick tremble. He grasped another rung and another, his breath huffing, biceps burning. He felt a hand slap at his boot, and he climbed harder, faster.

Reaching the monkey board he whirled around and sat on his butt, facing outward, holding onto the railing with all his might and began kicking at the man's face. He landed one solid blow and bought enough time to stand up on the board. He saw the second thug clinging to the ladder just below the big one. Far below he saw Brubeck fleeing down the steps from the drill floor.

He suddenly realized there was another sound—a ringing, a creaking of metal, a deep-seated moan far below, and a dreadful hissing. Even at his height in the derrick he smelled the hot, pungent stench of drilling mud. He pointed to the drill floor hoping the thug would realize the danger they were all in and abandon the chase, but he saw only a determined grimace and a bleeding gash on his face where Ethan had kicked him. The man cursed and reached for Ethan's leg.

Ethan turned and grabbed the rungs of the ladder leading to

the crown block. He had never been that high on the derrick. His heart raced. Sucking in gulps of air he scrambled upward, feeling the derrick waver and hearing the roar of gas that now muffled his pursuers' curses.

Reaching the top of the derrick Ethan grabbed a cable that dropped from the crown block and clung to it, violently scissoring his feet, hoping to land a blow on the thug's face. The man leaned backward to get a better view of Ethan clinging above him and to avoid the swinging legs. He let go with one hand and reached toward his belt.

Ethan glanced down at the rig floor to see what was happening and then turned back to the thug, looking straight down the muzzle of an enormous revolver. His breath seized. He saw the big hand gripping the pistol, saw the face grin. Ethan turned his head away and hid his face in his elbow.

A piercing blast of metal on metal jolted his body and nearly blew him loose from his perch. He opened his eyes and saw a shimmering geyser blossoming up toward him. The thug stole a glance over his shoulder, downward. The hot, gas-laced mud struck them with a thundering roar. Ethan saw the man lose his grip and totter backward, knocking the second man's grip loose. He saw the panic in the face, saw the loose pistol plunge. He saw both men plummet straight down into the geyser, careening off the swivel assembly, their limbs flailing, their bodies growing smaller and finally slamming onto the drill floor. He heard the pistol's report as it hit bottom. The darkness below erupted into a brilliant inferno.

Ethan turned his face upward, seeing only a disappearing starscape—a sky filling with a raging glow reflecting on streaming gas-laced mist. He dropped back down to the monkey board, reached out and groped for the Geronimo line as the heat built on his back and legs. He found it and grabbed the T-bar. It was designed to use with a safety harness, but Ethan had only his oily hands. He stabbed at the brake lever and threw the weight of his body into the T-bar.

His feet left the derrick and swung into the upward spewing hell, scorching his legs. Then he felt a rush of air. Moving backwards and down at a forty-five-degree angle he could see flames now as stout and as searing as a rocket plume roaring through the crown block where he had just been perched, turning the steel white-hot.

One hand slipped. He dangled with the other slimy hand. He reached back and tried to get another grip but couldn't. The rig slowly pulled away from him, as if he were stationary and it was moving away. Descending backward into darkness, he could see nothing else but a fire so brilliant he closed his eyes. Then the other hand lost its grip. He fell with his back down and opened his eyes for a final glimpse, waiting for the blow to his spine and head, hoping there would be no pain.

His landing was a thud, not a wallop, but the breath left him like a blow to the back with a two-by-four. When he opened his mouth it filled with gritty slime. His arms flailed but felt resistance, like swimming, but thicker than water. His lungs burned and quivered, trying to burst, to make him inhale the hot muck but he resisted. He pumped his legs and found a toehold on something solid. He paddled with his hands to an upright position and found the bottom with the other foot. His head burst up through the mud. His mouth exploded with slime and he gulped air laced with putrid smoke.

He wiped mud from his eyes and tried to open them, crying out as the bentonite stung his eyes. He looked behind, standing chest high in drilling mud, watching the furnace that had been Lucky Lucy.

The roar pounded him. Heat singed his face. He made swimming motions in the mud, trying to move, to get some distance from the inferno. Then he heard a thud behind him. He turned and saw a section of smoldering drill pipe sticking out of the mud at a crazy angle. His skin crawled when he realized what was happening. He looked up.

The night sky was filled with tumbling, flaming sections of

thirty-foot lengths of heavy drill pipe reaching the top of their arching climb, beginning their descent toward him. He gulped an enormous breath and ducked under the mud, folding his legs under him clawing for the bottom, desperate to get as deep as he could. He paddled the thick mud upward to stay submerged and heard impacts around him. When his lungs would stand no more he found his footing again, stood upright and burst out breathing. He wiped his eyes as best he could and looked about. Drill pipe lay contorted, bent and piled all around him, cooling, hissing.

The glow of the conflagration lit the cotton rows surrounding the drill site with a shimmering orange sheen. He picked a path through the jumble of pipe and made his way to solid ground.

A car roared past the parked Buick Roadster heading hell-bent away from the drilling rig. "Wasn't that Emmett Brubeck's car?" J.D. asked.

"Hell if I know," Grady said. They both watched it turn onto the highway and speed toward town.

"I don't like this," J.D. muttered. "Let's get over to the rig, now!"

They thumped their cigarettes away, and Grady started the car. Suddenly J.D.'s head snapped in the direction of the rig. "Holy shit! Look at that."

They both looked and saw the flames shooting up the derrick. Grady jammed the accelerator to the floor, skidding the Roadster's backend around and onto the rig road. He stopped about a hundred yards from the conflagration and both got out. They saw Ethan's car. They both shielded their faces from the heat and trotted to it. They looked inside and saw Ethan wasn't there. Grady yelled above the roar, "You go that way. Look for Ethan. I'll go this way." Grady ran off pulling at his pistol.

J.D. turned and trotted in the opposite direction Grady had gone.

Ethan climbed out of the hot mud and sat, heaving and coughing. He turned and watched Lucky Lucy melt. He laid his head back onto the bare ground and gulped more air. Someone grabbed him. "Are you all right?" J.D. yelled.

He grimaced at the sharp pains, all over his body, as J.D. tried to help him up. "No!"

J.D. looked over Ethan's body. "Hang on, Ethan. Hang on. Help's on the way. I see flashing lights coming down the road. Just hang on."

Headlights rounded the curve in the dirt road to Brubeck's cabin. The car slammed to a stop, spraying dust and gravel. Emmett got out and hurried to the cabin's porch with Benny trailing. After unlocking the door Emmett went straight to the liquor cabinet. He got out a bottle and two glasses. They both stood and brooded over their whiskey. Then Emmett smiled. "Your man Kidd came through for us," he said, nodding approval toward Benny.

"Yeah, boy," Benny said, grinning. "I told him to light that old busted down barn afire, shoot off a few rounds, and go to the store and call it in. I knew, when we saw Floyd's car start up and turn on his red lights and race off, that ole Buford had done good!"

Emmett eyed the phone. After draining the glass, the first of many he planned for the night, he picked up the phone and dialed with a shaking hand.

"Matt," he said. "This is Emmett. Bonner is dead." He paused to breathe heavily through an open mouth. "A fire, Matt. He burned up. That whole damned drilling rig caught fire. I barely got away from it before it blew up." He poured more whiskey while he listened, then took another sip. "No, Matt. I had to leave. I saw him go up the ladder to the top. He couldn't have lived through it."

He took another sip and listened. "No, it just blew up on its own. I don't know what happened, but the timing was perfect." Emmett's eyes bulged as he listened. "I think we got it done." He glanced at Benny. "I mean, yes, Matt, I *know* we got it done. I'm certain. You should have seen that fire. I've never seen anything like it. It looks just like an accident. Hell, it *is* an accident. That oil just spewed out of there and somehow it caught on fire." He listened and nodded, as if Chambers could see him. "That's right, Matt. We'll lay low for a while and then do a deal with whoever takes over—if anybody takes over." He chuckled nervously. "Hell, there ain't nothin' left of Bonner Oil Company now that he and his rig is gone. Just some investors. I'll find out who they are and offer them a buy-out." He took another sip. "Yeah, well. Thanks, Matt. I'll be in tou—" He looked at the phone, frowned, hung it up, and mumbled an affront to Chambers' sexuality.

Emmett looked at Benny. He chuckled. "We don't have to pay off the two thugs!" Both laughed, and raised their glasses.

"Emmett," Benny said, quietly, "you don't think them two escaped that fire, do you?"

Emmett's grin faded. He looked toward the window. He skewed his eyes toward the door, then the other window. He got up and went over to check the door lock.

Benny got edgy and started looking around.

Emmett reached with his free hand into his beltline and ran his fingers over the handle of his pistol.

Neither of them slept.

24

Ashes

Ethan's eyes opened. Laura took his hand, leaned over, and kissed his cheek. She smiled and whispered, "Welcome back."

She told him he was in the hospital in Mobile, that his arms and legs had suffered first- and second-degree burns, and that he had several broken ribs, a sprained ankle, a dislocated shoulder, and lacerations to his arms, legs, and face.

He grinned. "Does that mean I'm still alive?"

"That's right, partner," somebody said. Laura turned. Grady, J.D., and both crews shuffled in and spread around the bed. Grady stepped up close to him. "Now, didn't I tell you that rig was snake-bit?" The men chuckled. Ethan smiled.

Grady took off his hat. Laura got up and gave him her chair.

"What's happening out there?" Ethan asked with a weak, whispery voice.

"Well," Grady said with a sigh. "We lost the rig, as you know. Nothin's left. The derrick and substructure melted." He looked aside at the others. "Just flat out melted. Whew!" He paused. "There's a few tools and things left that are usable—from what we can see. Nobody can get close to it yet. The mud pumps and generators might be repairable. The only drill pipe that survived is a few joints we had left lying on the racks."

"But what about the well," Ethan asked.

"It's still blowing and burnin'. I called Myron Kinley's outfit in Houston. He sent a guy over to have a look—a feller named Red somethin' or other. He's up there now decidin' what to do."

"What do you think they'll do?" Ethan said, trying to raise up on an elbow, grimacing.

"Lie back down, now!" Laura demanded, helping him back down.

"He told me he'd probably use TNT or Nitro."

"Blow it out, then?"

Grady nodded. "He said it looked like a pretty simple job since the blow is coming straight up through the surface casing. He says he's got a control head that will fit over the casing."

Ethan stared at the ceiling then looked at J.D. "Will the insurance cover it?"

J.D. stepped forward, hat in hand. "Me and Grady read the policy. It only covers the loss of the rig. It doesn't include blowout control, Ethan."

Ethan's eyes cut to Grady. "How much?"

"Dammit, Ethan!" Grady said. "Don't worry about that. Myron always works something out. If you ain't got the cash, he'll take a loan or—or an override on production, or something. Just don't worry. Okay?"

Ethan looked back up at the ceiling and tried to laugh. "Don't worry, he says."

"Ethan, you're alive!" Laura said. "And you're going to be okay. That's all we care about."

Grady turned to the crew. "Come on, boys. Let's let the boss rest." They each wished him well and filed out. J.D. said, "I got to go too, Ethan. I rode with them."

In the hallway J.D. asked Grady if it was true, that Kinley's company made those kinds of payment arrangements. Grady shrugged. "I don't know. Probably not. I just didn't want to make him feel any worse than he is."

They passed Sheriff Tant coming into the lobby and chatted with him. Tant went to the room and greeted his niece, then Ethan.

"They told me you're gonna be okay," Hub said. "That's mighty good. Do you feel like answering some questions?"

Ethan nodded.

"Mister Whitley told me he saw a car that looked like Emmett Brubeck's leaving your rig site just before the explosion. Did you see Brubeck there?"

Ethan nodded. "We talked. He tried to get me to sign an agreement to give him half of all my leases."

"And did you?"

"No. I refused. That's when his two thugs came out of the dark and chased me up onto the rig."

"Why were ya'll there? You knew it was off limits."

"He insisted that's where we meet. And besides, I wanted to look things over. I was worried."

"So, you say two men chased you on the rig? Can you describe them?"

Ethan told him all he remembered about them. "They chased me up into the derrick even while the hole was spewing mud, because the oil and gas pressure was blowing it out." He tried to rise up again and grimaced.

The sheriff put his hands under Ethan's back. "Now, lie back down and be still."

"Remember, Sheriff? I tried to tell you I would lose that hole if you didn't let us stay!"

"And you remember I couldn't do it!" Hub sighed again. "Okay, they chased you up the derrick. What happened?"

"The big one tried to grab me. I kicked him. He fell back and hit the other one and they both fell all the way. I heard his pistol go off. I think it lit the gas."

Hub grunted. "How'd you get off of there before you got bar-be-qued?"

"The only thing that saved me was a north wind." He grunted again. "It kept the flames off to the side just enough to let me go for the escape line." Ethan told him about the Geronimo line and his fall into the pit.

Hub got up and looked out the window, rubbing his chin. He looked back. "Mr. Brubeck denied he was out there that night. Said he was coon huntin' with Benny Hull. And Benny confirmed it."

"It's a lie, Sheriff. Benny was there, too. He sat in the car while all this was going on."

Hub scratched the back of his head again.

"Say," Ethan said, "Did you find those two fellas that fell?"

"No. It's way too hot to get near that thing—if there's anything left of them. And if we don't find them, then this whole thing is just an accident. And you're the only casualty."

The sheriff bade them goodbye. Laura stayed at his bedside through the night.

They saw the black smoke column miles before they got there. Ethan sat silently in the passenger seat of Laura's car, staring at the plume, his mouth partially open, as if he wanted to say something but couldn't. Traffic was heavy and slow.

"Wow," Laura said. "Look at all these cars!"

As they approached the site, they saw parked vehicles lining the highway on both sides. People stood talking and taking pictures. He saw a few cars and trucks from newspapers and television stations. Here and there cameras with big long lenses sat atop tripods, all trained toward the place where Lucky Lucy had once stood.

In the distance a roaring red and orange plume stood straight up, a hundred or so feet, he guessed. Where the flames ended a billowing column of soot-black smoke boiled into the sky like a never-ending succession of giant burning mushrooms going up, one right after another. He cranked his window down, and the roar flooded in.

A deputy waved his arm at Laura as she slowed at the turn from the highway into the Shine farm. He bent, looked in, and tipped his hat. "Hi, Miss Hamilton." He nodded at Ethan. "Okay, ya'll can go on in," he said.

She parked beside Grady's Buick.

Very carefully, so as not to cause more side pain, Ethan got out of Laura's car and leaned into his crutches. Laura came around the car and joined him. They stood for a while looking at the destruction and listening to the roar. What was left of Lucky Lucy had been bulldozed to the side and pushed into a pile of twisted, contorted pieces of charred metal. A dozer sat near the pile. Ethan saw that corrugated sheets of metal had been welded to it to protect the operator from the heat. They watched the activity near the wellhead. A crane with similar protection for the operator was lowering objects next to the well.

Ethan hobbled toward a group of men. Grady, standing with the group, saw him coming and introduced him to the Houston men. Shouting to be heard above the din he yelled, "They're gettin' ready to put this candle out!"

Red, the site boss, explained that the crane was building a platform as close to the well as possible. Then the crane would place a 55-gallon drum next to it filled with TNT and nitro, wrapped in asbestos. High pressure water hoses would keep the drum relatively cool until the crane backed away. Then the explosives would be detonated remotely. If all went well the explosion would cause the fire to snuff out due to oxygen starvation.

Ethan shook his head. "Where did you guys get all this equipment?"

Red said the company kept equipment stored at different locations across the country.

"You guys are unbelievable," Ethan said. "But how will you kill the well after you get the fire out?"

Red said they would put a flange on the casing and then lower a valve assembly down and let the geyser of oil flow through it until they had it bolted in place. Then they would "kill" the well by pumping mud through an attachment on the valve until the formation was once again sealed off by the weight of the mud.

Red then urged them all to go back out to the highway. Before Ethan could turn away Red put a clipboard in his hands and asked him to sign a paper. It was an agreement to pay, although no amount was listed.

Red yelled and grinned, "We gotta eat, too!"

Ethan scribbled his signature.

Brubeck's heart nearly stopped when the shock wave slammed into his office window sending a planter plummeting to the floor. His secretary ran, terrified, into his office. "Oh, my God! What was that?" she shrieked.

He looked up from the busted planter. "They blew that fire out—I guess."

His phone rang. He snatched it and answered. "What the hell happened?" He listened, then said, "Stay close, Benny." He looked at his secretary and made a slight head motion toward the door. She got the clue and retreated, closing the door behind her. "I want to know the minute they find anything of our two associates, if there's anything left of them. Understand? I don't care how you do it, just watch and find out." In the manner of his boss in Mobile, he hung up without a goodbye.

He pulled out a drawer and took out a half empty bottle of Jack Daniel, poured it into a coffee cup and lifted it toward his lips but paused, looking at it. The cup shook. He couldn't stop it.

"The sheriff's coming over here," J.D. said, turning to Ethan in the back seat.

"Well," said Ethan. "Let's see what he has to say." J.D., Ethan and Grady got out.

Hub looked at the debris field. "The DA sent a couple of forensic guys up from Mobile, and they went through it with us. They found the gun. It was burnt pretty bad, but we could see that one round had been discharged. It looked like the serial number had been filed off. They will look at it in the lab and see if they can trace it back to somewhere or somebody."

Ethan let out a long sigh of relief. "Then you believe my story?"

"I got no reason to doubt your story," Hub said. "The report of a barn fire and shots over in the New Hope area pulled my deputy off. But that could be a coincidence, and just findin' that gun doesn't make this a crime site unless they find some evidence that somebody got hurt by it or killed here, and as of now they haven't found any of that." He nodded toward the scorched ground. "So far, this is just an accident. You can go in now."

The four walked the grounds in rubber boots, inspecting the wellhead Kinley's men had installed. They picked through the twisted, gnarled and charred wreckage of Lucky Lucy.

"Well, I'll be damned," Grady said. "Look a-here!" He kicked at something in the dirt until it was fully uncovered. He reached down and picked it up. Ethan stared at it and broke into a grin. He chuckled. So did J.D. Then Grady tilted his head back and cackled, followed by all of them, so loud the law officers standing a good distance away looked at them. It was the lucky horseshoe that Cuz had put over the doghouse door.

As they made their way to the trailer, Grady said, "I guess it's plain to see why you always put the trailer a good distance away from the rig." Inside, Ethan shuffled through his paperwork with his good arm.

J.D. picked up the phone. "Still works," he said.

Ethan looked around at the others and sighed. "I don't know what this fire is going to cost, but I suspect it'll be more than I've got or can get."

"Ethan, at least you know you've got a good well here. You can borrow some money on it and bring in a rig and complete it," J.D. said with an encouraging tone.

Ethan swallowed and looked away, then let out a cynical chuckle. "Who's gonna lend to me when I've got debts I can't pay and a cease-and-desist order still over my head?"

"But that order is not legal; it's political maneuvering. We know that. It won't last much—"

"It will last long enough for them to achieve their purpose,"

Ethan interrupted. "And that purpose is to make me go bankrupt and give in to their demands on the Hull leases." He looked at his friends one by one. "They have time on their side, and we don't."

From the coffee pot Grady mumbled, "We're out-gunned."

Ethan drew in a deep breath. "I need to figure out what's left of my cash and who it's going to." He glanced at Grady and added, "that is, after I pay my men."

The roar of a vehicle passing overhead on the Chickasaw bridge drowned out Brubeck's words. "What?" Ethan asked.

"I said, I see you're recovering nicely," Brubeck observed. "What's that bulge under your shirt." He pointed at Ethan's beltline. "You thought you might need that this time?"

"You're damn right I did!" Ethan blurted.

Benny paused from skipping rocks into the creek and looked their way. So did Grady, Cuz, and Tiny standing a distance away, arms folded.

"There won't be any need for it, or for your escorts. Our associates are gone, and Benny and I do business the gentlemen's way."

"Sure you do," Ethan mocked.

"Look, Bonner, I'm sorry you got hurt. I didn't plan it that way. But if you'd dealt with me before this affair got messy you'd be much better off than you are now. So let's get to new business. Here's the deal: You will assign both the Hogan and Hull leases to us. You get $50,000 and 1 percent overriding royalty interest. You ride into the sunset."

Ethan snapped, furiously, "You forgot to add that the attorney general suddenly realizes he didn't have the jurisdiction to shut me down on the Hogan lease, the judge lifts the injunction on the Hull lease, and you take over and start production."

Brubeck smiled. "I have no idea what you are talking about."

Ethan let out a hiss and looked toward the creek. "Fifty grand won't touch the debt I owe."

Brubeck shrugged.

Ethan blurted, "You take over all the debts. Everything I owe, and make it hundred thousand, and you pay Myron Kinley." He could hardly believe he said it.

"Who?" Brubeck asked.

"That company that put the fire out," Benny yelled.

"How much is that gonna cost?" Brubeck asked.

"I have no idea. I don't have the bill yet. And I don't care. You're going to pay it if you want the deal."

Emmett reached for a cigar from his coat pocket, took it out, glanced at the trio who had accompanied Ethan, bit off the tip, and spat. "Okay. Meet us back here tomorrow, same time. I'll have the cash and the assignments for your signature."

"And a letter," Ethan demanded. "A letter committing to pay for all outstanding bills plus the blow-out."

"Um," Emmett muttered. "That'll take some thought."

"No it won't. It'll be simple," Ethan persisted. "The letter will state that you, Emmett Brubeck, you—and him," Ethan pointed at Benny, "pay the invoices for putting out the fire, shutting in the well, and cleaning the mess up."

"What the hell?" Benny shouted.

"Shut up," Brubeck barked. He puffed at the cigar. "I don't have the authority to agree to that, Bonner."

Ethan turned and began to leave. "Wait," Brubeck said. "You tell me about how much all that is going to cost, and I'll run it upstairs."

"You mean upstairs to Matt Chambers?"

Brubeck shook his head. "My wife."

"A hundred and sixty thousand in obligations, and I'd say about five to ten thousand for the fire." Ethan knew it would be likely ten times that amount for the fire.

Brubeck nodded. "Oh, well. I'm as ready as you to get this over with. See you tomorrow."

25

Another Map

Ethan closed his suitcase and snapped it shut. He heaved it to his car with J.D. in trail toting a big cardboard box full of maps, logs, and notebooks. He looked over the Do-Drop Inn for a last time. The parking lot was packed with cars and trucks with the logos of several oil companies and service outfits. "When you and I rolled in here nearly a year ago, we had the only car in this parking lot."

J.D. nodded at the ground and took a drag from his cigarette.

"You know, J.D., despite all this activity it actually feels lonely around here, with our crews gone."

"They're not gone, fella," J.D. said. "Most of them are still here working."

"Yeah, but they're not working for me. That makes me feel lonely." He stopped scanning his surroundings and looked at J.D. "Hey, come here and look at something."

He reached inside the big cardboard box and pulled out a map. He unrolled it on the car's trunk. "Look. I'm gonna pay a visit to the Jurassic, J.D."

J.D. leaned across the map and looked at the title box. "Smackover? There ain't no Smackover oil in Mississippi. That's a crazy idea."

Ethan waved his arm around him. "That's what they said about what we did here."

"Oh, hell. Another crazy idea," a voice from behind boomed.

They turned. Grady walked up, coffee and cigarette in hand, peeking at the map. "Damn, I get the heebie-geebies when I see two crazy clowns looking at a geology map. "I take it that ain't around here."

"No, sir. It definitely ain't," Ethan said, rolling the map back up. "Grady, I tried to find you before leaving, but everybody said you were off working a rig somewhere, and I need to get on the road today."

"Yeah, I'm back on the console, for Mr. Mercer this time. Damn night tour. Ain't pushin' anymore, but that might change."

"Yeah," asked Ethan. "What you got going?"

"An old buddy of mine workin' down in Old Mexico has a rig for sale. Says I can get it cheap."

"Let me guess," said Ethan. "Stan Pickering?"

"You know him?"

Ethan shook his head. "Just heard of him."

"He's selling out."

"I think you should get it," Ethan said.

Well," mumbled Grady, looking at the ground, "I don't guess you got anything left to put up a loan for it."

"Grady, don't you realize that half the insurance money on Lucky Lucy, whenever we get it, is yours?"

Grady turned thoughtful. "Our deal wasn't a real deal. It was just a handshake. Not even that, hardly. It was just a bullshit session of a crazy idea. I ain't gonna hold you to that."

"Where I come from a handshake is stronger than any paper deal a lawyer could draw up. Lucky Lucy was half yours. You will get half of what's left after I pay the banknote off."

Grady's head went down. He stared at the dirt and wiped an eye with his sleeve.

"And if you don't wait too long, there'll be plenty of drilling work around here for a good while. You can put it to work right away. And besides," Ethan added, tapping on his map, "I might need you on this."

Grady looked up, grinned and nodded. "I'd like that. And maybe we might all get together one day and form up a company and start kickin' asses." He gestured toward J.D. "Him doing the land work, you the geology, and me the drillin'."

"Great idea," Ethan said. "I like it."

J.D. smiled and nodded.

Grady held his hand to Ethan, and they shook. "It's been a hell of a ride, sir. One hell of a ride indeed. I been reflectin' on how a man's life can change just by another man comin' into a bar and sittin' down beside him and sayin', *Come and go with me.* And that's what you did for me. I will forever be grateful."

As they watched Grady head to his car, Ethan turned to J.D. "I have one last job for you. I want you to assign my one percent override in the Hogan lease to Mrs. Shine. She needs it worse than I do."

J.D. slowly shook his head. "Well, I'll be. That leaves you with near nothing. I have never met anybody like you in my entire life."

"Naw, I've still got one percent in the Hull leases and some cash. It's not much but..." His voice trailed off as they both stood waiting for the other to say good-bye first. "Say," Ethan said, "you going to stick around a while? How long?"

"Oh, hell, I don't know, Ethan. There's plenty of work here for me. And, ah—well, you know."

Ethan smiled. "I know. Clarice."

J.D. smiled and nodded. "I found more than just a job here. I'm not gonna run out on that—like you're doin'. Ethan, why are you so afraid of commitment? Just go tell her you love her."

"J.D., I'm not even sure what that is. And I know she deserves a better life than to live out of motel rooms and be alone twenty hours a day." He let out a big sigh.

J.D. mashed out his butt.

"Well," Ethan said, "I guess I'll stop by and see her before I clear out."

They shook hands, then hugged. Ethan pulled back and

watched J.D. wipe his eyes. With a barely audible, cracking voice J.D. mumbled, "You saved my life."

Ethan felt his own eyes begin to water. He slapped J.D.'s shoulder. "You stay away from that who-hit-john, now. Ya hear?"

J.D. gave a subtle nod and turned back toward his room. Ethan watched him walk away, wondering if he would ever see him again.

He hadn't planned to tour the town and its growing oil field before leaving it, but his car seemed to have a mind of its own. Twice he drove past Laura's street without turning in to it, and finally he realized he was only stalling for time while he figured out what to say to her. But he had a long drive ahead, and the day was getting on. He turned back toward her house.

He slowed near her house and stopped short of her driveway. A car sat there that he didn't recognize. It looked to be brand-new—a gleaming red-and-white Dodge Lancer convertible. A lump grew in his throat. He drove through without a further glance at the car or her house.

"Laura, at least come out and see the car."

"Benny, just leave," she said. "Please."

"Laura, sweetheart, I'm set for life. You can have anything you want."

"I've told you before, it's over. It was over a long time ago. And don't call me that anymore!" She grabbed her door and jerked it open for him, just at the moment Ethan's car passed. She stood for a moment watching it disappear down the street, ignoring Benny's pleas. She looked at the Lancer and back toward the direction Ethan went. She turned back to Benny. "Let's go!"

Benny grinned. "Okay!"

She practically leaped into the car. Benny started to brag on the leather and the instruments, and she interrupted him. "Let's go! That way!"

He turned down the street, still giving her the verbal tour of his new ride. She had seen the boxes piled high in Ethan's back seat and had a hunch he was leaving town, and northwest to Mississippi would be his most likely route. Where they reached Highway 45 she commanded a left turn.

"Faster, Benny!"

"All, right!" he said, grinning. "And I don't even care if I get a ticket." The wind roared over their heads, and her hair swirled and fluttered. She thought about how messy she would look if she caught up with him. "Faster, Benny. Just don't kill us."

They roared around a slow car and swerved back into the right lane just in time to avoid an oncoming oil field truck. "Yahoo!" Benny yelled, glancing at her with a broad grin. She ignored his prattle as they sped northwest leaning left and right as he took the curves. She gripped the hand-hold on the door, wishing they had put body straps in these things. One wrong move out of Benny and they would be dirt cold dead.

Then she saw his car ahead. "Don't pass that one, Benny. Slow down." He did as she instructed. "Honk your horn, Benny!"

"Huh? Why"

She leaned over and slapped the horn on Benny's steering wheel. She saw Ethan's brake lights come on. Benny stepped on his brakes. "That's Bonner's car," he yelled.

"Yes it is," she yelled. "Now pull over!"

Benny let out some disgusted curses, and they followed Ethan onto the highway's shoulder. When the cars were stopped she leapt out, hurried forward to Ethan's passenger door and opened it. She slid in and slammed the door. A gigantic grin grew on Ethan's face as he watched her use her fingers as a comb. When she finally got her breath back she said, "Where are you going?"

He lifted his finger and pointed ahead.

She nodded. "I always wanted to go there."

Ethan revved his engine, popped his clutch, and sent dirt, rocks, and shark's teeth spraying onto Benny's new, handcrafted, ostrich boots.

The Citronelle Oil Field
Facts and Myths

The town of Citronelle, Alabama, located in north Mobile County, did have natural springs that were regarded as good for health and attracted visitors. Citronelle did have an oil lease auction in the early 1900s, which drew little interest from the fledgling oil industry.

In 1955, Everett Eaves, an independent geologist who had previously worked for Mobil Oil Company, became convinced there was a giant oil field under Citronelle but had trouble raising money to drill for it. His industry contemporaries considered the risk too high, but he managed to get a rig and start drilling shortly before his key leases and farm-outs expired.

The drill stem test on Eaves's well was a disappointment. But when the test tool was pulled, oil followed it up, spewed over the derrick and dropped into the town's streets. A crewman had indeed failed to open a critical valve.

The Citronelle Oil Field grew to nearly 500 wells. It was Alabama's first and only *giant* oil field—one that produces in excess of 100 million barrels. Citronelle is now near 200 million and still producing.

A group of Mobile investors—led by a man considered shady by the oil community—succeeded in gaining control of the Citronelle Field, though as far as we know, through legal means. The field's operator has changed hands a number of times.

A Citronelle used car dealer honored a previous handshake in the face of a much, much better offer. A man committed suicide, reportedly over oil money anguish. A New York newspaper sent a crew to create a feature story of how the giant discovery affected the town.

Dr. Walter B. Jones, Alabama's State Geologist from 1927 to 1961, is this story's only real character. He correctly predicted Alabama would one day become a significant oil and gas producing state and led the initiative to establish conservation and environmental rules governing the state's oil and gas activity.

Related: A man with little drilling and exploration experience found and rejuvenated an abandoned drilling rig in Louisiana, and built an oil and gas empire with it in north Alabama.

Ironically, thousands of tons of carbon waste from local coal-fired electrical power plants are being injected into Citronelle's depleted oil sands. It is one of the world's largest fully integrated carbon capture and storage project.

The salt dome below Citronelle is still growing.

ABOUT THE AUTHOR

I had two and one-half careers, maybe more depending on how you scrutinize it. I retired from the United States Air Force Reserve as a Lieutenant Colonel and pilot. My second career was at United Airlines, finishing there as a Boeing 767 captain. While serving in the Air National Guard and USAF Reserve I used my geology degree from the University of Alabama to explore for oil and gas. (At 13 years, that would be the half career). At one brief, very busy point in my life, I was juggling all three at once. These experiences proved to be fertile grounds for writing and storytelling.

Inspired by the great aviation authors, Ernest Gann, Richard Bach, Antoine de Saint-Exupery, and others of that tribe, I began writing in 1993 about my experience flying in the Persian Gulf War. That led to my first book, *Tail of the Storm*. Short pieces followed that garnered three awards. About that time, I became a newspaper writer doing local community interest pieces. Then came a string of magazine articles. In the late '90s I wrote a history of the oil and gas industry in the southern states, which resulted in *Drilling Ahead: The Quest for Oil in the Deep South*. I'm still tilling the literary soils.

I spend a lot of time dragging a travel trailer across America's back roads with Eleanor, my lovely wife of nearly 50 years, and current dog, Scout. My travels seem to be always centered on rocks. I still love geology. I fly recreationally, cruise the lake, work on my HO scale model railroad, and spend time with our grandkids. Boredom does not know me.

To find out more, I invite you to visit my author's website:

alancockrell.net

www.ingramcontent.com/pod-product-compliance
Lightning Source LLC
Chambersburg PA
CBHW030346200726
48286CB00013B/384